"For his initial foray into the w
Sometime After Midnight has woven an intricate plot that takes the reader through engrossing twists and turns in an unpredictable journey which concludes with an unexpected ending leaving me asking, 'I wonder what will happen next?'"

MaryBeth Hedstrom

"Robert Pugh has written a surefire hit with his first novel, *Sometime After Midnight*, which is sure to delight readers with his suspenseful plot and surprise ending! I am looking forward with anticipation for his sequel."

Virginia E. Trump

"The novel *Sometime After Midnight* truly characterizes life's experiences. It is a fast-paced human interest story that doesn't stop when you put the book down. Thanks for an ending that has left me ready for more."

L. Jean Cowart

Sheila —
Enjoy the story : it's
I've been told it's @
better than Sominex.
Hope you're doing well.
May God Bless You

SOMETIME AFTER MIDNIGHT

ROBERT R. PUGH

SOMETIME AFTER MIDNIGHT

Tate Publishing & Enterprises

Published by Tate Publishing & Enterprises, LLC
127 E. Trade Center Terrace | Mustang, Oklahoma 73064 USA
1.888.361.9473 | www.tatepublishing.com

Tate Publishing is committed to excellence in the publishing industry. The company reflects the philosophy established by the founders, based on Psalm 68:11,
"The Lord gave the word and great was the company of those who published it."

Book design copyright © 2009 by Tate Publishing, LLC. All rights reserved.
Cover design by Amber Lee
Interior design by Nathan Harmony

Published in the United States of America

ISBN: 978-1-60696-386-9
1. Fiction: Suspense
2. Fiction: Action & Adventure
09.02.20

This book is dedicated to my wife.

Thank you, Cindy, for your support and encouragement as I pursue my lifelong dream.

PROLOGUE

Generally speaking, we tend to define people by their roles in life. Take for example: a father can be known in a neighborhood as "Theresa's dad." Historically speaking, many people have been defined by their accomplishments, perhaps by even colossal mistakes or some misfortune. Traditionally, we may be defined by our associations with others. Regardless, we can get caught up in daunting circumstances—even an uncontrollable whirlwind, for that matter—where escape seems impossible.

For some reason, the early part of 1978 was one of those whirlwind times for the Carlisle family. They found themselves caught up in events beyond their control and couldn't shake loose of them.

Imagine a four-day period in your life where you had to deal with the murder of a dear friend and colleague, become involved in the investigation, and have incriminating evidence placed at your feet. No one, not even your friends and coworkers, would be immune to those circumstances. To make matters worse, your family would be placed at risk as well. Truly, this was not a rewarding time for Samuel Carlisle.

For the Carlisle family, New Year's Eve had come and gone with little celebration. A little less than two weeks earlier, snow had fallen in record amounts on Brooklyn, New York. Freezing temperatures and windy weather were still part of the daily forecasts—at least for the next several weeks. Yet in Florida, Daytona Beach was enjoying an early spring, profiting from a record number of breakers who were soaking up the sun, lounging on the beach, and making nightclub owners rich.

Samuel Carlisle, on the other hand, was beginning to feel the stress of his sixteen-hour workdays, with little or no time for enjoyment at the beach. His secretary, Lucille, was caught up in something larger than she was. She was determined to correct an injustice. Samuel's wife, Vicky, just wanted the upcoming trip to her in-laws to be part of history. Samuel's parents, Richard and Pat Carlisle, were looking forward to seeing their grandchildren. Basically, things were pretty normal for the early part of the year—at least for the Carlisles.

Samuel and Vicky's wedding anniversary was just four weeks away. Already what they were planning to give each other had become a part of their daily conversations. They had both agreed, two years ago, that it would be easier on everyone if his parents lived closer. To Samuel, it had always been about his parents leaving Brooklyn. To his parents, it had always been about starting over at their age. Now they just wanted this settled.

When attempting persuasive arguments with your mother and father, one of life's lessons is that it is not just a mind game—it demands preparation and confidence. Without either, your success rate is likely to be pitifully shameful because a rite of passage for parents is a presumed entitlement to become set in their ways. When discussions center on "who knows best," discussing the idea of starting over can be especially difficult. Consider yourself lucky if that is the only issue. Samuel, however, was convinced the results of his argument would be different this time. He was both prepared and confident. At least, he thought so.

He believed that his parents would have no choice but to recognize it was time for a much-needed break from their hurry-up lifestyle. Getting them to consider moving to Florida to be near their grandchildren had become one of Samuel and Vicky's goals. Plus, it was important to Samuel that his parents realize a more comfortable, less stress-filled, and more relaxed lifestyle they had not known most of their adult lives. Besides, the grandchildren would love being close to them. It just seemed like the perfect win-win situation to him.

During more recent visits with his parents, discussions about moving to Florida concluded as quickly as they had been introduced by Samuel. Conversations, whether initiated at the dinner table or over the phone, had proven ineffective. Still, he had great hope for his impending visit because the playing field was different this time.

Vicky, who hated making multiple trips during the year to New York, had tried earnestly on each of the previous visits to get them to discuss the possibilities of such a move. Samuel loved her tenacity. More to the point, he was grateful that he wasn't the one leading the charge on the upcoming trip. It wasn't that he didn't want to visit his parents. He just didn't want to go through the process of getting them upset and then, before returning to Florida, trying to smooth everything over.

This trip would be different, however. He would have to delay his flight for a couple of days to clear his calendar at work. This meant that Vicky and their two children, Rachel and Joshua, would have to fly to New York without him on Wednesday morning. They would fly from Daytona Beach early that morning, and he would join them on Friday afternoon. Although they believed their plans were solid, there was nothing usual about this trip.

Business at the law firm of Myers, Myers, and Associates had been brisk. The firm had been kept fairly busy. Unfortunately, Samuel's boss, Craig Myers, learned that Samuel had been offered a deal to go to work for Kevin Loebig in Tampa, Florida. Although Samuel and Vicky had discussed the offer and the many opportunities it would provide their family, Samuel had decided to turn it down, mostly because of his feelings of loyalty to Craig. Gratefully, Craig tossed a few more choice cases toward Samuel's direction. The idea was to keep Samuel busy and feeling more connected.

Vicky was not happy with that decision. In fact, she wasn't happy about much of anything in her life. Fortunately, she liked that business had been solid and their income had been steady. To her, Samuel's routine had become just that—a routine. She believed he deserved better. So did Samuel, but he wasn't keen on moving to Tampa, Florida.

Those next four days were supposed to be those of celebration and relaxation. Instead, the same events that demanded focus from the law firm demonstrated to the Carlisle family not just how fragile and transient life can be, but how much they needed each other. The Carlisles would soon learn some people just don't get it. When a person says no, it is supposed to mean, "No!"

Take, for example, the telephone conversation overheard by a member of a very distinguished law firm the day before Vicky left for Brooklyn:

"The best thing you can do at the moment is to shut up and listen."

"You can't talk to me that way, not after all I've done for you over the years."

"Really? In case you don't understand, try this on for size. You best get this fixed, or you'll leave me no choice."

"Don't threaten me. I know where the bones are buried, who buried them, and why they needed to be buried. I helped you to get where you are, and don't you forget that. Besides, there's nothing here I can't fix. You need to calm down and not go ballistic over the small stuff. There's plenty of time to get this thing done."

Each person knew what the other meant. Unfortunately, one of them was about to live the real meaning of the word "choice."

Funny how those things work out. You may never know what is best for you or all the choices you have—until it's too late. The two involved in that conversation were miles apart in their understanding yet too close for comfort.

Family roles were about to be redefined. Events were about to be more than demanding. The troubles that began for Samuel sometime after midnight on that Wednesday morning caught him off guard—and the Carlisle family would have to deal with the consequences.

CHAPTER 1

"Yes, Samuel is very successful, Pat," Vicky said resolutely. "He's very good at what he does."

"I know he's successful, but both of you have changed a lot over the last couple of years," Pat said quietly, while reaching for more flour.

"We can't always stay the same," she countered, sounding slightly irritated.

What a great way to start a family visit, Vicky thought as she turned to check on her two children, Rachel and Joshua. *This is just what I need in my life right now: a family gathering and an added bonus of my mother-in-law offering free psychoanalysis, which is sure to be followed by four fun-filled days of more than an adequate supply of life-sucking boredom. Isn't this just peachy keen?*

Typically, it took more than an hour before Vicky and her mother-in-law started with the back-and-forth wordplay. On this trip, however, it only took twenty minutes. Over the years, Vicky and Pat had developed their own set of rules and exclusive communication strategies, to such a point where the two of them had become predictable. The casual observer would swear there had to be some kind of rules of engagement, although unwritten, which had become second nature to them.

It had been over eight months since Vicky's last visit to Samuel's parents, but it seemed like only yesterday to her that she and the kids had just left. It wasn't that she didn't love his parents or that she didn't want them to see the kids. It just seemed that by the time she was on her way home after each visit, she was exhausted. Preparing for this trip and entertaining the kids, for what seemed an eternity during a not-so-pleasant flight experience from Florida, pointed everything toward another disastrous visit. She just knew this trip would result in her feeling punished rather than having enjoyed herself.

However, she knew this trip was both necessary and important for the future of the family. Besides, she had promised Samuel she would do as he asked. But before getting on the airplane Wednesday morning, her inner voice whispered loudly enough for her to know that this trip had life-changing events written all over it.

Samuel had hoped for several years that there would be a time when he could successfully approach his parents about moving to Florida. Only, he thought it would be better if Vicky would take the lead in talking with his parents. He recognized that she had a way of communicating with his mother that he didn't. The fact that he and his father were at odds had nothing to do with it. He intended to fix that issue, once and for all, sometime during his upcoming stay in New York. What worked best for him was knowing that Vicky spoke his mother's language fluently.

What made this trip harder for Vicky was that Samuel would not be able to join her for another couple of days. Try as he did, he was not able to break free from the court cases he had pending on his schedule. The fact that he would not be able to catch a flight until late Friday afternoon didn't help matters. She knew she shouldn't hold that against him, but she felt like everything surrounding this trip was working against her.

Knowing she would have to be cooped up with their children at his parents' place, facing the fact that his father would probably retell countless numbers of very dry and equally long stories about family history, she wasn't sure just how she was to help with the family gathering. From what she learned during the ride from the airport to her in-laws' home, what was supposed to be a family weekend get-together had developed into a half-blown reunion, which meant she'd be expected to help with the preparations. Her promise to Samuel was to get his parents to come around to the idea of moving to Florida. *All of this*, she thought, *is a bonus because I'm a good person.*

"Change happens," Pat said, while putting more flour into the bread dough.

"Look how little you and Richard have changed. Change is more likely to happen because of the circumstances people find themselves in," Vicky said, as she poured herself a glass sweet tea. She leaned on the counter and asked, "Haven't you ever wondered what things would be like if you and Richard sold the store and moved? I mean, Samuel is doing well, and we're likely to stay put where we are, at least for a little while. Besides, Uncle Patrick has grown such deep roots in California," she added sharply, knowing that Pat hadn't seen her brother in twenty-two years.

"Why ask such a question?" Pat inquired. Her discomfort with the question was evidenced by an increased and brisk-like handling of the bread dough she had been kneading for about five minutes. "Tonight's dinner waits for no idle conversations," Pat mumbled under her breath.

"You and Richard have worked most of your adult lives in the deli, without taking more than what, two back-to-back days off a year? What's it been now? Thirty-five years?" The look on Vicky's face was clearly understood by Pat.

"Look, this store has been our life. Without the store, we would have nothing to offer our children or our two beautiful grandchildren," she said, while smiling at Joshua, who was watching his grandmother's every move.

"That's just it. Because of all the changes over the years, you have everything to gain now by not staying here," she said, looking Pat straight in the eye.

"So, you think that we should move into some fancy condo," she said sarcastically. "Who wants to live in a condo?" she asked as she rubbed her nose with her right forearm instead of her dough-encrusted fingers.

"It doesn't have to be a condo. The two of you should look for a nice ranch-style house with a backyard. When the kids come to visit you, they could enjoy feeling green grass between their toes, instead of having to walk on nasty, dog-pooped, cluttered sidewalks. Besides, there are a couple of really nice places we've looked at that are close to us. The kids could visit with you and Grandpop almost every day."

"So, this is about babysitting service, huh?" she asked, with a wry smile on her face.

Vicky knew right then that it would be a long two days before Samuel arrived.

"What would Grandpop and I do after we got there? How would we make a living? How would we pay the bills?"

"He's planning to talk to you about this when he gets here. I just want you think on this," Vicky said as Rachel entered the kitchen.

Rachel, who had been standing in the doorway leading to the dining room and had overheard a portion of the conversation, had a curious look on her face.

"Mommy, do you think Grandmom and Grandpop would really move to Florida?" she asked as her face lit up with great anticipation.

"Honey, we just want them to think about it, that's all," Vicky said.

The look in her six-year-old daughter's eyes was unmistakable. Rachel dearly loved her grandmother and grandfather. She was the first granddaughter in the family, and Vicky believed that Rachel was being spoiled rotten by her grandparents from long distance. Still, Vicky would love for Rachel and Joshua to be able to visit with their grandparents more often.

"Rachel," Vicky said with great conviction, "we don't know how this will turn out, honey. We do know that Grandmom and Grandpop have never come to visit us in Florida. Wouldn't that be nice for a change?" she said, while avoiding eye contact with Pat.

Almost as if planned and on cue, the phone rang. It was Samuel checking to be sure that Vicky and the kids had arrived safely. As soon as Pat had picked up the phone, she began smiling, and her voice adopted an almost melodious tone. She motioned for Vicky to come to the phone. Before she could get to the receiver, however, Pat continued the conversation.

"Samuel, why didn't you come with Vicky and the kids?" she asked in a demanding manner. The manner in which she was holding the receiver, as if Samuel was standing right in front her, gave the appearance that she was disappointed.

"You shouldn't keep your mother waiting like this," she said sharply.

"Grandmom, can I speak to Daddy?" Rachel asked, reaching to get the phone from her grandmother. Vicky turned toward Rachel to keep her from grabbing the phone, while motioning for her to wait. Impatient and unwilling to wait in line to speak to her father, Rachel yelled, "Daddy, are you coming today too?" About that time, Vicky motioned to Pat that she should let Rachel speak to her father.

"Son, you worry me so," Pat said.

"Pat, hand me the phone," Vicky pleaded, while walking toward her.

While mumbling something about how she didn't get a chance to talk to her daddy, Rachel stomped out of the room. Fortunately, more attention was then focused on her little two-year-old brother, Joshua, who seemed to be amused by the whole episode.

During the brief phone call, Joshua had entertained himself with pieces of dough and butter, which he had been able to reach from the edge of the table. By the time Vicky and Pat remembered Joshua was in the room, he had managed to stuff dough in both ears, while pieces of it had become matted in his curly, dark brown hair. Pat found this to be humorous enough to laugh out loud. Vicky was not amused in the least, as she went about picking up Joshua and carrying him over her left shoulder toward the bathroom. Joshua laughed loudly enough, with that infectious laugh of his, that both his mother and sister couldn't stop themselves from laughing as well.

With Rachel and the children out of the kitchen, Pat returned to making bread and preparing for the evening meal. Her thoughts, however, became centered on the prospect of moving to Florida and all that would be involved in the process. Moving was not something she was used to doing. She believed she could handle the physical parts of the move; it was the rest of the process that she hated thinking about. She knew her husband would drop everything in a heartbeat, but he and Samuel still had issues that needed resolving. She could feel the tugging of her family's roots, which had established the business in Brooklyn almost sixty years ago.

The business originally started as *The Third Avenue Deli*. Pat's father and mother, Dallas and Brigitte Patterson, purchased the building on July 12, 1919, just eighteen days after they had been married. After repairs and remodeling efforts, they opened for business on October 6, 1919. It became known throughout the neighborhood as "Pat's Deli." On the tenth anniversary of its opening, her parents officially changed its name to *Pat's Delicatessen.*

To Pat, Florida meant starting over. Even though Samuel and Vicky had worked out some of the details, she knew there were several loose ends that needed to be thought about. Among the details, it had crossed her mind that before she and Richard moved to Florida, someone would have to buy their business in New York.

Equally as quick, other ideas came to mind, as she earnestly began considering a move to Florida. She saw these as opportunities to change some things in her own life. She even entertained the idea that she was still young enough to go back to school and finish her degree. She was comfortable with the thought of knowing their children were well established, with careers and families of their own. She and Richard were debt free and had developed a modest investment portfolio.

As she pondered all of it and prepared the bread dough for the oven, Richard came into the kitchen carrying Rachel on his hip. She could see how happy Rachel was to be with her grandfather. More importantly, she saw a side of him that she hadn't seen since their own children were Rachel's age. He was beaming and delighted in the time he got to spend with the grandchildren.

"I believe this little girl is getting prettier every day," he said before kissing Rachel's forehead. "She's as pretty as her mama and her grandmom too," he said as he lovingly patted Rachel on her head.

Pat stopped what she was doing and took in the moment. To her, nothing was more important than her family. From the time she could crawl, she had been taught about the importance of family relationships—and to protect them in whatever she did. Now the moment had come, and she felt ready to talk about it.

"Richard," she said, "we need to talk. There are a few things we need to deal with before he arrives on Friday. It's time … it's time," she said before hugging his shoulder and tenderly kissing his cheek. "It's time for us to think about what we really want to do."

"What do we really want to do?"

"It's time that you and I build some more," she said as she removed her apron and started walking toward the stairs. "I'm going to see Papa. I'll be right back," she said as she went down the stairs.

She felt it was time to set a few things straight. It had been a while since she had last visited her father's gravesite just to sit and "talk" with him. When she would visit, she would think about when she was a child. Often, she would recall tender memories of her growing up at the deli. She believed just sitting by his gravesite helped her to work through things, regardless of what the issue might be. This day would be no exception.

Before sitting down, she put some freshly cut flowers in a vase at the base of the headstone. After sitting for a few minutes alone, she began focusing on the prospects of moving and all that it would require. She tried hard to stay focused. Instead, her thoughts turned to how her life work seemingly was predestined to follow in her parents' footsteps.

She remembered fondly the day her parents insisted she should continue her schooling instead of working full time at the store. On that day, that notion had come as a complete surprise to her. She remembered hugging her father and mother and how overjoyed she had become when she learned she would get to go to college. She had shown such great potential with her schooling. Her parents believed she had much more to offer than slicing cold cuts and slapping condiments on bread.

With the sudden and unexpected death of her father, however, her opportunity to go to college vanished because she was needed to help run the family business. She remembered too her younger brother, Patrick, and his deep resentment for having to become a part of the family business. He had his heart set on becoming a pilot. He had no desire to be tied to a store, wearing an apron, and making sandwiches for the rest of his life.

She recalled so vividly how he would argue with their mother, practically every day, about how he wanted a life of his own. She recalled that warm day in April 1941 when he came home from school, announced that he had quit school to join the army, and was leaving for training the following day. She remembered that day because that was the first time she ever saw her mother cry.

Because of the feelings she had about her responsibility to her mother and the family business, her plans were put on hold. She wasn't the type to hold a grudge. She believed, however, there would come a time when Patrick would regret what he had done to their mother. *It is time to deal with this too*, she thought.

Looking off into the distance beyond the headstone, she thought about what she had always wanted to ask her father, but his death robbed her of that opportunity. Looking at her father's headstone, she thought, *how could you not say something to him, when you were alive? Papa, he would have listened to you. Mom didn't deserve what he did to her and to the family.*

The memory of her mother standing in the doorway, wanting to hug her son one more time, crying uncontrollably, was vivid. She remembered clearly how innocent Patrick looked as he left that day, while looking back over his shoulder only once. The memories of that day were bitter and lingered. For years, she fought back tears thinking that doing so would make her stronger. *Not today—not today*, she thought.

"It's time to settle this," she whispered.

She began to cry ever so quietly as she thought about how stubborn Patrick had been during his last two years at home. The memory was sharp and still somewhat painful. She realized that nothing could have stopped her brother from leaving the store. How small his world must have seemed to him. *Papa*, she thought, *I wish I could have been more like you in so many more ways. I wish I could keep focused like you did—how you remained emotionally honest and direct when it came to personal relationships. You seldom used upsetting words.*

She recalled the words she spoke in anger to him when he walked out the door that afternoon. Sitting there, looking at her father's head-stone, she whispered what she had shouted to her brother thirty-seven years ago: "Patrick, just what are you thinking? You selfish and uncaring fool. You only care about yourself. If you loved us, you wouldn't do this." She yelled those words in the spring of 1941 as he walked briskly to the bus stop. She wished she had been more like her father.

As she looked at the freshly cut flowers, she recalled the look on his face as he walked away that day. Here she was yelling at him, and he looked back at her with a look as if he had just shed a thousand pounds. At that time, her yelling those words to him felt right. Now, she wasn't so sure. *I just hope that he understands*, she thought.

She wasn't so sure anymore because as the years went by, other things began to be more important to her and to their family. Sitting that day at her father's gravesite, she realized that it had been long enough and that someone needed to do something about making things right.

Her thoughts turned from her brother, as she began reflecting on the mornings she attended college. To her, it felt like being paroled from prison. She managed a smile as she fondly recalled going to class. What she didn't know was that every morning as she would head off to class for those four hours or so, her father stood at the door of the shop with tears in his eyes, watching the little girl he loved so deeply drift farther and farther from his world. She recalled her mother explaining how he would stand at the door, watching her for as long as he was able, until she was out of sight, and how he would wipe away his tears with his apron.

Every morning she would leave to attend classes was pure agony for him. Pat never knew of this until much later, because even her mother had agreed that, in those days, some things just didn't need to be talked about. Besides, her parents were reconciled with the idea that she was older than her mother was when first starting out into the big world. Her success in college, however, was short lived.

Her thoughts turned to the morning she found her father's lifeless body on her parents' bed. She recalled the promises she had made to herself on that day. She fashioned the notion that when she had children of her own, she would do everything she could do to encourage them to leave home and make a life for themselves as early as possible. She remembered what her mother had told her: "Don't forget how small the world can become to a person. For some, the world already has stopped at the end of their block." She was grateful that her children had seen how big the world can be and that they had managed to make their own way through life.

She checked her watch, took a deep breath, and accepted the fact that it was time for her to get back to the deli. One last time before leaving, she bent over and scrolled her fingers over her father's name. It was as if to say, "I will always remember." One last tear fell upon the freshly cut flowers as she stood to go back to the deli.

"Papa," she said ever so softly, "I need for you to talk to me as we do this. I think I know what to do, but I need to be sure that it's the right thing to do," she said as she began to walk toward the cemetery's exit gate.

When she reached the gate, she felt a need to stop and respond to what she felt was an emotional nudging. She turned around, looked at the headstone one more time before leaving, and said, "I love you too, Papa."

She turned back around and walked a little farther to the exit. She could feel her father's presence. With each step she took, she could feel his instructive and loving manner embrace her. She slowed her pace, almost stopping, allowing for her to enjoy what was the moment. She felt safe. It was as if she was holding her father's hand and walking with him—just like she used to do when she was a little girl. She didn't know where she was going, but she knew she could trust her father to guide her.

She stopped, turned around once again, and said, "Thank you, Papa. I will say a prayer for you tonight."

CHAPTER 2

After speaking with his wife, Samuel could tell she was not having a fun afternoon. He figured he would call later that evening to see how the rest of her first day went. For now, he was thankful they had arrived safely.

Thinking that he could now concentrate on his work, he began to look at his day's schedule more closely. He just knew Friday would not arrive quickly enough for him. Having to get through the next two days to be reunited with his wife and children was not a thrilling prospect.

"Samuel," Craig said, after clearing his throat, "tell me we'll be ready with the brief for the Anderson case by Friday morning."

"I gave my notes on that case to Carrie yesterday. That should allow enough time for her to look over them. Once she's done, I'll see that they're cleaned up and typed. I also took care of the indemnification clauses as you had directed."

"Great! Now tell me we're going for drinks after work tonight," he said in his usual implied tone. The only thing missing from what he said to Samuel was the "or else" at the end of each of his sentences. Samuel never really appreciated the manner or the tone of voice that Craig would often use when he wanted something done. From time to time, even Craig's wife, Carrie, seemed to have trouble dealing with his manners. It was like he had to be theatrical and eccentric at the same time.

The night before Vicky left for New York, she'd had a conversation with Samuel about how annoyed she would get watching him dealing with Craig's rudeness. She wanted him to reconsider another firm's offer, the Loebig Group from Tampa, even mentioning that his rudeness should have helped him decide in favor of that offer. She not only wanted him to reconsider the offer, but more importantly, she thought his decision to turn them down seriously hindered his career advancement prospects.

She pointed out that not only would the money be better, but the contacts he would make through the Loebig Group would be more important to him later in his career. He liked the idea that he could be a little more selective in choosing cases. Plus, the idea of a full partnership within the next four or five years sounded great to him.

The partnership deal didn't matter to her, although the money and prestige did. What she didn't want was for Samuel to try to open an office and start his own firm. The idea of them starting over and being broke—again—did not appeal to her at all.

"Craig, do you remember that I will be flying out on Friday to visit my folks for a few days? Vicky and the kids are already there, but I will be back in the office Tuesday morning. I'll make sure that I am back in plenty of time to work with Carrie on the Kellerman contract too," he said, while leaning back in his chair.

"Just be sure that you're here on Tuesday morning by eight o'clock. We'll still need an hour or so before the nine o'clock meeting to go over our talking points. I want this deal signed and our clients smiling by noon."

Samuel called for Lucille over the intercom to come into his office. He wanted her to be aware of the schedule changes and that she would have to work later than usual next Monday evening. As she entered the room, he noticed her hair was styled differently, for the fourth time in two weeks. Like her last two efforts, it wasn't very attractive. So, he decided not to say anything, again.

"You might have to work late next Monday on the Kellerman contract. Would you mind staying that afternoon until it's finished?"

Leaning forward on the corner of his desk and smiling at him, she replied, "No problem, Mr. Carlisle. It shouldn't take too long for me to get it done and put it to bed."

Lucille Pierce was the epitome of efficiency. She knew her way around the workings of the legal system better than most lawyers. Also, she knew all of the clerks who worked in both the civil and criminal court divisions within hers and the connecting districts. She had started working for Samuel on the first day he went to work for Craig in the fall of 1972. Prior to that, she had worked as a paralegal for more than seven years.

Before making a name for herself in this business, she had wanted to be a court stenographer. She would tell anyone who would listen, however, that coming to work for Samuel was the best career move she ever made. He allowed her to really show off her abilities. Although recently having gone through an ugly divorce, she never let her personal life interfere with her work or job performance. The case involving her brother, Charles, was another matter.

"Will you be back on time Monday evening to work on the Kellerman contract as well?" she inquired, while walking slowly toward the side door that connected their offices. He was always amazed at how poised she was. She carried her six-foot frame with grace and such ease. As she placed her left hand on the doorknob, she turned toward him and asked appealingly, "Can I get you a cup of coffee or something?"

"No thanks, Lucille," he said as he stood from behind his desk to place a file on the credenza.

As she turned to go out the door, Samuel got her attention and said gratefully, "I won't be here Monday evening, but thank you for doing this."

She smiled and curtsied, as if to say, "Anything for you, Mr. Carlisle."

The morning flew by quickly, but he would rather have been on his way to Brooklyn. He hated having to wave good-bye to Vicky and his children. This particular morning had not been his usual "cup of coffee and an egg sandwich for breakfast" kind of morning. Instead, it started with having to watch his family leave, and then, after he got to his office a little after eight thirty, he had to deal with an inmate of the Florida prison system.

Charles Durham, Lucille's younger brother, had called to speak with him about the progress on the case. He had agreed to take his case after Lucille had asked him to review the transcript of her brother's trial. She believed the evidence presented by the prosecutor did not indicate what she thought was supposed to be a fair and impartial conclusion rendered by the jury. Instead, he was found guilty on two counts: burglary and second-degree murder. Charles needed help—and she wanted validation for him through the justice system.

It was a nice gesture on his part, thinking he could help Lucille deal with her brother's conviction. There was little room to believe that Charles was innocent because, to Samuel, the evidence appeared to be overwhelming. Still, some parts of the transcript were disturbing, but he couldn't point to any one specific piece of testimony that would offer solid ground for an appeal.

Throughout the entire trial, and even as he was taking up residence in prison, Charles insisted he was innocent. Lucille believed in him. She knew her brother and believed that he was not lying. She knew he might be considered a thief; she just could not see him as a murderer.

Samuel promised Lucille he would read the transcript again. His efforts were to make certain that the attorneys hadn't missed anything and that Charles had been represented properly. Each time he read the transcript, he found nothing on which an appeal could be filed nor any reason to change his feelings about the verdict. He had read it twice without changing his original opinion. After each reading, Samuel couldn't shake the feeling that Durham looked guiltier each time he read the transcript. He decided some outside help, to sort through the stacks of legal fine points, would be best.

As he sat in his office, with his thoughts wandering between the transcripts and his family, Samuel knew that Lucille understood her brother well enough to believe her when she said the case just didn't add up. Lost in thought as he sat and stared out his office window, he hadn't realized that Carrie had come in and tried to get his attention.

Seeing that his attention was elsewhere, she said, "A penny for your thoughts."

"I'm sorry, Carrie. I didn't hear you come in. I've been a little distracted today," he said, somewhat startled and apologetic. Although Carrie was not his direct supervisor, she was Craig's wife, a respected attorney, a full partner in the firm, and one attractive woman. Not only was she articulate and imaginative in the courtroom, he appreciated her taking time to talk with him about almost anything.

"You must have been on a mini vacation because you didn't hear a thing I said to you just now," she said as she closed the door behind her.

"I'm sorry. I was going over a few things about the testimony in the Durham case," he said as he stood to greet her.

"How exactly is it going? Have you found an approach to re-open the appeal process?" she asked, while walking past him to a chair by the side of his desk.

As she did so, her perfume caught his attention. *She not only looks great in that dark blue suit; she smells great as well,* he thought. An unexpected visit from Carrie was a day's reward for him, and he would not deny himself the pleasure of her company.

"Would you mind taking time to read over a portion of Durham's trial transcript just to see if maybe you can find anything that might help?" he asked, while handing the documents to her. "I am particularly interested in the part where he was being crossed on his whereabouts on that evening. It's on page sixteen, from line eight to line thirty-four. You tell me if you think there's anything there. Or tell me I've been watching too many detective shows lately on television."

Carrie read the specific area he had requested. She flipped a couple of other pages back and forth, as if she was looking for something that should have been there. While she was reading, Samuel studied her posture and facial expressions. He was looking to see if there were non-verbal clues he could observe. He was grasping at straws and he knew it. He didn't want to let down Lucille, but there wasn't much space left at the end of his proverbial rope. He was hoping that Carrie would find something. If this didn't work, he knew he would have to tell Lucille what he had suspected all along. Even though he believed such a conclusion might be a little easier for her to handle coming from him, it was one task he was dreading.

"I'm not sure what you thought you saw, but I don't see anything that jumps off the pages," she said as she placed the documents on his desk. Smiling one of those faint-hearted smiles, she continued, "I wish I could be more helpful. Let me think some more on this over drinks this afternoon. You will be there, won't you?"

"I guess so," he sighed. "I'm hoping that the loose ends of this day will get tightened up soon so I can feel less guilty about socializing. Besides, it would be my pleasure to toast the future success of your current case," he said, grinning as he picked up the pencil mug from his desk in a mock salute. The thought crossed his mind that he might actually enjoy the prospect of having drinks with the boss's wife.

Carrie wanted to stay and talk with him about other things, but she knew it was not the best time with such a heavy workload waiting for her in her own office. As she stood to leave, he stood as well and walked over to the door. She paused for just a minute, as if she had something else to say, picked up the files she brought with her into his office, and turned toward the door. He opened the door for her while watching her every move. He quietly breathed in the sweet fragrance of her perfume as she went by, even catching a quick glimpse of her smiling at him. He wasn't sure if he was blushing, but the room felt warm enough to him that he believed he should have been.

When Pat returned from her father's gravesite, she sought out Richard like a heat-seeking missile would its target. She was ready to approach the prospect of moving.

"Richard!" she called as she dashed up the stairs. "I've got an idea and I think it will work. Let's get a cup of coffee and work this out. Now!"

He could tell from the moment the front door to the deli had closed that she was working on something. The Dallas-like gait, the pronounced and protruding jaw, squared shoulders, and the directness of speech all told him she had reached a conclusion about something.

As she began to go up the stairs, he wanted to laugh. She hadn't noticed that he was on the other side of the shop. When she came into the shop in such a hurry, he had been kneeling down to adjust an air vent on the refrigerated display case. He stood up just in time to see her hurriedly climbing the stairs, almost taking them two at a time. He didn't have the heart to say anything.

Directing his voice to the top of the stairs, he yelled, "Pat, I'm down here." He started fixing each of them a cup of coffee.

She heard his voice and immediately stopped, turned around, and leaned against the wall for a few seconds, trying to catch her breath. She took out her handkerchief, which she always carried with her, and patted her nose and eyelids.

"I think it would be easier for you to come up here than it would for me to go down there," she said, while letting out a deep breath.

The next half hour brought back fond memories for him. It had been a good while since they had sat down and talked of future plans in the manner they did that afternoon. He remembered the last time the two of them had done something like this was when they had decided to buy out the owner of the duplex next to theirs. When they reached the decision to go ahead with the plan, he recalled the look that she had on her face. He had seen that same look just moments earlier as she dashed up the stairs. Whatever it was that she was about to explain to him, he knew she had her heart set on something that would be beneficial to both of them.

Richard had learned long ago that she was the one with the business sense in their relationship. He accepted his role with grace and humility because he loved her more than he was ever able to express in words. He found himself wanting to be more poetic and romantic in her eyes, but that just wasn't his style. Instead, he believed his role was to be that of a peace-maker. His ability to help others understand and express themselves was what he was best suited for in their relationship.

As he listened to her, he focused on her face. Usually he was a good listener—but not this day. He had focused so intensely on her face that he had not heard a word she said. He continued to smile, and even nod occasionally, to indicate his presence in their conversation. But it was her beauty, in spite of the wrinkles that had formed after thirty-seven years of marriage, that caught his eye. It was endearing how the corner of her mouth would curl upward when she would speculate on something. Her shoulders would rise, and her head would tilt slightly, as she expressed the ideas that just couldn't wait to be spoken. He knew he was still very much in love with her. He knew that whatever it was she wanted to do, he wouldn't stop her.

"Richard, what do you think?" she asked, taking his hands into hers.

"I think that if this is what you want, then this is what I want," he said, pulling her to him and hugging her tightly.

"Did you hear anything I just said?" she asked as she stepped back slightly and looked up at him.

"Not a word, but I saw the look and heard the passion. What else do I need at this point?" he asked, while smiling back at her.

Somehow, the two of them had been able to communicate with each other over the years clearly and with little effort. Although they would discuss the issues and express their concerns, the result would be a well-thought-out plan that could be accomplished in the manner they intended.

They always found a way to make things work. There were difficult times, but her faith and outgoing spirit coupled with his incomparable willingness to get things done, while seeing them through to the finish, was the bedrock of their success in business. They were a formidable team and understood that about themselves early in their marriage.

As they stood there, looking into each other's eyes, he saw her the same way she had looked on the first day they met. His thoughts were racing with all of the particulars that would have to be handled, including the many relationships the two of them had developed over the years. For just an instant, as he looked into her eyes, he recalled the first day that he came to work in the store with her—and all the obstacles he had to overcome. It was hard, at first, to remember all of the products and how to handle the equipment. He struggled with the inventory and the operations side of the business. But when it came to working with the customers, they were both remarkably skillful at engaging them in conversation and knowing exactly what it took to encourage repeat business.

As they stood there, for just an instant, they had looked deeply into each other's eyes and knew what the other was thinking. They both smiled at each other.

"Okay, then. Now let's figure out the details before we talk to the kids," she said as she leaned into his hug. She could feel the warmth of his cheek against hers.

"Are you sure this is what we really want to do?"

"Yes, I'm sure of it. It's time we both take a step back and look at what really is down the road. We're not getting any younger, you know," she said.

"Today, we start the rest of our lives together," he said, after kissing her forehead.

Four thirty that afternoon arrived quicker than Samuel had planned. He still hadn't finished reviewing the volumes of contract language for a client who should have been sitting in his outer office. As he picked up the two-inch thick folder and began quickly to review the documents, Lucille's voice could be heard over the intercom.

"Mr. Carlisle," she started," I think your four thirty just cancelled. Is there anything I can do for you before I pack it in and call it a day?"

"No. I'll see you in the morning."

He started packing as well, putting several documents in his briefcase. *Getting these done tonight will help me get a head start on tomorrow's schedule,* he thought. *I can't afford to get behind. There's too much depending on this.*

The social hour with Craig and Carrie, the office crew, and Lucille had been a nice distraction to end his day. The obnoxious behavior by Craig, Carrie's elusive presence, and the jokes told by Lucille were more than adequate entertainment for the evening.

It seemed obvious to Samuel that Lucille was trying too hard—and overcompensating because of her brother's circumstances. Carrie tried mostly to engage Samuel into less office-focused conversations by getting him to talk about his children. It worked—almost all too well. However, he knew the ride home would provide ample time for him to unwind and become human again.

After the reception and as he was driving home, he decided to visit with his longtime friend and mentor, Dr. Woodrow Rutledge. A thought had come to Samuel that Dr. Rutledge, known as "Woody" to his associates, just might be able to help him focus more on the content of the transcript and perhaps offer some insightful advice. Samuel not only respected Dr. Rutledge; he believed him to be one of the finest legal minds he had ever met. Their relationship over the years was defined by more than just legal issues or case law, however. Each had a fondness for the other that transcended the classroom or the courtroom.

Dr. Rutledge cared deeply for Samuel. He had taken an interest in his progress from the time he graduated in 1972 from Stetson University's School of Law. Now retired and living just three houses down the block from him, keeping track of Dr. Rutledge was not too difficult. Samuel's visits to Dr. Rutledge's house were always welcomed and enjoyed, no matter the length of the visit or the topics of the discussions that ensued.

When he pulled into the driveway, Dr. Rutledge was sitting in a lawn chair in front of his opened garage door and enjoying the early evening breeze. Each smiled at the other, while Dr. Rutledge motioned for him to come inside.

"It's a little late, so I presume the visit is one of urgency," Dr. Rutledge said as he leaned back in his easy chair.

"Not so much urgency, more like determination. I would like for you to read through a trial transcript to tell me what I've missed. I have read through it twice now and cannot find one avenue of approach that might last more than two seconds before an appellate court judge. I really want to help this client, but this one has me stymied," he said, while handing the transcript to him.

"It's good to see you're still direct and plain spoken, truly two of your better qualities. I promise to read through it, but only if you promise to tell me how your lovely wife and children are doing," he instructed as he stood up and walked toward the kitchen. "Would you care for a nice glass of lemonade?"

"No, thank you," he replied. "Vicky and the kids are doing great. They're in Brooklyn visiting my mom and dad. She's helping them to prepare for a family gathering of sorts," he said, while watching Dr. Rutledge move about the kitchen. "She's a little annoyed that I didn't go with her this morning, but I have several things to do here before flying out on Friday."

Continuing the conversation, Samuel said, "You probably see my kids more than I do, since I know they've spent most afternoons over here listening to your entertaining stories." Smiling, he just couldn't resist adding, "And I just know that every one of them are the truth and nothing but the truth, of course."

"Of course," Dr. Rutledge said, grinning from ear to ear. "They are such eager students and learn so quickly," he said as he sat back down in his favorite chair. "I believe your daughter will make a great defense attorney one day," he added.

"So...do you think you might have a chance to run through this by tomorrow evening? I'll be happy to stop by and bring dinner for both of us."

"Is it that urgent?" he inquired as he put down his drink and picked up the packet containing the transcript.

"Yes, I'm afraid it is," he said, while looking directly at Dr. Rutledge. "This case deserves everything I can bring to bear on it."

Almost as if on cue, he stood and instructed Samuel that if this transcript were to be read by him and ready to discuss tomorrow afternoon, Samuel would have to leave and go home. He thanked Dr. Rutledge, shook his hand as Dr. Rutledge patted him on the back, and said, "Thanks for stopping by. I will do my best to get this done this evening and be ready to discuss it with you by tomorrow afternoon. So as not to disappoint you tomorrow, I need to begin working on it right away.

Lights go out around here kind of early. By the way, when you speak with Vicky, please give her my best and have her hug the kids for me."

After arriving home and grabbing a bite to eat, the remainder of his evening was a bust. He tried to concentrate on the work he had brought with him, but his mind was elsewhere. So he decided to stretch out on the couch and watch television for a little while. Before falling asleep with the television blaring and several lights on in the house, he had managed to read over the Kellerman contract, make a few notes he wanted to be sure to discuss with Craig and Carrie, and had snacked on a bowl of popcorn.

Sleep came to him that evening, but rest was not to be found because the couch proved to be a poor substitute for his bed. An even greater impact on his not sleeping comfortably was his knowing that being by himself was not exactly his cup of tea. His last conscious thought was how much he missed his wife.

CHAPTER 3

Morning routines are supposed to be just that—routine. Maybe they aren't very exciting, but they make sure each day gets started on a familiar footing. In spite of a restless evening, the first part of Thursday started better than Samuel had hoped. After tossing and turning on the couch most of the night, he got up around six o'clock that morning. After his usual appointments with the toilet and a nice hot shower, he finished shaving and got dressed. Thinking he might have enough time for a cup of coffee and a quick glance at the sports section, he went out to retrieve the morning paper. Standing in the middle of his sidewalk while reading the headlines, he mumbled quietly, "So much for routine."

The headlines told it all: *City Councilman Arrested.* The front page photo showed Mr. A. J. Kellerman, whom Samuel was supposed to meet later that morning, in a set of shiny handcuffs, while trying to shield his face from photographers as he was being put into the back of a squad car. The little part of the news story that Samuel frantically read indicated that Mr. Kellerman had been arrested and charged with extortion and conspiracy to commit extortion.

Samuel quickly returned to his kitchen and made his way to the telephone. He tried to call Craig and Carrie at their house, but no one answered. He redialed, thinking he might have misdialed the number. He hadn't. No one was answering.

He then tried calling the office. Still no answer. Realizing it was probably still too early to catch someone at the office, he took one last sip of his coffee, placed the cup in the sink, and headed out the door with his briefcase in hand.

As he drove, his thoughts turned to how the firm might become entangled in all of this. Unfortunately, he had been hired to work on a contract for a person now charged and arrested for extortion. What worried him was the part about "the conspiracy to commit extortion." That thought disturbed him because the firm might be implicated or involved in this. He wondered what and how much Craig or Carrie might know and how deeply they were involved. He knew that Craig and Kellerman had a history of sorts, but he wasn't sure about Carrie's part in all of this.

While Samuel continued driving toward the office, he couldn't help but wonder if this would mess up his leaving for Brooklyn the next day.

By the time he got to the office, the cleaning woman had arrived and was already vacuuming the entrance area.

"Good morning, Mr. Carlisle," she said, raising her voice above the roar of the sweeper. "How are you this morning?" she said, almost yelling at him.

"I'm okay, Mrs. Cole," he replied, while quietly pasting a smile on his face.

Mrs. Cole had been taking care of the custodial needs for the office years before Samuel had come to work there. Her usual work schedule had her working in the evening, not the mornings. When working mornings, she always made coffee and tried to finish vacuuming the front office area before anyone else would arrive.

She turned off the sweeper and said, "It's a beautiful morning God has given us to enjoy today. You in a hurry?" she asked as she wiped her forehead.

"Has anyone called this morning? And by the way, why are you here this morning?"

"Not a soul called. I couldn't be here last night because of my son's birthday party. I traded last night for this morning," she said, while unplugging the cord to the sweeper. "Mr. and Mrs. Myers said it was okay."

After entering his office and putting his briefcase on his desk, he tried calling Craig at home. Again, there was no answer. Because of Craig's political connections with Kellerman, and given Craig's recent and public efforts to seek increased political influence, the lawyer part of Samuel was concerned about the possibility of the firm being sucked into some sort of front page news story for the next week. He wanted to know what the circumstances were and how deeply Craig might be involved. His lawyer instincts knew that the firm could be implicated, even if Craig was not. His experience knew that both the newspapers and television media could see to that.

The aroma from the coffee that Mrs. Cole had made earlier attracted Samuel and filled the office area. After pouring a cup for himself, he stopped by the filing room to get Kellerman's file folders. He needed the files to work on the contract issues he had promised Craig he would get done. He unlocked and opened the door to where all of the documents, for both the current as well as previous clients, were kept. Placing his cup of coffee on the top of one of the filing cabinets, he located the particular drawer where the contracts and other dealings with Kellerman were filed.

He had barely pulled the drawer open when he heard a voice from behind ask, "What do you think you're doing?"

He didn't have to turn around because he recognized the voice. It was Lucille's.

"I'm checking on something," he said quietly, while continuing to search through the folders.

"Have you seen the headlines in the paper this morning? Does this mean I may not have to work late on Monday?" she asked, while laughing softly.

He continued to search through the filing drawers while she continued asking questions. Unfortunately, he discovered all of Kellerman's folders were gone. Lucille, on the other hand, continued asking questions. Finally, he responded.

"There may yet be a change to your Monday evening schedule," he said candidly as he turned to look at her. "Apparently, we're missing some files, because I cannot locate the Kellerman files anywhere. Do you have any idea where to look?" he asked, while looking directly at her.

"Yes, sir, I think I do," she said as she moved to where he was standing. "Mr. Myers took several folders with him yesterday when he left in the afternoon to go home. He said he had some catching up to do. I thought it was kind of odd because lately he hasn't taken anything home except himself," she replied, while checking other cabinets. "Mr. Carlisle," she said, while quickly surveying the cabinets, "four of the filing cabinets are unlocked, and that should not be. I locked all of them yesterday before I left." He went behind her and checked them as well.

"When you left last night, did you set the alarm?"

She immediately shot back, "Yes, sir. The alarm was set, and the red light came on, just like it always does," she replied, pointing to the alarm panel on the wall.

"Get Craig or Carrie on the phone. I've tried twice this morning and couldn't get them. If you get a hold of them, let me speak with them," he instructed.

He decided not to call the police because he wanted to reach Craig or Carrie first. His lawyer instincts were kicking in again. He thought, *One of them might have the folders because more research or additional information for the contract was needed. Or maybe they had the folders because trouble was at their doorstep and someone needed to do a little house cleaning other than Mrs. Cole. Or maybe the folders just got up and walked out of the filing cabinet.*

He asked Lucille to check the other cabinets and to make a list of any files that were missing. Reaching for his coffee, he noticed a small stain immediately to his left, on the top of the filing cabinet. The outline was that of a particular coffee cup belonging to someone he knew who worked in the office. He decided not to disturb it. It might be the only evidence he had.

As Lucille began working on the names of clients whose folders were missing, he walked to his office, went over to his window, and watched as the sun rose higher in the sky. *It must have been a spectacular sunrise in Brooklyn this morning*, he thought. *I hope Vicky enjoyed it.*

"Mr. Carlisle, there are at least six other clients whose folders are missing from the cabinet drawers," she said, while handing him the list. "I'll need another hour or so before I can be sure that I have put the entire list together."

Samuel scanned the list, checking to see if any of the names had connections with Kellerman. Four of the six names could be loosely associated with Kellerman through city contracts and current projects under consideration. The other two names did not appear to have any immediate connection. What bothered him more at this point was the coffee stain he had found on top of the filing cabinet. The square-shaped outline left on the cabinet was no doubt that of Carrie's coffee cup. There was no other cup like it in the office complex.

"Could you ask Mrs. Cole to come to my office for a moment?"

"Yes, I think she's still here. May I refill your cup of coffee while I'm headed that way?"

"No thanks. Mrs. Cole will do for now," he said. "By the way, when you lock up at the end of each day, do you clean or dust any part of the office?" he asked in an off-the-cuff manner.

"No," she said, before adding, "that's why we have Mrs. Cole."

"When you're in the filing area, do you dust or clean in there?"

"I do if it needs it, Mr. Carlisle. Sometimes the tops of the cabinets get a little dusty, or someone will put things on top of them that make a mess. I wipe them down as best I can. It helps to keep the dust down," she said.

"Did you clean them before leaving yesterday?" he asked with raised eyebrows.

"Yes, as a matter of fact, I did clean the tops of all of them. Somebody spilled soda on the top of one of them and left a mess," she said, while once again walking toward the door to get Mrs. Cole.

He didn't know all of the story, but he did know that he needed to protect the firm from possible allegations. He knew there were a lot of questions that needed to be answered. At the moment, until he was sure that a crime actually had been committed, his one real concern was keeping the police at a distance.

When questioning Mrs. Cole, he learned that her daily assignments included cleaning the bathrooms, emptying the trash, vacuuming all carpeted areas, and dusting both the office and waiting room areas. She mentioned repeatedly that both Craig and Carrie had specifically told her that she was not to enter the filing room. When pressed about the instructions given to her concerning the filing room, Mrs. Cole said that Mrs. Myers told her to be sure that door was locked before leaving for the day.

It was evident to him that either Carrie or Craig was involved in what happened in the office. He wasn't sure which one, or perhaps both, but he knew they were the likely ones to be involved in this because of the key needed to open the filing cabinets. Someone else might have had a key to the filing room, but not to the cabinets. The only ones who had keys to the cabinets were Craig, Carrie, Lucille, and himself.

Pausing at the door to his office with her coffee cup in hand, Lucille asked, "What do we do now?" Before Samuel could respond, she leaned against the doorframe, took a sip of her coffee, and then asked, "Do you think this has something to do with the Kellerman contract?"

Samuel was thinking the same thing. He wasn't sure exactly what to say, but he felt Lucille deserved an answer.

"I'm not sure what this means or even if it means anything. What I do know is that we need to try to reach Craig or Carrie as soon as possible," he said, while walking toward his desk.

"There's just something not right about all of this," she said.

"I understand. I know … there are some questions that I would like to have answered too."

While making a phone gesture with his right hand to his right ear, he looked at Lucille and said, "The sooner you reach the two of them, or even just one of them, the sooner I will have answers to my questions," he said.

She knew what he meant and headed toward her desk.

As Samuel sat down in his chair, he let out a sigh. Traveling to Brooklyn on Friday seemed a much better prospect to him than his being at the office. Instinctively, he thought of calling Vicky to alert her about what had happened but decided not to because he really didn't have much to tell her.

The outline of Carrie's cup on the top of the cabinet needs more attention, he thought.

Just about the time he was able to collect his thoughts, she buzzed in on the intercom to tell him that she had reached Mrs. Myers at home.

"Mrs. Myers is holding on line two for you," she said casually.

"Thank you. Did you say anything about the files to her?"

"No. I just told her that you needed to talk to her right away. Then I put her on hold," she said, in her typical secretary's voice.

Before picking up the receiver, he thought again about how Carrie might be involved. Reminding himself to be as professional as possible about all of this, he picked up the receiver and said, "Good morning, Carrie. I'm sorry to have to bother you at home, but have you seen the headlines in the paper this morning? Kellerman was arrested last night and has been charged with extortion and conspiracy to commit extortion."

"Yes, both of us have seen the headlines. If you'll turn on the television, you'll get an eyeful of Kellerman because he's all over every channel's morning news reports. He's become quite the celebrity for the moment," she said sarcastically. "Craig and I will be in later this morning because Kellerman called late last night and asked us to represent him. We went down there last night and checked on his bail. This morning we need to speak with the district attorney about the charges. It will probably be after ten o'clock before we get there."

"Carrie, we have a situation at the office that you and Craig should know about. Some of the files from the cabinets are missing. We're concerned because Kellerman's files are among them," he said forcefully.

There was silence on the other end of the phone. Samuel paused for what seemed to be an eternity and added, "There's more, but it will have to keep until the two of you get here. I just don't want to do this over the phone," he said, while lowering his voice.

The silence on the other end of the phone was broken by Craig's unexpected interruption, saying, "Samuel, keep the police and press away from the office. We'll bring you up to speed when we get there. The most important thing for you to know is that we have this under control, and you'll just have to trust us for now," he said insistently.

Craig's tone of voice and choice of words were anything but comforting. He knew he would now have to confront both of them because there was little doubt that the two of them were involved in this matter up to their eyebrows. For some reason, the phone call just made things worse. After hanging up, he had Lucille redo his afternoon schedule.

Thinking his day had been salvaged, he turned his thoughts toward Dr. Rutledge and the Durham case. As he went about preparing a motion for appeal, the last thing he needed were distractions. It became increasingly clear to him, however, that the timing of the Kellerman charges could not just mess up all of his weekend plans, but they might cause Dr. Rutledge to become less involved with the case. *It isn't too early to call him*, he thought.

The concern he had was whether there had been ample time for Dr. Rutledge to come up with a wrinkle or two on the appeals issues. While glancing over his notes regarding the trial transcript, he asked Lucille to get him on the phone.

About that time, Lucille came in over the intercom, saying, "Mr. Carlisle, your wife is on line one."

The day began to go south from that point forward. He wasn't sure if she would go ballistic over all of this, but he wasn't taking any chances either. Knowing what was in store for him, both in Brooklyn and at his office in Daytona Beach, the rock-and-a-hard-place scenario was all he could think about before picking up the phone and speaking with his wife.

I can do this, he thought.

"Thank you," he responded. "Please call Dr. Rutledge and ask him if I can meet with him at his place this afternoon around five thirty. If he says he needs more time than that, just thank him and tell him I'll call him later this evening."

As he picked up the receiver, he tried to think of something to talk to Vicky about other than the morning's headlines in the newspapers.

"Hi, sweetheart," he said in a lively fashion.

"I miss you," she said softly. "I'm so glad that you'll be here tomorrow afternoon," she added.

"I've missed you too. How are the kids?" he asked, without giving her any room to talk about anything else.

"They're fine. Rachel fixed breakfast for everyone this morning, and Joshua helped me clean up the kitchen. You would have enjoyed seeing Rachel behaving like quite the cook in the kitchen," she said proudly.

He knew he was listening because he felt the grin on his face. He heard the part about Rachel and breakfast, but his recent run-in with missing folders, clients being arrested for extortion, and a transcript that might help him appeal a case for a convicted murderer kept him from totally focusing on what Vicky was saying. Apparently, she sensed it.

"What's wrong? Is there something wrong, honey?"

"Vicky..." he said, then paused to make sure that what he said next would be more informational than problematic, "there's been a little bit of a log jam at the office that might require more time than I want to devote to it. That's all," he explained.

"This is just great," she said pessimistically. "What happened that might take you longer than you expected?" she asked in a more stern yet whisper-like tone.

"I really can't talk about it at the moment, but I will call you later this afternoon. I need to make certain of my schedule for tomorrow; that's all. This is business and involves the lawyer-client privacy issue," he added, hoping this would reduce a barrage of questions that might be forthcoming.

"We need you here. Can't your work wait until Tuesday next week?" she asked, trying to remind him in a subtle manner about all that must be done over the weekend.

"I know; I know," he said respectfully.

This conversation is going nowhere, he thought. *I just wish she would let go of this thing right now and let me work this out today. I do not want this or anything else to interfere with my getting on that flight. Surely she must know that.*

"You can't be serious about something keeping you away from me and the kids. Certainly you must know how much your parents want you to be a part of this weekend. Besides, we discussed all this, and I

43

thought we worked out how you were going to talk with your father and mother about a bunch of other things too," she said matter-of-factly.

"Nothing has changed. Please don't jump to conclusions about any of this. I will know more about how this might play out later this afternoon. I will call you later, after I meet with Dr. Rutledge today…" he said, and added, "I promise."

Pausing for just a second, he tried to end their conversation at that point by saying, "I've got to hang up to take another call. I love you. Please give the kids a hug for me and tell them I will see them tomorrow, just like we planned," he said.

Vicky said her good-byes and hung up.

Gee, that went well, he said to himself sarcastically.

After hanging up the phone, he looked at his watch and decided to turn on the television to see if there were any updates on the news story. One of the local stations was showing the video clip Carrie had mentioned earlier. The reporter referred to Kellerman as "the councilman, whose alleged misconduct with certain companies resulted in charges being filed indicating that these same companies had to pay over eighty thousand dollars in payoffs and kickbacks to get projects approved and permits issued. In the statement released by the district attorney's office, the spokesperson indicated that more indictments may be forthcoming…"

"Mr. Carlisle," Lucille said, interrupting his thinking, "I brought some donuts this morning. Would you like one?" she asked, holding them close enough for him to take in both their freshness as well as her perfume.

His attention was focused on the part where the reporter said, "…more indictments may be forthcoming." That, however, did not stop him from his selecting one of the glazed donuts, thanking her, and sitting back down at his desk.

"Do you suppose that could mean Mr. or Mrs. Myers?" she asked, while watching Samuel take a large bite out of one of the donuts.

"I hope not," he mumbled, with a mouthful of donut. "The part about 'more indictments may be forthcoming' does not sound particularly good."

"I know Mr. Kellerman and Mr. Myers have been pretty buddy-

44

buddy lately, if you know what I mean," she said as she sat down in the chair next to his desk. When she crossed her legs, Samuel's attention was drawn to the ankle bracelet she was wearing.

That's a first, he thought. He did not recall having seen Lucille wear one of those before. *There's something very sexy about an ankle bracelet,* he thought, *especially worn by a long-legged woman whose legs are as shapely as Lucille's.*

The memory of when Vicky last wore an ankle bracelet came flooding back to him. She used to wear one every day, until she and Samuel ran into her old boyfriend, Douglas Waites, almost four years earlier. They were taking Rachel for an early evening stroll when they met Douglas Waites and stopped to chat about old times. Although Samuel tried to play nice during the four-to-five-minute conversation, he specifically recalled his being irritated to the core the entire time.

The problem arose when Douglas saw that she was wearing an ankle bracelet and just happened to comment that apparently she was "still his slave." That was a reference to when they had dated in high school. Douglas had given her an ankle bracelet during her senior year and used to brag to others how she was "his slave."

Funny, she doesn't wear that bracelet anymore. Douglas Waites was a jerk then and a bigger jerk now, he reflected. *Besides,* he mused, *that thing used to turn her ankle green.*

"Mr. Carlisle," Lucille said softly, "is there something wrong with my legs?"

Realizing his thoughts had been elsewhere at the start of the conversation, he glanced at the clock on the wall, trying to redirect his attention to something other than her legs.

"What do you mean?"

"You've been staring at them for several seconds. I'm not sure if there's a problem or if I should feel flattered," she replied whimsically.

"I'm sorry. I guess I was in another world," he said apologetically.

"That's okay. I feel flattered. And by the way, you're blushing," she said as she leaned toward him. "You've made my morning. Maybe I can make your afternoon for you," she said as she stood and walked slowly toward the door.

CHAPTER 4

"Pat, I just spoke with Samuel a few minutes ago. He said something came up at the office that he can't talk about, but he thinks he's still on for tomorrow's flight," Vicky said as she dusted and straightened mustard jars on the top of the display case.

"Did he have anything else to say? Or did he just clam up, giving the lawyer reasons he uses?"

"Apparently there's something going on that caused a log jam at the office. His words, not mine," Vicky added.

She knew the lawyer-client privilege phrase often helped him redirect a conversation. From time to time, she knew there were things he couldn't talk about as part of his work. Other times, she felt he just wanted to talk things out helping him to work through his thoughts. This morning she felt he sounded distant, where he was either reluctant to discuss the matter or could not be open with her. She wasn't sure whether to worry or not.

"I think something happened that he's just not able to talk about right now. He did say he would call me later today," she said, while continuing to dust and straighten the displays at the end of the counter. "He's probably trying to figure out the details right now so he can deal with whatever it is. If you ask me, Craig's probably got him heavily involved in whatever, just so he can keep his own hands clean."

Pat put on an apron and began cleaning the workstations behind the counter. While working on the displays, Vicky found an empty saltshaker, picked it up, went back to the storeroom, located the large salt containers, and began filling the smaller one.

It's odd how simple things like a saltshaker can cause memories to come flooding back. Holding that saltshaker reminded her of the day she and Samuel first met in November 1967. The two of them had never laid eyes on each other until each of them decided to spend time at the library on campus. He was in his junior year and stayed close to the other political science majors on campus. She was a sophomore who had not yet declared a major and stayed close to mostly a small circle of friends from her dorm.

She recalled that as that afternoon progressed, she had decided to take a break from her studies at the library and grab a bite to eat. The main cafeteria wasn't open, but the snack bar was, and she'd decided that would be sufficient for the time being.

The seating area wasn't full, but there were several students who were enjoying each other's company. There was a particular group of young women near the south entrance whose conversations mostly centered on school stuff. However, it would turn to young men—especially when one entered the snack bar. For Vicky, it was a cheap source of highly amusing entertainment. It helped to ease the tension she had been feeling about her grades and the work left undone in the library. On that afternoon, she decided not to join in on the fun, ordered a hamburger, fixed her drink, and then found a seat near the north exit door.

While waiting for her food, she recalled that her thoughts turned to her father, Norman. He had tried his best to convince her to become a chemist and go to work for his department at the Wilmington, Delaware, plant. Having been a chemist for over twenty-two years, he had made a good living and provided a nice home for their family. Sadly, it hadn't always been that way.

After twenty years of hard work, his department was one of the leading research divisions for the company. He knew that Vicky's math skills were more than adequate and that she was a natural in chemistry. He knew she would be extremely successful carrying on his work, as well as the work of many others in the research division.

Although she believed what her father thought was possible, she really wasn't interested in working in Wilmington, Delaware. Besides, like so many sophomores, she had not yet committed to a major field of study. What she knew—and her father didn't—was that her major field of study wasn't going to be in chemistry or chemical engineering. The recollection of her father's feeling of disappointment, a year and a half later, along with the look on his face when she told him she had decided not to finish school, had been etched into her memory. Instead, she had developed a plan of her own, hoping and wishing her parents would understand.

As she recalled the details of that day, she remembered looking through some notes, while sitting in the snack bar, that she had worked on earlier in the library. The girls near the entrance became noticeably hushed, and that's when she'd first seen Samuel. He had just entered the room wearing a pair of faded blue jeans, a light blue, long-sleeved shirt with the cuffs rolled up to just below his elbows, and a pair of black loafers with no socks. She also remembered her embarrassment when she became aware she had been staring at him for several seconds.

He too ordered a hamburger, got his drink, and then began surveying the room for a place to sit. He spotted a seat not far from Vicky—and then he spotted Vicky.

She remembered that as he walked toward her, he made eye contact and smiled at her. She watched with great interest, only to see him walk to the table behind her. The pretentious group of young women near the entrance saw the same. Vicky had forgotten until that moment, after so many years, how those girls began to move ever so slowly, seat by seat, attempting to find a vacant chair next to where he was planning to sit.

After setting down all of his books and his drink, he discovered there was no saltshaker on the table. After quickly looking at the surrounding tables, he discovered the only one in sight was on her table. So, he decided to approach her and ask her if he could borrow it.

"Do you mind if I borrow this?" he asked, while pointing to the saltshaker near the middle of her table.

She responded with a smile and nodded, as if to grant permission. He thanked her and returned to his table. As he went back to his seat, she remembered seeing him glance back at her. After pausing for just a second, he picked up all of his books, began balancing his soda, utensils, and the saltshaker, and then began walking toward her table.

"Do you mind if I join you?" he asked as he carefully started to put everything down on the table.

She remembered her feeling quite comfortable about his sitting with her. She also recalled her feeling almost stunned that he would do so. As the details came back to her, she recalled feeling very much at ease around him, even at this first meeting.

"Hi. I'm Vicky," she said, calmly extending her right hand to him. As she recalled, he went to shake her hand and lost control of the salt-shaker at the same time. It came crashing down to the tabletop. The noise it made was similar to that of a pile driver on concrete. To her the echo from the noise the salt shaker made hitting the table seemed to last for minutes. Salt flew everywhere.

"I'm so sorry," he said as he began to clean up the mess. It was when they both stood to clean the salt off of their clothes that their eyes met. What was noticeable was how quiet it had become in the dining area. Even the rowdy group of girls relished the moment as much as Vicky, she recalled.

"It's okay," she said, trying to diffuse the awkward moment and encouraging him to sit down.

"I can't believe I did that," he said, finally taking a seat. "Hi, I'm clumsy. Samuel Carlisle. You're Vicky..."

"I'm Vicky Fowler," she said, still looking attentively at him.

Just then, they were both called to pick up their order. He volunteered to go. On the way back, he picked up a mustard container before returning to the table.

"Thank you for allowing me to sit here with you. I really hate eating alone. Besides, I couldn't help but notice that you're really into the library thing today too. Exams or papers?" he asked before taking a sip of his soda.

"Exams," she said, and then added, "but I'm not sure I'm going to be ready for them. How about you?"

"I've waited, perhaps too long, to put together research on a paper that is due in less than two weeks. I'm confident I'll get it done, but I'm just not confident how effective it will be for Dr. Rutledge's class on nineteenth-century case law."

"Are you pre-law?" she asked, while handing him a napkin.

"Yes. How about you?"

"I haven't declared. I'm kind of hung up on what I want to do as opposed to what my parents ... let me correct that ... what my father wants me to do," she said, glancing over his left shoulder.

"I understand," he said, smiling ever so slightly. "I mean I've always wanted to be a lawyer, but I didn't want to go to those big schools up north," he said before taking a bite of his hamburger.

"Up north? Where's home for you?" she asked, even though she wasn't sure why she asked that question.

"I was born and raised in Brooklyn, New York," he said proudly. "Are you from Florida?" he asked, not knowing what else to say, while wondering where this conversation was going.

"No, I'm from a little place in New Jersey called Bridgeton. It's not too far from Philadelphia."

"I know where Bridgeton is. It's near a place called Fortescue, where we would occasionally spend our summers," he said, as he took another sip of his soda.

Vicky's time reminiscing about how she and Samuel first met was rudely interrupted when Pat entered the storeroom.

"Vicky," she said matter-of-factly, "I was beginning to wonder if you had gone to sleep back here. I could use a little help at the counter, if you don't mind."

"Okay, I'll be right there," she said as she glanced once more at the salt-shaker. She finally filled it, put the cap back on it, and walked toward the door. She stopped to adjust her apron, and she wiped the tears from her eyes.

For crying out loud, she thought. *I promised myself I wouldn't do this.*

CHAPTER 5

Not knowing Craig and Carrie's whereabouts, Samuel saw ten o'clock come and go that morning. He still felt he to needed to talk to both of them. Dr. Rutledge hadn't called him that morning either. Even though Lucille was trying to reach him, he wanted to clear at least one item off his to-do list. He figured Dr. Rutledge may have needed an extra hour or two to get through the transcript. To top it all off, he had had what he felt was a miserable conversation with his wife—plus a phone call from Charles Durham that left more questions than answers. *Two steps backward*, he thought. *The list will have to wait.*

While waiting for Craig to arrive, he began reviewing the trial transcript. He started at the point where Charles had taken the witness stand. He wanted to review how both the defense and prosecutor questioned Charles on the crucial elements of the case. This would help to impact the jury, and it would contradict any motive the prosecution might argue for murder. Thinking he would be less distracted as he read, he propped his feet on the windowsill and put his back to the door.

Although he trusted Lucille's instincts and her judgment, the first lesson learned in law school was to remain impartial. While reading, he focused on trying to find something in the testimony that would help him develop a stronger case than what had been presented in court. He was good at reading between the lines. If there was something there—anything—he believed he'd find it. It was a gift that he had learned to rely on. Over the years, he had learned to become comfortable with it.

As he continued to read, he recognized the prosecution had built a considerable circumstantial case for murder. Details and word pictures helped the prosecution to demonstrate for the jury a suspect who was not only capable of committing murder, but also that Charles was out of control during the two days preceding the crime.

Still, he knew he had not gathered enough information from the transcript to show where the prosecution had established any reasonable motive for the murder. One thing in his favor was how little evidence there was that Charles even knew or ever met the victim before the day of the murder. He scribbled a reminder to himself in the margins of the transcript to pursue this detail. There was something about the victim that caused him to put down the transcript and ask Lucille to find Lenny. He needed some background work done quickly. Lenny was good at it.

Leonard "Lenny" Yeager was a third year law student for the second time. Although very bright and capable, life kept getting in the way of his finishing the academic portion of his studies and finally graduating. He had not taken the bar exam for Florida, but he could probably teach the preparation for the exam better than some professors. He was a walking encyclopedia of information who knew his way around research material and the innermost workings of the Library of Congress. He was only four years older than Samuel but looked like he could be at least fifteen years his senior.

He had finished his first year at Harvard Law School in 1965. About three weeks into his second year of study, his family needed him to come home to help tend to the family business while his father recuperated from surgery. If given the chance in casual conversations, he would tell about how he used to practice his courtroom studies while standing in the middle of piles of cow dung. He spent countless hours memorizing case studies and federal court decisions while cleaning out stalls. All of this to try to keep up with his studies, but to little or no avail.

He was from south central Illinois. There, farming is as much a part of living as breathing and sleeping are to most people. He learned how to work hard while growing up on the family farm and held strong religious convictions from having attended church whenever the church doors were open. He was taught that his word was his bond. Indeed, the Yeager family was very proud of him. But he just couldn't catch a break.

After his father had suffered a mild stroke, he and his three brothers kept the business going. Even though his father was able to return to limited work before the year was out, Lenny still stayed home to help out. His mother helped make ends meet by selling her delicious canned tomatoes and creamed corn. Her specialty, however, was bread pudding that she would sell to the local diner. The family worked together and saved every dime they could. All of this, however, took its toll on Lenny's studies. It delayed his returning to Harvard for almost two years.

"Mr. Carlisle," Lucille said over the intercom, "Lenny said he'd be here in about fifteen minutes. I haven't heard anything further from either Craig or Carrie. May I get you anything?"

"No, thank you. Please send Lenny in as soon as he arrives," he instructed.

Samuel often wondered how or why Lenny ended up in Daytona Beach. He had decided long ago, however, that it might be best to leave that issue alone. Instead, he began jotting down a few thoughts about what he would like Lenny to do concerning the Durham case. It would require Lenny to spend some time at the newspaper archives and libraries in the area. He believed, if the information he needed could be found in the Daytona Beach area, that Lenny was the man for the job.

About thirty minutes later, Lenny reached the office complex and entered Samuel's office. Samuel had just finished editing a document that was due early the following week. When he looked up from his desk, he noticed Lenny's tattered and ragged appearance. It was outdone only by his tattered clothing and uncombed hair.

"Geez Louise, Lenny. What in heaven's name happened to you? Are you working undercover, working a second job you haven't mentioned, or is this just the new Lenny look?" he asked, rolling his eyes and trying not to laugh.

"I'm very sorry, but there was this couple who needed help with a spare tire…and it started to rain slightly. I did get here as quickly as possible though, as Lucille had asked," he said resolutely.

Lenny went to take a seat, only then to realize how grubby he actually was. He excused himself for a few minutes and went to the restroom. He returned a little less disheveled but ready to work. Lucille got him a cup of coffee and one of the remaining donuts. He took out his notepad, sat down in the chair, and said, "Okay, now, what's on your mind?"

"I'm looking into the Durham case for Lucille so she can feel a little better about her brother's fate. I've found a few items that I would like for you to dig into. I'm especially interested in the supposed victim, Herman Jackson. I've made a few notes to help you get started. First, find out what you can about him, and then go as far back to 1972. I believe he's originally from Miami. Check for any priors, known associates, and anything else you can dig up," he said, while handing him the piece of paper with his notes on it. "There's no telling where this might lead. Craig has been overly political of late and has had way too many visitors from town hall."

"I suppose you need this tomorrow, right?" Lenny asked, as he quickly looked over the information Samuel had given him.

"Actually, next Tuesday will do because I will be in New York starting tomorrow, and I will not return until late Monday afternoon."

"And to whom do I send the bill for this?"

"Send it to Lucille," he said, while smiling at him.

"Mr. Carlisle," Lucille said over the intercom, "Mr. and Mrs. Myers just came in. They should be in their offices by now."

"Thank you. I'll be there shortly," he said as he stood up and turned the intercom switch off.

After putting the paper into his shirt pocket, Lenny shook Samuel's hand and, as he stood to leave, said, "Thank you for the opportunity. I really do need the work, and I promise I will keep my nose to the grindstone on this."

"Just be sure you're as discrete as possible. I really don't want anyone other than you, Lucille, and myself to know what's going on. Here are a few extra bucks to help get you started," he said as he handed him an envelope containing four hundred dollars. "This will be deducted from any bill you send us."

After Lenny departed, he felt a little better about the prospects for the

Durham case. There were still many unanswered questions. He believed any information Lenny could find about Herman Jackson would help to give a more solid base for the arguments he was developing.

Samuel asked Lucille if she had heard anything from Dr. Rutledge.

"Nothing yet," she replied.

As Carrie was entering his office, Samuel said, "Lucille, Mrs. Myers and I will be in consultation for a while. With the exception of Mr. Myers and perhaps Dr. Rutledge returning my call, would you hold all calls and visitors, please?" he asked, while directing Carrie to sit down other than where Lenny had sat earlier.

"Yes, sir. May I get either of you anything?"

Carrie gestured she didn't care for anything. Seeing that, he said, "No, thank you," and turned off the intercom.

Carrie entered his office looking exhausted. *Holy moly, she looks like death warmed over*, he thought. *This is a picture that's got to be worth ten thousand words, if it's worth one.*

Carrie saw the look on his face and said, "Yes, I've had better mornings. I didn't get much sleep last night, and we had very little luck this morning at the state attorney's office." After taking off her right shoe, she bent down and began to rub her foot.

"Kellerman has really done some dumb things, but this could be the sorriest of them all. I think we're really looking at going to trial on this one," she said as she continued to rub her foot.

Samuel was listening to her and was somewhat amused as he watched her rub her foot. There was no question about it. Her appearance and posture contradicted her usual pristine and the classic Carrie-like composure. However, she never missed a beat while talking about the morning she and Craig had experienced downtown.

"The charges being brought against Kellerman are not likely to be dropped or even reduced as part of a plea bargain. They believe their case is solid and refused to discuss any part of the events," she said as she took off her other shoe and began rubbing her other foot.

"What about the discovery issues?" he asked.

"We discussed that on the way to the office this morning. We were told that any and all information pertinent to the Kellerman case would be made available to us by Monday afternoon. He's to be arraigned this afternoon at two o'clock," she said as she leaned back in the chair and let out a deep sigh.

He took in every bit of her as he looked her over from the top of her head to the tips of her sore feet. He couldn't help but think that even on a bad day she was gorgeous.

The conversation concerning Kellerman and her trip to the state attorney's office continued for another four or five minutes, leading nowhere. Samuel looked at the clock on the wall behind Carrie and thought this was as good as any time to get to the bottom of the open filing cabinets and missing files.

"Carrie," he said, pausing while moving to the chair next to her. Then, looking directly at her, he said, "When I came to work this morning, I found filing cabinets had been left open, and there were some clients' folders missing."

"You don't honestly think Craig and I have done anything wrong, do you?" she asked, tempting him to continue.

That was not the answer I was looking for, he thought. *She should know that I'm not going to debate this issue with her.*

"I am not sure what to think at the moment. I'd like to think the two of you were catching up on current casework. I think you owe me a more detailed answer than that," he said pointedly.

"You'll get your answer, but it will have come from Craig. I will tell you that we were in the office last night around eleven fifteen, after everyone was gone for the day. Yes, we went into the filing cabinets and took out Kellerman's files. We worked until almost three in the morning. We wanted to make sure we had what we thought we would need, in case his arraignment was moved to earlier in the day," she said, while turning to face him. "Craig will have to explain anything else because that's all I know," she said as she leaned toward him and placed her left hand on his left knee.

"I'm sorry, but I just have a feeling there's—"

Stopping him in mid-sentence, she said, "I really don't know any more about where you want to go with this or what you're implying. I just..."

She turned away from him. He could hear her crying gently and saw where tears had fallen on her skirt. He reached for a tissue and handed it to her. It was then that he realized Lucille was at the door. By placing his right index finger in front of his lips, he hoped she would know to wait and to be quiet. She understood. She nodded her head and went back to her desk.

"Craig has done something. I don't know what. I know he is in over his head right now. I just feel he's in the middle of some God-awful situation and keeping company with some sleazy individuals," she said softly. "I'm sorry," she said, while trying to gather her composure and turning slowly toward him. "I didn't see this coming."

He was at a loss for words and what to do. He reached for another tissue and handed it to her. As she took it from him, their hands touched. She clasped his hand with both of hers and looked at him with tear-swollen eyes.

He stood next to her, placed his hand on her shoulder, and said, "Maybe now is not the best time, but I do believe you and I need to spend some time talking. Not here. There are too many eyes and ears," he said as he glanced at the door. "Maybe later this afternoon would be better," he offered.

She stood, hugged him, and said, "Thank you. I know I can always count on you. Please ... please do not speak of this to Craig. I will talk with you later today, after the arraignment," she said as she turned to leave. She looked back for just a moment before leaving the room and said, "Time alone with you would be great."

He looked down at his feet to see if his teeth had fallen to the floor. He was stunned by her reaction and certainly by her words. Again, the picture he had of her was nothing like the woman who had just been in his office. She was not by any means the cool, composed, and professional person he knew. She was just not the type who showed signs of vulnerability.

This side of Carrie was something he found distinctively to his liking and very attractive. Although still cautious in his thinking about what just took place, he liked what he saw in the Carrie who just left his office.

"Lucille," he called over the intercom, "would you mind coming in here for a minute?"

"Is it safe?"

"Yes. And please bring that list of files that initially were missing with you," he instructed.

He sat motionless, staring at the seat where Carrie had been sitting, not really understanding what he was feeling. She had just revealed an unusual characteristic that was extremely different from how she usually presented herself to the world. In the previous conversations they had had over the years, she had never talked about Craig in such a manner. It now occurred to him that the conversations they had shared, as they sat and talked over the many years, were superficial, non-essential, feel-good details. This was different. It was as if she had stepped out of her world into his and had lost her way. He knew what to expect and how to manage those little tête-à-têtes they had had before. Those, he now could see, were casual and meaningless shared spaces and times. Now the rules had changed, and the playing field had suddenly become not so level. The prospect of their afternoon meeting, and his not really knowing how to handle it, scared him to death.

"What went on in here just now?" Lucille asked as she handed him the list of names he had asked her to bring.

"What would you say if I told you that Mrs. Myers was involved in something not of her doing and was not able to handle it?" he asked, while motioning for her to sit down.

"That's not the Mrs. Myers I know. The Mrs. Myers I know would tell you when to get off, where to go, and laugh about the prospect of your own imminent death," she said. "She's one beautiful human who could double as a black widow, if you catch my meaning," she added.

"I'm not sure how you interpreted what you saw a few minutes ago, but Mrs. Myers showed a side of her I've never seen before. I'm really concerned more about her involvement with the missing files than I am with Kellerman. She and Craig were in here working until three this morning, preparing for Kellerman's arraignment," he said as he looked over the list of names for the missing files.

"Mr. Carlisle," she continued, "the missing files belong to Sidney Dorn and Roger Matheny. I'll check to be sure that Mr. or Mrs. Myers didn't misfile them. Is there anything else you want me to do for you?" she asked as she stood up ever so slowly from her chair and leaned on the corner of his desk.

"Yes, there is something you can do. How about ordering lunch from Clark's, and I'll buy," he said, while handing her a twenty-dollar bill.

As she walked to the door, she said, "Mind your P's and Q's with Mrs. Myers. She strikes me as not really being exactly the kind of person who leans on others in times of need, unless there's something in it for her," she said.

As Lucille was walking toward the door, she turned toward Samuel, pointed her right index finger at him, began wagging it, and then said, "She's a user and a taker, not a giver and a maker." Smiling one last time, she added, "Now me, I'm a giver, and I'm really good at it too."

CHAPTER 6

Samuel picked up his briefcase and headed out the door for DeLand. The courthouse, which was about thirty minutes from his office, as well as the clerk of the court's office, was located there. As he walked by Lucille's desk, he looked at her and said, "I should be back by one o'clock. Let's eat and go over a few things about your brother's case … if you don't mind," he added as he continued toward the door.

"No, I don't mind. After I get back from Clark's with lunch … with it being such a nice day outside, maybe we could go across the street and have sort of a picnic," she said invitingly.

"Okay. That sounds like a plan," he said as he continued toward the door. "I will be in Judge Michaels' chambers dealing with the motion for the Dailey case. I'll see you in a little while," he said as he hurriedly went out the door and got into his car.

"Okay. Mr. Carlisle …" she said as she slowly got up from behind her desk and went to the door, thinking she might catch him before he got into his car. It was no use. Samuel had already begun driving toward DeLand.

As she turned to go back to her desk, Lucille could hear Craig's voice coming from Carrie's office. He was yelling, but it was difficult to make out all the words. She clearly heard Craig say the name "Matheny" just before she heard the unmistakable sound of a human hand striking a human face. The office complex went quiet; she could hear her own heartbeat pounding in her ears. She stopped dead in her tracks and, for what seemed forever, stared at Mrs. Myers' office door down the hallway.

She inched her way cautiously toward Mrs. Myers' door, never taking her eyes off of it. She could hear movement of some kind in the office, so she reached for the doorknob, but Craig bolted out of the door, almost knocking her into the opposite wall. Lucille steadied herself, looked into the office, and saw Mrs. Myers on her knees with her hands clasping her face. Her right shoulder was leaning against the base of her desk. She tried to muffle the sounds of her crying, but her body motions betrayed her.

Lucille got on her knees next to her and put her arms around her. Carrie drew away, began crawling awkwardly to the sofa, pulled herself up to it, and slumped onto the cushions.

"Mrs. Myers," Lucille started, "let me get you a washcloth with some ice in it," she said, while handing her a tissue.

"I'll be fine," she said as she took the tissue from her.

Lucille could see the welt that had formed on her left temple as well as the clearly identifiable imprint of Craig's hand on the left side of her face. It had begun to swell such that Lucille got up and went out the door saying, "I'll be right back with some ice."

As she walked to the kitchen area, she heard what she thought was Carrie attempting to dial a number. What she heard next startled her. It sounded as if Carrie had thrown everything that was on her desk on to the floor. There were two or three seconds of quiet before the sound a heavy thump against one of the walls, followed soon after by another one on the floor, and then silence.

Lucille rushed back to the room to find that she was on the floor behind her desk and unconscious. She checked her pulse and found that Carrie's heart was still beating, although faintly. She picked up the phone base and the receiver from the floor and set them on the desk. She wasn't sure who to call first, so she called a number she knew by heart and one that would get Samuel back to the office quickly.

The person on the other end of the phone line was new to the clerk's office. She was just filling in until Mr. Bernard Stockton, Clerk of the Court, would return from lunch. Lucille had her take a message to give to Samuel, making sure to tell him that it was an emergency. Then she asked for her call to be transferred to Judge Michaels' chambers.

While she was holding for Judge Michaels' secretary to pick up, she heard Carrie moan slightly and watched her roll over as if she was trying to sit up.

"Carrie, I wouldn't try to move too quickly," she said.

Carrie raised herself to a sitting position and attempted to steady herself.

"All I see are bright shooting stars," she said breathlessly. "How long have I been out?" she asked, slurring her words with a heavy tongue.

"Oh, just a few seconds. As soon as I finish with this call, I'm taking you to the hospital," she said firmly. "Your head has taken enough for the day."

Lucille spoke with Judge Michaels' secretary and explained the situation. She was assured that Samuel would be notified as soon as he arrived. She hung up the phone and helped Carrie stretch out on the sofa. Lucille managed to get a washcloth packed with ice so that Carrie could begin to deal with the swelling to her face.

Totally unaware of what had occurred, Samuel continued to drive to DeLand. He expected the hearing before Judge Michaels to be over quickly. His business with Mr. Stockton wasn't expected to take very long either. With Lenny beginning the background work and Dr. Rutledge helping with both the motive and appeal issues, he was beginning to feel like he could offer Lucille a little more than rhetoric about her brother's chances. In spite of more recent events, he felt like he was making some headway in the Durham case.

Once I get back to the office, he thought, *I'll speak with Lucille and let her know what's being planned for her brother's case. That should help things a lot.*

He arrived at the courthouse and went directly to Judge Michaels' chambers. As he entered the outer office area, the judge's secretary handed him the note about what had happened after he had left his office.

He asked to borrow the phone so he could call Lucille. Trying to act as if nothing was wrong, he dialed the number while politely smiling at the secretary. He knew, however, she would not have called unless it was truly an emergency. While standing there waiting for the phone to be answered, he tried to compose himself for what Lucille was going to say to him. He wondered if Vicky had called to tell him there was a problem. Or were there concerns about the plans they had worked out for the coming weekend? He speculated that maybe Dr. Rutledge had called with some valuable information. Maybe Lucille called and there was something pressing with the Kellerman case that he needed to handle while he was at the courthouse.

He wasn't sure what to think because, until today, he had never known her to use the word "emergency." He knew enough to know it was serious. Not knowing what Lucille had to say started his thoughts racing such that he hadn't realized Lucille had already started speaking to him.

When he finally focused on her voice, he began to hear of the events that happened a few minutes after he had departed. He was stunned. While he and Lucille went back and forth on the phone putting the events together, what hit him most was Craig's alleged actions and involvement with what Carrie called "sleazy" people. He picked up the base of the phone and sat down in a chair near where he had been standing. The realness of his being pulled into the events of Wednesday night hit him in his gut like a solid one-two punch. There was no telling where this was headed and whom he could be dealing with along the way.

He told Lucille to get her to the hospital and that he would meet them there when he had finished with his business in DeLand. He coached her on what to say and what not to do while at the hospital. Lucille indicated she understood and that she would take care of what he had asked her to do.

Fortunately, the hospital emergency room wasn't very busy. There were only a handful of patients sitting in the waiting area, while an orderly damp-mopped one of the corridors leading to the exam rooms. Lucille steadied Carrie as she walked into the waiting area and helped her take a seat at the receptionist's desk. Carrie's face had swollen considerably, causing her speech to be distorted and difficult to understand. Lucille, in her usual effective manner, took over the intake process so that Carrie could get to see a doctor quickly. Lucille would not let her say anything about how it happened or who had done this to her. She was absolutely brilliant, almost lawyer-like, handling it for Carrie.

Carrie was told to go immediately to exam room three, where one of the nurses would check on her. She was told the doctor who would examine her would be available in about ten minutes. With that done, an orderly helped her into a wheelchair and headed for exam room three.

Exam room three had the usual gurney and cabinets full of medical items. There were a few other things that Lucille wasn't exactly sure would be used for, but she knew getting Carrie to the hospital was better than hanging around the office. Carrie indicated that she felt nauseous before the orderly helped her out of the wheelchair. Once she was seated on the gurney, the orderly handed her one of those kidney-shaped bowls. She rolled her eyes at Lucille as if to say, "I hope I don't need this thing."

"It won't be too long now before the doctor sees you," she said, while holding Carrie's left hand.

Lucille watched as Carrie tried to speak. It was obvious that talking would not just be difficult for a while, but it would be painful too. She understood her as she tried to tell her how embarrassed she felt about having to be taken care of as if she was a cripple. What was interesting to Lucille, even causing her to smile slightly, was a sudden thought she had about how their roles had been reversed.

Carrie saw the smile. She got Lucille's attention to let her know that she saw the smile and wondered what she was thinking.

"I thought it odd how lawyers are called 'mouthpieces' and that now I'm yours," she said as she fought back a smile.

Carrie started to grin, but that resulted only in more pain.

Finally, the doctor showed up.

CHAPTER 7

"Samuel is going to think I've fallen off the face of earth," Dr. Rutledge said, speaking to his pet cat, Jingles. "A little milk is just what the judge ordered," he said as he set a bowl of warmed milk on the floor next to the refrigerator.

Jingles wasn't just his pet. Jingles had become his companion and best buddy. Dr. Rutledge's wife of forty-nine years had died suddenly four days after he had retired from teaching. It had been almost two years to the day when he rode in the ambulance to the hospital with his wife, holding her hand the entire way, never thinking it would be the last time the two of them would be together. Jingles helped to fill a void in his life.

Jingles' favorite trick was nudging him with a cold, wet nose each morning so he would get up, refill the food bowl, and empty the litter box. Jingles had done his job well at six o'clock this Thursday morning. It allowed Dr. Rutledge to continue his reading of the transcript, while Jingles went back to sleep in Dr. Rutledge's lap.

Reading through the transcript for Samuel had taken longer than he had expected. He had fallen asleep in his chair the night before while attempting to read through sixty pages of testimony. He had forgotten how dry these things could be and how poorly trained some of the attorneys had been in courtroom questioning strategies. He had ended up grading the attorneys on their questioning techniques rather than doing what Samuel needed him to do.

Nonetheless, he awoke earlier than usual to finish those portions Samuel had asked him to read. In the process, he found an odd statement made by the defendant when questioned on the time of the burglary. Charles was, he learned, a two-bit burglar who had two convictions for petty theft and one for larceny. His record was not about murder, assault, or any other crime that involved violence. He had concluded that Charles was basically a thief. Because of his confidence on this point, it presented an opening for him to explore a hypothesis that came from statements made by most of the victim's associates.

Herman Jackson's associates were all somehow connected to the construction industry. Based on these witnesses, it seemed an unlikely connection because Jackson's line of work generally wasn't related to the construction industry. Besides, Charles' primary character trait, assigned by Dr. Rutledge, was that he had never worked a day in his life with his hands, unless he was taking something that belonged to someone else. *He may be Lucille's brother, but he's probably more related to the milkman than to Lucille*, he thought.

He was beginning to put together a theory about Charles and the circumstances surrounding the case. He knew that if he made too many assumptions, the theory would never hold up when debated before a judge. Before calling Samuel, he needed an illustration or flow chart of what he knew, how it could be tied directly to testimony, and to be able to explain it so that Samuel could develop his brief for a judge.

He began with the names of persons identified in the testimony by all of the witnesses. He then linked them to the victim by their testimony noting work relationships, places frequented, personal habits that might have been mentioned, and other pieces of information that were descriptive and specifically identifiable to them. Then he went back and circled all words, phrases, events, and locations that were the same or similar. Using those as his reference points, he connected the names based on the time frame, which had been established so dramatically by the prosecution. This, he figured, would then give him the names of individuals who should either be questioned or at least investigated more thoroughly. What he saw, as he began connecting the names mentioned through testimony about Herman Jackson, was enough evidence for Samuel to begin developing an argument before a judge. The picture puzzle was complete.

Starting with the assumption that Charles was not the type who went around leaning on people with the intent to do bodily harm, Dr. Rutledge believed he had a workable premise with some details that he could discuss with Samuel. He dialed the number to Samuel's office and learned that both Lucille and Samuel were not there. He left a message asking to have Samuel to return his call before six o'clock because Thursdays were Dr. Rutledge's nights out for the evening meal.

Reviewing his outline, he discovered something else about the connection between Charles and his associates. The name T.D. Zeigler was mentioned four times, while the name Art Yochem came up just once. There were no other places in the transcript, at least where he had read, where these names surfaced. These were individuals who had been connected to Herman Jackson—who was supposedly connected to Charles. Dr. Rutledge was not sure, but he believed Zeigler and Yochem were pawns for someone much more powerful and far more removed from these events. Yet they had to be involved up to their necks in what had happened. He tried to reach Samuel once more but ended up leaving a second message for him to contact him as quickly as possible.

Carrie's initial physical examination took about fifteen minutes. Several questions for the doctor were answered by Lucille and confirmed by Carrie's nodding. The question of how she had been injured was responded to by Carrie—as best she could—and interpreted by Lucille, as best she could. The doctor did not seem convinced but continued with the examination.

They learned that her examination would not be able to be completed until the doctor had an opportunity to see the X-rays taken of her head and neck areas. He indicated to Carrie that he was certain her jaw was broken. Also, he was referring the case to someone else who specialized in head injuries. What Carrie learned was that she had suffered a concussion. The doctor was concerned there could be complications because of that injury alone.

"Carrie," Lucille whispered, "don't you worry about a thing. I'll stay right here with you. I know Samuel should be here any minute." Carrie nodded her head and tried to smile, but both actions only caused pain.

When the doctor returned, he had with him an associate who informed Carrie that she would need to stay in the hospital overnight until further tests could be run and evaluated. Based on the X-rays, both doctors believed that the concussion might be more complicated. Observation and further testing would be the prudent things to do.

With that understood, Lucille, who had been seated next to her and holding her left hand, looked at her and told her not to worry. Lucille was thinking the same thing Carrie was: what if Craig showed up at the hospital? What would he do to Carrie if no one else were around?

Carrie's expression said it all. Lucille could see the relief on her face knowing she wasn't going to stay in her house that night and that someone would be with her. Craig had demonstrated his violence once, and she wanted no more of it. Right now, the last thing she needed was to have to deal with Craig. Although she knew a time would come, she had no desire to confront him about his actions without Samuel in the room with her and the authorities nearby.

She motioned to Lucille to get some paper and something to write with.

Lucille handed her a small notepad and pen that she always carried in her purse. Carrie began scribbling on the pad, wanting to know if Lucille had tried to contact Samuel. She informed her of the phone calls but that she hadn't heard from him.

Carrie scribbled another note on the pad and held it up for her to read. She wanted to know if she had called the police. Lucille indicated she had not and that Samuel advised her not to report anything at this point. The problem, however, was that the doctor wanted to know how this had happened. Lucille told the doctor that she didn't really know because all she saw was Carrie on the floor when she had entered the room. Lucille hadn't lied; she had just sent the truth on a brief vacation until Samuel could get there.

Before Carrie was wheeled to her room, she signed her admission papers. Lucille followed close by believing that Samuel would be able to find them. As the orderly wheeled Carrie into the elevator, Lucille thanked the nursing staff for their kindness and attentiveness to Carrie. Carrie, who had closed her eyes, hated hospitals. She hated having to be in it more than she hated the idea of needing it.

Samuel was on his way back to the hospital when something on the car radio reminded him of Catherine. He wasn't exactly sure what triggered his thinking about her, but his memory of Catherine was still very clear and real to him. Her features were still clear to his mind's eye, and even his memory of her perfume came back to him. It was as if she was sitting next to him as he drove back to Daytona Beach. His day had been hectic, and this memory of her was a welcomed relief. Although interrupted by approaching police cars with their sirens blaring, it was a break he welcomed.

Once the sirens were behind him, however, he recalled the time he and Catherine were at her house playing cards with her brothers. It was getting late, and he knew that he would have to leave soon or be in trouble by the time he got home. His parents did not like for him to walk home by himself after dark. In those days, just being with Catherine, though, was worth it. As he reminisced, he knew his mother and father were right. He just hated to admit it.

As he recalled the events of that afternoon, he remembered that after the card game ended and it came time for him to go home, her brothers went upstairs. The two of them were alone for the first time, and he was itching to steal a kiss from her. As soon as she was sure that her brothers were out of sight, Catherine put her soft hands on Samuel's face and pulled him toward her. She kissed him squarely and passionately on his lips. It took his breath away. At the time, he thought he was going to faint.

She let go and took a step backward. He went over to the sofa and sat down.

"What's wrong, Samuel?" she asked as she went over and sat beside him.

"Nothing. I've never been kissed like that before; that's all," he said as he let out a very long breath of air.

He leaned over to her, put his left arm around her, and pulled her closer to him. As he did so, she leaned toward him and placed her arms around him as well. They just sat there, both enjoying the moment—a brief but memorable moment.

She reminded him that he had to go because he would be late and certainly get into trouble. As she walked him to the door, they hugged each other before kissing once again. This time he kissed her back. That's when their fate was born.

Before opening the door and saying goodnight, he remembered putting the index finger of his right hand on her lips and saying, "You're wonderful."

As he approached the hospital, those words were resonating in his ears. He had known Catherine from the time they were in grade school. There seemed to be a history between them from the moment the two of them sat next to each other in Miss McCauley's ninth grade English class. By the time they were juniors in high school, everyone expected them to get married and live in Brooklyn forever. They had become inseparable and seemed like the perfect couple headed for wedded bliss—only life intervened.

As he parked his car and walked toward the emergency entrance, he wondered how Catherine was doing and if she had decided to follow her dreams. Right now, he knew he had to regain his focus on the tasks at hand and by Friday afternoon be on that plane for Brooklyn.

He asked the receptionist where they had taken Carrie. He learned that she was now on the fourth floor in room 412. He headed toward the elevator trying to think of what he was going to say. He wasn't sure how he would begin the conversation; he was just hoping he knew how he was going handle all of this. He always felt inadequate in hospitals. He didn't like hospitals any more than Carrie did. His uncle Ted had died in a hospital, while Samuel was in law school. The problems between his father and himself started in a hospital and grew worse on the day they buried his uncle.

Exiting the elevator on the fourth floor, he was impressed with how quiet everything was. As he walked by each room, all he could hear were the televisions and the occasional paging for a doctor. He arrived at room 412, stood outside the door for just a moment, and tried to muster his courage. That's when Lucille saw him.

"Samuel!" she exclaimed as she briskly walked over to him and hugged him. "You're finally here," she added, while locking elbows and practically dragging him from the corridor and into the room.

"Carrie, Samuel's here!" Lucille said excitedly.

Carrie reached out her hand to Samuel and tried to smile. He took her hand and sat down in the chair next to her bed. Lucille moved to the other side of the bed, near the window, and sat down as well.

"Carrie, do you know where Craig is?" Samuel asked, while looking at what had been a beautiful face, which was now swollen and bandaged.

She indicated that she did not, while glancing at Lucille.

"Lucille," Samuel began, "please go try to reach someone at the office and see if Craig has returned. And see if anyone might have any idea where we might find him," he said, urging her with a jerk of his head toward the door.

Lucille gathered her belongings, reassured Carrie she would be back in a little while, and headed for the waiting area on the first floor of the hospital. There, she knew she would find plenty of pay phones and a restroom nearby.

Samuel looked at Carrie's injuries, and a feeling of queasiness came over him. This was the part of the hospital visits he hated. He knew he'd be okay, but at the moment his stomach was doing back flips. He felt like he might have to be sick.

Carrie could see his distress, both on his face and in his posture.

71

She squeezed his hand and tried to say, "I'm okay," but he was not able to understand what she said. Samuel's expression told her of his anger toward Craig and his sorrow for her pain. She wanted to try to comfort him, but he began pacing slowly by her bedside.

"Carrie, the firm is probably in deep trouble. I'm not sure what exactly is happening, but I am sure that we need to be prepared to circle the wagons. Before Lucille comes back, you and I need to agree that no matter what, and I mean no matter what, the two of us will stick together in our dealings with the authorities. This matter needs to be reported," he said as he sat back down. "Craig needs to be dealt with professionally and personally. I know he's your husband, but for God's sake, look at what he did to you. There's no telling what he might do to someone else or you, again," he said.

Carrie knew all too well what Samuel meant. She knew that Craig was into something, that he could not handle it, and that it was bigger than she wanted to imagine.

Carrie picked up the notepad Lucille had left and began writing. Samuel watched as she wrote. Carrie had written a brief note telling him not to worry. As he held Carrie's hand and told her how sorry he was that this had happened to her, Lucille returned with a message for Samuel.

"Craig has not returned to the office," Lucille announced as she entered the room. "In fact, no one has heard from him or knows where he went. And Samuel," she continued, "Lenny needs you to call him when you get a moment. He's found something while going through old newspaper articles in Stetson's library. And, oh yes, call Dr. Rutledge too," she added.

Carrie heard Lucille mention Lenny's name. Samuel could see there was an immediate interest by Carrie in what Lenny might have discovered. Lucille had let slip that Lenny was working for him. He looked at Carrie and tried to explain that it had nothing to do with Craig. He explained that he was working on the Durham case to see if an appeal or reversal was possible. Still, Carrie had a look of concern—and she motioned for Samuel to hand her the notepad and pen.

She wrote on the pad and gave it to him. He read it, looked at Lucille, and looked again at Carrie. She had written, *Craig was in on the Durham trial.*

"Are you sure? How do you know?" She immediately began writing a response.

The note read, *Anthony Dortch knew and was in on it. Trust me.*

Samuel asked Lucille to step outside to talk to him without Carrie hearing. He gave her instructions that he wanted her to follow exactly the way he had given them to her. He made her repeat them to him so he was sure that she understood what it was she needed to do first. He gave her fifty dollars and watched as she walked toward the elevator. He noticed she was still wearing her ankle bracelet, but somehow it looked good on her now.

When he went back into Carrie's room, he saw that she was crying. He told her everything was going to be all right and that she should trust him to handle these matters.

"Carrie," he said, while holding her hand once more, "it's time we had our little talk. Maybe it's not exactly what you and I might have had in mind earlier today, but right now and right here is when it needs to happen. Here's your notepad and pen. I'll talk and read; you listen and write. Together we're going to work this out, whether Craig likes it or not."

The next two hours Samuel spent with Carrie revealed much of Carrie's recent life, and several things, for Samuel, became clearer. He accepted everything Carrie had related to him as true. He could tell that she was genuinely afraid of Craig and needed to be reassured. He was concerned that Craig might try to get at her while she was in the hospital. So, he convinced Carrie to let him contact the police and file a report. He called it in using the phone in her hospital room.

While they were waiting for the police to arrive, they both just sat there comforting each other over the mess in which they now found themselves. She knew that there would be rough times ahead for her, and he knew that he better be on the plane for Brooklyn by tomorrow afternoon. They both knew that Craig was a loose cannon.

Carrie fell asleep quickly, after unloading so much on Samuel. She was finally able to tell Samuel about Craig's dealings and how it had been eating at her for months. Getting rid of all that guilt and deceit she had been carrying must have been like ridding herself of a ton of bricks. Managing to fall asleep was a welcomed relief and was sorely needed.

While she was sleeping, Samuel decided to slip out of the room to call both Lenny and Dr. Rutledge. He might not reach Lenny by phone at the moment, but he knew how to find him. If Lenny had found something that could help shed light on the Durham case, Carrie's revelation about Craig's involvement would be the icing on the cake. He needed to call Lenny first, even though he knew Dr. Rutledge would soon be headed to his favorite Thursday evening watering hole. That's what Dr. Rutledge did every Thursday evening at six o'clock. His call to Lenny would have to be quick in order to catch Dr. Rutledge still at home.

As he headed toward the first floor and the telephones, it bothered him greatly that Craig could do what he did to Carrie. Samuel had not seen this coming, and Craig's action had crossed a line with Samuel. Although initially perplexed, Samuel knew now what Carrie had been dealing with for several months. There was no more confusion. Justice was to be served to Craig—and Samuel would see to that for Carrie's sake.

Samuel was able to reach Lenny on the first try. Lenny began telling Samuel about what he discovered looking through the newspapers at the library. While researching an article on Jackson, he came across a front page story about Kellerman and some shady construction-contract issues.

"Samuel, a story on Kellerman was in a news article about three years ago. He and someone named Roger Matheny were being investigated for bid-rigging on a large contract proposal down in Orlando," he explained. "The authorities could never build a case against Matheny, but there is evidence, of sorts," he added.

"Did you find anything on an Anthony Dortch while you were looking?"

"No. Should I keep looking until I do?"

"Yes. See if you can find a connection between Dortch, Matheny, and Jackson. Somewhere, I believe their paths probably crossed, maybe within the last three years or so. Also, keep looking to see if you can link Kellerman to any or all of them as well. If he's dirty, these guys are likely to surface somewhere," he instructed. Lenny began to understand what Samuel was trying to do.

"No problem. I may need to end up in Orlando. It has much more research capacity. I'll keep looking, and I'll call you as soon as I can find something," he said on an upbeat note. "A trip to Tallahassee may not be out of the question either," he informed Samuel. "There's no telling where I might find the scent."

When it came to unearthing someone's efforts to hide or drop off the face of the earth, Lenny was better than a bloodhound. To Lucille, Lenny had those big, sad looking puppy-dog eyes, like those of a hound dog. To Lucille, it was important to notice things like that.

CHAPTER 8

Pat was in the middle of preparing supper when Vicky came into the kitchen carrying Joshua and playing Joshua's favorite game, "make Joshua giggle." As Pat continued to peel carrots, Joshua continued his infectious laugh such that Pat could not resist any longer. She stopped what she was doing to hold him for just a few minutes. Vicky picked up with the carrots where Pat had left off, and Joshua continued his giggling without missing a beat. The Carlisle home was filled with laughter and smiles that late Thursday afternoon. Business had been brisk, and everyone was looking forward to Samuel's arrival on Friday.

After dinner was over and the dishes had been cleared from the kitchen table, Pat poured a cup of coffee for Richard and herself before sitting back down at the table.

"Vicky, would you like to join us?" Richard asked, directing his voice toward the hall leading to the living room.

"I'll be there in a minute," she replied, while she finished folding a load of clothes.

Pat and Richard smiled at each other. They had spent the better part of the afternoon talking over what they were about to explain to Vicky. They needed to enlist her to help diffuse any of Samuel's concerns that might come up over the course of the next few days. What they were about to do would require the help of the entire family, and it wasn't something that Pat and Richard wanted to do by themselves anyway. The two of them agreed that it was an all-or-nothing proposition for the family.

After finishing her conversation with Rachel, who had remained in the living room, Vicky entered the kitchen, sat down, and began putting cream and sugar in her coffee. As she was pouring the cream, she looked at Richard and then glanced at Pat. She sensed something was going on by the way Richard kept looking at Pat and then at his coffee. They just sat there without saying anything. *Something's not right*, she thought.

Finally, Vicky spoke. "Okay, what did I do?" she asked, thinking that she had done something wrong.

"Nothing, nothing at all," Pat said, while trying to fight back a smile.

"Honey, we just want you to know we love you; that's all," Richard said.

"Okay, now you're scaring me. What's going on here and what haven't you told me about?" she demanded.

"Vicky," Richard said, while lifting his coffee cup to take a sip, "Pat and I have something to tell you, and we want you to hear us out before you say anything. Do not judge what we say; just listen," he said before taking a very long drink of his coffee.

"Seriously?" Vicky asked as she leaned back in her chair.

"We're as serious as Kosher is to pastrami," Pat said. "What we want to talk about is us selling the store and moving closer to you and Samuel," she said, while slowly stirring her coffee.

Vicky should have been shocked. Instead, she was relieved and over-joyed at the same time.

"This is wonderful," Vicky exclaimed. She got up out of her seat, went over to Pat, and hugged her. Then she quickly moved to where Richard was sitting and hugged him too. Pat and Richard were relieved as well.

"This is just amazing," Vicky said, while hugging Richard's neck. "Rachel and Joshua are going to be absolutely ecstatic."

"We haven't finished all the plans, but Richard and I are hoping that when Samuel gets here tomorrow, we can all talk things out. I know there are things we have to do. I mean there's the business, the house, and..." Pat continued, as Vicky sat and listened. She didn't mean to tune out Pat. Instead, she began to focus on Samuel's arrival on Friday afternoon. She knew this would be such great news to him.

"We're going to need your help to be sure that Samuel understands the reasoning behind what seems to be such a sudden decision. I know we may have appeared to not be interested when this topic came up before, but things are different now. We're not looking to retire. We're looking just to change location. We still want to work. Besides, it'll help us. We're excited about this. What do you think?" Pat asked as she reached for Vicky's hand.

She took Pat's hand and smiled. The prospect of their moving to Florida was huge. There was so much that needed to be done.

"Have you considered a time frame or date for all of this?" Vicky asked.

"Yes, we have," Pat responded. "We're thinking about putting the business and the house up for sale tomorrow, after we talk with Samuel. He'll know what to do. In fact, we're counting on him to take care of the Brooklyn end of all this while we relocate. Of course, we'll gladly pay his fee," she said, while pouring herself another cup of coffee.

"I can help with getting you settled in Florida," Vicky suggested.

Richard got up from the table and stood behind Pat, placing his hands on her shoulders. He began rubbing her neck and shoulder area, and then he said, "What we would like to do is to take a couple of weeks and go looking for a place where we can relocate our business. We don't really want to retire," he said, while continuing to rub Pat's shoulders.

"We'll need to stay with Samuel and you for a little while, until we find a place of our own," Pat said as she closed her eyes and began enjoying the massage.

Vicky understood and nodded in agreement. The likelihood of their moving might take a couple of months, but it would be worth it in the scheme of things. Then the "little while" notion, mentioned by Pat, hit her.

She quickly began to think of things that might hinder the move: the store could take longer to sell than they had hoped; interest rates still were climbing on mortgages, and inflation was wiping out any gains they had recently made. In addition to what seemed like major issues to her, she realized that Pat would need to learn how to drive. She hadn't driven a car in years.

"Okay, it's settled! We're moving to Florida," Richard declared. Pat stood and embraced him. Pat and Richard both started crying as they began to celebrate their decision. Vicky began to cry as well. Richard extended his right arm to Vicky, and she went to join them. All three stood quietly for a few moments in the middle of the kitchen, crying and sharing a hug about the future events starting to unfold.

Meanwhile, Samuel finally reached Dr. Rutledge.

"Dr. Rutledge," Samuel said, relieved that he had finally reached him by phone, "I received your message. I'm sorry for taking so long to get back to you, but the day just flat exploded on me. Will there be time for me to visit with you this evening?"

"Better than that," Dr. Rutledge replied. "I'd like for you to join me for dinner tonight on my nickel."

"I'd love to, but only if you let me pay."

"No, I insist," Dr. Rutledge said more forcefully than before.

Samuel gave in, only to keep the phone conversation short, because he still had other calls to make. He agreed to meet him for dinner at the Water's Edge Restaurant. He knew this was Dr. Rutledge's favorite eatery, easy to get to, and it wasn't more than a fifteen-minute drive from the hospital.

After hanging up, he hurriedly dialed his office, hoping to catch Lucille still there. She was still there, working on the things that Samuel had given her to do, which was cause for Samuel to take a deep breath.

"Lucille, how are things progressing?"

"Mr. Carlisle, I'm almost finished. As soon as I do, I will head to the hospital," she said as she continued to type.

"No, you need to come now, Lucille, because I need to leave in about thirty minutes to meet Dr. Rutledge," Samuel insisted. Lucille quickly finished what she was doing, put away the folders she was working on, and began straightening her desk when she heard the rear door to the office area open. Knowing she was the only one who should be in the office at that time, she quietly got up from her desk and went into the restroom at the end of the receptionist's work area. She opened the door just enough so she could see who was in the back area of the office. It was Craig. From her vantage point, she had an unobstructed view.

Craig entered his office and left the door partly open. Lucille took that moment to slip out of the restroom, gather her things, and sneak out the front door. She moved as fast as she dared, hoping not to attract attention to herself, because she had no plans to hang around to see what he was doing. She knew, however, that he was speaking to someone—either on the phone or someone in his office. She wasn't waiting around to find out.

As she was about to start her car, she saw the lights come on in Samuel's office. She instinctively reacted by quickly ducking down in the front seat. She slumped lower in the driver's seat, hoping that he wouldn't notice her. She came back up just enough to see what was happening. She could see Craig clearly as he walked by the front door heading toward the rear exit area. Within a few seconds, the building went dark. She sat back up, started her car, edged into traffic, and left the area grateful that she had not been seen—at least she thought she hadn't been seen.

While Lucille was driving to the hospital, Samuel had gone back up to Carrie's room. The sun was nearly gone, and the main sources of light that remained in Carrie's room came from the light poles on the streets and headlamps of passing cars on the streets below. He picked up the chair that was near her bed and moved it behind the privacy curtain where he could watch Carrie and be out of view of someone who might enter the room.

As he sat in the darkness, he felt a deep and profound sadness for Carrie. He had never understood how someone like Carrie could be attracted to, let alone marry, someone like Craig. Although he didn't realize it at first, Craig was a power-hungry fanatic with money who just happened to land Samuel straight out of law school. She, on the other hand, was not only gorgeous but was not appreciated by Craig for who she was and how much she brought to the law firm. Samuel knew

Carrie was as big a social climber as Craig, but the only things Samuel wanted to see him climb were prison bars.

It had been a while since he had sat in the darkness of a hospital peering out a window. As he sat there watching the shadows form on the wall, listening to Carrie's relaxed breathing, wondering what Carrie was going to do when this was over, he saw shadows appear at the bottom of the door to her room. He sat still, watching to see if the door would open. He could hear voices outside the door, but he was not able to make out whom it was. He rose from his chair and positioned himself against the near wall so that when the door opened, he would be behind the door, out of view to whoever entered the room.

The door began to open slowly. Samuel reached around the door, grabbed the arm of the person, and pulled. He turned on the lights only to discover that it was the nurse's aide who had come to pick up Carrie's dinner tray.

"Who are you?" she asked Samuel, with an indignant look on her face.

"I'm terribly sorry, but I didn't know one of the staff was coming to check on Mrs. Myers," he said apologetically. "I'm Samuel Carlisle, Mrs. Myers' associate," he explained, "and I was waiting for my secretary to get here to sit with Mrs. Myers this evening.

"Are you nuts? You could at least keep a light on," she said as she picked up the dinner tray and then moved toward the door.

Looking at her nametag, he said, "Ms. Porter, I'm very sorry. Mrs. Myers was hurt badly today by someone who might try to hurt her again. Would you mind asking for someone from security to come to the room? I need to make arrangements with them for Mrs. Myers while she is in the hospital," he explained, hoping to help her understand why he had taken such precautions.

"Mr. Carlisle, you sure have a funny way about you," she said as she left the room.

He stepped into the hallway and glanced in both directions before returning to the room. He was beginning to worry about the amount of time remaining before he would have to leave to meet Dr. Rutledge. He didn't want to leave without talking to Lucille, yet he didn't want to be late.

A couple of minutes later, the security guard entered the room and discussed the situation with Samuel. Explaining all that had happened, Samuel was relieved when the guard agreed to stay at the nurses' station until Lucille arrived. With that settled, he wrote a brief note for the guard to give to Lucille. As he left the room to go meet with Dr. Rutledge, he glanced once more at Carrie, who appeared to be peacefully asleep, thinking she was safe and that she would get a good night's sleep. *Okay, everything's covered*, he thought.

With that, he thanked the guard and headed toward the elevators.

CHAPTER 9

Lucille drove into the hospital's parking lot later than she had wanted. She gathered all of the items from her car that Samuel had told her to bring and headed for Carrie's room. The little run-in at the office with Mr. Myers had thrown her off just enough to make her feel disorganized and behind schedule. Samuel's insistence for her to leave the office when she did, however, actually helped matters.

When she finally arrived at Carrie's room, the guard stopped her and asked for her name and identification. Assured that he was speaking with Lucille Pierce, he handed her the note that Samuel wanted her to have. She thanked him, went to the room, and sat down quietly so as not to disturb Carrie.

"Lucille, is that you?" Carrie asked, with a raspy, almost airy-like voice.

"Yes, Mrs. Myers. I'm back, and I am spending the night with you. It'll be like a sleepover," she said as she took Carrie's hand.

"I must have dozed off while Samuel was here. What time is it?"

"It's just about six thirty. Have you had anything to eat? Because I brought a bunch of stuff," she asked, digging into a large, suitcase-like straw handbag.

"Yes, but I couldn't eat very much of it. I ended up drinking my dinner tonight. I guess I will be drinking my meals for a while."

Not thinking, Lucille turned on the wall lamp near Carrie's bed. The bright light caused Carrie to cover her right eye until it had become accustomed to the glare. Her left eye had been bandaged over because of the injuries Craig caused earlier in the day.

"Mrs. Myers, I am so sorry this happened to you. Did the doctors say anything about surgery or whatever they're going to do?" she asked as she offered Carrie a sip from the apple juice container left behind by the nurse's aide.

Carrie took a quick sip of the juice, commenting that it felt good going down her throat. She had to build up her courage, but she finally explained that the doctors were supposed to come back with the results of the tests and their diagnosis. She indicated that she had not seen them and knew nothing different from what she and Lucille already had heard. Lucille recognized the anxiety in Carrie's voice.

"I have a splitting headache," Carrie said as she gently put her head back on her pillow.

"Let me see if I can get you something for that," Lucille said as she pushed the call button for the nurse.

For the time being, Samuel actually felt at ease with Carrie's situation. Knowing that Lucille would be staying with Carrie and that security at the hospital had been alerted to the circumstances, he was able to think about his dinner with Dr. Rutledge.

As he drove to the restaurant, he recalled the time the two of them had shared a lunch together on campus. Not only did they share a lunch, they ended up discussing one of Dr. Rutledge's favorite subjects, "Rules of Evidence." As Samuel recalled the events of that afternoon, he remembered how engaging Dr. Rutledge could be. Not only did the time go by quickly that day, Samuel learned a great deal from him too. Just recalling that time brought a smile to his face.

When he reached the restaurant's parking lot, he recognized Dr. Rutledge's car and parked in a vacant spot next to it. As he entered the building, he knew this was not going to be a cheap dinner. He had eaten at this restaurant, when he and Vicky had celebrated their sixth wedding anniversary. He remembered the menu prices were pretty steep. As he started to look for where Dr. Rutledge was seated, he remembered the food and service were superb, however. *They ought to be, at these prices*, he mused.

He made his way to where the head waiter was located, mentioned he was with Dr. Rutledge, and was shown where he already had been seated. Dr. Rutledge had selected a booth, well removed from the general flow of the waiters and other customers, and had already ordered a glass of wine for both of them.

Samuel had been looking forward to this occasion as much as Dr. Rutledge. They greeted each other casually, as two friends would do. While they were exchanging handshakes, the server waited until they were seated, and then handed each of them menus and explained that he would return in a few minutes to take their order.

"Samuel, it is good to see you, my boy. I have so much to tell you that I really don't know where to begin. The obvious would be with this glass of wine, as I toast you and Vicky," he said as he lifted his glass toward Samuel.

Samuel lifted his glass, in return, and saluted Dr. Rutledge. Their glasses touched and made that unmistakable ring that only fine crystal can make.

"Dr. Rutledge, I've had a day that is hard to explain," Samuel said as he placed his wine glass on the table. He continued telling Dr. Rutledge about what he had learned from Carrie about Craig, the events at both the office and the hospital, and Lenny's first bit of information regarding the Durham case.

"My goodness," Dr. Rutledge said, raising his eyebrows. "You have had quite a day. But, my dear Samuel, it is just beginning," he said as he leaned forward.

As he began to explain what it was that he had found in the transcript, the server returned. He leaned back, stopped talking, and waited until the water glasses had been filled and a basket of freshly baked rolls had been placed on the table. When the server was out of earshot, Dr. Rutledge resumed by describing to Samuel the process he had used to arrive at his conclusions.

As he listened intently, Samuel could tell that he had become captivated by the case. The prospects of getting Durham's verdict reversed or thrown out by a judge had become not just a possibility for Dr. Rutledge; it was fast becoming a mission for him.

His body language indicated a high degree of intensity and sincerity in what he was saying to Samuel. The tone and the pace of his speech were not the usual relaxed, and somewhat methodical, manner that Samuel was accustomed to hearing. It was now evident that he had become the advocate that Samuel had hoped for and the one he would need as an expert witness for testifying in court or arguing before a judge in chambers.

To Samuel, the case now had progressed into the next level. Now he had what he needed to present a believable and reasonable argument to a judge, support the possibility of reasonable doubt, and provide meaningful and conclusive evidence to that end. Things were looking up for Lucille—and especially Lucille's brother.

"Samuel," Dr. Rutledge continued, "Durham is not a murderer. He's a thief and always will be a thief. The fact that he was in Jackson's house makes perfect sense. The assertion that he murdered Jackson makes no sense at all," he reasoned. "Durham was there to steal, not to murder. Thieves usually take off at the first thought of their being caught in the act. Besides, the prosecutor's idea about Durham's connection to the murder weapon was weak at best. There were no prints on the weapon. So, he was supposed to have stopped stealing and turn into a murderer?" he asked sarcastically.

"It doesn't make sense," Samuel said as he took a sip of his wine. "What escapes me is why he would have stayed in the house once he heard Jackson's car approach in the driveway," Samuel said, acting as if he was thinking out loud.

"A good point, but take it another step by examining the testimony more closely," Dr. Rutledge said, while motioning for him to continue.

"I'm not sure what you mean," Samuel admitted.

Dr. Rutledge placed a copy of the transcript on Samuel's plate. It was opened to a particular passage that he had circled, and he asked Samuel to read it aloud.

Samuel picked up the manuscript and read the part where Durham was responding to a series of questions about his arrival and entry to the house. Samuel began reading:

Prosecutor: What exact time did you arrive and enter Mr. Jackson's house?

Durham: Sometime after midnight.

Prosecutor: Was anyone home?

Durham: No.

"Did you hear what you just said, Samuel?" Dr. Rutledge inquired.

"Yes. He said he got there sometime after midnight. And this is important because..." Samuel said to Dr. Rutledge, expecting him to complete the sentence.

"Samuel, my boy, you'd make a lousy thief or cat burglar," he said, as if to scold Samuel. He pointed once again to the passage and said, "The time frame for the prosecutor was never made. Durham couldn't recall what exact time it was when he went into Jackson's house. Thieves, especially those who are good thieves, always know the routine of the people who live in a targeted house. The best Durham could come up with was 'sometime after midnight.' That's not the correct answer. He's either lying about the time or dumber than we want to believe. Burglars know the time because their livelihood depends on not having people around when they are working," he explained, while pointing to the transcript.

Samuel began to understand what Dr. Rutledge was describing to him. The prosecutor in the case never really nailed down the time—the exact time—because Durham was not able to tell him. Samuel looked at him and said, "This means what?"

"It means that Durham's full of it. It may mean he's the fall guy in this and is taking the heat for someone else, if he's truly innocent. Only Durham knows the truth about that," he said, while buttering one of the warm dinner rolls.

It was as if a light bulb over Samuel's head had been turned on. The time frame, which the prosecutor had worked so hard to lock in place, could very well be different than what was presented at trial.

"Samuel, Durham didn't really know Jackson all that well. Sure, he had a little run-in with him two days before, but that was over a paycheck that Durham felt he was owed. The bottom line is that there is a hole in the testimony, a small hole, but still big enough that talking to Durham might help," he said before he sampled more of the dinner roll.

"I agree. Lenny and I are doing just that next Tuesday. We're headed to Starke to question Durham. Only this time, I hope Durham understands what's at stake."

"I would love to tag along, if it's okay with you," Dr. Rutledge said.

"Only if you allow me to buy you lunch that day," he said as he lifted his wine glass once more to toast Dr. Rutledge.

"If you insist," Dr. Rutledge said, returning Samuel's salute.

The rest of their time together that night was spent developing and discussing the questions that Durham would need to answer. Samuel hated that the evening had to come to an end. He knew he still had a lot to do before getting ready to leave for Brooklyn the next day. The hard part for him in all of this was not being able to shake feeling guilty about leaving Lucille in a tough spot.

CHAPTER 10

Dinner with Dr. Rutledge proved to be exhilarating for Samuel. With all that had gone on during the day, having some time with Dr. Rutledge that evening turned out to be exactly what he needed. Not only did he enjoy the meal and the surroundings at the restaurant, he left there with hurriedly scribbled questions on several sheets of paper, which Durham would need to answer. Before saying good-bye to each other, they had agreed upon the sequence of those questions that would help make their visit to Raiford Prison in Starke, Florida, worthwhile. At least, that was the plan.

Samuel drove home that night thinking about how difficult it would be to leave behind all that was happening, get on a plane the next afternoon, and go to Brooklyn. His concerns focused on Carrie's injuries and Lucille's role in keeping her safe. Equally troubling were Craig's whereabouts and what his next move might be. Then there was what Lenny might find over the weekend that might require a prompt reply, possible instructions, or perhaps even his presence. Seemingly lost in the shuffle, there was the reason for his trip in the first place—his parents. All of this wasn't overwhelming to him, but he was stressed, and he knew it.

While he began packing for his flight to New York, he called Vicky to say goodnight to her. Richard, however, answered the phone.

"Dad," Samuel said, "can I please speak with Vicky?

"Sure, son, hold on," he replied.

Samuel stood quietly. It hit him that his father had just called him "son." He hadn't heard his father call him that since the day before the family buried Uncle Ted. The events of that day, which occurred on January 16, 1971, had redefined their relationship for over seven years. During those years, neither of them could find understanding in their hearts for the other, but something in his father's voice, just moments before, was different on this night.

"Samuel, you'll never guess what happened right after dinner tonight," Vicky said excitedly. "We were sitting there, sharing a quiet moment over a cup of coffee, and your parents said they decided they wanted to move to Florida and open a business. They even thought about putting the store up for sale tomorrow," she said, without taking a breath.

He could not believe what he was hearing. Vicky had accomplished exactly what they had wanted to do—and had done it in less than two days.

"Slow down, Vicky, and tell me about the selling of the business and the opening of another business," he responded.

She began telling him, although terribly out of sequence, the details about the decisions Pat and Richard had made that afternoon. As she explained all that she could remember, Samuel began thinking more about what his father said to him. He had to interrupt her, at least to try to get a quick word in somewhere during the phone call.

"Vicky, what exactly happened today?" he asked curiously. "What did my father say or do that would have him call me 'son'?"

"I'm telling you, Samuel, it was like night and day happened all at the same time. All I know is that after dinner tonight, your parents sat down to have a cup of coffee with me, and blam! It was like I magically lost ten pounds and two dress sizes all in twenty minutes. We talked for over two hours about the plans they had already discussed earlier in the day. They actually are excited and motivated about this. Oh, I do wish you had been here to see the look on their faces. We all cried and hugged. It was wonderful!" she exclaimed.

"Vicky, do you realize the last time my father called me 'son' was the day before our family buried Uncle Ted? He's barely recognized the fact that I'm alive, let alone that I am his son. Today, out of the blue, he takes this change of course. I don't know what happened, but I'm sure I will have to deal with this tomorrow," he said as he began pacing in his bedroom. "How am I supposed to deal with this? I mean, it's not that

I don't have enough on my plate, for crying out loud. Now what am I supposed to do?" he asked, almost painfully.

"I guess you should thank your lucky stars and get over it," she said curtly, trying to coach him. Vicky explained to him that maybe Pat and Richard were serious about trying to put their family back together—in one place—with a single purpose.

He asked her to tell him about the other events that happened during the day. When she had finished, she asked him how his day went. It was then that he realized he needed to tell her everything, without leaving anything out or to chance. After he explained the incident at the office, the hospital, and all of the other details that were somehow all connected, he waited for Vicky's reply. There was silence on the other end of the phone for several seconds.

The only thing that she could think to say was, "Samuel, I'm so sorry."

"Vicky, you don't have anything to be sorry about. When we get back next week, I may need your help. Lucille is going to be tied up with a few special assignments to help with the Durham case. I promised Carrie that I would help cover her casework until she is able to come into the office. In the meanwhile, I need to try to keep our office out of the newspapers. With any luck, this thing will blow over and not amount to much. The unknown in all of this is just how deeply Craig is involved in all of this and, as of now, exactly where he's hiding."

"Samuel, what about Carrie? Is she going to be okay?"

"The doctors are keeping her in the hospital for now. Surgery is probably going to be the answer because of her broken jaw. They were mainly concerned about the concussion she suffered. She should know more in the morning. Lucille is at the hospital and will spend the night with her, just in case. Security has been alerted, and they are aware of Craig's situation. I have filed a police report, and charges are pending. Again, we'll know more in the morning."

They both realized that they had been on the phone a while and that it was getting late. She wanted to continue the conversation, but she could tell that Samuel's day was beginning to take its toll on him.

His voice sounded tired. So, she said her good-byes, telling him that she loved him and missed him. Samuel responded by asking her to hug the kids and to kiss them goodnight for him.

"Vicky, I love you. It'll be good to see you tomorrow." Then he asked her to do something he hadn't asked in a long time. "And by the way, would you tell my parents that I love them?"

"I'll do that and one more as well. I will give them both a hug for you."

With that, he told Vicky he loved her and hung up the phone. He placed the phone back on the nightstand. Then he turned his attention, once again, to the suitcase that he had barely touched during the phone call with her.

In the meantime, Lucille began to make herself comfortable for the evening. She found a blanket and a pillow in the closet that looked as if they had been issued in World War I. She used the bathroom in Carrie's room to take a very long, hot shower, and then dressed in a pair of walking shorts and an oversized blouse. After putting on her slippers, she sat down in the chair preparing to read a book she had just purchased. She figured that if the book was any good, she could stay awake that much longer, helping her to get through the night. If the book wasn't any good, she guessed she would probably fall asleep, still helping to make the evening pass quickly. Either way, she wanted the night to go by quickly.

The nurse came in around eleven o'clock to check on Carrie. Carrie was resting comfortably and Lucille had fallen asleep in the chair. So the nurse pulled the covers up on both of them, turned off the lights, and closed the door behind her after exiting the room. She completed her rounds and returned to the nurses' station to update her patients' charts. The floor was quiet. All of the patients, as well as Lucille, were sound asleep.

Samuel awoke to what he thought was his alarm clock ringing. Realizing it was the telephone, but still half asleep, he rolled over and answered it. He glanced at the clock and saw that it was three thirty in the morning.

"Samuel," Lucille said excitedly, "you need to get down here to the hospital now! Craig was here … and he's … done something … to Carrie," she said, sounding as if she was out of breath.

Somewhat alarmed but not surprised, he asked, "Is she okay?"

"I'm not sure. The doctors are in with her at the moment. He held a gun in my face and taped me up so I couldn't speak. He threatened to kill me if I made a sound. After he gagged me and bound me to the chair, he stuck her with a long needle. Samuel, it was huge, and it was so dark, and I was so scared. I'm sorry, Samuel," she said as she broke down in tears.

"Lucille, it's okay. I will be there in about twenty minutes," he said as he jumped out of bed and hurriedly began getting dressed. Actually, it only took him sixteen minutes to arrive at the nurses' station on the fourth floor of the hospital.

Lucille had been taken to the emergency room to be examined. The nurses recognized Samuel and explained that Carrie was undergoing treatment at the moment in her room. The doctors had been in the room already for over thirty minutes, without coming out. Only one hospital orderly, who had been summoned to bring a collection of medical items, including syringes and two different procedural trays for the doctors, was allowed to enter the room.

Samuel thanked the nurses and explained that he would be downstairs in the emergency room checking on Lucille. He demanded that if there was any news on Carrie's condition, they were to contact him immediately.

When Samuel saw Lucille through the glass partition that separated the hallway and the emergency room, he could see she was still trembling. She still had a small piece of tape in her hair, where Craig had taped her head to the back of the chair. She was bleeding from the corner of her mouth, and her left cheek area was raw from where he had taped her mouth shut. Still dressed in her walking shorts and oversized blouse, she looked distressed and disheveled. This was not one of Lucille's finer moments.

She finally saw Samuel as he approached. She jumped down from the gurney, ran to where he was, and leaped into his arms. She and

Samuel stayed that way for several seconds. He patted the back of her hair, and she cried with her face buried into his left shoulder area.

"Lucille, it's going to be okay; it's okay. I need for you to get a hold of yourself for now and tell me everything that happened," he said, while still holding on to her.

Lucille broke down again. He escorted her to a chair, just outside the examining area, and sat quietly there with her for over five minutes. He thought it best just to let her get this out of her system for now. They could talk later. And they did.

After a few more moments, Lucille was calm enough to ask in a whimpering voice, "Is Carrie okay?"

"At the moment, the doctors are in there working on her. We should know something before too long. How are you?" he asked as he helped to wipe her tear-stained face. He had never noticed the freckles that she had managed to hide, for all those years, under her make-up.

"Is she going to die?" she asked, while looking at him through tear-filled eyes.

"Lucille, don't worry about such things. I need for you to tell me what and when this happened," he said, trying to keep her focused on things other than how Carrie was.

"I honestly don't know. It was dark, but not dark enough that I couldn't tell whom it was that did this. That monster Craig did this to us. Oh, Samuel, he stuck her in the neck with a very long needle; that's all I can remember. I must have passed out. When I came to, I was tied tightly, and I couldn't move anything except my feet. So I beat on the wall with my feet until one of the nurses showed up and untied me. You know the rest," she said as she leaned forward and placed her head in her hands.

He walked her back into the examining room and asked the doctors if there was a reason they couldn't be excused and return to the fourth floor nurses' station. Lucille was told to stay put until the police arrived. Samuel told her to tell them exactly what she had explained to him and to try to remember every possible detail.

"Samuel," she sobbed, "what are they going to do to me?" She began to tremble once again.

"Nothing, Lucille. Just tell them what happened and don't leave out anything. I will be upstairs for a few minutes to see how Carrie's doing. Just answer their questions."

When the doctors came back into the examining room, Samuel headed back upstairs. Lucille had been roughed up, but she was going to be okay. He didn't know how Carrie was doing or what her problem was. When he reached the nurses' station, the head nurse motioned for him to join her in the waiting area, on the other side of the hallway.

"Mr. Carlisle, Mrs. Myers' condition is critical. I guess you've figured that out by now. We're not going to know anything until—" She stopped speaking when she noticed that the doctors, who had been treating Carrie, had come out of her room and were walking toward the elevator. Samuel saw them and went over to meet them.

"Mr. Carlisle?" one of the doctors asked. "I'm Dr. Phillips, and this is Dr. Yu and Dr. Nevins. I'm afraid we don't have much to tell you at the moment. Whatever it was that was injected into her has paralyzed her. She's breathing on her own for the moment, but we have called for a specialist from Ft. Lauderdale to meet us here as soon as possible. In the meanwhile, please know that we are doing everything possible to treat Mrs. Myers."

Samuel was taken aback by the news. He managed to steady himself enough to ask, "Will she be okay?"

"She's a fighter. We believe that once we can identify the substance that was injected into her system, she will respond favorably to the treatment," Dr. Nevins said.

"Is there anything I can do to help?" Samuel asked.

"If you know any prayer warriors, contact them and tell them it is time for them to go to work. I'm afraid that's all we can do for the moment. We'll know more after the specialist gets here and has a chance to examine her. In the meanwhile, we are running a battery of tests. The results won't be ready, though, for several hours," Dr. Nevins said.

Samuel thanked them and then asked the head nurse when he might be able to visit with Carrie. She said he could stay the rest of evening, if he desired to do so. He decided to stay, hoping it might give him some time to think.

As he sat next to Carrie's bed and listened to her struggling to breathe, he could feel the rage begin to build in him. Craig had hurt two of the people he held dear in his life. Carrie was a target because she knew too much for his liking—about where the bones were buried—and she was an extremely dangerous liability to him. He threatened Lucille because he knew he could. Samuel wished that Craig would be foolish enough to come after him. He wanted one chance—one opportunity—to make sure that Craig was not denied his just reward—and Samuel wanted to deliver it personally.

"Craig has to pay," he mumbled under his breath. "This is twice he has gotten away with an attempt on Carrie's life. Now he's threatened to kill Lucille," he muttered.

Turning to Carrie and holding her hand, he added, "I will find him, and he will pay. One way or another, he will pay."

CHAPTER 11

First light on Friday morning was a welcomed sight to Samuel. Although his morning had started earlier than he would have liked, he just was glad that the misery of Thursday's agenda was over. The few hours of sleep he did manage to get came only because of sheer exhaustion. For now, a couple of hours of sleep were about all he could afford.

As he awoke slowly while trying to focus on his surroundings, he did not remember Lucille's curling up and sleeping next to him in the chair. She had placed a pillow between herself and his shoulder, which made a perfect resting place for her head. When he saw out of the corner of his eye that she was sound asleep and even snoring slightly, he chuckled quietly so as not to wake her. As he started to slide out of the chair, her eyes opened long enough to see that it was Samuel. She closed them gently and, with a pleased smile on her face, quickly went back to sleep.

Carrie lay motionless, stretched out in her bed and not making a sound. He watched carefully, making sure he could see the movement of her chest as she inhaled and exhaled. Thankful that she was still alive, he got out of his chair, stood next to her, and looked down at her as she slept. He noticed her skin color was jaundiced and that she had at least four different bags of fluids hanging from a steel pole on the back corner of her bed. The doctors had inserted a catheter during the evening and placed restraints on both of her wrists. To Samuel, she looked more like an experiment than a patient.

He went over to the sink and splashed cold water on his face, hoping it would help him wake up. As he patted his face with the towel and turned to walk back to his chair, he saw Carrie's fingers move slightly. Remembering that the doctor mentioned she had been paralyzed by some drug, he went immediately to the door and excitedly called for the nurse from the doorway. She saw the movement as well, only this time fingers on both hands moved. Using the phone in the room, she called for Dr. Nevins, who was still on call, to come to the room, "stat."

With all the commotion, Lucille woke up and asked Samuel what was happening. He explained what he had seen and that the doctor was on the way. The nurse, during all of this, began taking Carrie's vital signs and recorded them on her chart. Samuel sat back down near Carrie's bed and held Lucille's hand as they both watched Carrie for other signs of movement. The monitor near the IV bags indicated that her oxygen level was above ninety-six percent—far better than it had been at four o'clock that morning.

When the doctor entered the room, he asked the nurse to escort both Samuel and Lucille to the waiting area and to contact Dr. Yu immediately. Samuel stopped at the concession area, just outside the waiting room, to purchase a cup of coffee for himself and a soda for Lucille. She was accustomed to drinking sodas first thing in the morning, often referring to them as the "inexpensive high octane of the working masses." He settled for coffee from the machine instead of going downstairs to the cafeteria. He was afraid that he might miss something.

Lucille turned on the television to watch the morning news. The Friday morning news worked better than the caffeine in either the coffee or the soda to jolt them both back to the reality of the moment. The reporter was speaking about an attempted murder at the local hospital involving members from a local law firm. Samuel missed the first part of the report, but Lucille had not.

"Where did they get this information? Unless somebody at the hospital has talked to the press—" she said irritably, stopping in mid-sentence.

"I don't know," he said, with a quizzical look on his face. "It may be that someone in the hospital leaked the information, or it's possible that someone in the hospital is working with Craig. Did you notice that Craig's name wasn't even mentioned but that yours and mine were all over the screen?"

"I'm not exactly sure what's happening here," she said as she went over to the television and turned up the volume.

Samuel went to the nurses' station and asked to speak to the administrator of the hospital, but he learned that Mr. Courson was not expected until a little after nine o'clock that morning. He went back to the waiting room and told Lucille he was going home to check on a few things. He instructed her to go home as well, take a shower, and to put on some clean clothes. Then she was to return to the hospital to learn as much information as she could from the doctors and plant herself in Carrie's room.

He spoke with the nurses and the security team, hopeful they wouldn't allow Craig anywhere near Carrie. He hadn't noticed in all of the rush of the morning that there had been a police officer stationed outside Carrie's door. Samuel spoke with the security guard and learned that only four other people, other than doctors and nurses, were allowed in the room. Samuel was told that only Lucille, himself, Sergeant Rothermel, and Lieutenant Howard were granted access to Carrie's room.

It's about time somebody around here got serious about this, he thought as he headed toward the elevator. *There's no telling what Craig might try, especially since he may know by now that his attempt to kill her failed.*

The trip to his house was sobering. He still had to finish packing and put his house in order before leaving for the airport later in the afternoon. Also, he wanted to go by the office to pick up a few items he could work on while in Brooklyn. He really wanted to have time to speak with Lenny and Dr. Rutledge too, to get the plans lined up for their trip to Starke. Sometime in the course of the morning, he wanted to call Vicky.

He decided his first order of business would be to stop worrying about Carrie. He didn't need anything else on his plate. *I've got enough to deal with for at least an hour or so*, he thought. *What I really need is for the police to find Craig before I do.*

Vicky woke up early that Friday morning as well. The anticipation and excitement of Samuel's arrival and all that had occurred the previous day for the Carlisle family caused her to toss and turn most of the night. She finally got up around five o'clock, thinking she'd put on a pot of coffee and watch the morning news for a few minutes. As she was sitting at the kitchen table waiting for the coffee to brew, Rachel came into the room dragging her blanket and rubbing her eyes.

"Mommy, I can't sleep," she said as she climbed into her mother's lap.

Vicky put her arms around her and cradled her like she used to do when she was just a little baby. She took Rachel's favorite blanket, wrapped it around her shoulders, and began a slight rocking motion.

"Mommy," Rachel said as she looked up at her mother, "when will Daddy be here today? Are we going to be able to meet him at the airport?"

"Rachel, honey, Daddy's flight will arrive at the airport at six o'clock this evening. And yes, we'll meet him at the airport. You'd like that, wouldn't you?" she asked before kissing Rachel on the nose and continuing the rocking motion.

Rachel's eyes had closed ever so gently, as she managed only a mumbled response to Vicky's question because the rocking motion was doing the job Vicky had intended. She stood up slowly, carried Rachel to the bedroom, and then placed her gently on the bed. After pulling the covers up about halfway, she leaned over and kissed her on the forehead. She checked to be sure that Joshua was still asleep, then quietly tiptoed out of the room, and left the door open slightly.

As she headed back to the kitchen, her attention turned to the family pictures in the hallway. She had walked by them hundreds of times, but this morning she stopped to look at one in particular. It was the picture of Samuel's seventeenth birthday, where family and friends had gathered to celebrate. He appeared wonderfully happy in that picture. His mother and father were both holding the birthday cake, where the burning candles cast a glow on each of their faces. There were presents at the end of the table, and some of his friends were seated at the table with him. The picture showed the leftovers of what must have been a feast that had been enjoyed by all. Then she saw something that caught her eye.

Standing in the background, toward the right edge of the photograph, was a young lady about Samuel's age, dressed in a short-sleeved dress, holding a small sign. She looked familiar somehow, but Vicky was not able to recall how or why. She couldn't make out the first few words on the sign she was holding in the picture, but the last word clearly spelled out the name Samuel. Then she noticed that all of the others in the background of the picture were holding signs as well. Only, Samuel's name was the first word on each of the signs they were holding.

"That's odd," she said as she quietly entered the kitchen. *I guess the girl in that picture was different, but I wonder how?* she thought. As she poured herself a cup of coffee, Vicky thought to herself, *That girl was cute, and her dress was just darling.*

With coffee in hand, she went into the living room, turned on the television, and sat down in one of the overstuffed chairs. As she began to watch the news, she couldn't help but think about the breakthrough that had occurred the day before. She was excited for Samuel and the children because it meant that Grandpop and Grandmom would be close by every day. Their selling the business in Brooklyn was the biggest of all the surprises. She knew that would be hard for Richard and Pat. Once that was done, however, she just knew there would be no turning back.

It wasn't long before Pat came into the room with her cup of coffee and sat down to join Vicky. There was something different about this morning. Vicky felt it, and so did Pat. There was not just a sense of warmth in the room, there was a deeper regard for each other as well. Vicky looked at Pat and smiled in such a way that Pat got up from her chair, went over to her, and kissed her gently on the top of her head.

"Vicky, thank you. I want you to know that Richard and I can't thank you enough for helping us like you did yesterday," she said as she looked down at her. "We've needed to do this for years but were afraid. I know this decision is right because I slept very well last night. In fact, I haven't slept that comfortably in years. Richard is in there right now sawing logs," she said, while chuckling.

"Pat, I'm so glad and happy for the two of you. I have to tell you, though, that Rachel and Joshua are going to be wild about this news.

Maybe we ought to wait until Samuel gets here later today before we tell the children."

"That will be hard, but you're right. The biggest problem will be keeping Richard from talking about in front of the kids," she said, lifting her cup as if to salute Vicky. They both smiled because they both knew Richard couldn't keep a secret, even if his life depended on it. Vicky leaned over and extended her coffee cup to Pat. The noise the cups made as they brought them together may not have been that same distinguishable sound that crystal glasses make when coming together, but it was a very happy and joyful noise to both of them.

After arriving at her house, Lucille went immediately to the bathroom and turned on the shower so the water could warm up. She went about packing into that very large handbag a couple of extra undergarments, make-up, and a pair of sandals. Then she checked all of the doors and windows, making sure they were locked, returned to the bathroom, and then locked the door behind her. She felt safe enough now where she could take a quick shower in peace.

As she was drying herself with an oversized beach towel, the phone rang. She let it ring twelve times before picking up the receiver. Her mother had taught her to do that. *Anyone who really wants to talk with you,* she recalled her mother telling her, *will let it ring at least twelve times, thinking that when the phone starts ringing, you might not be able to get to it right away. Besides, the caller who's trying to sell you something won't usually allow that many rings because time is important to them. The more calls they make, the more money they make.* True or not, she wanted to make sure someone really wanted to talk to her before picking up the receiver.

Samuel was on the other end. He was calling from the office to remind Lucille about her statement and to go by the police station to see Lieutenant Howard. He had stopped by the office to pick up a few things but would be at his house in a little while.

"Samuel, you're checking up on me, aren't you?" she asked, in a cute kind of way.

"Of course I am," he said, and quickly added, "I care about you."

"Oh, Samuel, that's so nice of you," she said, using a poorly attempted Southern accent. "Here I am dressed only in a towel, and you call. My, my, my. What an opportunity missed," she said, almost laughing.

"Enough of that, Lucille, this is serious. Just keep your wits about yourself and what you do. Craig is a dangerous man right now and there's no telling what his next move might be," he said forcefully.

Samuel hung up the phone and started going through a couple of files, when the idea of searching Craig's office came to mind. He knew he could be fired or possibly brought up on charges for this kind of misconduct, but somehow he just didn't seem to care too much about that at that moment. The idea of finding something that could possibly lead him to Craig was worth the risk to him. Finding Craig was critically important—especially with leaving these things behind for Lenny and Lucille to handle. Plus, he believed that Carrie and Lucille were not safe until Craig was behind bars.

Craig's office door was locked, and none of the keys that Samuel had with him would open the door. That seemed strange to him because one of the keys on his key ring used to open Craig's office door. *He must have had the lock changed*, he thought. *I wonder what else Craig has been up to around here.* He rushed toward the door, trying to kick it open. Instead of the door crashing open, all he managed to do was leave his shoe print near the doorknob. He tried three more times before having to stop because he was out of breath. The last attempt bruised his heel.

He went over to the receptionist's desk, thinking that there might be a set of keys hidden somewhere in one of the drawers. He spent another fifteen minutes looking through the two closets located in the hallway and the restroom at the end of the hall.

He went back to Craig's office door. He decided to try kicking in the door one last time before discarding the idea of searching Craig's office. He just didn't want the last half hour to have been wasted.

He charged the door once again, only to leave one more footprint on what undoubtedly was one of the most secure rooms in the office complex.

As he stood there, bent over with his hands on his knees and looking at the floor, Lucille entered the receptionist's area and saw Samuel in the hallway.

"Are you okay?" Lucille asked as she began walking toward him.

"I'm fine. I just tried to do a kung fu on the door. I now realize that either I must be watching too much television, or I'm getting old," he said, while turning to face her. "What are you doing here?" he asked, with a surprised look on his face.

"I thought you might need someone to watch out for you," she said, smiling. "Obviously your key no longer works, right?" she asked as she located her set of keys. She tried to open the door, but her key didn't work either.

"I wonder when he changed the lock," she said as she walked toward the kitchen area. "I've seem him not be able to get into his office, go into the kitchen, and come out with a key that would open this door," she said, looking directly at Samuel. "It must be in there somewhere," she concluded.

Samuel followed Lucille into the kitchen area, and they began their search. He started with the cabinets on the left side of the room and Lucille with the sink area on the right. They both searched carefully and skillfully but with no immediate results. They continued until they had searched all of the easily accessible areas.

"I believe that key is in this room, Samuel," she said as she opened the refrigerator door and searched it.

While Lucille checked the refrigerator, Samuel began searching a freestanding storage cabinet that was next to the coffee maker. When he pulled on the right-hand door to open it, he noticed that the cabinet rocked slightly. He continued his search of the cabinet, when Lucille said excitedly, "Eureka!" She had reached behind the same cabinet that Samuel was searching and had found the key hanging on a clip attached to the back of the cabinet.

"Thank God," he said. "We could have been here forever trying to find that key."

By the time Samuel caught up with her, Lucille was out the door and had already unlocked the door to Craig's office. They entered the room and found what looked like the aftermath of a tornado.

"Someone has not been playing nice," Lucille said. "Should I call the police?"

"Not yet. I'm thinking that as sneaky as Craig is, he's probably hidden, in an unusual location, what I am trying to find in this office. Now, if I were Craig, where would I hide something that was valuable to me and that I didn't want anybody to find?" he asked, while looking at Lucille with a puzzled look.

"Definitely a safe," Lucille said as she stared at the wall space to the right of the desk.

Stepping over books and papers that were scattered everywhere throughout the room, Samuel went over to the desk, stood behind it, and looked back at Lucille.

"Lucille, I'm thinking that it is within a step or two of where I am standing," he said. "It would make sense that it would be smaller than a bread box but concealed in such a manner that it blended in with its surroundings."

He scanned the walls behind him and immediately to his left. Lucille, standing near the doorway and just inside the room, watched as Samuel ran his fingers over the wall space above the two-drawer filing cabinets and checked behind a couple of pictures.

"What are you doing?" she asked.

Samuel had placed his right cheek on the wall, closed his left eye, and looked to see if there were any protrusions from the wall. Then he placed his left cheek on the wall, closed his right eye, and surveyed the wall in the other direction.

"Lucille, come here and stand where I tell you to," he said.

She carefully walked around and over items that were on the floor and made her way to the location where Samuel directed.

"I want you to pull the filing cabinets away from the wall," he said.

"Are you nuts? Those things weigh a ton," she said, almost laughing.

The look on his face, however, told her to go move the filing cabinets. When she reached down and pulled on the cabinets, it surprised her how easily they moved. That's when she discovered what Samuel had seen. There was a wall box of some kind behind the cabinets. She knelt down and saw that it was closed and locked.

"Samuel, it requires a key," she said.

"Maybe it doesn't, Lucille. I'll be back in a minute," he said as he hurriedly left the room. She heard him go out the front door. That bothered her because he was gone and out of sight for what seemed to her to be more than a minute. When he returned, however, he had a crowbar in his hand, and instructed Lucille to stand back and to stay out of the way.

Jamming it into the edge of the crease between the box and the wall, he began leaning on the bar, which forced the door of the box to open. He looked up at Lucille and smiled.

"Aren't tools great, especially when you have the right tool for breaking and entering?" he said. He laughed.

He opened the door to reveal the contents of the container. He grabbed the items that were on top, including an expanding file. He asked Lucille to get the cash box that was still in the wall container. They placed the items on the desk and began looking through them. Lucille opened the cash box and stood there motionless for several seconds. Finally she said, as she began counting the neatly wrapped bills, "Samuel, there must be over three or four hundred thousand dollars here."

He heard what she said, but his eyes were fixed on a copy of a contract bid that was for a construction project in Tallahassee. He found another one for a project in Miami—and one for Orlando. There were others from Fort Lauderdale and Tampa, plus one from St. Louis, Missouri—and even one from Patterson, New Jersey. As he scanned the documents for names and dates, he discovered that Kellerman had been connected to a couple of them and that Jackson and Matheny were linked as well.

He turned to Lucille and said, "How could we have missed this? How has he been able to get away with this, and we had not one clue to any of this?" he said, with contempt in his voice.

"What do we do with this, Samuel?" she asked as she continued counting the money.

"We do nothing for now. This information is valuable to us, whether Craig knows we have it or not. Lucille, real power is having knowledge of something that others do not and knowing how it will impact not just us, but them as well. What we do with this now is not as important as what we will do with it later. We can make an extra set of copies of these documents later. The real documents will be needed for court. Right now, we need to get this to a safe place, and sooner is better than later," he said as he began gathering all of the documents.

"I've counted over two hundred and seventy thousand dollars, so far. There may be about another fifty or so to go," she said as she closed the lid to the cash box and followed Samuel out of the office. Before they left, Samuel tried to close and lock the wall container. It locked, but it probably would require the crowbar, instead of a key, to get into it again. He made sure the office door was locked, returned the key to its rightful place in the kitchen, and instructed Lucille to accompany him to the bank, where he would put these things in a safety deposit box under his name.

"What do we do about the money?" she asked.

"We make sure that it stays out of the conversation," he said, while looking directly at her. Lucille thought that was kind of odd, especially knowing that Samuel was a decent man who played by the rules.

"I guess we'll just have to trust you," she said.

He nodded in agreement. He knew what she meant, but that was a lot of money for someone to be carrying around. The sooner he could get it into a safe place, the sooner he could focus on his afternoon flight. He knew that if he wanted to get everything done before leaving for the airport, he would have to make the remaining time work for him.

CHAPTER 12

Vicky, Pat, and Richard were sitting at the kitchen table, about a half hour before opening the store, sharing a freshly brewed pot of coffee, when Richard asked, "Pat, is there any particular realtor you know in the business?"

"Adrianna Berteloni's brother, Carlitto, is in the business. Why don't we call him to see what he says? He might give us a deal," she said as she shrugged her shoulders.

"I'll call him a little after nine o'clock," he said as he began thumbing through the phone book.

Vicky watched the two of them as they went about getting both their business and home put up for sale. They seemed so business-like about the whole thing. She knew that the two of them had decided to do this, but they were actually doing what they said they were going to do. To her, they were going about it in what seemed like such a detached manner. Just twenty-four hours before, this whole thing was just talk. Now, their whole life was about to change with a single phone call.

"Pat," Vicky whispered, "what have you decided to do with all of your furniture? I mean, when do you plan to contact a moving company?"

"No, we'll do that after we spend a couple of weeks in Florida. We don't think the store will sell that quickly, especially for what we've decided to ask for it. We both agree that we need to check out locations in Florida before we make any real decisions up here. First the business there, then the business here," she said, while clasping Richard's hand and glancing at him. "Expansion is not out of the picture. There's nothing that says we can't open a business in Florida and keep the business here."

The idea really hadn't occurred to Vicky. As she considered the possibility, Joshua came into the kitchen hugging his blanket, climbed up into the chair where his booster seat was, and made eye contact with each of them.

"Would somebody please feed this poor waif?" Richard asked as he reached over to tickle Joshua.

Vicky stood up from her chair and poured milk on Joshua's cereal. Then she said, "This poor waif would eat you out of house and home, if you'd let him."

"Vicky," Pat said as she helped Joshua with a spoonful of corn flakes, "the idea of opening the business in Florida and keeping the store here is the risky part of the whole thing. We think we can pull this off, but it'll require the right setup here. Since we will be in Florida, we'll need the right folks here at the store."

"Who'd run the store up here?"

"We haven't come to that part, at least not yet," Richard said, and then added, "That's why it's still risky."

"First the business in Florida, then the business here," Pat said as she wiped Joshua's face.

Vicky could see that they had a plan. Although not all of the details were clear, the big picture was in place, and she could visualize it. She was excited about what she had heard so far of the plan, knowing that Samuel would be pleased with what they had accomplished in such a short time. Still, no one was certain how long all of this would take. That was really what was of concern to her.

"Pat," Vicky began with a curious look on her face, "who's the young girl in the picture with Samuel, you know, the one of his seventeenth birthday?"

"You must mean Cathy, Catherine Bennett," she replied in a casual manner.

"Is she related to the family?"

"Probably would have been, but no, she's not," Pat replied.

"She was Samuel's girlfriend all through high school," Richard said quietly before taking a sip of his coffee.

"What do you mean, 'probably would haven been,' but she's not?"

"Everyone expected them to get married one day and settle down in Brooklyn, but that didn't happen. Life's funny that way," Pat said matter-of-factly as she started running water in the sink to wash the breakfast dishes.

"Did Samuel love her?" Vicky asked as she leaned back in her chair.

"I think he was head over heels in love with her back then," Richard said, as he got up from the table. "I'm sure they're still friends, but he loves you," he said, pointing his finger directly at Vicky. "I'm going to get the mail," he said as he walked toward the stairs.

"The two of them were just really good friends. It wasn't what you would think of as an engagement, but they really didn't date anyone else or want to be with anyone else. They just seemed to like the same things, and they felt comfortable around each other. I think it was puppy love because she was his first real girlfriend. But they did make a handsome couple."

"Is she still living in Brooklyn?" Vicky asked as she gave Joshua a glass of juice to drink.

"No, she moved about six years ago to somewhere in Jersey, I think," she said as she rinsed off the silverware before placing it in the drying rack. "And before you ask, no, I don't know if she's married or not. Why all the questions?"

"Oh, no reason. I'm just curious; that's all. He hasn't said much about her over the years. I know she was really pretty because she's gorgeous in the picture," she said as she began to help dry the dishes.

"Funny, I don't remember her as gorgeous. She was cute, though," Pat said as she wiped Joshua's face and hands with the dishrag.

She could tell from Pat's voice that Catherine held a special place in her heart. Although their relationship occurred years before she and Samuel met, for some reason she felt slightly jealous about that connection, as if it still existed after years of marriage. She didn't think that Samuel was in love with Catherine, but she knew that first time relationships can be both memorable and haunting.

Richard returned with the morning mail and placed it on the table.

Noticing that one of the envelopes had a California return address on it, he picked it up and said, "Pat, you may want to open this."

"No, my hands are all wet. You open it and read it to me," she said, without looking.

He opened the envelope and pulled out a single piece of paper, which he unfolded.

"It's from Patrick," he said as he held the letter out to her. "Here, you read it."

She dried her hands and sat down before reading the letter. When she had finished, tears ran down her face and fell onto the table. She handed the letter to him, motioning for him to read it. Joshua, who had been watching all of this, became upset as he watched Pat sobbing. He began crying too. Vicky picked him up, reassured him that everything was okay as she left the kitchen with him, and headed for the bathroom.

"Your brother wants to visit you," he said as he hugged her shoulders.

"All of a sudden, he wants to visit me," she said as she wiped her face with her apron.

"Yes, your brother wants to visit you. He also said he wants you to meet his wife, their two children, and his granddaughter. It looks like he's trying to make things right between the two of you. Isn't that what you've always wanted?" he asked, as he sat down and held Pat's hands.

"Yes," she said as the tears returned. "But why now? There's so much we have to do, and now this. He always did have perfect timing," she said sarcastically, while attempting a smile. She looked at Richard for comfort but found that he too had tears in his eyes. He tried to smile, but she wiped away a large tear rolling down his face.

"Sweetheart," he said as he wiped the tears from his eyes, "this is a good thing. It's taken years for this to happen. A few more days are no big deal. I'll help you with this, if you let me," he said.

"I know you will. And yes, I will need your help," Pat said.

After leaving the bank, Lucille knew she needed to see Lieutenant Howard to provide the police with her statement about the events that occurred at the hospital. On the way to the station, she replayed the events of both the evening and the early morning that led up to her confrontation with Craig. It helped her to focus and to see what she could remember. Realizing that some of the details were not clear because everything had happened so quickly, she figured she might not be very much help at all. By the time she had arrived at the station and parked her car, she had begun mumbling to herself, repeating what she could remember.

She entered the building, walked to where an officer was seated behind the main entry desk, and said, "I'm here to see Lieutenant Howard." The officer picked up a phone, dialed the number to Lieutenant Howard's office, and advised whoever was on the other end of the conversation that "there's someone here Lieutenant Howard is going to want to meet."

While waiting for him, she walked around the lobby area, looking at the pictures and plaques that decorated the room, thinking that Craig was not likely to do anything stupid at a police station. It bothered her that he was still on the streets and nobody knew where he was or who he might be with.

"Mrs. Pierce? I'm Lieutenant Howard. Thank you for coming in this morning," he said as he extended his right hand to greet her.

Lucille was taken back. She could not believe that she was meeting a man who was absolutely striking. *Definitely a twelve*, she thought. Realizing he was trying to shake her hand, she dried her right hand on the skirt she was wearing and returned the kindness.

"Mrs. Pierce, we'll be done and have you on your way in no time at all," he said as he motioned for her to follow him.

"Lieutenant, please take your time. I'm in no hurry," she said.

He took her to a quiet part of the station where they could sit and talk. They spoke for about two or three minutes before another officer brought her a couple of forms and a pen and placed them on the table in front of her. She was instructed to write down anything she could remember about the events that occurred.

"I don't know how he got into the hospital, but he woke me up from a sound sleep by placing his hand over my mouth," she explained as she leaned forward and pointed to her lips. She wanted the lieutenant to take a good look at her lips—especially where Craig had mashed his hand down hard over her mouth. There was no apparent bruising, but she had just put on fresh lipstick before coming to the station and figured it wouldn't hurt for him to look at her lips. She added, "I was scared to death."

"Mrs. Pierce—" he started to say, when Lucille cut him off.

"Lieutenant Howard, please call me Lucille," she said, while running her hand through her hair. "May I call you Joseph?" she asked as she moved slightly closer to him.

"Yes, ma'am," he responded.

Lucille was mesmerized. Writing anything at the moment that might make sense was going to be a difficult task. She was captivated at how virile he looked in his uniform. It had been altered perfectly to fit his muscular and trim body. He too was taken with Lucille from the moment he met her. He was six feet, four inches tall, and her six-foot frame was refreshing to him. The fact that he had been attracted immediately to her didn't hurt either. They were both attracted to each other—only Lucille wanted to make sure he knew it.

When she finally began her statement, he left for a few minutes and returned with a soda for each of them. She started her statement at the point that Craig had sneaked into the room and placed his hand over her mouth. She began writing the events in a story-like manner, leaving nothing out, in a surprisingly crisp, well-scripted style.

The more she wrote, the more clearly she began to remember. She recalled that Craig's initial actions startled her enough to make her want to yell, but he told her that would get her killed. She was so frightened that she didn't see the gun pointed at her until he raised it and put its barrel on her left cheek. She had lost all track of time but knew it had to be sometime after midnight when he entered the room. She didn't hear anything until he woke her rudely and forcefully. She remembered his exact words.

"Lucille, don't make a sound. I don't want to hurt you, but I will if you make so much as a peep," he whispered.

She recalled she had been asleep and, apparently, hadn't heard a thing up to that point. She remembered that clearly because when he put his hand over her mouth, she began to gag as she tried to breathe. His hands smelled of stale cigarettes and beer, which made it that much more difficult for her. She tried to move to make it a little easier for her to breathe, but the pressure being applied over her mouth only got worse. As more of the details were recalled, she figured it must have been the sound of Craig's voice, the same voice that Carrie had heard for fourteen years and was easily recognized by her, that caused Carrie to wake up.

"Craig!" Lucille remembered hearing as she watched Carrie trying to yell but only speaking his name. Her jaw was still swollen, and the bandages that were wrapped tightly around her head and neck area to keep her jaw somewhat immobile made matters even worse. She remembered the intensity in Craig's eyes as he wheeled and clamped his hand down hard over Carrie's mouth, causing her to let out a throaty moan from the pain.

Lucille tried to get out of the chair to help Carrie, but Craig quickly pointed the gun to her head and said, "Don't you move one inch, or I'll blow a hole clean through you. I'm not here for you. I'm here for Carrie. Stay out of this, Lucille."

Carrie's pain was so intense that tears rolled down the side of her face. She began crying almost uncontrollably. Lucille wanted to comfort her, but all she could remember seeing was the wrong end of a barrel belonging to a .357 caliber handgun. So, she decided to become a permanent part of the chair from that point on.

She remembered that Craig switched the gun into his left hand and took out a very long syringe with an equally long needle attached. Lucille described it, in her statement to the police, as "huge."

The next few seconds of Craig's actions were difficult for her to write. As she tried, everything seemed to come back to her in living color—only in slow motion. She remembered how he removed the safety cover for the needle with his teeth, squeezed off a little of the serum from the syringe, and jammed the needle into the left side of Carrie's neck. That's when things became harder to remember. The last thing she remembered was Carrie's body becoming rigid before it went limp. Lucille figured she must have fainted a few seconds later too. When she regained consciousness, Craig was gone, and Carrie wasn't moving at all. She discovered that Craig had used duct tape to immobilize her to the chair, making it difficult to call for help. That's when she started kicking on the walls, attracting the nurses' attention.

"Joseph, that's all I remember. It happened so quickly," she said apologetically. "Will this help you and the case?"

"Yes, Lucille, you've been a big help. Thank you for coming in this morning to take care of this," he said as he stood.

"It has been nice meeting you, Joseph," she said as she pushed the chair back, enough to allow her to swing her legs free of the table. She then extended her right hand to him. Before standing, she looked up at him and smiled invitingly. Lieutenant Howard took her hand and helped her up from the chair. He thanked her for coming in and, while pointing out the directions to the front door, escorted her to the waiting area.

She began walking toward the swinging doors, which separated the office area from the entrance, when she heard him ask, "Lucille, do you mind if I call you sometime?"

"I would mind if you didn't," she said, while smiling back at him. She placed her hand on the door leading to the main entrance and said, "Joseph, I left a phone number where you can reach me at the bottom of the statement. Once you've read the statement, you may need to call me just to make sure that you get answers to any questions you may have about my statement. Sometimes, answering questions are easier for me if they're done over dinner," she said as she went through the swinging doors.

"How about seven o'clock tonight?" he asked.

"That'll work," she said.

CHAPTER 13

It didn't take Lenny very long to establish a connection between Herman Jackson and Kellerman. He found several articles in the local newspapers on Kellerman that were mostly focused on the slightly less-than-respectable characters that were often seen with him. The majority of the articles Lenny found could not be considered flattering for someone who was a public servant like Kellerman.

Jackson, on the other hand, was not viewed in the same manner by the public. His reputation had been established in the early 1950s, helped by his notoriety throughout central Florida in union building. He was viewed as a community-minded individual whose power base had grown considerably in just a few short years. Lenny found numerous articles about how Jackson was out to help the "little guy" and often was successful in promoting himself as someone to call when you needed help.

Kellerman and Jackson were constantly seen together, especially at city council meetings, talking about city improvement projects. One photo showed the two of them at a fundraising activity in the Orlando area, where they had been credited with raising over eighteen thousand dollars for the construction of a park facility. The park, which was to include several pieces of playground equipment, never materialized, and the funds that were raised could not be found.

Lenny traveled to Orlando late Thursday afternoon. This was where the trail took him, and he was on the scent. The leads he had developed in Daytona were plentiful enough, but they all pointed to Orlando and a person named Roger Matheny. Lenny learned that Roger Matheny somehow was connected to Kellerman because, just like Kellerman, Matheny was an elected official and had been previously defended, in a dispute over contract irregularities, by Craig Myers in 1969. Like so many other reports he found, the stories just seemed to fade away, and no charges were brought against any of those involved. Other than connecting Kellerman and Matheny through Craig Myers as their attorney, there was no single direct relationship between the two of them that he could find through the resources in Daytona. Once the courthouse in Orlando opened up, Lenny believed he could find something that would provide background on the contract issues that never seemed to gain momentum in the Daytona newspapers.

The drive from Daytona usually took an hour and a half, but traffic had not been kind to him along the way. He hated the stop-and-go traffic on the interstate, but there was nothing he could do about it.

By the time he got to a motel that looked like a place where humans could survive and not cost a fortune, he was tired, hungry, and miserable. Dinner that night consisted of a day-old turkey sandwich and a soda he bought at a convenience store in Sanford when he had stopped to gas up the car.

He checked into the motel around nine fifteen Thursday evening. He wanted nothing more than to take a nice long shower, read the local paper, and get a good night's sleep.

After getting his room key, he carried his overnight bag and typewriter into his room. He flopped down on the bed, feeling exhausted and spent, and lay there motionless. At that moment, it was all he could do to get up from the bed, take a shower, and lay out his clothes for the morning. As soon as he finished typing his notes for the day and putting them in his notebook, he got into bed thinking that the next eight hours belonged to him.

Friday morning started early and rudely for him. Shortly after four o'clock that morning, he was awakened by loud noises originating from the adjoining room, which sounded like a large group of children fighting over a single toy—and each one wanted it.

With each utterance, the high pitched, shrill-like sounds reverberated with greater intensity than the ones before. He rolled out of bed onto the floor, found one of his shoes, went over to the door that separated the two rooms, and began beating on it repeatedly. Finally, the noises coming from the other room stopped. At that point, he hoped that someone in the other room would have complained. Fortunately, for all concerned, the noises vanished, and Lenny was able to resume his well-earned night's rest.

Later that Friday morning, at seven thirty, he was ready to face the world. After checking to make sure that he had not left any of his belongings in the room, he went to pay his bill and turn in his room key. The clerk apologized for the noises earlier that morning but refused to lower the bill for the room. He did, however, give Lenny a coupon for a free breakfast at a diner located not far from the motel. He assured him the food and service were excellent.

As Lenny got into his car and began driving to the diner for breakfast, he began planning his day in more detail than he had the evening before. Having time for breakfast in his daily routine of things was unusual. Lunch was usually his first meal of the day. This morning, however, he believed he had earned a free breakfast, and he was going to make the most of it.

The first thing he thought of upon entering the diner was how much the aroma and décor reminded him of his mother's kitchen back home in Illinois. The soft light, which was created by the sun's early efforts, was being filtered through the curtains and onto the black and white linoleum floor. The soft padded cushions in the booths all helped to bring back comforting memories. The waitress behind the counter told him to sit wherever he wanted and that someone would be with him in a moment or two.

As he walked to a small booth at the end of the counter, the customers sitting at the counter all smiled and greeted him with a friendly "Good morning." Another waitress brought him a glass of water, asked him if he would like to read a section of the morning newspaper, and told him his waitress would be there shortly.

I could get used to this, he thought.

While he was looking at the front page of the newspaper, Sheri introduced herself.

"Hi, I'm your waitress this morning. Do you know what you'd like, or do you need another minute or two?"

Lenny never looked up from reading the paper. He indicated he was not ready to order, agreed that two more minutes would be a good thing and that he wanted a cup of hot tea, and placed the coupon on the corner of the table so she couldn't miss seeing that his breakfast was supposed to be on the house. He watched, however, as Sheri walked away from where he was sitting and noticed she was limping. Initially, he didn't think much of it, until she returned with his tea and her order pad.

"Sheri, is your ankle or foot bothering you?"

"No, I've walked this way most of my life," she responded, while setting a small, white, porcelain-like teapot, a large white ceramic cup, and a shiny teaspoon on the table in front of him. "I got hurt when I was three years old."

"I'm sorry; I didn't mean to meddle," he said apologetically.

"That's okay. It was nice of you to ask. Have you decided on what you'd like for breakfast?" she asked.

"I'd like a couple of eggs over easy, grits, and toast, and keep the hot tea with lemon coming, please. Do you have any apple butter?"

"Why, sure, and it's homemade. Poppa makes it fresh twice a week," she said.

Sheri seemed so down to earth. *She has a beautiful smile,* he thought, *and gorgeous eyes. I could really get used to eating at this diner.*

"Sheri, would you be able to join me and maybe have a cup of coffee?" he asked, with a pitiful-sounding plea in his voice.

"If you'll stay for about another half hour, I'd be happy to, only I don't like coffee. I'd be more inclined to share a pot of hot tea with you. We're a little busy right now, with the breakfast crowd and all, but I'm sure Poppa wouldn't mind. Things ought to slow down a bit, and my brother should be here to help by then too," she said.

"Great. Besides, I'm new in town, and maybe you could help me with directions and stuff," he said, without thinking. He couldn't believe he was going to be joined for breakfast by such a captivating woman. Also, he couldn't believe he had just told her he was new in town, because he knew Orlando better than he knew the back of his hand.

Sheri went to turn in his order, and he continued to read the local news sections of the paper. It wasn't too long before she returned with his breakfast and put it on the placemat before him. For some unknown reason to him, it was hard for him to take his eyes off of her. He knew he was probably staring, but it didn't bother him in the least. She didn't mind that he was staring at her either, while tending to other customers. Lenny didn't seem to notice her limp as much as he had a few moments before, but contemplated how her eyes had become more inviting to him. *She cuts a nice figure*, he thought.

On several occasions while tending to other customers, she glanced quickly in his direction. Her smiling at him acknowledged his presence and that she was looking forward to joining him for tea. Lenny enjoyed that thought as much as he did his breakfast.

The half hour soon turned into forty-five minutes before she was able to join him. *No matter*, he thought, *as long as she still gets to sit with me.*

"So, you know my name is Sheri. What's yours?" she asked, while sliding into the opposite side of the booth.

"I'm Lenny, Lenny Yeager," he said as he raised his cup to take a sip from it.

"Obviously you're not from around here. Where do you call home?" she asked as she poured herself a cup of tea from the pot she had just placed on the table.

"Sheri, I live in Daytona Beach, but my job takes me to different places. Originally, I'm from Illinois," he said.

"What brings you to Orlando?"

"I'm on a fact-finding trip for my boss. Say, are you originally from this area?"

"We moved here from Zolfo Springs when I was four. My father bought this business, and our family moved here," she said, while refreshing his cup of tea.

"It sounds like you would rather be in Zolfo Springs than in Orlando," he concluded from the tone of her voice.

"All I've known is working in this diner seven days a week, fifty-two weeks a year," she said matter-of-factly.

"How long have you worked in the diner?"

"I've worked for my dad for twenty-three years," she said as she refreshed his cup of tea.

He glanced at her hands and noticed they were not as young and smooth looking for someone her age. But she wasn't wearing a wedding ring, her nails were shaped and manicured, and her nail polish matched her lipstick. Doing what math he could put together from their conversation, he figured she was around his age, maybe just a year or two older.

While studying her hands, he said, "What do you do for recreation?"

"I love to sew and read. I like to take long walks on the beach, when I can get to the beach," she added, while smiling and looking at the cup of tea she was holding with both hands. "How about you, Lenny? What do you like to do with your spare time?" she asked, while looking directly into his eyes.

"I really love to garden, but my job doesn't allow much time for that. I like being a part of the earth and seeing things grow. Like you, I enjoy taking long walks on the beach, especially in the evening around sunset."

The small talk continued for another thirty minutes. Finally, he glanced at his watch and admitted that he had to get to the courthouse and start his day's work. He asked if she would mind his coming back and having lunch with him later. She thought it would be nice, but she wanted him to be sure to come after the lunch rush. They settled on one thirty and that Lenny would pay his way. Lenny thanked her for the meal and asked for the bill. She promptly reminded him that he had given her a coupon for the free breakfast. He insisted on paying for the meal, however.

After bantering back and forth about the bill, she relented and allowed him to keep his coupon and pay for his meal. She refused the tip, however, and said, "Sharing tea with you this morning was special. A tip would ruin it." He took the hint and extended his right hand. She refused his hand. Instead, she leaned forward, gave him a kiss on his left cheek, and said, "I'm looking forward to lunch, and I'll try to make sure I don't keep you waiting."

"I'll be here. You can count on it," he said, sensing he was blushing.

"Why, Lenny, are you blushing?" she asked in a charming Southern accent, while looking directly into his eyes.

"Why, Sheri, I believe I am," he said as he picked up his belongings and headed out the door.

He waved good-bye as he went down the front steps toward his car. When he finally sat behind the steering wheel of his car, he noticed she had been watching and waving at him through one of the front windows. He waved back, hoping that the next few hours would go by quickly. He was glad that he had lunch plans for the day—and that Sheri would be a part of them.

The next half hour was spent trying to make his way around a town filled with one-way streets and very few available parking spaces. The courthouse was busier than usual that morning, and open parking places were almost non-existent. Instead of fighting it, he decided to go on to the library and begin his day's work there.

Once inside the library, he made his way to the research and micro-fiche sections. He believed the answers to questions that had surfaced while researching in Daytona would be found in these sections and at a much faster pace. He found a comfortable and quiet location where he could use his typewriter, hoping it wouldn't bother anyone.

His first few efforts of looking through newspapers and periodicals, dating as far back as the spring of 1969, produced no results. Knowing he would have to be more selective in determining what year he should focus his inquiry, he began by searching all years ending in odd numbers. After an hour of fruitless efforts, he decided to continue his searching, but would begin by looking through the 1973 articles.

As his luck would have it that morning, the November 16, 1973, issue of a local newspaper had started to run an investigative series on problems surrounding the construction industry and local governments in Florida. He spent the next hour recording as much detail as possible and getting as many copies of the articles from the microfiche as he could. He knew what he found was important. He just didn't know how important.

Researching that two-week time span, from November 16 through November 29, he located eleven news articles and four leading stories, in three different newspapers and magazines, concerning Herman Jackson, A.J. Kellerman, and Roger Matheny. In three of the articles, there were featured stories on Herman Jackson and Roger Matheny. They all dealt with a legal dispute over workers' compensation issues. In three other stories, Roger Matheny was connected with someone named Jevon Mayer, from Tallahassee, about a dispute regarding deliverables on several proposed construction contracts. Apparently, front money was paid by a group of investors from Myrtle Beach, South Carolina, for thirteen hundred acres of land that was to be developed by two separate construction companies. The name that surfaced in the middle of these stories was someone named T.D. Zeigler from Winter Park, Florida.

T. D. Zeigler was indicted twice, within a three-year time span, on two separate counts for fraud and conspiracy to commit fraud. The co-conspirators in the indictment included Roger Matheny and a real estate investor named Thomas Pruneda. The story that surrounded the charges focused on Zeigler's money handling and Pruneda's connection with several offshore bank accounts in the Cayman Islands. Matheny was the political front guy who would get investors interested enough to provide advance money and secured deposits. Pruneda would appear to invest the funds only to seemingly run into a series of unfortunate circumstances. The money would be lost because of those circumstances. Each time Zeigler would offer an attempt to investigate the events, he never found any irregularities or wrongdoing in any of the activities.

The indictments never went much beyond the three of them being served subpoenas on the charges. Out of the blue, charges would be dropped. In one particular case, the charges were thrown out with an apology from the judge. The attorney of record for that case, who was able to keep the case from going to court and make the district attorney's office look foolish in the process, was Craig Myers.

Lenny now had documented evidence, although not terribly strong, connecting Craig with Matheny, Zeigler, Jackson, and Kellerman. In each of the cases where Craig's name appeared as the attorney of record, issues of money laundering, fraud, and conspiracy to commit fraud were woven into the fabric of his activities. He found no link to the Durham case, which would have strengthened the idea that Craig had something to do with the murder of Herman Jackson. Still, Lenny believed there was enough smoke surrounding the information he had discovered that there had to be a gun somewhere. He believed, with little doubt, they were all up to their eyebrows in Jackson's murder.

While researching the articles and gathering the information, it occurred to him that he should contact the reporter whose name appeared on the byline for several of the articles. Lenny thought that Hank Watson, a well-established reporter with over twenty years of experience in the news industry, had done a superb job on the series and decided to contact him to discuss the articles. Today, however, it would have to be by appointment because he wasn't going to miss having lunch with Sheri. Realizing it was already after the noon hour, he finished typing his notes and went to get copies of the articles for Samuel.

While he was waiting for the library assistant to retrieve his copies of the articles, he asked if he could borrow the phone to make a local call. Upon looking up the number to the newspaper, he dialed the number and reached the switchboard at the newspaper's head office. He asked to speak to Mr. Hank Watson but was transferred to the editor's desk.

"May I ask who is calling?" the voice on the other end of the phone asked.

"I'm Lenny Yeager. I'd like to speak to Hank Watson, the reporter who wrote a series of articles about five years ago on the Matheny cases," Lenny said.

"I'm sorry, but Hank Watson died last year in September."

"What do you mean, he died?"

"It's what usually happens when you are run over by a car," the other voice said.

"Who am I speaking to?"

"I am Chris Owens, managing editor for the paper," he said sternly. "What is it that you do, Lenny Yeager, and why are you asking about Hank?"

"Mr. Owens, do you have time to meet with me later this afternoon to discuss this matter with me? I'd like to explain in more detail what I am doing and why. I believe you and the paper could be of great assistance to me with the inquiries I am making."

After much insistence and explanation of the work he had already begun, Lenny was able to get an appointment to continue the discussion. He wanted to make sure that there was ample time to meet with Sheri and not have to rush their time together. He had developed a superb lead, hoping he had turned a corner on his assignment.

Before hanging up, Lenny asked, "Mr. Owens, where was Hank killed?"

"In Boca Raton, while on vacation," he responded.

"Did they ever find who did this?" Lenny asked.

"Yes, but he was not charged. It was ruled as an accident. The name of the guy involved was Anthony Dortch."

"Thank you. You've been a big help."

Lenny knew he had to reach Samuel right away but wasn't anywhere near a place he felt comfortable speaking to him over the phone. He knew Samuel's rule about relaying information over the phone, and that meant he needed to find a payphone near the diner. Also, he knew he would have to sit tight until Samuel gave him instructions—that meant he'd have to spend more time with Sheri. *It's a tough job*, he thought, *but somebody has to do it.*

By the time he was able to get out of the library, he figured the courthouse wasn't an option on his schedule. It would take him at least another twenty minutes to get back to the diner and another forty minutes or so to order and eat lunch. By then, he figured Sheri would be able to join him for a cup of tea—at least that was the plan. With Samuel's flight looming for three o'clock that afternoon, there was much that needed doing so he could enjoy the time with Sheri. The last thing he wanted to do was to keep looking at his watch while he was with her.

He gathered his things and headed out of the library to his car. He hadn't noticed anything in particular, but he had an uneasy feeling come over him as if he was being watched or followed—or both. He had learned long ago to trust his instincts in these situations, so he stopped and bent down to tie his shoelaces. He glanced casually around to see if anything looked unusual or out of place. He spotted a beige-colored two-door sedan parked near the side entrance of the library with someone sitting behind the steering wheel. He looked across the street and saw a plumber's truck, with two men in work clothes carrying varied lengths of pipe, a man sitting on the bench reading a newspaper waiting for the bus, and two women walking their dogs and chatting with each other.

Thinking he was okay and not being followed, he continued walking to where his car was parked, got in, and drove off toward the diner. He decided to change directions a few times just to see if anyone had been following him. After driving for fifteen minutes and after making several turns, the beige-colored two-door sedan appeared in his rearview mirror. Seeing that car in his rearview mirror confirmed his feeling that something was not right.

He began plotting how he would learn who was following him and why. First, he had to get to a safe place, call Samuel, and tell him of the events of that morning. Time was getting short, and he was beginning to feel pressured, especially since he had uninvited company hanging around.

As he continued to lead whomever it was following him to no particular place, he decided to stop at one of the shopping centers to make his phone call. Remembering there was a payphone at a nearby clothing store that would allow him to make his calls and keep a clear field for him to see what the other guy was up to, he calmly drove into the parking lot and parked near the clothing store. Keeping a cautious eye on the car that had been following him, he walked toward the phone mounted on one of the columns outside the store. He noticed the driver of the other car stayed close enough to view what Lenny was doing but far enough away that Lenny could not recognize facial features or other personal characteristics. *This guy is good*, Lenny thought. *I've got to figure out who this guy is and who hired him.*

As he picked up the receiver of the phone to begin making his calls, the driver of the other car moved his vehicle behind a large semi. The trailer was just long enough to provide him just enough time to run into the store directly behind him while not being seen by whoever was following him. When the car came to a point where the driver should have been able to see him at the phone, it looked as if he had disappeared.

Meanwhile, he dashed inside the store and was hiding off to the side of the large front windows. From that vantage point, he was able to see every move the driver of that mysterious car was making. Not knowing where he had disappeared to, the driver began to circle the area, giving him ample time to catch several glimpses of the license plate—and a fairly good look at the man in the car. It wasn't too long before the car was parked so the driver could easily spot Lenny leaving the store.

He asked one of the clerks if he could borrow the phone to make a few calls. He even offered her a twenty-dollar bill to cover any costs for using the phone. He asked her to let him know if someone with brown hair and a green shirt came into the store. He explained briefly whom he was, showed his identification to her, and made sure she understood how important it was. Hesitantly, she agreed. She positioned herself by the front door. This allowed Lenny to watch her and complete his calls at the same time.

He first tried dialing the office number, but no one was answering. Using the phone book on the desk next to the phone, he looked up the number to the hospital where Carrie had been admitted. The switchboard operator, after much insistence by him, connected him to Carrie's room, where Lucille answered the phone.

"Lucille, where's Samuel? I've got to get in touch with him before he gets on that plane this afternoon."

"He should be headed back to his house to pack and get ready for the trip. You should have seen what we came across in Craig's office," she said excitedly.

"If he should get in touch with you before he leaves, please tell him to call me at the Holden Avenue Diner at the corner of US 441 in Orlando," he said quietly, and then added, "And be sure to tell him to call at about one forty this afternoon."

"What are you doing in Orlando, Lenny?"

"Don't worry about that. Just tell him I've got information that he needs. Besides, I need for him to tell me what he wants me to do next."

"Try him at his house first. If you miss him there, you can probably catch him at the airport between two o'clock and two thirty."

"By the way, how is Carrie doing?"

"She's breathing better than she was earlier this morning, but she hasn't recovered from whatever Craig did to her. It's got her looking like a lemon, and she hasn't moved anything but her fingers this morning."

Lucille quickly looked up the phone number to the airport for him and suggested that Samuel might head back to the office before going to the airport. She continued to update him on Carrie's condition. Also, she explained to him how the doctors seemed confused by the jaundice. She indicated that they had called in a specialist from Ft. Lauderdale, and his flight would arrive Friday evening, sometime after midnight.

While listening to Lucille, his eyes were focused on the front door and the sales clerk. He quickly looked at his watch and realized that if he did not get out of the store, he was going to be late for lunch with Sheri. He said good-bye to Lucille and tried to reach Samuel at his home. He let the phone ring three times and hung up. He redialed the number and let it ring twice before hanging up a second time. The third time he let it ring until he was satisfied that Samuel was not at his house. Knowing nothing else was possible, his attention immediately turned to his getting out of the store without being seen by whoever was following him.

He motioned for the sales clerk to come to him. He asked her if there was a rear door he could use to leave the store without being seen.

She explained to him that she was not allowed to open the rear door except in an emergency. He finally persuaded her that this was a life-or-death situation and that he needed to get out that door. He went back to the phone, called for a taxicab, and instructed the dispatcher to have the cab driver pick him up at the rear exit of the store.

When it came time for him to leave, he handed the clerk an extra twenty dollars, gave her a big hug, and dashed out the door to the waiting cab. He ducked down in the back seat and instructed the driver to go around to the front parking area. This way, he could point out the beige sedan to him. The driver spotted it almost immediately, telling him that there were two guys in the front seat.

"Did you say two guys?"

"Yes, there are two guys in the front seat. One of them has on a green shirt, and the other guy is wearing a white shirt and tie."

"I want you to get us out of here, and make sure that car does not follow us," he said sternly.

"You're the boss, and it's your money. Where do you want me to take you? I've got to report my destination to the dispatcher," he said as he picked up the microphone to make the call.

"Tell him you're taking me to the motel on Oak Ridge Road," he said. "But I want you to drive around a little to make sure that car does not show up tailing us."

"I didn't know there was a motel on Oak Ridge Road." Then it hit him what Lenny was doing. He just smiled and eased the cab into traffic.

Lenny sat up enough to see out the windows but otherwise kept a very low profile in the backseat of the cab. He figured he would catch another cab to come back to his car after lunch. By then, the two men who were waiting might have given up and left. Even if they hadn't, he figured he would have accomplished three things by the time he got back to his car: he would have had a nice lunch while spending at least a couple of hours with Sheri, caught up with Samuel before he caught his flight to New York, and would have been able to run down the license plate information on that beige sedan.

He knew Samuel would want the information he had found earlier in the day. He also figured that Samuel would want to know who those two guys were who were following him. He was not used to the intrigue and gumshoe tactics, but he believed Samuel would help him through all of this. His expertise was finding information in courthouses and libraries, not trying to outrun or hide from people who were trying to find him. He never did like that part of what he did. Always before, however, Samuel had known exactly what to do.

He asked the driver how much of a tab he had already run up on the meter.

"At the moment, you're at four dollars and sixty cents."

"Keep turning and using side streets until you get to Azalea Park. Then turn around and head to the east end of Harden Avenue. You can let me out there, and I'll walk the rest of the way. If you see the beige car anywhere in the area, do not stop; just keep driving," he said as he placed a ten-dollar bill on the seat for the driver.

"Mister, you keep putting Mr. Hamilton's face on my front seat, and I'll take you wherever you want to go," he said, almost chuckling.

"Drive on, but do not speed."

"No problem. I have never gotten a speeding ticket in my life, not even as much as a parking ticket. Like I said, you keep putting Hamiltons on the seat next to me, and I will push this car if I have to. I will be happy to help you any way I can."

Lenny wasn't totally reassured, but he felt better knowing that the cabbie had a sense of humor—and understood what he was trying to do. It was important to him that he remained incognito and that very few people knew where he was—or what he was up to.

CHAPTER 14

Richard looked at his watch and realized the day was getting away from him. He wanted to make sure that he and Carlitto Berteloni had spoken before Samuel arrived later that evening. He was hoping that Carlitto would ballpark the dollar figure for the property and the store while Samuel put together an estimate for the business end of the package. With those two pieces of information, he and Pat could be more selective when looking for a new location in Florida. He understood that real estate in Florida was moving fairly well, but the current interest rates on business loans were extremely high. Still, he believed that once Samuel knew what he and Pat had been planning, and should a real opportunity present itself, the two of them would be able to move quickly and decisively.

"Richard," Pat said, while fixing Rachel and Joshua a sandwich for lunch, "has Carlitto called back?"

"No, I haven't heard from him. I think I'll call after lunch just to see if he's coming this afternoon," he said as he poured a glass of milk for Joshua.

"Maybe you should call Adrianna instead," she said in a caustic tone.

"He'll call. Just give him another hour or so," he said as he lifted Joshua into his booster seat and pushed the chair up to the table.

"I say it's even money, Richard, that he doesn't and Adrianna should," she said as she extended her right hand, attempting to close the bet with him.

"No way! Just wait and see," he said confidently.

She just smiled as she placed the sandwiches in front of the two children. She glanced at Richard and noticed he was smiling at her. He knew full well that if Carlitto didn't call back soon, he would never hear the end of it. He excused himself and headed back downstairs to the shop.

"Do you have Carlitto's phone number with you so you can call him now?" she said, while raising the level of her voice and laughing quietly to herself.

"I do, and I'll let you know what he says as soon as he calls," he yelled back, while smiling the entire time.

"Pat, why don't you just call Carlitto yourself and be done with it? It just seems that the two of you are at odds over this," Vicky said.

"Believe me, Vicky, we're not at odds over this. In fact, this is a diversion that we've become accustomed to, and it works for us. You and Samuel probably play a similar game, only with different rules and perhaps under different circumstances. Still, the call that needs to be made will be made, and we will both come out winners. You'll see," she said proudly.

Richard went to the back storeroom and called Carlitto's office once more. After speaking with the secretary, he learned that Carlitto was somewhere in Queens but that he intended to be at the deli around two thirty that afternoon. She assured him that if he was going to be late, she would call and let them know. She reiterated that Carlitto appreciated the opportunity and that he would see them today.

That's perfect, Richard thought. *That should be more than ample time to come up with a rough estimate for us. The real piece of information we'll need is how long he thinks it will take to sell the business.*

"Vicky, what time did you say Samuel's flight is due to arrive?"

"He's supposed to get in at six o'clock on the dot. Of course, we will have to get his luggage and clear the parking lot, but we should be home around seven-ish," she said as she took a bite out of Joshua's sandwich.

"Is his flight non-stop, or is it one of those that has to go through Atlanta?" Pat asked, while refilling Rachel's glass with milk.

"It is supposed to be non-stop. It's the only one out of Daytona Beach during the entire day," she said in an irritable tone. It hit her as soon as she had spoken those words that if he missed that flight, it would be after ten o'clock that evening before another flight out of Daytona Beach could connect in Atlanta with one headed toward New York.

Pat figured as much and sensed what she was feeling. "Thank goodness the airline has at least that one," she said resolutely.

Meanwhile, recent events forced Samuel to reorganize his afternoon activities before he could get on that plane. After leaving the bank, he went back to the office to work on a few things for a couple of his own clients whose cases would need his personal attention by the middle of the next week. He planned to stay at the office until a little after one o'clock, go home to finish packing, and then go to the airport. Other than checking with Lucille at the hospital, he decided to spend any remaining available time at the airport.

While he was finishing with his paperwork and putting things away in the filing cabinet, the phone rang. He went back to the comfort of his own office before picking up the call.

"Myers, Myers, and Associates," he said, very businesslike.

"Samuel, Lenny needs to talk to you right away. He's in Orlando, and he's got information for you," Lucille said urgently.

"Okay, I'll call him back in a little while," he responded. "That must have been his call I missed just as I was getting through the front door to the office."

"He sounded like he was in trouble, Samuel," she said.

"That's just Lenny being Lenny. Don't worry about him. When I speak to him, I'll be sure to tell him that you're concerned."

"Samuel, please be careful," she said, with concern in her voice.

"Don't worry, I will."

After a few more minutes of updates about Carrie and what the doctors were doing, he was relieved to know that the specialist was still very much in the picture. He thanked her for the update and advised her to stay at the hospital for a couple of nights, thinking that maybe the police would have found Craig by then. After reassuring her once more, he thanked her and said good-bye.

Before he went home, his thoughts turned to the events of the day and how much had happened in just a few hours. He thought about what new information Lenny might have to share regarding the Durham case. He thought about a lot of things as he went about stacking case files on his desk. Mostly, he remembered that this started less than two days ago because of a simple coffee stain on top of the filing cabinets. He was concerned about the amount of cash that he and Lucille had carried out of the office. He knew that the cash didn't belong to him, but he sure didn't want Craig to get his hands on it either. His thoughts turned to the documents that he had found in the wall safe in Craig's office. *They are more valuable than all of the cash*, he thought.

That thought led him back to Craig's office for another quick search. Since he knew where the key to the door was located, he retrieved it and went back into the room. Something was bothering him about the wall safe, so he headed to it first. After another quick application of the crowbar, he was able to access the wall box. He inspected it carefully, thinking there might be something they had overlooked in their haste. While thoroughly inspecting the box itself, the tips of his fingers found what seemed to be a small button on the very back top left-hand side of the safe. He pushed it, and the right-hand side wall fell to the bottom of the safe. There, no longer hidden, he saw a .25 caliber handgun, clips of ammunition, and several more newspaper clippings—some even dated as far back as April 1970.

He thumbed through the news articles quickly. The one that caught his eye was an article about a two-bit hoodlum named T.D Zeigler and someone named Kurt Stevens from Tallahassee. Both had been defended by Craig. That particular clipping had a phone number that he didn't recognize as a local number written on the bottom of it. He noticed several of the clippings had that same phone number written on them as well. He gathered all of the clippings, put them and the gun in his briefcase, and then pushed the false wall back into place. He grabbed the crowbar, which he had forgotten the first time he had gone into the room, retrieved it as well, and headed to the door.

As he was about to exit the room, he glanced around one more time to make sure he hadn't forgotten anything else. He turned off the lights, closed and locked the door, and then returned the key to its rightful place in the kitchen area. He knew he had found damning evidence, but without a search warrant, it was worthless in any kind of case he could build against Craig. He wasn't sure about what to do with the handgun, but he figured that Dr. Rutledge would be his best advisor on that issue. He was more than willing to turn the gun over to the police because the gun could bring about a great irony that he could enjoy. He knew the police would want to get their hands on the weapon because it probably wasn't registered—and the serial numbers were still intact. The prospect of Craig being done in by his own weapon was too delicious and brought a smile to his face. As he went out the back door of the office complex and got into his car, his smile had grown into a full grin.

The ride to his house was uneventful, until he turned onto the street where he lived. He was trying to be cautious as he approached his driveway. He had taken a different route from the office and made sure he stayed well under the speed limit. The last thing he needed was to be pulled over with Craig's handgun in his possession. He spotted two cars parked on the street across from his house, but no one appeared to be in either one. There were children playing in their own yard two doors down from his, and his next-door neighbor's dog was sleeping on their porch—much like he always did. *Nothing seems out of the ordinary*, he thought. *I think I will drive around the block one more time just to be sure.*

As he drove by his house, one of the parked cars started up and drove off in the opposite direction. He looked quickly into the rearview mirror on the driver's side of the car and saw a man in a dark grey suit get into the second car and drive off as well. It appeared to him that the man had come from the back side of his house.

He slammed on the brakes, stopping abruptly in the middle of the street, put the car into reverse, and gunned the engine. The smell of burning rubber and the noise from the squealing of the tires filled the inside of his car. When he was even with his driveway, he wheeled the car off the street and into the driveway, grabbed his briefcase, and ran through his carport to the side door of the house. He fumbled with his keys but finally got the door open.

Upon first inspection of the house, everything seemed to be in order. Nothing had been turned over or ripped open. His house appeared much the same as he had left it earlier in the day. He continued to look through all of the rooms, checking windows and doors to be sure they were shut and locked.

Satisfied that the house was secured, he sat down on his bed and breathed a sigh of relief. Wondering who that guy was, he realized he hadn't gotten a good look at the guy. Plus, he failed to get the license plate number for the car. He did remember that the first car was a two-toned 1973 Chevrolet Impala, and the second car was a solid white 1977 Pontiac Bonneville, with white walls and a dark blue or black interior. *Not much, but it might come in handy later*, he thought. He wrote down all he could remember, including a rough description of the guy he saw get into the car.

His thoughts turned to the tasks he needed to get done before leaving for the airport. While he returned to packing his clothes, he thought about calling Dr. Rutledge to get some advice about the gun. The more he considered the idea, the more he figured it was a bad idea to involve him. Craig was still on the loose, and Dr. Rutledge would be easy prey for him. He couldn't leave the gun at his house, and the news clippings were too valuable for someone else to get their hands on them. He figured out a plan for what he would do and decided to call Lucille one more time.

The hospital switchboard operator connected Samuel to the nurses' station, where one of the nurses put him through a battery of questions before being allowed to speak with Lucille.

"Samuel, is that you?" Lucille asked, clearly surprised.

"Yes, I have two more things for you to do before I leave. First, I want to make sure you have my parents' phone number. And second, tell me, why did this phone call not go to your room?"

"Mr. Courson decided that, as part of the security process, all calls were to be screened first through the nurses' station. Personally, I think it's because he's afraid of a lawsuit. Samuel, he's concerned because everything that has happened has involved attorneys. Don't you find that kind of funny?" she said, laughing out loud, while looking directly at one of the nurses seated at the desk area near Lucille.

"Lucille, that's not funny. Well, maybe just a little. Listen, make sure you call me if anything, and I mean anything, comes up. If Lenny should call you, tell him I'm on the way to the airport and should be there by one forty-five. I will call him as soon as I call you back for the contact information, get my luggage checked in, and pick up my ticket," he instructed.

"Okay, I'll take care of things here. You be careful. I'm a little uneasy about your leaving. A few days away from this, though, might be a good thing for you," she admitted.

She started to tell him the phone number to the diner, but he broke in quickly and said, "Not over this phone. Nobody needs to know where Lenny is at the moment. If Craig finds out that he's begun to put the puzzle together, he will not stop until he gets to Lenny."

Realizing what she had almost done, she apologized and said, "All right, but he said he needs to talk to you before you leave for New York. He said it was urgent."

He hung up the phone and, once again, started packing his suitcase. Since he had planned to return Monday evening, his needs were few. Besides the suitcase, he decided to take his briefcase and a carry-on bag so he wouldn't have to stuff everything into the suitcase. He gathered his toiletry items, enough socks and underwear to last him for five days, and two t-shirts that had been given to him by Rachel. He finished packing his business clothes, closed the lid of the suitcase, and sat back down on the bed for a few minutes to collect his thoughts.

After speaking with Lucille, he decided to deal with the events of the day and engage the police in the process. He picked up the phone, dialed the police, and asked for Lieutenant Howard. When he finally got to the phone, Samuel asked him if it would be possible to have an increase in the patrol activity around his house. He explained what had happened less than a half hour earlier, thinking that the increased patrols might discourage would-be break-in attempts. He reminded him that Craig's whereabouts were still unknown and that he was dangerous. Although not sure if it was the best thing to do, he told him about finding the handgun and asked for assistance with it.

"Where's the weapon now?" Lieutenant Howard inquired.

"I have it with me. I was careful to use a handkerchief—" he explained.

"Stay put, Mr. Carlisle. I will be there in about ten minutes," Lt Howard said before hanging up the phone.

His coming to Samuel's house was not on Samuel's agenda at this point in the day. He only had about an hour to get to the airport, get checked in, pick up his ticket, and find Lenny. Every minute was becoming critical to him. While he was waiting, he decided to take a closer look at the clippings he had found in the safe.

Although slightly discolored, they were actually in very good shape. As he inspected them, he began putting them in chronological order, accounting for twenty-three in all. Seventeen of them had the same phone number at the bottom of each clipping. He recognized the area code as that for calls to Tampa, Florida. He was sorely tempted to call the number just to see who would answer, but his phone rang, putting that thought on hold.

It was Vicky. She had called to see if everything was okay.

"Yes, everything's okay. I will tell you all about it when I see you in less than six hours."

"I tried the office, but nobody answered, so I got a little worried. How come there's no one at the office?"

"We've shut the office down until Monday. I'll explain it totally to you when I see you," he said firmly.

"What's wrong, Samuel?"

"I can't tell you over the phone. I will explain it all to you when I see you later today," he said, slightly distressed.

"Okay, okay. I get the hint."

Lieutenant Howard showed up two minutes early. The doorbell ringing was clearly heard over the phone by her, prompting her to inquire who was at the door.

"I think it's Dr. Rutledge," he said alertly. "He's probably come to say good-bye. I'll see you in a little while. I love you. Bye," he said and then hung up the phone. He hated having to do that, but he would explain everything to her later.

He went to the front door, let Lieutenant Howard inside, and explained to him that he had a plane to catch and a few extremely important calls to make.

"It would be best if you hand over the weapon to me. I'll get it to ballistics as well as the forensics team. Where did you say you found the weapon, Mr. Carlisle?"

"It was plainly visible in an opened wall safe in Craig's office," Samuel replied.

"What were you doing in Craig's wall safe, and what else did you find in the safe?"

"Nothing, except for some ammunition for this gun, some contracts he was working on, and some other business-related papers. I have the gun and the clips in my briefcase in the bedroom. Let me get them for you," he said as he headed toward the hallway, followed closely by Lieutenant Howard.

He went into the back bedroom, where he had put both his briefcase and his luggage on the bed. Before opening it, he turned the briefcase slightly away from Lieutenant Howard, which would limit Lieutenant Howard's ability to view its contents. Using a handkerchief, he picked up the gun by the grip and handed it to Lieutenant Howard, and he put it in a brown evidence bag. He also put the two clips in the same bag, making sure that his fingerprints were not on either the weapon or the clips.

"What time does your flight leave?"

"It leaves at three o'clock, but I have some phone calls to make from the airport before boarding."

"One of my officers will be posted on the outside of your house for the next seventy-two hours, just to keep an eye on things. We've got a twenty-four-hour guard on Mrs. Myers and Lucille at the hospital. The guard, by the way, has been instructed to stay there until further notice."

"Thank you, Lieutenant. I really appreciate all you are doing. But I really have to leave now in order to get my phone calls completed. I don't want to appear paranoid, but I think it is best not to make calls from my home phone, at least until Craig is behind bars. Is there anything else you need from me?"

"Yes. You need to give me a statement about all of this, including the safe, its contents, and any additional details concerning the car and mysterious man you saw. You never did tell me why you were in Craig's safe."

"I will have my statement for you on Tuesday morning next week. Will that be okay with you?"

"Come by the office first thing Tuesday morning, and we'll talk. I need a phone number where I can reach you. Right now, though, you need to tell me why you were in Craig's safe."

"I work there, Lieutenant. When I went to retrieve a file from the room directly across from his office, I noticed several footprints on the door, as if someone had been attempting to kick down the door. Knowing where he kept the key for his office, I opened the door to find the room in a mess. It was evident that someone had been looking for something in the room. The safe was opened, the handgun and clips were in plain view, and I didn't touch anything else," he said, knowing he was stretching the truth about as far as he dared.

"What day did you say you were returning to Daytona?"

"I'll be back late Monday night and in the office on Tuesday morning," he replied as he glanced at his watch, once again hinting that he had to leave.

"Just be sure that you bring a statement with you by Tuesday morning around nine o'clock."

"Yes, sir, that will not be a problem."

Samuel shook the lieutenant's hand, picked up his luggage, and walked to the car. After putting his luggage in the backseat of the car, he watched as the lieutenant drove off. *That's one piece of the puzzle completed*, he thought. He went back into his house, checked everything once more, locked the front door, got in his car, and headed for the airport.

Twenty-five minutes later, he had parked his car and was walking up to the airline's ticket counter—right on schedule.

CHAPTER 15

Twenty-seven dollars later, Lenny finally reached the east end of Harden Avenue. He and the cabbie had been watching carefully for the beige-colored, two-door sedan for at least twenty minutes without seeing it anywhere. Feeling confident enough to instruct the cabbie to pull over a block away from the diner and that he would walk the remainder of the distance, he paid the cabbie the amount owed, got out of the cab, and began walking toward the diner alert to both his surroundings and all approaching persons and vehicles.

Harden Avenue, which was no more than a side street off of US Highway 441, was lined with parked cars on both sides of the street. The diner, located in a semi-residential area of duplex-styled townhouses, reminiscent of what one would find in downtown Brooklyn, was positioned in an advantageous location from which to observe the coming and going of both vehicular and pedestrian traffic.

When he started walking, his pace was quick and rhythmical. By his demeanor and stride, it would not be hard to imagine he was listening to a cadence being barked by an invisible drill sergeant. Still sensing that he was being watched, he turned around and surveyed the area behind him with almost every other step. He continued walking quickly and rhythmically, all the while assessing the distance to the diner and the slightest of changes to his surroundings. The same shadows on the south side of the street, which provided some comfort against the early afternoon sun, helped to conceal his presence. The sun's rays, bouncing off the buildings on the other side of the street, were sharp in contrast to the shadows. He was hidden somewhat by the glare off the buildings, making it slightly difficult for anyone to see him.

With each step, the length of every stride he took wanted to out-distance the previous one. His focus was zeroed in on the entrance to the diner. His senses were heightened and being tested with each step. The least little noise caused him to flinch, then locate the source of the noise and stare intensely in that direction to determine if it was a threat to him. The last thing he wanted to do was to attract attention to the diner and cause problems for Sheri.

As he closed in on the diner, his pace slowed, allowing him one more thorough assessment of the surroundings. Just before he reached the steps to the diner, he leaned against a parked car, took out his glasses as if to inspect them, began cleaning the lenses, and then put them on. As he studied the parked cars to make sure no one was sitting in them, he was certain that his trail had been covered and that he had not been followed.

He turned quickly, went up the steps to the diner, opened the door, and went in. Once inside, he was glad to see the same booth where he had sat some four hours earlier was available.

Meanwhile, Samuel had entered the airport and had gone directly to the ticket counter. The clerk went through the usual particulars to process his ticket and baggage. After paying for his ticket and having collected the receipts for his luggage, he began looking for the nearest phone booth. Before calling Lenny, he wanted to check in with Dr. Rutledge one last time to remind him of the schedule of events for the next four days and alert him that there would be noticeable police activity in the neighborhood.

Although he figured Dr. Rutledge would probably be resting, he dialed the number, thinking that this message was worth his hearing.

"Hello," Dr. Rutledge said, sounding tired.

"Dr. Rutledge, did I wake you?"

"Almost. After all, it is nap time," he said sharply.

"Dr. Rutledge, I wanted to make sure that I explained a couple of things before I leave for Brooklyn. I'm at the airport and will be boarding my flight in a little while. Do you have the phone number for my folks in Brooklyn?

"Let me look, Samuel. I'm sure I do, but I better check to be sure. Hold on a minute," he said, placing the phone down.

Samuel could hear music playing in the background and the sound of what he thought was a desk drawer being opened. What he heard next was beyond his understanding.

It was the unmistakable blast from a shotgun that came across the phone line, deadening Samuel's left eardrum. Its fierceness was pronounced and marked by its proximity to the phone. The sound exploded from the earpiece and was heard clearly by two women walking near the phone booth. Then an uneasy silence followed by what sounded like footsteps, which could be heard approaching the phone. Then the phone line went dead, disconnecting Samuel's call.

Samuel was stunned. *This can't be happening*, he thought.

Immediately, he dialed the police and reported what he had heard, provided Dr. Rutledge's address, requested an ambulance be dispatched as well, and then asked to speak with Lieutenant Howard. He was told that Lieutenant Howard was not in but that the dispatcher would raise him on the radio and have him meet Samuel at Dr. Rutledge's address.

Samuel bolted out of the phone booth and began running to his parked car. As he ran, his thoughts turned to Dr. Rutledge's condition. Praying on the run was not one of Samuel's areas of expertise, but it was all he could think of to do at the moment. As he cleared the initial traffic in front of the airport and jumped a row of small hedges, he saw a policeman sitting in a parked patrol car not far from where the exit would be for him to leave the parking lot.

At first the officer thought Samuel was some kind of nutcase, until Samuel asked him to check with the dispatcher. Once the officer had confirmed what Samuel had explained to him earlier was in fact the truth, he agreed to provide Samuel with an escort to Dr. Rutledge's house. It was all the officer could do, however, to keep up with Samuel's driving, once Samuel pulled out of the parking lot.

It had taken Samuel twenty-five minutes to get to the airport earlier. It took less than twenty minutes with a police escort to reach Dr. Rutledge's house, which was only three doors down from Samuel's. Other squad cars and an ambulance already had arrived at the scene. There were several of Samuel's neighbors standing across the street straining to see what had happened in what was otherwise a quiet neighborhood. The local television crews had not yet arrived, allowing the police ample time to cordon off the area and protect the crime scene.

After Samuel's car screeched to a halt on the driveway pavement on the east side of Dr. Rutledge's house, he hurried from his car and headed for the front door. What he saw next was even more amazing than what he had heard just twenty-or-so minutes before.

As he reached the top of the steps to the house, Dr. Rutledge met him at the front door.

"I heard the shot and thought…" Samuel said excitedly with an incredibly unbelieving look upon his face.

"You thought what?" Dr. Rutledge asked.

Samuel was at a loss for words. He reached out for Dr. Rutledge and embraced him. "I am so grateful you are okay."

"My boy, I have never been better in all of my days," he said quietly to Samuel as he patted him on his shoulder.

With his arm around Samuel's shoulders, the two of them entered Dr. Rutledge's house and stood in the foyer staring down a central hallway that connected the entrance area to the back end of the house. As they attempted to bypass a couple of police officers who had been assigned for security purposes, Samuel saw the lifeless body of an adult male lying on the floor in the middle of the living room.

"I got him clean," Dr. Rutledge whispered to Samuel. "The problem, Samuel, is that he might have been a part of the puzzle you and I have been working on. I'm waiting for the coroner's team to make some kind of ID on this guy, but I have been told to mind my own business. I thought that since you are here, you could act on my behalf, as my attorney, to find out a few things they are not willing to tell me."

Samuel was restrained from approaching the body by one of the police officers. His initial visual inspection of the living room area from the hallway showed a massive blood flow on the carpet and a huge blood splatter pattern on the wall just above the console television. Dr. Rutledge had answered the phone about ten feet from where the body was found.

"When did you have time to get your shotgun?" Samuel asked.

"Unfortunately for him, I had finished cleaning and loading it just before you called," he responded.

"I thought you said I just woke you?" Samuel said, with a look of confusion on his face.

"You did, and your timing could not have been better. That's when I saw him turn the corner with that weapon," he said as he pointed to a revolver near where the body was located. "He must have come in the back door," Dr. Rutledge said, while shaking his head. "I must have left it unlocked again. Too bad for him, huh?"

Samuel went to the back end of the house to inspect the rear door. He wanted to see that location before the police would make him leave the area entirely. Neither the back door nor the outer screen door had any markings of being forcibly opened. *I definitely want them to check for prints on the door, the doorknob, and the door casing as well,* he thought. He continued to scan the room to see if there was anything that stood out from the rest of the surroundings. What he concluded was that Dr. Rutledge kept everything in the house spotless. *Your could eat off this floor,* Samuel thought.

As he left the back of the house and rejoined Dr. Rutledge in the dining room, Samuel began to ponder the possibilities of who would want to harm Dr. Rutledge. *Obviously, they meant to harm him in some manner,* he thought. Several questions came to mind—especially if Craig had been behind these events. Samuel began wondering, *If Craig was behind this, why did he feel Dr. Rutledge was a threat to him? What did Dr. Rutledge know that Craig felt was not just a threat to him but enough of a threat that he felt he had to kill him?*

He walked back to the front of the house, found Dr. Rutledge sitting in the dining room, and asked, "Why do you think this guy showed up at your house?"

"He wasn't here to play cribbage, that's for sure," Dr. Rutledge said as he turned toward Samuel. "That's the sixty-four-thousand-dollar question," he added as he stood up and walked over to the wall area nearest the living room.

"Samuel," Dr. Rutledge said as he pointed to a part of the wall near the front door, "I believe I have some major repair work to do." The wall had been peppered with buckshot and was covered in bloodstains.

As the two of them inspected the wall, Lieutenant Howard and Sergeant Rothermel came in the front door, stopped to speak with the two uniformed officers at the door, and then started walking toward the living room.

"You've been a busy boy, Samuel," Lieutenant Howard said. "I thought you had a plane to catch."

"That's right, Lieutenant, and I was just about to leave," he said as he shook hands with Dr. Rutledge then began walking toward the front door. "My flight leaves in about forty minutes, and it is about a thirty-minute ride to the airport," he said as he continued out the door and toward his car.

Lieutenant Howard, puzzled by what Samuel was doing at a crime scene when he had a plane to catch, started after him to speak to him. Dr. Rutledge, thinking he could help cover Samuel's exit and get Lieutenant Howard focused on the investigation of the events at the house, approached the lieutenant hurriedly.

"Lieutenant, let me explain what happened here," Dr. Rutledge began, "so you'll know exactly why he ended up here instead of at the airport. I had been cleaning my shotgun..." he said as he drew attention to himself and away from Samuel.

Samuel managed to get back to the airport with just enough time to call Lucille. Finding a public phone directly across from the waiting area where he would board his flight, he dialed the number and waited for her to pick up. Instead he got one of the nurses, who told him that she had stepped out to go to the cafeteria. He gave the information to the nurse and asked her to make sure that Lucille received the message.

He wanted the nurse to understand the importance of the information, so he used the phrase "life-and-death emergency."

When he asked the nurse to repeat the information back to him to ensure she had written it down correctly, he heard his flight being paged in the background. He thanked the nurse, picked up his briefcase, and walked to the check-in counter for his flight. *Isn't this just great? Now I've missed my chance to get together with Lenny this afternoon,* he thought.

After selecting a seat for the flight and grateful that his ticket was in order, he exited through the doorway leading to where his plane was parked. The noise of the jet engines warming up, the smell of jet fuel, and low-key conversations in the cabin of the plane were all familiar things to him. He was glad to be on the aircraft, but he was concerned about having to leave Lucille, Carrie, Lenny, and Dr. Rutledge behind. There was no telling what Craig had in store for them.

As he took his seat and buckled his seatbelt, he looked out the window. He watched as the ground crew finished the final preparations for the aircraft. All he could think about was hoping that Lucille had made contact with Lenny, shared his information with Lenny, and hope that Lenny understood it. *I hope he gets it right,* he thought.

As the aircraft began backing away from the gate area, Samuel leaned back in his seat and let out a long, muscle-relaxing sigh. He closed his eyes and took a couple of deep breaths, trying to relax himself and become comfortable in his seat. The plane, which had continued to back away from the gate area, managed to clear the other aircraft on the tarmac. After it came to a complete stop, it remained motionless for a few seconds. Then the plane moved forward slightly as the engines began to rev up. It continued rolling, with increased engine noise, as it made its way to the runway. *At last, I'm on my way to Brooklyn—finally*, he thought.

Lenny's entrance into the diner had been exactly what he had hoped for. Most of the lunch crowd had already departed. By the time he sat down, he noticed there were only two other groups of customers in the diner. After looking out the window and checking to see if he had been followed, he decided to move away from the front window and closer to Sheri's workstation. He felt much more comfortable knowing that he was in a safe place, near a phone, and that he would have plenty of time to talk with her. He believed Craig and his henchmen had no idea where he was—and he liked it that way.

Sheri came out from the kitchen carrying a tray, filled with glasses of iced tea and water, for one of the groups sitting on the far side of the diner. She spotted Lenny right away, smiled at him, and motioned to him that she would be there in a minute. He watched her as she walked toward the group. He saw that her limp was noticeably worse than it had been earlier in the day. *She's had a rough day,* he thought. After delivering the drinks to the customers, she motioned to the other waitress that she was going to sit down for a while and then walked over to his booth.

"Hi, Lenny," she said as she sat down next to him. "I wasn't sure if you were coming. I thought you might have changed your mind. I mean…" she said, stopping in mid-sentence.

Lenny had not expected her to sit next to him. He didn't move, but he did have to clear his throat before responding.

"No, I have been looking forward to this since I had to leave this morning," he said as he looked directly into her eyes.

She, not knowing exactly what to say or do, smiled back at him and, while glancing downward, said, "I kept watching the clock and wondering if I had been too forward this morning or something."

"Not at all," he responded quickly. "I just got hung up with some work, and the time got away from me. Can I buy you lunch to make it up to you?" he asked.

"Buy me lunch? Lenny, my father owns the diner. I eat free, and so will you today."

"I couldn't and I shouldn't. Please, it's very kind of you, but I think it is best if I pay my way today," he said, not realizing that someone had walked up behind him.

"I like this guy already," the man said as he sat down in the seat on the other side of the booth. "Sheri, aren't you going to introduce me?"

"Lenny, I want you to meet my father, Mr. Thomas O'Bannon," she said, which was quickly followed by, "and Poppa, this is Lenny, Lenny Yeager."

Shaking hands with her dad wasn't as bad as he imagined it would be. He was grateful to get all of the protocols and social graces displayed and out of the way. He wasn't sure exactly what to say because it hadn't occurred to him that he would be meeting her father on the same day that he had just met her. He didn't mind the idea. He just wished he had taken the time to freshen up and put on some clean clothes.

"So, Lenny, what do you do for a living?"

"I am a paralegal and conclude research projects for attorneys," he said as he handed Mr. O'Bannon one of his business cards. "I'm currently working a case that brought me to Orlando last night and to your diner this morning. Not only was the meal very nice, but it was a pleasure to meet Sheri. So, I've decided to be a repeat customer, if that's okay with you."

"I appreciate your business. She told me what you did this morning with the coupon. And I heard just now, with my own ears, how you like to pay your own way. That's not only refreshing to me, but it is something I believe a person usually learns early in life. Where are you from, Lenny?" he asked. Before Lenny could respond, Mr. O'Bannon pointed to and gestured for another waitress to bring each of them a glass of sweet tea.

"I'm originally from a small town in the central part of Illinois called Oakford. My parents have lived there all their lives, farming, mostly," he added.

"How did you end up in Florida?"

Sheri leaned in closer toward Lenny to make sure she didn't miss a word of what he was about to say to her father.

"Mr. O'Bannon, I came to Florida in the summer between my second and third year of law school to work for an attorney. When I finally got situated in Daytona Beach, a job offer from a really prestigious law firm was very hard to turn down because the money was extremely good. After three similar opportunities for those attorneys, I had other offers from larger firms that eventually kept me busy enough to take off from law school for a couple of semesters."

"When do you plan to finish law school? You do plan to finish law school, don't you?"

"All I lack, basically, is to take a few exams at the school, pass the bar exam, and hang out a shingle."

"Lenny," Mr. O'Bannon said as he served one of the iced teas to Sheri and the next one to Lenny, "just what are your intentions with my daughter?"

"Poppa, you're embarrassing me," she said as she swiped at her father's arm.

"All I want to know is what he's thinking. He waltzed in here this morning from who knows where, and we don't know him from Adam," he said as he looked directly at Lenny.

"I assure you, my intentions are honorable. It was a very nice breakfast, plus I enjoyed visiting with your daughter this morning," he said, and immediately followed it with, "And I'd like to get to know her more, with your permission, of course."

"Sheri, I told you I like this guy," he said as he turned toward Lenny. "Just be sure you understand that my daughter is very special to me, especially since her mother died twelve long years ago."

"I'm sorry. I had no idea..."

"I know you didn't, but now you do," he said as he stood to leave.

"Just be sure you remember that it is a good idea to talk with me once in a while," he said as he walked toward the kitchen.

"I'm so sorry about that," she said as she placed her hand on his.

"It's okay. I have no children, but I think I understand how he feels, and that's okay with me."

Realizing he should already have heard from Samuel, he asked Sheri if anyone had taken a call for him. She was sure no one had called asking for him. She explained that if he needed a little privacy, he could use the office phone. He thanked her for the offer but declined it, indicating that he was expecting someone to call him.

"What would you like to eat while you're waiting for the call?" she asked as she stood next to the table.

"Whatever you're having is fine. I would like a cup of hot tea with it, however."

"How does the O'Bannon luncheon special sound to you?"

"Perfect, as long as you'll be back to sit with me."

"I'm looking forward to it. Just let me get your order in and get your tea, and I'll be right back," she said, while smiling at him. She reached out and placed her hand on his shoulder. He leaned over and placed his cheek on her hand.

Sheri asked, "What are you up to, Lenny?"

"Nothing, I'm just enjoying this time with you."

She was at a loss for words as she walked toward her workstation.

He knew the others in the diner were watching his every move, but he didn't care. Sheri was special to him. Not knowing why, he just felt there was something more he wanted and needed to know about her. His lunch that afternoon, although later than he had planned, was something he wanted to enjoy—with her. He felt comfortable around her, and he wanted to build on the budding relationship the two of them had begun earlier in the day. It wasn't about the lunch. To him, it was about where he was having lunch and with whom he would be sharing lunch. *What a great place for some down time,* he thought. *I just wish Samuel would call.*

CHAPTER 16

While Carrie was undergoing additional blood tests and neurological assessments, Lucille decided to get some lunch. She had been sitting in the chair in Carrie's hospital room without a break for three hours. *A change in scenery would be great,* she thought.

She had been reading out loud to Carrie to keep her mentally active and engaged with her surroundings. Plus, she thought it was doing something worthwhile for Carrie. It was hard to just sit and wait because the whole event seemed so unreal to her. So, she decided to go get something to eat and headed to the cafeteria.

When she entered the cafeteria, she went directly to the coffee urn, poured a large container of decaffeinated coffee for herself, paid for it, and found a vacant table in the far corner of the dining hall. She began watching two young children, who were sitting quietly at a nearby table, waiting for their mother to bring their trays to them. While sipping her coffee, she recalled a similar time she and her brother went to the hospital with their mother. Seeing them watch their mother's every move brought back memories of when she, her brother, Charles, and her mother were eating in a cafeteria, at another hospital, in another city, over thirty years earlier.

Her father, who had been rushed to the emergency room from his worksite, had suffered a severely broken leg and internal injuries. She and her brother were in school at the time of the accident, making it even more memorable. They had to be picked up from school by their grandmother, which had never happened before, and taken to the hospital. They had gathered with their mother in the waiting room just outside the trauma center. Charles had started crying in the car, thinking their father was going to die. Lucille, not really understanding the severity of their father's injuries, tried to comfort him by telling him that everything was going to be okay. *That's what big sisters are supposed to do*, she thought as she began recalling the details of the event.

When you're only nine years old and you don't know any better, you do what you've seen your mother do for other people, even when someone's heart ached worse than the pain from the injuries. Still, the memory of that day was very real to her—even recalling the antiseptic smell of the emergency room, the muffled sounds of sirens, and the ambulances as they approached the emergency room. She remembered how brave and how in control her mother seemed to be, in spite of all that had been happening around her. Somehow, today, as she sat in a hospital cafeteria, she needed to draw from her mother's strength to get through all that was happening. She wanted to believe that she could somehow help Carrie.

Staring at the wall across the room as she sipped her coffee, she recalled the nurses hurrying supplies into the emergency room while tending to her father that afternoon. She remembered watching the staff as they wheeled her father out of the emergency room, into the elevator, and finally into the operating room. She and her mother went together and followed the gurney onto the elevator. She especially remembered how quiet her father was and how ashen the color of his skin appeared. She recalled vividly the bloodstains on the white sheets and that his left leg had been elevated. She recalled how her mother wiped away several tears and how she clenched her handkerchief, as if someone was trying to wrestle it away from her.

Watching the two young children eat their lunch with their mother rekindled the memory of seeing her mother talk with the doctors before her father went into surgery. Her memory was clear. She recalled how her mother and the doctors stood in the hallway outside the emergency room, their voices low, almost whispering, which made it difficult for her to hear what they had been saying. She never heard what the doctor said to her mother, but she recalled the look on her mother's face and how her knees weakened slightly. She recalled the doctor holding onto her mother's left arm to steady her and keep her from collapsing to the floor.

She had not recalled that particular detail of those events until now. It caused goose bumps to shoot up and down her right arm. She remembered watching as her mother listened to the doctors, while they explained the surgical procedures and the risks involved. The memory of her mother sitting next to her outside the operating room, pulling her close, kissing her on the forehead, and telling her, "I love you," was vividly clear and unmistakable.

Tears began to run down Lucille's face while she sipped her coffee and remembered the events of that day from so many years before. Tears came uncontrollably and streamed steadily down both sides of her cheeks. She couldn't stop the tears that day long ago, when she learned that her father had died during surgery, and she couldn't stop them now. She used a napkin from the container on the table to help wipe her eyes, but the tears continued.

The young children noticed what was happening, and they started whispering to their mother about what they had seen. Their mother motioned for them to continue eating and not to pay attention to her. Of course, it only made them want to watch even more. It was then that she decided to refill her coffee, inspect the serving line, and consider if there was anything that she might find appealing for lunch.

After selecting a few items and paying for them, she returned to her seat. Although not very hungry, the food tasted good, and her appetite began to return with each additional bite. It wasn't too long before she decided she had not put enough on her plate. As she started toward the serving line, two doctors in surgical gear entered and went directly to the woman. She watched with interest and began to feel her anxiety return. Somehow, she just knew what was about to happen.

She returned to her seat and watched with concern as the doctors explained to the woman what had happened. The children were unaware, at first, of what all of this might mean. Lucille knew what it meant, and she wanted to go over to that table in the worst way.

Knowing what was happening to that family was none of her business, but that didn't matter. When the little girl began to cry, Lucille got out of her seat and went over to where the family was sitting.

By the time she got there, the woman had collapsed into the chair, grasping at her chest, and was having difficulty breathing. The little boy had gotten out of his chair, taken a step backward, and then stood motionless. The little girl stood near the table crying and looked at everyone in the room, as if pleading for help. One of the doctors, taking his stethoscope, began listening to the woman's heart. The other told the cashier to, "Call the emergency room. Have them send a crash cart and gurney, stat!"

Lucille stood next to the little girl, knelt down, and took the little girl's hands into hers. Compared to hers, the little girl's hands were cold and trembling. Both Lucille's and the little girl's eyes were reddened from crying. She reached up with her right hand and placed it on the little girl's left shoulder, telling her, "I know; I know."

It was then that the little girl turned, reached out to her, and hugged her tightly yet lovingly. She buried her head in the nape of Lucille's neck, sobbing all the while. She motioned to the little girl's brother that she would hug him too.

"It's okay. I have enough hugs for both of you," she said, while trying to smile and yet not cry at the same time.

Instead of coming to her, he took another step backward, not certain of Lucille's gesture. His demeanor was guarded, and he showed little emotion. It was evident that he was more concerned about watching what the doctors were doing to his mother than anything else.

After what seemed to Lucille to be forever, a crew from the emergency room finally entered the cafeteria, and one of the doctors began telling them what to do. Once the woman had been placed on the gurney, they all began moving toward the exit. As the little girl watched her mother being wheeled from the cafeteria, she began crying even louder and reached out for her mother over Lucille's shoulders. Lucille stood up, holding the little girl securely.

"Come on, we're going too. I think I know where they're taking your mother. You'll see; it will be all right," she said as she began to follow the doctors to the emergency room.

The little girl looked back at her brother.

"William!" she yelled, while holding an outstretched hand, gesturing for him to come with them.

Lucille stopped, turned around, and went back to where he was standing.

"William," she said, almost whispering his name, "your sister and I are going to see your mother. Wouldn't you like to come with us?" she asked, while smiling at him. She knelt down and put the little girl next to her brother.

He nodded that he did, but he stood still by what he had seen and heard. The little girl took his hand and then reached for Lucille's.

"William," the little girl insisted, "come on. This nice lady will help us," she said as she gave a tug on her brother's hand. Cautiously, he took a watchful step along with his sister, and all three headed toward the exit.

Lucille knew all too well how to navigate the corridors that led to the emergency room. She dreaded thinking about what might be waiting for them at the end of their little journey.

"I know your brother's name is William," she said as she looked down at the little girl. "What's yours?" she asked, trying to coax a smile from her.

"Paula," she replied quietly, while clutching Lucille's hand and looking up at her.

"Oh, what a pretty name," she said. "How old are you, Paula?" she asked as they continued walking toward the emergency room.

"I'm almost six, and William is almost three. His birthday is next week," she added.

She looked at William and then Paula and said, "We're almost there. When we do get there, we'll need to be really quiet. Until the doctors tell us about how your mother is doing, we'll sit in the waiting room. How about we get something for your mother from the gift shop before we sit down?"

"Okay," Paula said as she continued walking with her and tightly holding William's hand.

The diversion proved helpful for the children and to her as well. They were able to think about something other than what had just happened in the cafeteria. It helped to take their mind off of what might be happening in the emergency room. Just being in a quiet place, where there were so many shiny and colorful items to consider, helped them to focus on something pleasant—even if it would be for just a few minutes.

William decided he would watch as his sister decided what to do. He remained quiet during their time in the gift shop. He followed his sister as she went methodically up and down each aisle, looking carefully for just the right gift for their mother. She spotted a small, furry, powder blue teddy bear. It had a card attached that read *I Wuv You, Mom*. Lucille noticed it too and asked, "Is that what you would like to get for your mother, Paula?"

"Oh yes. It's just like the one my father gave me when I was little," she said with such glee. "It's perfect."

William smiled for the first time as he reached out to hold the teddy bear. Paula gave it to him and said, "Go with this lady because we have to pay for it."

She paid the attendant for the bear, while Paula and William waited patiently by the exit. She was pleased that he had smiled and that Paula was willing to speak with her. She moved toward the exit, thanked the attendant, and directed the children to follow her so they could go see how their mother was doing.

With each step Lucille took toward the same emergency room she had been in earlier that day, her anxiety level rose. She was fearful that the news would not be good and that the children would not handle it well. When she looked at the children as they continued their walk, she had to paste one of those "It's okay" types of smiles on her face for fear that she might break down right there in the middle of the hallway.

When they approached the double swinging doors to the emergency room, it occurred to her that she did not know their mother's name. Paula was not able to provide her with a great amount of detail, including how her father was somewhere in the hospital—as Paula put it, "to be operated on." Armed with very little information, they went through the doors and headed for the nurses' station.

Lucille recognized one of the doctors who had been in the cafeteria and asked if he would not mind speaking to her. She could tell he was hurried, but he had slowed down enough to listen to her. From the corner of her eye, she could see Paula watching everything from just inside the entrance area, while William sat quietly hugging the stuffed animal and rocking himself against the back of his chair.

"Doctor, these children belong to Mrs. Joyce Lester, you know, the lady who was just brought in here from the cafeteria. Would you mind telling me how she's doing so I can speak to the children? They're a little anxious for her. Plus, their father was admitted today for surgery, and I do not know how he's doing or what room he's in," she said.

"Are you related to Mrs. Lester?"

"No, I am just trying to help the children with a tough situation," she said firmly.

"I cannot speak to you about another patient's condition without the family's consent."

She could feel the irritation beginning to build and tried once again to inquire about the condition of the children's mother. Although polite, he refused and walked behind the counter area as he wrote on a patient's chart. He looked up a moment later and saw her standing there with two children. She looked at Paula and said, "Go ahead, Paula."

"Doctor," Paula started, "how is my mother?"

The doctor called for one of the nurses to take Lucille and the children to the waiting room. Lucille decided it was better for her not to make a scene in the middle of the emergency room, so she left with the nurse, telling the children that they would have to be a little more patient. There she learned that Mrs. Lester had been taken to the Critical Care Unit on the third floor. The nurse gave her the name of the doctor who had been attending the children's father and advised her to contact the nurses' station for that floor.

When the nurse left the waiting room, she turned to the children and said, "I think we need to just sit here for a few minutes. Paula, I have to make a phone call. Will you and William stay here while I go make that call?"

Paula and William sat quietly as she stepped into the hallway and went to the phone bank just outside the door. She deposited a quarter into the slot and dialed the number.

"Hello," the voice on the other end of the line said.

"Mom, I need your help," Lucille said. "You're not going to believe this, but…"

CHAPTER 17

"Mr. Myers, I don't know how to tell you this, but Jack was killed by that nutcase you sent us to talk to," Anthony said.

"What do you mean he was killed?" Craig asked angrily.

"That guy didn't give Jack a chance to say anything. He just opened up on us and cut Jack in half."

"How in God's name did he know the two of you were even coming?"

"I don't know, but when we first got there, it looked like he was sleeping in his chair in the living room. We had just entered the back door when we heard the phone ring. The next thing I hear is the blast. I went out the way I came in, only on the run, and I didn't look back."

"This changes everything. Get back to the garage area, and be sure you're not followed. I've got a house call to make," Craig said as he slammed the phone down on the table.

"Do you believe this?" he said as he turned and looked at Todd. Todd Koehler was Craig's inside contact with the local thugs in the Orlando area. Craig's "other life" included the likes of Todd Koehler, Jack Ussery, and Anthony Dortch.

"Todd, get yourself to the garage area and meet Anthony there. I'll join the two of you at the garage area later. In the meanwhile, keep out of sight."

Knowing how Anthony could go off, Craig turned to Todd and said, "If it looks like he's going to flip out, give him one of these to calm his nerves." He opened a small pill bottle and handed Todd one of the capsules.

"I wouldn't advise you to take this. It might make you permanently dead. Use it on Anthony if you have to, but just make sure you don't lose it."

After Todd departed, Craig attempted to call his office to see if anyone was answering the phones. He wanted to go retrieve the cash box from the safe and take care of a few details. He knew it would be risky, but he had no choice. He couldn't count on anyone except for Todd, and he needed him to keep Anthony under control. He couldn't stay at his brother's winter home any longer. He didn't want to take a chance on being identified by someone in the neighborhood. It had been the perfect hideout for him. There, he could collect his thoughts and sleep, without worrying that someone might sneak up on him. None of his neighbors knew who he was or seemed the least bit interested. *Besides,* he thought, *the only one who knew about this place was my darling wife, and she's as good as dead.*

Before leaving the house, he went about wiping fingerprints off the table and phone, collected the newspapers he had touched, and wiped down the rest of the furniture to remove any possible fingerprints. As he was preparing to leave, the phone rang. He decided to wait to see what the caller would do. The phone rang four times and stopped ringing. A few seconds went by and the phone rang again. This time, on the third ring, he picked up the receiver and said, "Speak."

"Mr. Myers, what am I supposed to do now? I lost Lenny. He gave me the slip when he stopped to use the phone." Frenchie Puska, who had been tailing Lenny most of the day, knew Craig was not happy. He figured, however, that he had better report the events and get his instructions for Saturday.

The news was just one more thing that Craig didn't need. He paused for a few seconds, trying to put everything into perspective.

"Okay, so we can't find Lenny. My guess is he's not too far from where he landed last night. Where's he parked?"

"His car is just outside a small store on the east side of town."

"Get back to it and sit on it. He will come back for it sometime today. But," he continued, "be sure that you change your clothes first and use a different vehicle. Farm boy grew up around cows, but he is not as stupid as he looks. Just follow him. Do not try to approach him. Call me using the other phone number I gave you this morning, once you pick up his trail. I need to know where he is and what he is doing."

"Mr. Myers," Frenchie said, before clearing his throat, "I picked up some help today. I asked Ricky Sims to help me out. Is it okay if he stays on this with me?"

"Yes, but tell him nothing. Just have him help keep an eye on things and follow instructions. He's your responsibility, and if he screws up, you'll answer to me."

"Yes, sir. Don't worry. He'll be fine."

Craig hung up the phone, wiped any possible prints from it, and headed out the door one more time. He walked quickly to his car, which was parked between the side of the house and a row of hedges that separated him from his neighbors. The house was perfectly located for him to stay out of the public's eye, allowing him relative isolation and anonymity. It had worked perfectly. It was time, though, that he relocate for his own good.

As he drove toward his office, sporting sunglasses and a hat to help disguise his appearance, he couldn't help but think about Carrie. In the early years of their marriage, she was the love of his life. Having to kill her was not in the plans, but she knew too much—especially where to find things that would incriminate him in a heartbeat. He risked a great deal going into the hospital, but Carrie was a liability to him at that point. However, he hadn't expected to find Lucille in the room. *I should have silenced Little Miss Do-Goodie while I had the chance,* he thought. *Depending on how things develop tomorrow, I may have another opportunity.*

He turned onto the street that would take him to the back entrance of his office building. Trying not to attract attention, he slowed the car to almost a crawl, scanned the surroundings cautiously, and especially made sure there were no policemen who might be waiting for him. He decided not to park in the small lot at the back entrance. Instead, he pulled over into one of the parking spaces on the side of the street. From that location, he had a line-of-sight advantage point. He brought the vehicle to a stop but left the engine running. As he sat in his car for about six or seven minutes, his eyes moved methodically back and forth, surveying the area—especially the back door to his office.

Nothing that caught his eye looked suspicious or out of place to him. He turned off the engine, gathered his briefcase, exited the car, and moved quickly to the rear door of the office. While looking around to make sure no one had spotted him, he unlocked the door and entered the building.

Once he was inside, he went immediately to his office, unlocked that door, and stood motionless for several seconds as he stared into what once was a spotlessly kept office. Fearing the worst, his eyes fixed on the safe as he walked toward it. He bent down and pressed the release button, only to find that the money and gun were gone.

"Samuel!" he said under his breath. "Only you could have done this," he said resolutely.

He recovered the phone from the floor, dialed off a series of numbers, and waited for the call to connect.

"Hello," the person answering the phone said.

"We have a problem that is greater than I figured. We're going to need to switch defense strategies," he said.

"Understood. I will get in touch with the coach and get back to you. In the meanwhile, go to the locker room and prepare your sequence of plays. The rest of the defense will huddle and will make a substitution or two."

"I will wait in the hallway." He hated the cloak and dagger routines, but he was in too deep now to do anything else. For him, it was all about the rules and procedures. The secretive language served its purpose. He was certain that by now his office was bugged. Even if it wasn't, he wasn't taking any chances.

He had no choice now. He knew he had to get back to the garage area as soon as possible. Craig gathered a few papers that would be important and come in handy to him later. He closed and locked his door, slipped out the back door, and headed for his car. Halfway between the door and his car, he spotted two men dressed in suits standing near his vehicle. Immediately, he took cover behind one of the large metal garbage containers so he could hide and watch what they were doing. The two men casually walked farther up the street, apparently searching for something.

When he felt they were far enough from him, Craig left his concealment and made a beeline for his car. Just as he got into his car and had started the engine, one of the men turned and began sprinting toward him. He gunned the engine in an effort to escape but was not able to out-race the bullet that shattered the rear window of the car and lodged itself in his right shoulder. The bullet crushed his right collarbone but did not exit his body.

The pain was intense, but he remained focused on keeping the car moving away from the second and third bullets headed his direction. The third bullet went through the right-hand passenger window. He heard a fourth shot but wasn't sure if it hit the car. He continued driving, but his shoulder felt as if it was on fire. He could feel his shirt becoming soaked with his blood as he continued to maneuver through the side streets, all the time headed toward the garage area. He needed another four or five minutes before he would feel safe. He just didn't want to pass out from the pain.

The two men ran to their vehicle and began to give chase. The driver turned the wheel hard to the left, attempting to make a u-turn. When he did so, the car was hit in the right quarter panel by a motorcyclist. The rider was thrown over the hood of the car and landed twenty feet from the left front of their vehicle. Their pursuit had stopped as quickly as it had begun. The driver threw the car into reverse, changed directions, and sped off in the opposite direction from where Craig had gone.

Craig slowed his vehicle so as not to attract immediate attention. *I can't stay in this car the way it looks and with my shoulder feeling like mincemeat,* he thought. He knew he would have to change vehicles, but he'd have to reach the garage area first.

As he approached the garage area cautiously, he was sure he had not been followed. He drove up to the entrance door, honked the horn once, and waited for the door to open enough for him to drive under. Once inside, he parked the car near the first office area, pushed open his car door, and gingerly slid out of his seat. As he tried to stand up, he felt like he was about to pass out. Todd and Anthony rushed to him and, lifting him under his arms, managed to get him inside the office and onto the sofa.

"Get hold of Doc Lafferty and tell him to get over here now!" Craig said to Todd. "Anthony, I need for you to take care of two suits who probably are looking for my car. It would be nice for you to set them up and use the car for bait. I need at least one of them alive, so be careful and use your wits about yourself," Craig added as he placed a pillow under his right arm to relieve some of the pressure he had been feeling.

Anthony caught the keys to the car that Craig had tossed him and drove the vehicle out of the garage. Todd helped remove Craig's coat.

"Mr. Myers, we need to get the bleeding slowed down before you pass out," Todd said as he walked quickly to a storage cabinet. He grabbed several boxes of bandages and a roll of tape. He helped him sit up and began bandaging the gunshot wound. He handed a large bandage to him and said, "You're going to need to hold this in place while I wrap you up as tightly as you can stand it. Doc Lafferty may not be here for an hour or so."

"Tell that quack to get here now, or he'll need these bandages worse than I do. I pay him good money not to sit on his butt and push pills."

Todd continued wrapping and taping, until the wound was covered and direct pressure could be applied. Craig began to feel faint and told him that he needed to lie down. He thought he was about to pass out. Todd tried to keep him as still as possible while continuing to apply pressure to the bullet hole. Craig, however, would not cooperate. Instead, Todd ended up placing a pillow under Craig's shoulder thinking his own body weight on the pillow would actually help with the pressure.

"Mr. Myers, I just called the doctor. He said the best thing you can do right now is lie still and not get that wound bleeding badly. He said he'd be here. He also said to make sure you don't get anything to eat or drink until he gets here," Todd said as he adjusted the pillow under Craig's right shoulder.

"Those guys who tried to take me out were not cops. How do you suppose they knew where I was? And who are they working for? They weren't playing around. They meant business," he said as he moved slightly, trying to get comfortable.

"Mr. Myers," he said, pausing slightly and then continuing, "maybe you should head back to the safe house until you're able to figure out who's behind this. Maybe when Doc gets done taking care of you, he might need you to lay low for a while. The house would be easier for you to manage. I imagine he's going to need to do some work on that shoulder before you get better."

"Never mind about that."

Just as Craig had finished saying that, he and Todd heard a car drive up on the east side of the building. There was only one entrance on that side of the building, and it required a key. They both looked at each other, not sure what to expect. Todd looked at Craig and threw his hands up, as if to say he had no idea who that could be. They both knew it was too soon for Doc Lafferty. Craig pointed to him for him to hand the revolver, which was on the table near the door to the office, to him. Then he instructed him to stand off to the side of the entrance.

They could hear whomever it was starting to unlock the door. Craig cocked the hammer on the revolver, and Todd pulled his .45 caliber pistol from its holster. They both looked at each other, and Craig motioned for him to stay where he was.

After the door had opened a few inches, they both heard, "Is anyone home?"

"Get in here," Craig said. "And close the door behind you."

"Well, that's a welcome if I have ever heard one," Verna said.

Verna turned to lock the door when she noticed that Craig was bandaged heavily.

"What happened?"

"I got shot; that's what happened," Craig said in a sarcastic tone.

"Does it hurt?"

Craig couldn't believe she had asked that question as he looked at Todd in disbelief.

"Verna, sometimes you say the stupidest things."

She walked over to him and said, "I'm sorry. I didn't mean for it to come out that way. Can I get Doc Lafferty?"

"He's already been called," Todd said. "The biggest thing you can do is keep Mr. Myers on the couch and keep him still. He's lost a lot of blood and doesn't need to be moving around a lot."

Verna Gordon and Craig knew each other from when they were in grade school together in Savannah, Georgia. She moved away during her junior year in high school. Her father had taken a job in Atlanta working for a major food company. Craig lost track of her for a couple of years until they unexpectedly ran into each other in Tampa, Florida, during the summer of 1958. He had taken a temporary position completing a practicum, which was part of a course he was taking for his senior project. She was working a summer job as a legal secretary for W.C. Loebig, a well-known attorney on the west coast of Florida. It was during that summer they resumed their high school romance. Once again, they were viewed as a couple by their friends and associates at work.

Craig ended up having to go back to Gainesville in August that fall to finish his senior year of undergraduate work. She wanted to move in with him until he finished that year plus the three years of law school that were in his plans. He decided that it would be best for them to slow down and not rush things. There were times over the next several years that he regretted that decision.

She met and fell in love with W.C. Loebig's son, Kenneth. He started and ran one of the largest private airlines in Florida. They dated heavily in the fall of '58 and got married in a very plush and elegant ceremony in Tampa, less than ninety days after they had met. The first few years of their marriage were fun-filled, almost dream-like. Eventually, they ended up in Miami, Florida, where he started all sorts of cargo and passenger flights to Venezuela and Colombia. His business flourished such that he began running flights from Miami to Mexico City, as well as Caribbean cities, and began working with the government of Peru. He was so busy with the airlines that he was never home to notice that she had developed several connections for herself.

"Craig, what can I do to help you?" she asked, while rubbing his forehead.

"First, how did you find me? And where did you get a key to this garage?"

"Finding you was easy. You used to speak about this place when we dated. Getting a key was easy. I ran into Jack earlier today and asked for one. He gladly gave me the key."

"Verna, I hate to tell you this, but Jack's dead. He was killed earlier today trying to get information to locate Samuel Carlisle and to figure out what he knows. Everything has kind of gone downhill since then, until you arrived," he said, forcing a smile. "Why are you here, anyway?"

"Ken and I have called it quits. He's never home anymore, and he's got trouble with a couple of his pilots. I came here to see you about getting a job or something, maybe even fanning an old flame or two," she said before kissing him on the cheek.

"I'm kind of in a pinch at the moment," he said quietly. "Your timing couldn't have been better, however."

Just then the phone rang, startling all of them. Craig motioned for Todd to wait to see if the caller would hang up and call again. Within a couple of seconds, the phone rang once again, and Craig instructed Todd to answer it. Verna went to the bathroom and picked up a washrag, rinsed it in cold water, walked back to where Craig was, and applied it to his forehead. Its comfort brought a smile to his face.

Todd picked up the receiver and said, "Okay, now it's your turn to talk."

It was Frenchie Puska calling to tell Craig he would need a few bucks to spread around trying to pick up Lenny's trail. He had reached a dead end, and Lenny had not yet returned for his car.

"Todd, tell him to get back here. We need to circle the wagons for a while until I can get a handle on things. Besides, Lenny probably already has what he needs to go to the police. We need to figure a way out of town and a place to go to where we won't attract a lot of attention."

"Craig, why don't we go back to Savannah?"

"Too much history, and a lot of people know about that history," he said.

Todd finished speaking with Frenchie and hung up the phone. He turned to Craig and said, "My brother has a place over in Suwannee County that would be perfect. Once Doc has you ready to travel, I think that would be off the beaten path enough for you to lay low and yet stay close enough to keep an eye on things."

"Not a bad idea. Give him a call and find out more about the place. Just make sure he doesn't hear or see more than he needs to. Things like that could be unhealthy, if you know what I mean," he said as he moved slightly on the sofa trying to find a comfortable position. The pressure on his wound was causing it to throb.

"Craig," Verna whined, "Suwannee County? There's nothing over there but woods and more woods. The big activity on Saturday nights is a raccoon raiding a garbage can," she said, while lighting a cigarette. "Seriously, why don't you stay at my place in Tarpon Springs? You're close enough to the gulf that if you need a quick escape, you're on the water, and my boat can take you anywhere in the world," she said as she wiped Craig's forehead with the washcloth. "Besides," she continued, "the place is a fortress and is equipped with an alarm system that is state of the art. It could be like old times for us. One thing is for sure, Doc Lafferty would only be but about four hours away, unless you wanted to use Ken's quacks," she said, puffing on her cigarette.

Her offer intrigued him. Everything would be on someone else's nickel, and it would be a place where few people would even begin to know where to look for him. The only one who might figure it out would be Carrie. *She is not likely to do that from a morgue,* he thought.

"Lady, as soon as Doc Lafferty says I can travel, we're going to your place at Tarpon Springs. We'll need to take care of a few things here in Daytona before we leave. Besides, we can't stay here much longer anyway because my face will be all over the news by tonight."

"Mr. Myers, Doc Lafferty just drove up," Todd said.

"I haven't seen him in over ten years. Do you think he'll recognize me as a brunette?"

"Of course he will. He'd know your cloud of smoke anywhere," Craig said.

CHAPTER 18

"Pat," Richard called out as he walked up the stairs from the deli. "What time did you say we were planning to pick up Samuel?"

"His flight is due in at six o'clock. We'll need to leave here by five for sure to get there in plenty of time, find a parking place, and get to his gate," she answered, while folding work aprons she had just collected from the dryer.

"I just wanted to make sure that our help knew we were closing early today, unless you've made other arrangements," Richard said.

"We don't need to close early. Daniel said he could stay until six thirty, and Angel and Rosa will close for us tonight. When is Carlitto due here?"

"I am expecting him at two thirty," he said pointedly.

"I guess we'll meet in the office area," she said as she folded the last of the aprons and closed the dryer door.

He turned around and went back downstairs to continue working. He figured that if he stayed upstairs, any continued conversation would be mundane at best. He recognized the look that was in her eyes. He understood how she had been looking forward to Samuel's visit for several weeks and that he and Samuel finally would have to work out the disagreements in their relationship. He wanted to make sure that what was being planned for their family would be received by and acted on as something good for the entire family. He wanted this visit to go well for everybody's sake.

Richard went about his business making sure the shelves were stocked and that workstations were as clean as possible. He never knew when the health inspector might show up. It hadn't been a problem, but he didn't want it to become one either.

As he worked that afternoon, his thoughts turned to what he would say to Samuel and how he was going to approach him. He readily admitted the two of them needed to sit down and get things worked out. The harsh reality for him, however, was that Samuel was not just his son, but he was a grown man now with responsibilities too. Richard, believing he had not fully lived up to being a father to his very successful son, struggled with finding the right words that would help break the ice.

He had just finished wiping down the double sink area when the phone rang. He took the call and began taking a customer's order. About halfway through getting the order written, Carlitto Berteloni entered the front door. His entrance was as if he were the be-all and do-all for the Carlisles.

"Richard, my friend, I came as soon as I could," he said as he closed the door.

"Carlitto, you're early," Richard said with raised arms.

"For you, anything," Carlitto said, reaching out to hug Richard.

"Thank you, my friend. Let me get Pat from upstairs, and we'll sit together in our office. Have you had lunch yet?"

"No, but I was hoping—"

"Hope no more. Daniel will fix you up right away," Richard said, while pointing at Daniel to start fixing a house special for Carlitto. "How about something to drink to go with that?"

Carlitto nodded in agreement and followed Richard into the office area. Before sitting down at the desk, Richard asked Rosa to tell Pat that their guest had arrived. Carlitto sat down on the sofa and put his valise on the end table.

"So, I understand that you want to sell the business. Is something wrong, or are you and Pat just anxious to retire?"

"Nothing's wrong, and we're not planning on retiring anytime soon. We may want to sell, but we need to determine and discuss what options we have."

Pat, who had been in the back storeroom, entered the office area, handed Richard a cup of coffee, and took a seat next to Carlitto. Daniel brought Carlitto's sandwich and an ice-cold soda, placed them on a tray, and put the tray next to Carlitto.

After taking a sip of coffee, Richard turned to Carlitto and said, "We need to know what this place is worth on the market."

"Who does your books for you?" Carlitto asked as he took a huge bite out of the sandwich.

"Wilhite and Sons in Manhattan. Why do you ask?" Pat asked before taking a sip of her coffee.

"If you are planning on selling the business, you're going to need to have the books open. If all you are thinking about is selling the building, that's something else entirely," Carlitto said, in between bites of his sandwich.

"We figured that," Richard said. "What we need is for you to give us a price on the building, and you know, what the market value is."

"No problem. I could probably get that for you early next week. I will need to walk around the place, take a few pictures, ask a few questions, and check out a few other things. Off the top of my head, your building is easily worth two hundred grand, and that's without digging around a little."

"If we got that much for it, how much is your commission?" she asked.

"Five percent of the agreed upon price and two percent for advertising and expenses. Seven percent in all."

Pat looked at Richard, then turned to Carlitto and said, "If you get us two hundred and fifty thousand, we'll given you seven and a half percent." Richard smiled, knowing full well what she was up to. She had a business nose and knew how to make a buck. Her deal perked up Carlitto's ears enough for him to put down his sandwich and look seriously at Pat and then Richard.

She continued, "If you're able to get us three hundred, we'll pay you a flat eight percent."

Carlitto's eyes lit up. He leaned back and looked again at both of them. He reached over the end table, grabbed his valise, pulled out several sheets of paper, and said, "I want you to go ahead and fill out these.

I'm gonna make a couple of contacts and check on a few things. May I borrow your phone for a few minutes?"

Richard handed him the phone and directed him to sit at the desk. He and Pat sat together on the sofa, watching while Carlitto began working his magic.

Pat whispered to Richard, "Do you think he realizes that the three hundred thousand figure is the lowest figure we're going to accept?"

He looked at her, smiled briefly, and then whispered to her, "He doesn't have a clue." With that they stood up, gesturing that they were going back to work, and left Carlitto as he negotiated with a contact over the phone. Richard followed her upstairs, both with their coffee cups in hand.

When they had reached the kitchen area, they refreshed their coffee and sat at the table, not saying a word, just smiling at each other. Vicky came into the room after getting Joshua to finally fall asleep for an afternoon nap.

"What?" she asked as she glanced at both of them. "The two of you look like you just found out that Peter Pan really can fly."

They both broke out in laughter. They finally told her what was going on in the office downstairs.

"He never had a chance," she said as she too smiled about what was happening. "Do you think Samuel will believe this?"

"I hope so, because we're counting on him to close the deal for us," Pat said.

The rest of the afternoon went by quickly. Carlitto finished doing his preliminary calculations and gave them an initial figure of three hundred and fifty thousand dollars for the building. It was conditioned such that they would have to be willing to take care of a couple of plumbing items in the deli, and they would have to do some work on the trim of the building. The amount was more than Pat needed for the move. It was more than what she had planned. That kind of money would not only take care of their journey to Florida, but it would open up several new options for consideration.

Before realizing how late it was getting, they had spent most of the rest of the afternoon talking about and planning what their next steps should be. They began to appreciate that selling the business could be a good thing—only it had its own set of problems. One of those dealt with how and when to tell their help, because Carlitto had left with signed papers in hand. They both knew the word would spread like wildfire in the community. Then there were the movers who would need to be contacted and the bank to deal with. Of course, there were so many friends, many of whom were regular customers, whom they would have to contact. They knew they would probably have to answer the same questions a thousand times. And the biggest problem of all: Samuel was going to have to get a handle on all of this, and several other pieces of family business, almost as soon as his plane would land later in the day.

Meanwhile, the weather in Daytona Beach was overcast, but not enough of a problem to stop his flight from leaving. Samuel's plane was poised at the end of the runway to take off. The captain had announced that there would be a four- or five-minute delay, since smaller aircrafts were in the area. It only took a little over two minutes before the plane was ushered to the end of the runway to begin its journey to New York. He could hear the engines begin to roar as the pilot eased the throttle forward to start the plane moving. As the engines responded, he could feel the aircraft lunging forward, faster and faster as it rumbled down the runway. The bumps and dips in the runway could be felt as the plane gathered speed. With every second, the speed of the aircraft forced itself into the airspace in front of it. The plane started to drift slightly right and then left, as the captain would correct the direction of the aircraft. With each second, it pushed itself farther down the runway—closer and closer to the point of no return.

As he looked out the window, he could see his world going by so quickly. Finally, the nose of the aircraft pointed upward, and he knew he was now airborne. Faster and higher it flew. He could breathe now.

His knuckles loosened their grip on the armrest that separated his seat from the one next to him. He began to flex his fingers, which allowed the blood to once again flow to the tips of his fingers. Flying commercially was not one of his stronger points. In fact, flying commercially was something he could do without in his life.

He finally got comfortable and tilted his seat back slightly. He continued to look out his window. He saw the clearly distinguishable coastline of Florida and the far reaches of the Atlantic Ocean. The plane continued to gain altitude into and through a series of broken and intermittent clouds. He leaned back and breathed a sigh of relief as the aircraft made a sweeping turn to the north.

"Not into flying, are you?" said the woman sitting on the aisle seat to his left.

"No, it isn't my thing," he responded.

"I'm not sure I will ever get over the anticipation and anxious moments before taking off and becoming airborne. Each time is as bad as the first," she said as she unbuckled her seatbelt.

"I know exactly what you mean," he said.

That was enough conversation for him. For three hours he preferred to keep to himself, without a lot of talking or answering questions. To help her get the message, he took out a set of documents from his briefcase and began reading. Apparently, she was not well practiced on picking up subtle, conversation-ending clues.

"Is this a business trip or pleasure?"

Samuel studied the lady before answering. He figured her to be in her mid-sixties, grandmotherly, and that quiet was not something she enjoyed. He humored her for about five minutes, enough so that she finally decided to take out a book, purchased for the trip, and began reading it. He saw that the author was one of those writers whose style was wordy, and the plot was generally tortuous with details. He smiled, however, as if the book she held in her hands was a jewel.

"Enjoy your book," he said as he continued to review the documents he had taken from his briefcase.

"I just love this author. He writes with such authority and great tempo. His plot development is thorough and telling," she said as she opened the book to the first page.

He began to tune her out—not that he wanted to be rude, but he just wanted to be left alone to endure the misery of this flight in solitude. He felt this lady was not just invading his time but that she was generating memories he would rather have never chosen to be part of this flight.

Does she have an off button? he thought.

"You know," she continued, "I didn't catch your name, young man."

That does it, he concluded. He looked for a vacant seat in front of and then behind where he was sitting. As luck would have it, the only vacant seat remaining on the aircraft was on the other side of where she was already sitting. *I will try not to be offensive or too terribly rude to her,* he decided.

"My name is Cautious, Cautious Mann," he said, while trying to fight back a muffled chuckle.

"My, what an unusual name. I've never heard of anyone named Cautious. What's the origin of your name?" she asked, in such a serious tone.

"I'm from Iceland. My mother was from Greenland, and my father was Irish."

This is too easy, he thought. *I should be ashamed of myself. This is probably someone's grandmother, and I should be more respectful.*

"I've never met someone from Iceland. Is it really cold there?"

He was beginning to become slightly more annoyed. The conversation, to him, seemed to have been commandeered by her, leaving him without any control in the matter. He gathered his senses about himself, smiled at her, and said, "If it's all the same to you, please excuse my brusqueness, but I really have a lot of work to do. So, if it's okay with you, would you mind giving me some uninterrupted time for me to do my work? Seriously, I really need to get these done," he said as he pointed to the documents in his other hand.

"Well, why didn't you just say something? Of course, I will be more than happy to just sit in this seat and tend to my own business."

"Thank you," Samuel said. *Peace at last*, he thought.

Once he had restored some relative quiet in his life, he actually did get into his work. It wasn't until the aircraft hit a little bit of turbulence that he noticed how much he had completed. He was still working on the contracts that Craig wanted to have done by the following Tuesday, when the sudden turbulence caught all of the passengers off guard.

The turbulence, however, was helpful to him because it brought him back to reality. He began to think about Carrie, Lucille, Craig, and Lenny. He thought about having to meet with Lieutenant Howard on the events that involved Dr. Rutledge. Somewhere in his schedule, he had to complete his work for his other clients and prepare for an upcoming pretrial hearing. *All in due time*, he thought.

Once again, he turned his attention to the world outside his window. Given the manner in which he was staring at the clouds, anyone nearby him would know he was lost in thought. He had managed to shut out all of the noise and distractions in the cabin of the aircraft and become fixed on the few clouds that seemed to rush by his window so quickly. Mostly, he began to focus on the brutality of Craig's attack on Carrie. He felt responsible, for some reason, for the whole mess. *If I had just forced the issue with Craig, he would be the one in the hospital instead of Carrie*, he thought.

After several minutes, he returned to his work in front of him. He tried to focus on getting other items finished before landing in New York. Between his listening to the constant whirr of the plane's engines and taking a short break to enjoy a cup of coffee the stewardess brought him, his thoughts drifted again toward Carrie and Lucille.

These two women were very much a part of his life. He loved Vicky, but he held a deep affection for the other two. He worried for them, knowing that Craig was still on the loose. He worried for them because of the things that Craig was capable of doing. He worried because he was not able to be there for them. It was important to him that they felt safe, that they felt cared for, and he wanted them to know that.

○

Doc Lafferty took one look at Craig and knew this was not going to be pretty. He asked Todd to get a few things from the car. He directed Verna to clean off the table near the door to the storage unit. He helped Craig sit up to get a better look at the gunshot wound and removed the makeshift compresses that Todd had used.

"Craig, you've lost a lot of blood. The wound doesn't look all that bad, but without some X-rays, I can't tell what internal injuries you may have suffered. You'll need to go to my office. We'll get you put back together there."

"It'll have to wait until dark. Just get me settled here for a while. I need to take care of a few things before we leave. Verna and I are planning on heading to the west coast later tonight, and I'll need you to stay close to me. That means you'll have to come up with something for the hospital. Don't you have a sister over in Pasco County?"

"Yes, I do. She teaches school there," Doc said as he began to clean the wound.

"Perfect. Call her and tell her you'd like to visit with her for a while, but tell her nothing else. I am going to need you nearby until I can travel."

"I just can't up and leave my practice. I've got patients to tend to and rounds to make. I've got seriously ill people to take care of at the moment, and they are counting on me."

"I hope you included me on that list. Right now, you're going to need to be gone from here, and you're going to have to make arrangements. Don't worry. I will compensate you handsomely for your efforts. Besides, your partner, what's his name, has never suspected anything. If you'd like, I can take care of him for you," he said as he tried to slide slowly off the sofa.

"Craig," Doc said decisively, "you'll do no such thing. His name is Dr. Preston Cantlon, and he's not for sale. I'll handle him," he said.

Verna, with Doc's assistance, helped Craig to his feet. They quickly moved him to the table that Verna had cleared off. He rolled onto the table while Verna put a pillow under his head. Todd pulled the cushions off of the sofa, helped prop Craig into a sitting position, and started to help Doc Lafferty tend to the wound.

Doc located the probe from his medical bag and began to search for the bullet lodged somewhere in Craig's back. It took about thirty seconds, but the sound of the bullet hitting the bottom of a glass jar was like music to Craig's ears.

"Doc, you're the best," Craig said, just before passing out.

"Verna, before we try to move him to my office, we've got to stop the bleeding. I want you to hold this compress over the wound and apply constant pressure. We'll bandage him up later. Right now, I've got to call Preston and have him cover for me at the hospital. Todd, I need for you to run over to my office and keep an eye on the place. The last thing we need right now is to be caught helping Craig," he said, while looking directly at Verna.

"Don't make it sound so dirty, Doc," she said.

CHAPTER 19

"Lunch was really good. Thank you," Lenny said as he took the last slice of bread and sopped up the remaining tomato sauce from his plate. "Your father's a great cook."

Sheri, looking directly at him, said, "He's an even better baker. There's cheesecake for dessert. Sit tight. I'll be right back with some for both of us."

Before he could tell her he was really full, Sheri was gone. He had eaten his fair share of meatloaf, rice, and tomatoes, and three large chunks of cornbread. Even Sheri's father made light of the fact of how much such a thin guy like Lenny could eat.

While she was in the kitchen getting the cheesecake, he looked up the phone numbers for Lucille and for Samuel's parents. He wanted to ask Lucille how Carrie was doing and tell Lucille that he would be spending the night in Orlando. Within just hours, Lucille had become his lifeline for information between himself and Samuel.

Before calling Samuel by noon Saturday, he would have to get to the courthouse no later than ten o'clock in the morning. Knowing that the records department of the courthouse closed at noon on Saturdays, he felt he could afford a few moments of downtime with Sheri, which would allow for a pleasant break from the case. However, he would first have to force down a healthy serving of cheesecake.

When Sheri returned to the table, she was carrying two exceptionally large servings smothered in blueberries. She placed one of them in front of Lenny, handed him a spoon, and managed to refill his iced tea—all at the same time.

"Lenny, you mentioned to my father that you are from Oakford, Illinois. What's it like in Oakford?" she asked as she cut into the cheesecake.

"It's a small town mostly. The population is somewhere around two hundred or so, if you include the cats and dogs, I guess. My folks grew up there just like their folks grew up in that area, as did many other generations of Yeagers. Our family has raised dairy cattle and planted corn in Oakford since sometime in the early 1830s. When we were kids, my brothers and I would dream of living in a big city. We would talk for hours about not having to get up every morning at five o'clock to do our chores," he said as he shoved another piece of cheesecake into his mouth.

After wiping his mouth with a napkin, he continued by saying, "The winters were cold and often harsh, especially mornings when chores had to be done before sunrise. The wind would whip pretty quick sometimes. But Oakford was a great place where kids felt safe and everyone knew everyone else.

"It hasn't changed much over the years. With the pressure on the price of milk and beef, real estate has gotten a little pricier, and a few of the farms had to be put on the market. They just couldn't meet the bank payments anymore. I miss the memories of the way the town used to be. The farther I travel from Oakford, the more real its memories become to me in my thoughts and dreams."

"Why did you leave Oakford, Lenny?" Sheri asked before taking a sip from her glass of sweet tea.

"As a kid, my parents encouraged me to be somebody. They wanted me to make something of my life so I wouldn't have to work hard like they had to. My folks worked hard for me to go to school. They never had that chance," he said, just before taking a drink of iced tea.

"The first time we visited Chicago," he continued, "I knew right away that I wanted to live and work in a bigger city. Getting out of Oakford seemed like the thing I was meant to do. My mother, though, likes it when I come home to visit for a while, especially since Dad died. My brother Louis, who helps Mom keep the place going, still lives there with his wife and three children. I guess it just wasn't in the cards for me to hang around there."

Sheri had hardly touched the rest of her cheesecake. She sat quietly listening to Lenny talk about something she could tell he still loved and that was still very much a part of his life.

"What about you, Sheri? Why Orlando? Why haven't you moved on?"

"We don't grow anything, but we sure end up cooking the fool out of it. Like your family, our family business is our life here in Orlando. When our family moved here from Zolfo Springs, Poppa spent every dime we had and put it into the diner. We slept at the diner until we could afford to finally buy a house. We moved here in 1946 just after Poppa got back from the war. We didn't move into our house until I was almost eight years old. I guess it's just home. I mean, I've been to Atlanta and other big cities, but I'm not much for that kind of lifestyle. As it is, the traffic around Orlando has gotten to be more congested, with all the growth and everything. The business at the diner, though, is better than ever."

"I guess it's been kind of rough since your mother died," Lenny said, just before taking one last bite of the cheesecake.

Sheri looked away and focused on something beyond the table on the near the wall.

"It's been harder on Poppa than the rest of us. He and Momma had been through a lot together. He's lonely, and I guess the diner has become his life. He works every day. I bet he hasn't taken two days off in a row in almost five years. Since Momma died, all he can think about is work. I guess that's his therapy, because that's all he ever talks about."

"He's an excellent cook and a wonderful baker," Lenny said as he tried to find words to comfort Sheri.

"What about your folks, Lenny?"

"Like I said, my younger brother Louis lives there with his wife, Beth, and their three children. Dad died in 1971 from a failed heart. One of my brothers, Michael, was killed in Vietnam in 1968. My youngest brother, Grant, lives and works in Washington, DC. Mom manages the business end of the farm for Louis, but he does the labor mostly. Beth has been so kind to Mom, and the three kids have helped to keep things lively. They have worked out a great relationship, and the place looks great. They all seem to be happy with the arrangement."

Lenny began to realize how comfortable he was becoming around Sheri. She too felt comfortable and at ease as she talked with Lenny. There was a feeling of acceptance between them, without an apparent need for conversational masks or hidden agendas.

Their conversation about themselves and their childhood memories continued for almost two more hours. It was nearly five o'clock before Lenny realized how late it had gotten, and he had yet to call Lucille. Neither one of them had noticed that it had been raining steadily for almost an hour.

"Sheri, I must apologize, but I've got to make some phone calls and tend to business for a while. Besides, your dinner crowd will be in before too long. Do you think it would be okay for me to use the office phone to make my calls? I promise to charge the calls to my account."

"My goodness, Poppa will be back in a few minutes, and I've got so much to do. Come on. Let me show you where the office is. Just promise me that you won't leave, because I would love to continue this conversation. Maybe we could meet after I finish my shift?"

"What time do you get off work?"

"Seven o'clock sharp!"

"No problem. Before I can get back, I've got to pick up my car and run a few errands. I will be back by seven. I promise."

Sheri walked him back to the office area. Just before leaving the office, she turned, kissed him ever so tenderly on his left cheek, and whispered into his left ear, "I could really get used to waiting on you."

She smiled and went out the door. Lenny was breathless as he watched her return to the counter area.

When his senses fully returned a few seconds later, he sat down, dialed the operator for calling assistance to charge the call to the office number, and asked the operator to connect him to the hospital, where Lucille was staying with Carrie.

The call finally connected to the switchboard operator at the hospital. Then, after at least four separate attempts and two failed connections to different stations, he finally reached Lucille.

"Lenny, where have you been? Did you know that Lieutenant Howard is looking for you? He wants to talk to you about what you might know. Somehow he got your name from somebody, and he said he wants to talk with you right away."

"Who's Lieutenant Howard, and why would I want to talk to him?" he asked.

"He's the lead investigator for Carrie's attempted murder case and the death of Jack Ussery at Dr. Rutledge's house earlier today."

"Lucille, did you say Jack Ussery? That's not good news. That means that Craig will be looking to get even. Jack and Craig are linked and have been for years. Is Dr. Rutledge okay?"

"Yes, Dr. Rutledge is just fine. You need to reach Samuel as soon as you can. I suggest you stay away from Lieutenant Howard until you talk with Samuel. Samuel's plane is supposed to land in New York at six o'clock. I also suggest you call his folks' place around eight thirty or so tonight, without fail."

"Okay, okay. I've got the number. I will call him later tonight. How's Carrie doing?"

"I'm afraid the news is bad. She has been placed on a ventilator, plus they've changed her medication. Something about an irregular heartbeat. The doctor recommended that we call her next of kin, but I haven't been able to reach her mother or her sister. Unless the specialist can think of something these doctors have not, I'm afraid there won't be anything left for them to do for her. Lenny, I'm afraid she's not going to make it. I've never seen anyone die before."

"Lucille, I will contact you later tonight, once I get settled for the night. I have yet to figure out where I am going to stay, but I've got a lot to get done in the next two hours."

"Just stay away from Lieutenant Howard, Lenny, until you talk with Samuel. Promise me that, Lenny. Promise that you'll not talk to Lieutenant Howard until you talk with Samuel."

"I promise," Lenny said.

Just as he finished speaking with Lucille, Sheri's father entered the office, closed the door, pulled up a chair, sat down directly in front of the door to block Lenny's exit, and offered Lenny a cigarette.

"No thank you, Mr. O'Bannon, I don't smoke," he said.

"Good. I don't smoke either. At least, I haven't in seven years. I keep a pack around because every once in a while I just want to smell the tobacco," he said as he put the pack of cigarettes back into his shirt pocket.

"Tell me, Lenny, what's going on here with you and Sheri? Have you got some kind of spell on my little girl? She's all kind of silly since you came in this morning."

"No. We just seem to enjoy each other's company. And Mr. O'Bannon, may I say I also enjoy your cooking?"

"Both smooth and gracious. You may be someone I have to watch out for. This has been coming for some time, and I knew this day would get here eventually. All I am asking is that you tread carefully how you deal with Sheri and the road you choose to travel with her. I want to make sure that she doesn't get hurt by you or anyone else she favors. She deserves the best life has to offer. Her happiness means everything to me. Do you know what I'm getting at here, Lenny?"

"Yes, sir, I do. I've only known her for a few hours, and I know exactly what you mean. She is very special."

"Just make sure you keep that thought. In case you did not understand what I meant earlier, anyone who begins a relationship with my daughter begins a relationship with me. Clear?"

"Yes, sir, I understand. If you're trying to intimidate me, it's not working. I can accept that there exists a special relationship between you and your daughter. What you do not realize about me, sir, is that I learned a long time ago from my folks about treating people respectfully and without intimidation, especially those who show you no ill feeling.

It's worked for me for most of my life, and I'm not planning on changing it any time soon."

"Good. You and I are going to get along just fine."

A slight smile came to Lenny's face as he asked Mr. O'Bannon, "Does Sheri know this?"

"She will in the next few minutes," Mr. O'Bannon said as he stood up, returned the chair to its original place, opened the door, and headed toward the front counter.

Lenny just sat there, somewhat amused by what had just happened. He wasn't really sure how to take Mr. O'Bannon's actions. He'd met fathers like him. Some of them thrived on using intimidation and harsh rhetoric. Some of them attempted to make these tactics work, but wimps were wimps—especially fathers who couldn't look you in the eye and say what needed to be said.

Mr. O'Bannon kept his eyes straight on me and never blinked, he thought. *He's serious about what he said; at least, it sounded real, felt real, and looked real. No matter,* he concluded. *There is something very special happening here, and I don't want to mess it up.*

Lenny called a cab to come pick him up, gathered his things, and met Sheri at the diner's front door. He extended his right hand to say good-bye to Mr. O'Bannon. They shook hands before Mr. O'Bannon looked Lenny square in the eye and said, "It's been a pleasure. Come back and visit."

Lenny then turned his attention to Sheri, took her hand into his, and held it tightly. He smiled at her and said, "I will be back by seven o'clock. If for any reason I'm going to be late, I will call you."

Seeing that the cab had pulled up in front of the diner, he said good-bye to her father one more time and then turned to speak to Sheri.

"I want to finish our conversation, but we both have work to tend to."

With that, he turned and went out the door. He covered his head with his coat to protect himself and his briefcase from the rain.

When he got into the backseat of the cab, he was slightly taken aback, realizing that the same cabbie who had dropped him off at the diner earlier was still in the area and had answered the call.

"I heard the call over the radio for a single passenger at the diner. I just knew it had to be the same guy who kept feeding me Hamiltons. I love Hamiltons. Where to, Mr. Hamilton?"

"Let's go get my car," Lenny said as he leaned forward and placed another ten-dollar bill on the front seat.

"Yes, sir, Mr. Hamilton. Would you care for the scenic route or a more direct route this time?"

"How long will it take for the straight route?"

"About fifteen to twenty minutes."

"That'll work. Drive on, James."

Sheri watched Lenny's cab as it pulled out into traffic. She turned and looked at her father, who was still standing right behind her, and said, "Poppa, he's a nice guy. He's not like the others. I hope you can see that."

"Just be careful, darlin.'"

Lenny scrunched down in the backseat of the cab as it drove away. All he could think about was getting his work done so he could be with Sheri. The cabbie was talking non-stop about his and Lenny's adventure and how it had made him feel so alive. Lenny reminded him to make sure he watched the road and to watch for that two-door beige sedan that had hung around the parking lot earlier.

When silence returned to the backseat of the cab, Lenny's thoughts returned to Sheri. He believed he had found a real person to share his dreams and thoughts with. To Lenny, Sheri represented all that could be good in his life and something he wanted to hold on to.

Her father calls her "darlin,'" he mused.

He reached into his pocket and pulled out a twenty-dollar bill, placed it on the front seat near the cabbie, and said, "This is for you, provided you keep yourself available for my transportation needs over the weekend. Another one will be yours on Sunday evening if this arrangement can be worked out."

"I thought you said we were going to get your car?"

"We are, but it will be parked in a different place to attract a few people. I need to make sure they don't show up where I am planning on hanging out."

"I get it. It's bait, right?"

"Hook, line, and sinker," Lenny said, while smiling from ear to ear.

"Mr. Jackson, meet Mr. Hamilton. Come to Poppa," the cabbie said.

"There won't be any room for much of anything other than staying near the radio and waiting for my call. What's your call number?" Lenny asked.

"Ask for driver twenty-seven. Make sure you say my name too. They know me as 'Scooter.'"

"Okay, Scooter."

Fifteen minutes later, they approached the shopping area where Lenny had parked his car earlier in the day. The cabbie asked if there were any specific instructions about anything he should know before entering the parking lot.

Lenny asked him to drop him off by his car. Before leaving, the cabbie was to wait until Lenny had unlocked the car and was seated behind the steering wheel. Also, Lenny wanted him to park some place across the highway. This would allow him to observe Lenny and anything that might happen. He was to make sure that Lenny's car had started and was moving before accepting his next passenger. Also, Lenny told him, "If you see anything that looks suspicious, like someone holding a gun to my head, call the cops."

Most of the stores were still open, and the parking lot had several cars still parked throughout it. Without being told to do so, the cabbie entered from the nearest entrance and began circling the parking lot. He was looking for the two-door beige sedan. Lenny stayed out of sight in the backseat as the cabbie continued to drive slowly.

"I do not see the car, Mr. Hamilton," said the cabbie.

"Thank you, Scooter."

Lenny, feeling a little more secure at that moment, sat back up, pointed out his car to the cabbie, and asked him to get as close to his car as he could.

The cabbie pulled up next to the driver's side of Lenny's car, settled the cost of the meter, and reminded Lenny to take all of his belongings with him. Lenny bolted out of the car with his car key in hand. He attempted to open the driver's door and then tried the other three doors, but to no avail. Someone had broken off objects in each of the door locks.

He scurried back to the cab, getting soaking wet from the torrential downpour, jumped into the backseat, and quickly closed the door.

The cabbie asked, "Where to now?"

Lenny, with his clothes drenched from the persistent rain, said, "The nearest phone, please."

CHAPTER 20

"Yes, Rachel, we're almost there, sweetheart," Pat said as she caressed Rachel's shoulders.

"Are you sure we're going to the airport? It doesn't look like the same way we came to your home," Rachel said, somewhat puzzled.

"We're just fine," Richard said. "In fact, the traffic is kind of light for a late Friday afternoon. We only have about another five or six minutes before we get to the parking facilities."

"I can't wait to see Daddy," Rachel said excitedly.

"It won't be too long," Pat said.

Vicky sat quietly, on the rear bench seat of the van, serenely watching Brooklyn go by. For someone who was supposed to be excited about seeing Samuel, she really didn't have much to say. It had been only three days since saying good-bye to him, but to her it seemed like a month.

She had so many things to discuss with him. From his parents' decision to move, them selling the business, and to what was going on at his office, she wasn't sure where to start. *So much has happened in these three days*, she thought. *It would be a shame not to find a quiet time and place to talk with Samuel about all of these things. Sooner would be definitely better than later*, she thought.

Richard turned the van off of the parkway and on to the entrance road leading to the airport parking facilities. The closer he got to the airport, the busier the traffic around the airport had become. Traffic had increased considerably in the past few seconds, as several flights were landing and taking off around the six o'clock hour. As he moved the van closer to the gate for the short-term visitors' parking lot, he spotted the perfect parking spot that would allow for easy access to the terminal and be within a comfortable walking distance for all of them.

The crowds arriving at the curbside had increased as well. The baggage handlers were jockeying for position by the curb, trying to snag arriving passengers for handsome tips. Fortunately, Richard's parking spot was ideal. They could walk to the lower level, take the escalators to the flight levels, miss the congestion at the curbside, and avoid the passengers clearing their baggage at the exit levels.

They all got out of the van. Richard blazed the trail from the parking lot to the airport's entrance, while Pat and Vicky each had one of the children in tow by the hand.

Once they entered the lower level, Richard looked for the flight information and the allotted gate for the plane's arrival.

"His flight will be arriving at another concourse at gate five," Richard said to Vicky as he picked up Joshua. "It might speed things up for us if I carry Joshua."

"He looks like he's ready to go to sleep. He was mighty quiet on the way over here tonight," Vicky said.

They only walked for a few minutes before arriving at gate five. The waiting areas were a welcomed relief, as they each found a seat. Fortunately, there was a television near their seating area that helped to distract both Joshua and Rachel.

"We should be able to see your daddy's plane out these windows," Richard said to Rachel, pointing to the covered gateway extending from the terminal.

"How long will it be before we see his plane, Grandpop?" Rachel asked as she walked over to the large series of windows and gazed intently at the flight line.

"His plane should be touching down in about four or five minutes. All total, it should be at the gate about ten minutes from now," Richard added.

As Samuel's plane continued to make a circling descent toward the airport, the stewardess went about getting the passengers and the cabin ready for the landing. She made several trips up and down the aisles checking seatbelts, making sure overhead compartments were secure, and collecting the last of any trash that passengers would need to put into a large gray plastic bag. The captain's voice came over the intercom, saying, "We should be on the ground in about five or six minutes. We are in the pattern and are currently circling, awaiting clearance for our final approach. Please listen to and follow the instructions of your stewardess. Again, thank you for flying with Eastern Airlines, and enjoy your stay in New York City."

Samuel couldn't help but chuckle. He was not particularly happy about his having to stay at his parents' house, but he was extremely happy about his being able to spend time with Vicky and their children. He was hoping that they would have time to see some of the sights. They even might get to take the children to the Bronx Zoo.

He finished making a few notes on the last of his documents, put them back into the filing pocket of his briefcase, and closed and locked the case. Being a dutiful passenger, he brought his seat to the upright position, checked his seatbelt, and then glanced outside to see what he could of the skyline as he eagerly waited for the plane to land. It hadn't been all that long since he was last in New York City, but there was something about the magnitude of it all as he watched from his seat.

The plane began a slow descending right turn and then leveled out for about fifteen seconds. Then it made a wide, slow descending left turn before leveling out once again. The captain announced over the intercom, "Ladies and gentlemen, we have been cleared for landing and have begun our final approach. Please be sure to follow all instructions given to you by your stewardess and remain seated until the plane comes to a complete stop."

Samuel glanced outside the window and marveled at the magnificent beginning of a beautiful sunset. As he continued to watch, he could see the headlights of several cars becoming more identifiable as they motored about on the freeways below. As the aircraft descended slowly, with its wings dancing in the air currents, the nose of the aircraft tilted up slightly. As it approached the runway, he felt the plane shake slightly from the landing gear being lowered and locked into place.

So far, so good, he thought.

As always, his hands began to tighten their grip on the armrests of the seat. He leaned back in his seat, took several deep breaths, and clenched his teeth out of nervousness. Once he heard the wheels touch down and the nose gear of the aircraft gently touch the runway, he relaxed his death-like grip on the armrests, took a couple more deep breaths, and let out a muffled sigh of relief.

Thank God we're down and in one piece, he whispered to himself. *I'm glad I don't have to do this too often. But the captain did do a nice job.*

The engines began to roar when the captain initiated the slowing process for the plane. The plane shook somewhat while the brakes were applied to slow the aircraft. Still, Samuel knew there were a few minutes remaining for the aircraft to taxi to the gate before he could relax.

Flying should be left for the birds, he said to himself.

The stewardess began going through the usual end-of-the-flight jargon by saying, "Thank you, ladies and gentlemen, for flying with us this afternoon. The temperature outside is currently fifty-four degrees, and no rain is forecasted for the next couple of days. If you are connecting with flight 876 to Saratoga, New York, your connecting flight is awaiting you at gate six. Please be sure to check in with the attendants at gate six for assistance. All passengers, however, are to remain seated until the aircraft comes to a complete stop. Enjoy your time in New York City."

Samuel couldn't stop thinking about those poor travelers who had more flying ahead of them. *I wonder how many of those transferring will arrive on time in Saratoga, but their luggage will be somewhere on the ground or headed to Chicago,* he mused.

Samuel stood, gathered his belongings, and waited for the stream of passengers at the front of the cabin area to begin getting off the plane after arriving at the gate. As if perfectly rehearsed, each row of seats emptied. Finally, it was his turn to slide into the aisle and begin moving toward the front part of the aircraft.

As he did so, he said his good-byes and thanked the stewardess for her kindness. When he reached the door of the aircraft, he felt the crispness of the cool air. The heavy odor of jet fuel and the exhaust fumes from the engines made their presence known. He wasn't sure whether he was excited because the flight was over or because he was about to see his wife and children. All that joyous thinking came to an abrupt halt, however, when he remembered that his father would most likely be there too. He still wasn't sure what to say or how he should respond to what his father might say or do.

As he walked up the gangway toward the waiting area, the loss of what to say to his father fueled his mixed emotions. He could see the doorway ahead of him, and, in between several passengers who had exited before, he caught a glimpse of Rachel peering through the crowds. She clapped her hands and yelled, "Daddy! Daddy's coming!" Those who were standing near her smiled and watched with great interest to see who this little girl's daddy was when he came through the door.

Samuel went straight to Rachel and picked her up, spun her around once, and then put her back down. He reached over to Joshua, whom Vicky was holding, and kissed him on the cheek. Vicky put her right arm around Samuel's shoulder, looked up to him, and said, "I love you. I am so glad that you're here." They kissed, while Joshua patted his daddy's hair.

Pat and Richard stood behind them, waiting patiently for Samuel to finish greeting his family. The smile on Pat's face told it all. Samuel had come home—even if it was for only three or four days. Richard, last in the line of greeters, smiled as well.

Samuel went over to Pat, gave her a warm and loving hug, and then kissed her on her right cheek. He stepped back slightly, as other passengers were hurrying to get by them. Richard's eyes locked onto Samuel's. They both stood motionless for a few seconds. Then Richard stepped forward and hugged his son.

"I love you too, Son. Welcome home," Richard said.

All of the anticipated scenarios Samuel had explored and worried over for the last several days, as well as all of those that had built up into obstacles and headaches for him, melted away when he heard his father say, "I love you too, Son."

He returned his father's hug and said, "Dad, I am so sorry."

Pat began crying softly, with tears running steadily down her face. Rachel asked, "What's wrong, Grandmom? Daddy's here. Why are you crying?"

"Rachel, honey, Grandmom is happy to see her little boy too. These are tears of joy. Your grandpop and grandmom love your daddy very much," Pat said, while looking down at Rachel.

Vicky took Samuel's hand into hers as they began heading toward the baggage claim area.

Richard turned to Pat and said, "I'll meet you on the lower level at the passenger pick-up area. After I get his luggage to the car, I'll keep circling through the pick-up area until I see you." He turned to leave, but Samuel would not have any of that.

"Dad, it won't take long to get my suitcase. How about we all go down there together?"

To say the least, the ride home from the airport was much more talkative and enjoyable than Samuel had imagined it would be. Joshua was wide awake now that he was being held by his daddy. Rachel had squeezed herself between Samuel and Vicky, while commenting on how pretty the sky was just minutes before.

"Samuel, are you hungry?" his father asked.

"Yes, the snack on the plane was just that: a snack. What's for dinner?"

"I have made your favorite," Pat said. "Meatloaf, potato salad, pickled beets, and homemade yeast rolls."

"And I helped with the rolls," Rachel said.

"And I stayed out of the way," Richard added.

Vicky leaned over and whispered to Samuel, "Find a few moments for us to talk. There is much you need to know about before speaking with your mother and father."

As the van continued its journey home, the conversation remained lively. Nothing, however, was mentioned about the impending move, the plans, the business, or any other topic that addressed the reason for Samuel's being in New York in the first place. Vicky's comment piqued Samuel's curiosity enough for him to finally whisper to her, "I'm sure there is much to discuss, but I have news as well."

CHAPTER 21

After first making sure his handgun was loaded and securely in its holster under his navy blue blazer, Todd drove out of the garage area and headed for Doc Lafferty's office. Since it was only an eight-mile trip, he attempted to blend into traffic as best he could. Doc Lafferty's last instructions to him emphatically included making sure that he did not get stopped by the cops for speeding. His primary mission was to get to Doc Lafferty's office, lay low until Craig showed up, and to keep an eye on the place. For Todd, the idea of keeping out of sight appealed to him. He had no desire to have any kind of run-in with whoever shot Craig.

Strange how Mr. Myers is the one who should get shot. I always figured it would be me and Anthony.

"Craig," Verna said softly, while trying to wake him. "Craig? Wake up, Craig," she said, shaking him slightly.

"Verna, he's going to be out for a little while. I gave him a pretty decent sedative to make dealing with him a little easier for us. He can be such a jerk sometimes. Right now, his bleeding is under control, and it needs to stay that way. Waking him would encourage him to think that he's superhuman. He probably wouldn't listen to a word I told him."

"Okay, Doc. But let's not tell him about the sedative," she said. "Let's just keep that our dirty little secret."

They both started collecting bloodied bandages and towels, initially used by Todd to dress the wound, and placed them in a plastic garbage bag. Verna used a bottle of bleach water to clean up the areas where Craig's blood was evident. Knowing that fingerprints and blood evidence would not be a good thing to leave behind, she wiped down every suspected surface, including door frames, doorknobs, chairs, and especially the tables where Craig had been.

"Doc, what do we do about the sofa that Craig bled all over?" she asked, while standing in front of it and staring at the evidence of severe blood loss.

"I guess we'll need to send Todd back here later to dispose of it."

Verna decided to take a break for a few minutes. Her curiosity had gotten the best of her, so she decided to strike up a conversation with Doc.

"Doc, how did you get wrapped up in all of this with Craig?"

"He and I met about a year or so after he had passed the bar exam and started practicing law. I was on the wrong end of a lawsuit, and he had just started his practice. That's when I hired him to represent me," he said as he checked Craig's pulse. "It was just about the same time that you and Craig ran into each other at one of those reunion gatherings in Gainesville. In fact, that's where he and I first met. I was invited by one of the young ladies that I had met earlier at a medical symposium. I had only been practicing a short while. He was available to represent me at a substantially reduced fee, and one thing led to another."

"I remember that time. Craig wouldn't have anything to do with me anymore because I had already married Ken. I know I shouldn't have to ask this, but how did the lawsuit turn out?"

"The case never made it to court. To this day, I do not know how he managed that."

"Let me guess. He helped you then, and you owed him big time. Am I right? Believe me, he likes it that way. It gives him the opportunity to manipulate people so he can accomplish what he wants, usually under the table and in the dark of night," she said as she started to light a cigarette. "All he has to do is do what he does best, and he's got you. Then it goes on forever from there," she said.

"Verna, put that thing out. Don't you know those things can kill you? Besides, he doesn't need the smoke in his lungs."

"You're as bad as my husband. Ex, that is," she said.

"Speaking of your husband, does he know you're here?"

"He doesn't know where he is half the time. Of course he doesn't know. I left him yesterday. He hasn't been home in over five months, and a girl can get kind of lonely, you know. So, I decided to come see an old flame."

Doc Lafferty, while turning toward Verna and looking directly at her over the rims of his glasses, said, "I don't remember the exact circumstances, but my recollection is that you and Craig seemed more like a couple way back then."

"We dated pretty seriously back in high school, before moving to Florida. We were quite the couple. We went everywhere together back then."

"What happened that the two of you parted company?" he asked as he checked Craig's blood pressure.

"One thing led to another. I married Ken, and Craig married the law and some gal name Carrie."

"What law?" Doc asked sarcastically. "He's been subjecting the law to his whims since I've known him. Don't get me wrong; he pays me well. But he ends up dictating my life to me from time to time, especially when it best suits him more than me. It can be mighty inconvenient at times. Just like right now, for example. But he is a phenomenal lawyer, and his expertise in the courtroom is unparalleled. Plus, this man has more connections than China has tea leaves."

"Doc, you don't sound very pleased about all of that, and yet you marvel at his ability. Have you ever told him just to go take a long walk and forget the way back? I mean, you control his life at the moment. It wouldn't be too hard for you slip him a hypodermic cocktail that would free his spirit," she said as she began wiping down parts of the office area again.

"I took an oath, Verna, and I intend to honor it."

"Okay, he defended you in a lawsuit. What started the other part of the relationship? You know, the taking care of his needs that usually are less than open and above board?" she asked.

"Actually, I came to a man's aid thinking I was doing the right thing. We were playing poker one evening at Craig's house when one of his associates—"

"You mean one of his henchmen?" she said, interrupting him in mid-sentence.

"No, when one of his business associates from Ft. Lauderdale, at least that's what I thought at the time, collapsed at the card table. He suffered what appeared to be a stroke and needed immediate medical care. I didn't ask who he was or what he did for a living. There wasn't a lot of social chatter going on at the table that told me he was a criminal. I instinctively began CPR. I finally got a pulse, and he began breathing again. That's all I did. The problem was that this man, whom I knew only as Vincent, wasn't supposed to be in Daytona Beach. He was under house arrest pending a trial date in Broward County."

"That's cute. What happened next?"

"I started to call for an ambulance, but Craig said that was out of the question. So, we transported him to my office where I could get a good read on an EKG and do other tests. From there, his so-called 'friends' arrived several hours later, put him in the back of a converted ambulance, and took him home."

"So what was the big deal? I don't understand," she said in a caustic tone.

"About a week later, I was handed a package by Craig containing fifty thousand dollars, a gracious thank-you note from Vincent Nicoletti, and a picture of me treating him in my office. From that day on, I have pretty much been at their mercy. They've never acted on that little-known fact, but I haven't given them any reason to either."

"Do you know who Vincent Nicoletti is?" she asked.

"I do now, but I didn't then."

"He's one of the biggest mob boys in the South Florida area there is. He's connected all the way to Los Angeles and New York, even Mexico City. I know, believe me. My husband, soon-to-be ex, has done business with that man for years. He's into drugs, guns, prostitution, kidnapping, slave trade, and a host of other civic services. It's a good thing you did save his life. I mean, if you hadn't, they would have whacked you on the spot."

"Comforting thought," he said sarcastically.

"No. Seriously, Doc," she said, staring directly at him. "Those people don't play around. Unless you are part of their family, they're cold and uncaring. Outside the family, you mean nothing to them, unless you can either be used to their own design or you own something they want. I've heard about things they've done that would curl your eyebrows, Doc."

"Verna, what made you want to hang around that lifestyle?"

"Doc, the money was great. All I had to do was play nice. I've ended up with a lot of nice toys, and I call my own shots. Can you say that?"

"Well, then, in common terms, you were bought and were paid well for services rendered, huh?"

"That doesn't sound so bad," she said, laughing softly. "Just like you said, I'm paid well."

"Haven't you ever wanted something else other than this? I mean, haven't you ever wanted a career of some kind, or kids?"

"At one time, I wanted to go on to graduate school and get my master's degree. Life, however, didn't work out that way."

Doc just shook his head and continued to tend to Craig. Now that he had stabilized Craig from the gunshot wound, he felt better about Craig's prognosis. The bleeding was under control, but his blood pressure seemed low, and his pulse was still weak.

"Tonight, Verna, I'm going to need your help to get Craig put back together. Do you think you're up to the task?"

"Of course! I was born to do this kind of stuff… if I don't faint."

Just then the phone rang. Verna answered it.

"Hello, may I help you?"

"I need to speak to Doc. This is Todd."

She handed the phone to Doc and then went over to one of the chairs near the office door and sat down.

"Todd, where are you?"

"Doc, I'm at the office and parked by the side door. Is there anything you want me to do before you get here?"

"No. Just make sure you don't answer the phone under any circumstances. If I need to reach you, I will call on a separate line. My calls will show up on line three. Any calls coming in on lines one or two are to be ignored. Is that clear?"

"Yes, sir. Answer only calls on line three," Todd responded.

"And Todd, turn on only the lights in the reception area," Doc continued.

"Got it," he said.

After hanging up, Doc turned to Verna and said, "We're going to try to move him around seven o'clock tonight. I need to contact my partner just to make sure he's got my patients covered during rounds at the hospital. To move Craig, we're going to need a station wagon or van. Got any ideas?"

"You're in luck. Let me call a good friend of mine who has a very bad memory," Verna said, with a hint of humor. She reached into her handbag, pulled out a small address book, and said in a guilty manner, "I haven't spoken with Gina in a while."

"I hope you're serious about this person having no memory," Doc said.

"There she is!" Verna said excitedly. "This one still lives in the area and drives a long-bed van. You're welcome, Doc," she said as she walked toward the enclosed office area. She picked up the phone and dialed the number.

"Hello," responded the person on the other end.

"Hey, Cootchie, this is Verna."

"Hey, gal!" she responded. "How are ya doin'? I haven't heard from you in a long time. Too long."

"Look, I need a favor that requires your van and a short memory."

"No problem. Where and when?" she responded quickly.

"I'll give you the address and time later. Right now, I just want to catch up on what's happenin' with you, lady."

Doc busied himself with Craig's vital signs. Verna and Gina started catching up right away. Their conversation was lively and exceptionally animated.

Doc tried not to listen to their conversation, but Verna's animated antics and provocative language kept his attention. He could tell these two were best of friends. Not meaning to eavesdrop, the memories and events he heard them rehash during the course of their conversation seemed more typical for one who had grown up in what Doc thought would have been a normal household. *You wouldn't know it by the way Verna lives her life these days,* he thought.

All this only made Verna more of a mystery in his eyes than she had ever been.

Verna finished her conversation with Gina, turned to Doc, and said, "Okay, we're set. She will be here with her long-bed van at seven o'clock sharp. She said she's even got a small gurney we can use."

Doc just shook his head and started getting Craig ready for the move.

"Verna, grab one more blanket from the back of my car. We might need that. While you're getting the blanket, how about also bringing in the sack of burgers I left in the car? I completely forgot about them, and I am famished," he said.

"No problem, Doc. Did you know those things can kill you?" she commented, while grinning from ear to ear.

CHAPTER 22

Lucille had been sitting with Carrie for most of the afternoon. In between the calls from Samuel and Lenny, she dozed off a couple of times while trying to read a poorly written spy novel. She felt a little guilty about her pending date with Lieutenant Howard, but not enough to cancel it to stay and sit with Carrie. She was looking forward to getting to know more about him, even though it would take her a few hours away from Carrie.

Lucille got out of her chair and stood next to Carrie's hospital bed, placed her left hand into hers, looked down at Carrie, and said, "I really hope you understand, but I am attracted something fierce to this guy. I'll only be gone for a little while. Besides, this place has become a fortress with all of the police and hospital staff on alert. I promise I'll be back by ten thirty tonight. I promise, Carrie."

Having eased her conscience and unloaded a ton of her own guilty feelings, Lucille turned to go out the door. Dr. Yu and one of the nurses entered the room.

"Dr. Yu, anything new to report?" she asked.

"I'm afraid the news is not good. The blood work-ups are showing a deteriorating immune system, and her heartbeat is showing signs of arrhythmic disorders. The medications we've tried have been ineffective so far, and her breathing has become increasingly shallow. We believe the big picture is that she will not be able to maintain an acceptable oxygen saturation level on her own. At the moment, she is hanging on to life by sheer will."

"This morning you sounded so hopeful, and now you sound like she's got one foot in the grave. Which is it?"

"I don't want to mislead or offer you any sense of false hope, but she's critical, and her vital signs are weakening by the hour. Unless we can find some way to improve her breathing and improve her circulation, her organs will soon suffer irreparable damage, and she will begin to spiral downward quickly. If there is any ray of hope, it will come when the specialist arrives later this evening. I'm told sometime after midnight."

"What do we do in the meantime, doctor?"

"May I suggest you spend some time in our chapel downstairs?"

With that, he walked over to Carrie's bed and checked her pulse. The nurse began injecting medication through the IV tubes. Dr. Yu then began a shortened series of neuromuscular examinations that produced no response from Carrie. The nurse and Dr. Yu updated Carrie's chart before continuing additional tests.

Lucille stood motionless during the time they worked on Carrie. Finally, she decided it would be better to spend time in the chapel than to stay in the room and watch Carrie be used as a pincushion.

About the same time she decided to leave, the head nurse opened the door and told Lucille she had a phone call.

"Who's calling me now?"

"He just said to tell you it's Woody."

She thanked the nurse and asked if the call could be transferred to the phone in Carrie's room. Within a few seconds, the phone rang.

"Dr. Rutledge, is there something I can do for you?"

"Yes, you can first start by calling me Woody. Then you can tell me what the latest is on your brother's case," he directed.

"Okay, Woody. I know that Samuel is working on Charles' case. At the moment, he's in New York, or soon will be, and he has Lenny tracking down several leads. I know that he took a portion of the transcript to reread and that he has been in touch with the state attorney's office about reopening the case. Did he talk with you about the newly discovered connections between Jack Ussery and Anthony Dortch?"

"I have not heard that. I've got Samuel's phone number, but I cannot remember when his flight is due to arrive in New York."

"He won't be there until after six o'clock this evening."

"Thank you. Then I will try to reach him later this evening. If you hear from him, please tell him I called and that I have a few questions for him."

Lucille gave Dr. Rutledge the phone number for Samuel's parents, hung up the phone, and started to leave the hospital.

As she walked toward the elevator, she wondered how Paula, William, and their mother were doing. After checking the time, she decided she would make a quick visit just to see how things were working out for them.

She went to the front desk in the lobby and learned that Mrs. Lester had been transferred to the second floor, where surgery patients were usually kept. She inquired as to the well-being of the children, but no one seemed to remember either of them or anything of their whereabouts. So, she got back on the elevator and went to the nurses' station to ask to visit Mrs. Lester.

"You said your name was Lucille Pierce? How are you related to Mrs. Lester?" one of the attendants asked.

"I'm not immediate family. I was with her and her children when she suffered a heart attack in the emergency room. Can you at least let me visit with her?"

"I'll have to check with her doctor to see if it's okay."

Lucille stood there for several minutes before learning that Mrs. Lester had been heavily sedated and was not receiving visitors. She was instructed to contact the social worker on the second floor to learn more about the children and Mrs. Lester's condition. It didn't take long for her to find that office.

She was informed that the children had been picked up by their aunt and uncle, Grace and Bernard Korczak, about two hours earlier. She asked for their address and phone number, but the social worker would not release it, explaining that hospital rules and guidelines prohibited her from doing that.

Lucille thanked her. As she headed for the elevator, she saw a bank of phones and several phonebooks, which had been stacked on top of each other. It occurred to her that she didn't need the hospital's permission to use the phone books. After all, she could figure out how to spell their name.

In a few minutes, she had the name of the family she was looking for and was certain they lived in New Smyrna Beach, not very far from the hospital. She decided there wasn't enough time remaining for her to drive to New Smyrna Beach to check on the children, drive back to her house, take a shower, do her hair, and change clothes before her date with the lieutenant. Instead, she began dialing the number to the house.

"Hello," the person answering the phone said softly.

"I'm looking for Grace Korczak, also known as Aunt Grace to Paula and William Lester. Is she at home?" Lucille asked.

"Why, yes, I am she. Who's calling, please?"

"I'm Lucille Pierce. I was at the hospital when Paula and William's mother suffered a heart attack earlier today. It took a while, but I'm glad I found you. I just wanted to know how the children are doing," she said, fighting back a tear.

"For now, they're doing about as well as anyone could expect. They've had a pretty tough day today."

"Listen, if you need anything, and I mean anything, to help with these children, please call me. I will be more than happy to help you."

"Who did you say you were?"

"My name is Mrs. Lucille Pierce. Ask Paula if she remembers me from the gift shop. I was the one who helped the children at the hospital when their mother collapsed in the cafeteria."

"Yes! I remember Paula telling me about a nice lady who was very kind and loving. She couldn't remember your name. I am so glad that you called, because both Paula and William have been asking about you. I just didn't know what to tell them. Would you like to speak with Paula?"

"Of course I would. I would really like that," she said with great interest.

She waited for Paula to come to the phone. She could hear Mrs. Korczak calling for her to come downstairs and speak with "that nice lady." She heard footsteps coming at a rapid pace down what sounded like wooden stair steps.

"Hello," said a very young voice.

"Paula? This is Lucille, you know, from the hospital. I'm the lady who took you and your brother to the gift shop. Do you remember me?"

"Oh yes, I remember you. I am so glad that you called because my brother and I want to thank you for what you did. Do you think you can visit with us today?"

"Well, today will be kind of hard for me because I have so much to do here. How about I speak with your aunt about visiting sometime tomorrow?"

"Yes; yes, please! That would be super!" she said as she handed the phone to her aunt.

"Ms. Pierce, Paula is so excited about something you said," she declared.

"Mrs. Korczak, would it be okay with you and your husband if I come to visit with Paula and William tomorrow, perhaps in the late morning?"

"That would be okay with us."

She gave her phone number and address to Mrs. Korczak, just in case there was something she could help with. They both agreed that they would keep in touch with each other regarding Mrs. Lester's condition.

After hanging up, it hit her that she hadn't asked about the children's father.

The rain continued to pour down heavily, with no let-up in sight. Lenny figured he had two choices: he could get his car fixed right away or ride in a cab and burn up his expense account quickly. He realized that cab fares would begin to eat into his profits, and he still had not made arrangements for a place to stay for the evening.

He directed the cabbie to pull up to a public phone not far from where his car was parked, leaned forward in his seat, and said, "Wait here. I need to make a few calls." He bolted out the right rear door and ran toward the phone booth.

After calling three different locksmiths, he found a local one whose address was less than twenty minutes away. He made arrangements for the locksmith to meet him at the car, hung up the phone, and made a mad dash back to the cab. Once back in the cab, he instructed Scooter to take him back to the parking lot where he could meet the locksmith. He wanted this afternoon to be over with because it was beginning to look as if it would eat into his time with Sheri.

"Did you have any luck?" Scooter asked.

"Yes, I did. They said they should be here in about thirty minutes and that it would take a good hour and a half to get done with all four locks. But so be it. Can you believe this is going to cost me thirty dollars a lock?"

He tried to relax, but the thought of having to pay that kind of money took the adventure out of the moment. When it came to money, he knew when he was being taken. He knew the value of certain services. In this case, all he could think about was getting back to the diner so he and Sheri could start their date. At the moment, he was willing to pay twice whatever the cost might be. It was hard for him to let that go and move on, but money was money, and his motto had always been that it was better in his pocket than in another's. Being with Sheri, however, was his main objective at the moment, and nothing was going to interfere with achieving it.

After waiting for over forty-five minutes, the locksmith showed up and began to work on the car doors. He tried several remedies to fix the first door he attempted until one finally worked. The first lock took about twenty minutes to return to working order. The next three took only thirty minutes in total. He could not believe that he still had to pay the total amount, when it only took him less than half the time he was originally quoted over the telephone.

"Mister, I will be more than happy to put those plugs back into your locks and call it even," the locksmith said sarcastically.

He understood that if he wanted to see Sheri tonight, he had better pay the man and move on to another task that needed doing. He got a receipt because he intended for this bill to be included in his business expenses.

He paid Scooter what was due him and finally got into his own car.

As he drove out of the parking lot, he knew he only had about an hour remaining before he was due back at the diner to meet Sheri. He still needed to find a motel, get cleaned up, and make a few phone calls.

I can do this, he thought. *I just hope Samuel appreciates what I am going through at the moment.*

No sooner had he finished that notion than he thought he heard the distinctive sound of a tire blowout. He pulled over to the curb as quickly as traffic allowed. There was a noticeable tilt to the car, clearly identifying that his left front tire had gone flat.

He raised his hands and asked pointedly, "Okay, God, what else is in store for me today?" He put his head into his hands, leaned forward on the steering wheel, and sat there wondering how long this was going to continue.

"This is not what I planned for the day," he said dejectedly.

It took about three or four minutes of his sitting there, enjoying the beginnings of a full-blown pity party, before finally opening the door, walking to the rear of the car, and opening the trunk. He started gathering the equipment he would need to fix the flat tire.

"At least I have what I need," he said thankfully. While walking toward the front of his car and watching others drive by him without so much as waving or offering some kind of assistance, he muttered to each of those drivers, "An umbrella would be nice."

As he went about repairing the tire, the rain continued to fall without mercy. Within the first two minutes of his efforts to change the tire, he had become thoroughly soaked. By the time he finished some thirty-five minutes later, his clothes felt as if they weighed an extra fifty pounds. Soaking wet, the kind of wet where your shoes ooze water with every step, he got back into his car and began looking for a phone. He wanted to call Sheri to let her know what was happening and that he would be late. Also, it occurred to him that her father might not know of his ordeal. He figured that Mr. O'Bannon could think he was trying to weasel his way out of seeing her.

This is not good, he thought.

It took another few minutes, but he finally found a public phone at a gas station just down the street.

When he was able to connect to the diner, the line was busy. He waited another minute or two before dialing the number again. The line was still busy.

While trying to redial the number, there was little protection available from the rain. *What the heck, I might as well take out a bar of soap and finish taking a bath*, he mused.

Finally, on the fifth try, he was able to reach someone at the diner. He just happened to reach the only waitress at the diner who, luckily for him, had been instructed by Sheri to give him her home phone number, address, and directions to her house. The waitress explained that Sheri wanted him to meet her at her house before they went out for the evening.

He thanked the waitress and got back into his car. She lived near the east side of Kissimmee in a small housing development, which was located about twenty minutes from the diner. He decided to go first to her house, explain all that had happened, and then beg for mercy. At least that was his plan. He wasn't sure of anything beyond that point.

For the moment, he was back on track for his date with Sheri. His attitude was improving with the passing of each minute as he drove toward her house. The day had been filled with accomplishments as well as his fair share of disappointments. He had been looking forward to this time with her. Still, he knew he needed to talk with Samuel. Although not important at the outset of the day, there was something that continued to bother him about Dr. Rutledge's shooting of Jack Ussery. He was troubled about why Jack Ussery would be at Dr. Rutledge's house. There was something missing, and he couldn't visualize it. It was as if a piece of the puzzle had been left out that contained the clue to the next question.

As he continued driving toward Sheri's house, he realized a connection between Jack Ussery being at Dr. Rutledge's house and the Durham case was not clear. It didn't seem logical that they would somehow be connected. He just figured that if he could establish a connection between them, there might be an easier solution to the rest of Durham's case. There were no solid reasons why Charles Durham happened to be in Herman Jackson's house the night that Jackson was allegedly murdered. And there were no solid reasons, as of yet, why Ussery was at Dr. Rutledge's place. All he felt and believed was something was not right—about all of it.

It took him a little over thirty minutes to find her house on East Water Oak Road. As he turned from the road and into her driveway, he saw her looking through the curtains of what appeared to be the living-room window. A smile came to his face. He brought his vehicle to a stop just short of the carport, got out of the car, and walked to the front door.

As he approached the door, the porch light came on, clearly helping to identify Lenny for all of the neighbors, and anyone else who happened to be looking his direction, to see. After knocking on the door, he could hear her walking toward the door. He took a step backwards the moment the door opened.

"Oh my," she said, and then began to laugh openly. "Look what the cat dragged in. I wonder if I should take it in and feed it?" she said as she went about inspecting his wet clothes.

"I am so sorry, Sheri," he said as he began to remove his outer coat.

"Never you mind. Come in, and let's get you out of those clothes. You're going to catch your death of pneumonia."

He smiled again.

"You need some dry clothes. Besides, you are not coming into this house and dripping everywhere," she said as she pointed for him to stand on the welcome mat. "You'll feel better once you've dried off," she said, while closing the door.

Lenny, whose clothes were drenched and whose hair was matted, sneezed.

"See," she said as she handed him a towel.

CHAPTER 23

"Dinner was great, Mom," Samuel said as he folded his napkin and placed it on the table. "The rolls were perfect."

"Would anyone care for a cup of coffee?" Pat asked as she walked toward the table carrying the coffee pot in her left hand.

"I would," Richard said as he picked up his coffee cup from the table.

"Me too," Samuel added.

Vicky, wanting to be sure to have time after dinner to talk with Samuel and his parents about the impending move to Florida, saw a great chance to get the kids bathed and in bed without a great deal of fussing. Instead of staying and listening to the conversation, she said, "I'll join you in a little while. I've got to get these two bathed and headed off to bed. It will soon be past their bedtime." Rachel lagged behind, wanting to stay with her father a little longer, and climbed into her father's lap.

"Rachel, honey," he said, "I'll be here when you've finished your bath."

"I'll be in to help you in a minute," Pat said to Vicky as she filled Richard's coffee cup.

The two men sat quietly at the table, each not making eye contact with the other. Samuel, a trained and experienced trial lawyer, was at a loss for the right words to say to his father. He wanted to start a discussion about Uncle Ted's funeral and all that came from it. Richard sipped his coffee without saying a word, and Samuel stared out the window. Pat saw what was happening, so she decided to get things rolling because they had more important things to tackle.

While picking up the remaining dishes from the table, Pat looked at Samuel and said, "Son, it is so good to have you with us, even if it is only for a few days. Your father and I have so much to talk over with you. We're going to need your professional help with some of it. Why don't you and your father go to the living room and get out into the open what's been causing the two of you to sit in here looking like you've been constipated for two weeks? Richard, why don't you put down that cup of coffee for a minute and talk to your son? Isn't seven years of being put out with each other enough?" she asked. "I mean, after all, we've got things to deal with here, other than the two of you stewing in your own pucker juice. Apparently, you aren't willing or can't get it out into the open now. Lance this boil and be done with it."

"Thank you, Pat, for making this so easy for me. I just don't know what I would do without your subtle yet all-too-trying manner sometimes. You're about as subtle as a twenty-pound sledgehammer," Richard said, while staring at her. "Sometimes you can make walking barefooted on broken glass look like a welcomed addition to life's rewards," he said as he stirred his coffee.

She smiled as she returned the coffee pot to the stove, took off her apron, and, as she left the kitchen to help Vicky with the kids' baths, dropped it on Richard's head.

"Dad, I really would like for us to talk about this," he said as he let out a sigh. "It's just that I don't want to say the wrong thing to you. I'm afraid that what I have to say might make things more difficult than they already are. I just know that when Uncle Ted died, I was in the middle of one of the most difficult classes of my senior year, and I was about to fail the class big time. On top of that, my relationship with the professor was strained. Plus, I was really sick, physically ill. I wanted to be with the family, but getting to Uncle Ted's funeral wasn't meant to happen for me. I'm sorry, but I felt at the time that I needed to stay at the school."

"Look, Son, I have tried to deal with this and really don't want to drudge up old arguments and feelings. Instead, I'd rather accept what you just told me and move on. I know that we argued at the time. I apologize as your father and as your friend for my conduct."

He took another sip of coffee before continuing.

"I can't tell you how many times I wanted to call you and speak with you to get beyond this. Sitting in this room, in my own house, right now and not being able to speak to you openly and comfortably is killing me. I want you to know that no matter what you think or believe, I have always loved you, and I have always been proud of you. Your uncle Ted was very dear to me. I watched him follow your accomplishments from the day you were born. You were very special to him, and he was very proud of you. I'm sure you know that."

"I know, Dad, and he was special to me too."

Richard, with his eyes focused on his coffee cup, said, "The family expected you to be there for the funeral, and I ended up having to make one excuse after another for your not being there. Your aunt Linda was devastated by Ted's death. Every time she turned around, she wanted to know when you were going to be there."

"Dad," he began, "I said I was sorry, and I meant it. I am sorry that Aunt Linda wasn't able to understand, but I've spoken with her many times since the funeral, and she doesn't have a problem with all of this now. She seems to have moved on with her life."

Richard sat there, trying to think of something to say that would reel in where this conversation was going. He did not want this to become an argument. He did not want this to be another fruitless effort, leading only to more frustration, where both of them would end up feeling empty. He looked at Samuel and said, "Do you want some more coffee?"

"Yes," he responded, while holding up his cup.

Richard retrieved the coffee pot from the stove and filled Samuel's cup and then his own. They each shared the creamer and then stirred their coffee, almost in a synchronized fashion. Silence ruled the kitchen area, until Pat returned from helping Vicky with the kids' baths.

"Well, do the two of you have this thing settled?" she asked as she retrieved a towel and headed to the bathroom. Before she left the room, Richard broke the silence.

"Yes, we've revisited this. And the fact that we have sat down as two men to deal with this, openly and honestly, tells me we don't need to deal with this any longer. It's time we put this behind us."

He reached across the corner of the table and placed his hand on top of Samuel's. Samuel placed his other hand on top of Richard's and said, "I'm sorry for letting you down, Dad. I am sorry for having disappointed you."

Richard's eyes welled up. His face showed a great relief, as if a thousand pounds had been lifted from his shoulders. Samuel could see the change in his father's posture, and he responded by clasping his father's hands even tighter.

"I'm sorry, Samuel. I don't know what else to say except that you are not a disappointment to me. You've never been a disappointment to me or to your mother. It was hard for me that day; that's all. I guess I needed you there to help me deal with burying my brother. Your not being there wasn't your fault; it wasn't anybody's fault. I guess I just didn't handle it very well," he said as he lowered his head.

"Dad, I don't know what else to say," he said as he patted the tops of his father's hands.

Refocusing on Samuel, Richard looked directly at him and said, "Son, family is the most important thing you have in this life. Without a sense of family, there is nothing of significant value left. I want you to know how important it is to me for you to understand that. One day, down the road, you will be the head of this family, and the responsibilities of the family will fall to you. This includes taking care of your aunt Linda and your other relatives."

Pat, who had entered the room without having heard all of the conversation, knew what he meant. She was glad to know that Samuel, now, was at least aware of their feelings.

Richard looked at her, stood, put his arms around her, and hugged her. Samuel instinctively stood and hugged them both. The three of them stood quietly in the kitchen, each feeling the years of unspoken and buried frustration melting away. The last time they had hugged each other like this was when the family had been notified in 1968 that one of Samuel's older brothers, Frederick, had been killed in Vietnam.

She lifted her head and looked into Samuel's eyes before saying, "Son, your father and I love you so much. We are so proud of you."

"Look, Mommy!" Rachel said as she entered the kitchen fresh from her bath. "Can I hug all of you too?" she asked as she tried to put her arms around all three of them. "Grandmom, are those tears of joy too?" she inquired. Her question was heard, but no one answered.

"Daddy," Rachel continued as she looked up at her father, "Grandmom said she had tears of joy when we were at the airport tonight. Is that what these are too?"

"Yes, sweetheart, they are," he said as he patted her on her head.

A few seconds later, Joshua and Vicky entered the kitchen and joined the family hug. The Carlisle family stayed motionless for several seconds, until Rachel inquired boldly and directly of Richard by raising her head, looking at her grandfather, and asking, "Can we have dessert now, Grandpop?"

Pat couldn't hold back her laughing at what Rachel said. It brought a smile to the others as well.

"Rachel, honey, we're all going to have some ice cream. We're going to enjoy having our family together tonight too," Richard responded.

Samuel leaned toward Vicky and whispered into her ear, "I need to tell you about Carrie and Lucille. I am expecting to hear from them about what's going on at the hospital. Maybe Lenny will call as well," he added.

"We better put the kids to bed before getting into that. Besides, your mother and father need your professional help. You need to hear all about today, and tonight would be better than waiting 'til morning."

No sooner had she completed her sentence than the phone rang. Although Samuel was glad to hear from Dr. Rutledge, he was not prepared to discuss any new information about the Durham case. He remained cordial during the conversation, answered all of his questions as best he could, and tried to stay on point. He shared what he had learned about the connections and associations between Craig and others, what he had learned about Craig's involvement in dishonest activities, and mentioned his discussion with Lucille earlier in the day. Samuel focused the last part of their conversation, as he attempted to bring the conversation to a close, on Dr. Rutledge's schedule and the upcoming trip to visit Charles.

"Samuel, my boy, we have much to do over the next few weeks, but I wouldn't miss that trip to Raiford for all the tea in China. By the way, Lieutenant Howard called just a little while ago to tell me that the ballistics report on Ussery's weapon found at the scene points to its involvement in an unsolved murder case of a reporter named Hank Watson. Guess who one of the primary suspects in the investigation was back then?"

"Try this on for size," Samuel said confidently. "A wild guess might be somebody named Anthony Dortch," he said, whispering his name.

"How did you know that? They never had enough real evidence tying him to the case, until now. Seriously, how did you know that?"

"Lenny and I have seen that name surface, and Craig's name wasn't far behind. We're working on widening the circle of our investigation. Anthony Dortch needs to be in the circle. Speaking of Lenny, I haven't heard from him since this afternoon. Have you?"

"No, I haven't heard anything from him. If he calls, I will pass on that you are wanting to hear from him."

"Dr. Rutledge, are you staying at your house tonight? You know you are more than welcome to camp out at our place. Please feel free—" Samuel said, interrupted abruptly by Dr. Rutledge.

"I am fine. I promised Lieutenant Howard that I would stay in the back area of the house. I've got my shotgun, and the police have stationed a uniformed officer outside the door for the duration of the weekend. That should be more than enough for now."

"If you change your mind, please call me," Samuel insisted.

Their conversation lasted another fifteen minutes, with Dr. Rutledge going over the crime scene at the house and what their next moves might be. With each part of the conversation being overheard by Vicky, she couldn't wait for Samuel to get off the phone and explain the crime scene issues and how all of this related to Dr. Rutledge staying at their house for a few days.

After telling him good-bye and hanging up the phone, Samuel

turned to Vicky and said, "Let's get the ice cream out of the way and the kids to bed. Then I can be a little more candid about things."

Dr. Yu phoned Lieutenant Howard's office. The lieutenant was coming out of the police station's locker room freshly showered, shaved, and sporting a new turtleneck sweater for his date with Lucille when one of the duty officers informed him he had a phone call.

Lieutenant Howard picked up the in-house phone and said, "This is Lieutenant Howard."

"Lieutenant, this is Dr. Yu. I hate to have to tell you this, but Mrs. Carrie Myers died tonight at 7:01 p.m. of complications from the attack on her person yesterday. Her body will be transported to the county morgue as soon as you sign the release form. You, sir, are the only one we will release the body to for now. Would you mind coming in tonight to sign the authorization for this move?"

Pausing and taking a deep breath before sitting down on one of the benches, he said, "No problem. I won't get there until after eight o'clock because I need to get in touch with the rest of my team. Plus, I have to take care of a few personal items on the way. Tell your team that I will get back to you in about an hour or so."

After hanging up, he set into motion events that would require several people to begin processing, in greater detail, a murder investigation. It meant that he would have to intensify his search for Craig and see that an autopsy be completed quicker than usual. Not sure if Carrie's parents were still alive, he instructed one of his desk-type officers in the squad room, who just happened to be on duty that night, to begin researching for someone, other than Craig, who might be her next of kin.

The last of the immediate things for him to do was the one he wished someone else would do for him.

"Who's going to tell everyone that Carrie died? This is not the way I wanted to start a date night," he mumbled as he headed out of the squad room. "Man, this stinks."

CHAPTER 24

It took Lucille over twenty minutes to do what normally she would do in just five. She knew that Lieutenant Howard would be picking her up in about an hour, but she found it impossible to rush herself to get ready for his impending arrival. She wanted everything to be picture perfect, and she knew not to rush perfection.

As she stood in her bathroom, looking at her reflection in the mirror, she carefully applied her eye shadow and touched up her eyebrows. She struggled with the decision on what shade of lipstick to use but finally selected a color she had never before used on a first date.

"This one should be perfect," she said softly, while taking the top off of the tube. "'Eden's Journey' hopefully will do the trick tonight," she said as she prepared to apply the lipstick. "I hope he asks what the name of it is," she said as she separated her lips slightly and then applied the lipstick slowly and accurately.

After blotting her lips with a tissue, she stood very still inspecting the person staring back at her, carefully taking in the whole picture and trying to decide what else she needed to do. After several seconds and a concentrated effort toward detail, she raised her eyebrows as if to say, "You look great."

Satisfied that she had disguised the dark rings under her eyes and that her makeup was just right, she slipped into the dark maroon dress she had been saving for just such an opportunity as this. She reached around back, zipped up the back of the dress, and turned to check her appearance in the floor-length mirror hanging on the back of her bathroom door.

Turning from side to side, she inspected every inch of her appearance. Aware that there were only fifteen minutes before Lieutenant

Howard should arrive, she smoothed the front of her dress, walked to her bedroom closet, and slipped into the pair of shoes that completed her outfit. Feeling very pleased with her finished preparations, she thought, *I might even ask me to dance tonight.*

She entered her living room area and placed her folded evening jacket on the back of the sofa. She looked out her window to determine if she should take a small umbrella with her. Just as she turned to retrieve the umbrella from the hall closet, the phone rang.

Thinking it might be someone from the hospital, she quickly went over to the phone and picked up the receiver.

"Hello, this is Lucille."

"Lucille?"

"Somehow, I don't think this is good news," she said, recognizing the lieutenant's voice.

"I'm very sorry to be the one to have to tell you this, but Mrs. Myers died. I knew you would want to know right away. I've sent a car with a couple of officers to take you to the hospital. They ought to be there any minute now. I know this is such short notice, but I just learned of this a little while ago. We'll need to call Samuel once you get here."

She thanked him for calling. She wasn't sure what she was feeling, except she knew Carrie's death would immediately change things in the lives of several people. With the telephone receiver still clutched in her hand, she replayed her last few moments at the hospital with Carrie. She took a couple of deep breaths and leaned against the doorframe to the hallway.

"Lucille, are you still there? Are you okay?"

She paused for a few more seconds, gathered her composure, and replied, "I'm fine. I guess I'll see you at the hospital in a few minutes."

"Lucille, are you sure you're okay?"

"Really, I'm fine."

As she was finishing the conversation with him, a car with two men seated in the front pulled into her driveway. She explained to him that she needed to hang up the phone because the car he had sent to pick her up had arrived. She hung up the phone, reached for her evening bag, picked up the evening jacket that she had placed on the back of the sofa earlier, went out the front door, and walked toward the car.

Maybe I should call Samuel about the news, she thought. *No, I'll wait and call him from the hospital.*

One of the men got out of the front seat on the passenger side and opened the right rear passenger door for her. She thanked him, slid into the middle of the backseat, and got as comfortable as she could.

"Thanks for the ride, guys. That was quick. I mean, I just finished talking with Lieutenant Howard a few seconds ago."

The man who had opened the door for Lucille and closed the door behind her walked around the back of the car, opened the rear door on the driver's side of the car, and got in. When he sat down, he placed himself tightly against her and said, "This is not Lieutenant Howard's pimp mobile. You just sit there quietly, and you'll be fine. If you make any sudden gesture or effort to scream out, I will sedate you, at least until we get where we're going. Do you understand?"

Even Lucille's perfectly prepared makeup could not hide her terror. She heard the word "sedate" and recalled what she had seen happen to Carrie. She froze, and then muttered, "You won't have any problem from me. Just don't hurt me."

As the car began backing out of the driveway, she recalled those recently imprinted memories of Craig standing over Carrie's lifeless body with a very large syringe in his hand.

"Who are you, and where are you taking me?"

"We're not going to hurt you, unless you give us no choice. You're going to go visit with someone tonight. Just sit back and enjoy the ride. You'll be back in a couple of hours. We're not here to hurt you, unless we have to."

"Look, I am supposed to meet Lieutenant Howard, you know, with the police. I'm supposed to meet him in about fifteen minutes. If I don't show up, he's going to get extremely jealous about my being in the company of two rather large men who are breathing my air space, and one of them happens to be touching my left thigh," she said as she shifted slightly to her right.

"Really?" responded the man sitting next to her. "I believe your date with the good Lieutenant Howard will have to be slightly postponed. Now shut up and just sit there, or it's goodnight for you."

She could tell he meant what he said, so she began concentrating on the surroundings and where she was being taken. Although it was almost dark outside, she was able to make out street names and locations fairly easily. It took about six or seven minutes into the ride, but the man sitting next to her caught on to what she was doing. A couple of seconds later, he pulled a large piece of cloth out of his coat pocket, wrapped it around her head, and completely covered her eyes.

"Easy," she said, "you're messing up my hair. Please be careful."

No sooner had she finished saying those words than he gave one final hard yank on the cloth to pull it tightly across her forehead.

"I told you to sit there and shut up. Another peep out of you, and I will put you in la-la land. Do you understand?"

She nodded her head. She didn't dare make a noise.

For the time being, Lieutenant Howard thought he had everything under control. It wasn't until he got to the hospital that he learned his dispatcher was on hold and needing to speak to him.

"This is Lieutenant Howard. Go ahead, over."

The dispatcher at headquarters asked him to stand by, as she had a call being patched through to him from an officer on the scene at Lucille's house.

"Lieutenant Howard, no one is answering at any of the doors, and there are no lights on anywhere. I searched the outside of the premises to see if there was any forcible entry, but there are no signs of that either. What do you want me to do?"

"How long have you been there?"

"We got here six minutes ago."

"Stay put. I will call you back," he said in a commanding voice.

He checked with the folks in the emergency room, as well as the front desk volunteers, to see if she might already have arrived at the hospital. Not able to locate her anywhere in the hospital, he sent one of the officers standing near the emergency room entrance to check the parking lot. A few minutes later, he was informed that her car was not anywhere on the grounds.

Lucille, he thought, *what are you doing, and what's going on?*

He picked up the phone, dialed the dispatcher at the station, and asked her to contact the officers who were at Lucille's house. He instructed her to tell the officers to stay there until he personally arrived at the house. He also instructed them to check with the neighbors to determine if anything had been seen by them.

Lucille was uncomfortable sitting blindfolded in the back of an unmarked car. Further, it was discomforting to know that the two strangers were anything but gentlemen. As she listened intently for any sounds that might help identify where it was they were taking her, she was able to recognize the sounds of several vehicles, especially after twenty minutes or so into the trip, traveling at a very fast speeds. What concerned her most was the amount of time she had already spent in the car without hearing any conversation between the two men.

The possibility of her being on either I-4 or I-95 then became a reality to her. The question she wasn't able to answer was which direction she was traveling.

"Hey, would one of you guys at least tell me what time it is?"

"Sister, you've got to be kidding," the man who was sitting next to her said.

She could smell the sweetness of his cologne and felt his breath on her face.

His cologne smells fairly familiar, she thought. His breath smelled of alcohol and peppermint. His voice characteristics were becoming more engrained in her memory each time he spoke.

She was beginning to paint a mental picture of him, memorizing the brief glimpses she had of him before being blindfolded. What the two men didn't know was that her professional training was filled with forensics coaching. She had developed an ability to sequence, code and decode, and quickly summarize events that later would produce plausible situations for juries to find believable. She was a master at taking the not-so-obvious and re-creating situations. For seven years as a paralegal, before coming to work for Samuel, and with extensive trial preparation practice over as many years, she had an advantage that these two men couldn't understand or appreciate. Although blindfolded, she could see clearly, in her mind's eye, what was happening. With little effort on her part, she would be able to re-create almost a minute-by-minute historical account of the event.

I've got them right where I want them, she mused. *One of them is bound to slip and give away where they're taking me and hopefully whom I am going to visit.*

"You're soaked and dripping wet," she said, finding some sense of comedy about it all.

"I'm sorry. You would not believe what I just went through on the way here. You must admit, however," Lenny said as he turned and allowed her to help him take off his rain-soaked trench coat, "my being late on our first date is better than my not being here at all."

"My, aren't we confident tonight," she said. "Listen," she said, while taking both his coat and shirt from him, "I've got plenty of my brother's clothes you can use until we can get yours dried out. He's a little bigger than you are, so they should fit comfortably on you. Let me go get you a pair of pants and some boxers for you to use. I'm sure I've got a shirt that will fit you as well."

He decided not to argue the point because a chill from his recent adventure with the torrential downpour was beginning to take hold. He could feel himself shivering slightly, and he knew that was not a good thing.

"Do you mind if I use your bathroom? A quick shower would really help me warm up a little."

"It's halfway down the hallway on your left," she said as she headed to a closet in the back room.

"Do you mind if I use one of the towels in here?"

"That's fine," she responded as she continued to look for a pair of pants to go with the shirt she had selected for him.

Undressed and shivering slightly, he stepped into the shower, positioned the shower curtain such that the water would not run out on to the floor, and eased into the water's warm flow. He put his hands out and leaned on the wall in front of him. The warm spray of water started at the top of his head and cascaded down his entire body. He didn't move for several seconds. The water felt like waves of warm sunlight running down his neck, his back, his legs, and finally on his feet. He could feel the chill subside as his body temperature began to rise.

When he stood upright, the flow of the water warmed his face and chest. The frustrations of the day, the rain-soaked quest he endured getting to her house, and the anxieties he had been feeling about the case he was working on all began to melt away around him.

Knowing that he had closed the door before taking off his clothes, he felt somewhat secure in the thought that he would be able to finish his shower without any interruptions. Not so.

He heard the knocking on the door, followed by Sheri asking in an irresistible voice, "Are you decent?"

He responded curtly, "How can anyone be decent standing butt naked in a shower, behind a shower curtain that could double as a piece of clear plastic wrap, and no clothes within reach?"

"Perfect," she said as she slowly opened the door and entered.

He knew she wanted to check him out, so he decided not to move. She, on the other hand, kept her eyes glued to the floor while retrieving the rest of his wet clothes.

"Here," she said as she picked up a washcloth. "I thought you might need this."

As she handed the washcloth to him from around the edge of the shower curtain, she could see the outline of his body and the unmistakable tan lines from his waist up and mid-thigh down. When he reached to take the washcloth from her, she noticed how tanned his arm was—except for where he wore his watch.

"Nice tan, Lenny," she said jokingly but somewhat nervously.

"Thank you. There are other endearing characteristics about me too," he said, somewhat sheepishly.

She could tell she was blushing and decided it was time to leave.

"Where are you going?" he asked.

"Do you do this on all of your first dates?" she asked coyly as she turned to exit the room.

"Actually, no. This would be a first," he added as he looked out from behind the curtain he had pulled back slightly.

Too late—she had already exited the room and closed the door behind her.

CHAPTER 25

"Doc!" Verna said excitedly. "Gina's here with the van, and she's right on time." By the time she had finished saying those words, she had opened the garage door and dashed outside to greet Gina.

"Gina, I haven't seen you in so long. It seems like forever, girl," she said.

She started opening the rear door of the van and added, "You're a sight for sore eyes."

They hugged each other and smiled at each other, as two friends would do after having not seen each other in several years. After the second hug, it was all business.

"Verna, what's this all about, and why so secretive?"

"You'll see in a minute. Right now, help me get this thing into the garage," she said, while trying to pull the gurney from the van. As she pulled the gurney toward her, the wheels locked in place on the asphalt beneath it. She began pulling it into where Craig was resting while Gina went about securing the van.

Doc had placed a blanket under Craig to help with transferring his body from the table to the gurney and eventually onto the table at Doc's office.

Gina followed Verna into the garage area and walked over to where Doc was standing. Doc's first glimpse of Gina told him two things. First, her taste in clothing and makeup were not things she and Verna had in common. The two of them were the same age and had been friends long before high school, but one of them dressed the way they had in high school. Verna, although able to afford the best of what the clothing designers could offer, always chose to downplay that part of her life. On the other hand, if the skirt that Gina was wearing could be any tighter, there could not possibly be any circulation to her legs. Secondly, Gina had a pair of legs that were long, shapely, and caught Doc's attention.

Doc's eyes followed Gina's attractive legs, which were accentuated by the three-inch heels and the tan shade of nylon stockings she was wearing, from her heels, then to the curves of the back of her calves, to the back of her knee, and then to what he knew had to be a twenty-four inch waistline.

"When I count to three," he said, first admiring Gina's legs and then looking directly at her, "one of you two grab the blanket where his feet are, and the other one grab hold of the blanket in the middle. I'll take the part nearest his head. We'll move him onto the gurney on the count of three and strap him down after that. Is that clear?"

Gina had noticed Doc's interest in her legs. She decided to brush by him slightly, making sure she touched his right forearm with hers. As she did, she made eye contact with him to let him know she appreciated his interest.

"Verna, who is this delicious man, and will you share him with me?"

"He's a big boy. What he does with his time is his doing," she said, while both she and Doc situated the gurney near Craig. Verna continued, "Honey, meet Doc Lafferty. Doc, this is Gina Barber."

They smiled at each other and politely, yet sensually, shook hands. Gina backed up slightly, wanting to get a better look at this person standing in front of her.

Realizing both he and Gina shared somewhat of an interest and curiosity about the other, Doc decided he had better stay focused on what he needed to do.

"Gina, I'd love for us to get to know each other a little better, but right now we have things we need to get done," he said, reaching for the gurney. She looked at Verna, while gesturing as though she had done something wrong. Verna shrugged her shoulders at Gina and motioned for her to move toward the other side of the gurney.

"Here," he said as he handed a pair of rubber gloves to each of them. "Put these on. There's no sense in us taking any chances leaving any fingerprints at this stage of the game."

After positioning the gurney, they managed to lift Craig and situate 231 him fairly easily. Gina began coupling the straps. Doc and Verna gathered the items they would need for the trip and a few extra supplies and realized they still had to deal with the large garbage bag near the door.

"Doc," Verna began, pointing to the trash bag, "shouldn't we take that with us?"

"I guess so. We can dispose of it later. Anyone feel like a wiener roast?"

With Gina's help, he began wheeling the gurney toward the van. Verna had been the one selected to turn off all of the lights, secure the door, and grab the remaining items before leaving to get in the van.

Not one of them, however, saw a patrol car as it turned into the driveway, until it had flashed its spotlight on Gina.

"What do we do now, Doc?"

"Just let me do the talking and follow my lead. Keep your mouths shut, unless I ask you a question," he shot back at her.

Before the patrol car came to a stop, Officer Marcus Grasso checked his shift's information alert sheet to see if the van was listed as being stolen. Not finding it on the list, he called in the license plate numbers to see if there were any outstanding tickets or warrants connected to it.

"The van is clean," he said to his partner, Officer Peter Stiles. "Stiles, keep the doors open to this vehicle while we approach them on foot to secure the area."

They got out of their vehicle and both began walking toward Doc and the two women. Gina, who had already opened the door to the rear of the van, turned toward the officers and smiled at them. Doc Lafferty finally managed to roll the gurney to the van and began pushing it into the rear of the flat bed, while the officers approached with hands on their revolvers and their flashlights shining directly on the ladies.

"What can I do for you, officers?" Doc asked as he made sure the gurney was all the way into the van.

"How about explaining what's going on here?" Officer Grasso instructed.

"Officers, I am transferring my patient to the hospital with the help of my nurse and her friend who is assisting," he said as he closed the rear door of the van.

Officer Grasso's attention turned to Verna, who was walking toward the van, carrying the garbage bag filled with incriminating evidence. He shined his flashlight at her to get a quick glimpse of what she looked like and what she was carrying. Officer Stiles began walking toward Verna, but Gina came from around the other side of the van, drawing his attention away from her.

Gina had taken off her coat and had placed it on the driver's seat, before walking to where the officers were standing. Without her coat, her shapely body was enhanced such that very little was left to one's imagination. It caught Officer Stiles off guard. He shined his flashlight toward her, causing Officer Grasso to react.

Verna, taking advantage of the break in direct attention from the officers, opened the rear door of the van, put the garbage bag of damning evidence at the foot of the gurney, walked over to where Gina was standing, and said, "Good evening, officers. May I help you?"

Officer Grasso moved toward Verna and said, "Is everything okay here?"

"Of course it is, Officer. The doctor decided it would be best to get some tests run on his patient that can only be done in an isolation ward at the hospital."

"Isolation ward?" Officer Grasso asked, while turning to Doc Lafferty with an inquisitive look on his face.

"Yes. I believe it is in my patient's best interest, as well as those who might come in contact with him, to keep him someplace where we can control who actually has access," Doc said as he turned and spoke directly to Officer Grasso.

"Is he contagious?" Officer Stiles asked as he approached his partner and stood behind him.

"I'm not sure. I only know his symptoms indicate that he could be highly infectious through physical touching. That's why we're wearing gloves. It's only a precaution, but we probably should all be wearing masks as well, until we can confirm a diagnosis."

"What did you say your name was?" Officer Grasso asked, while looking directly at Doc.

"I'm Doctor Kenneth Lafferty. This is Verna, my nurse, and her friend Gina."

"Do you need any help?" Officer Grasso asked.

"Actually, no. We've got things pretty much under control for the moment. We're not far from the hospital, and there is no real emergency for now. Thank you, but we'll be fine."

"Are you sure?"

"Yes. We'll be fine, but thank you for stopping and checking. If it's okay with you, we'll go ahead and leave now."

Officer Grasso, acting as if all was well, directed his partner to head to the patrol car so they could get back to other things. Verna got into the van and closed the sliding door. Gina got behind the steering wheel, and Doc sat in the front passenger seat.

As Gina began to pull the van out of the parking area and onto the street, Doc waved and smiled at the officers, all the while quietly saying to Verna, "That was good, really good. The only problem now is what happens if they decide to contact the hospital."

"No problem, Doc," Gina said. "I'll just turn on the scanner and see if there's any action on the airwaves tonight."

Doc turned to Verna and said, "She's going to work out just fine, just fine."

Some twenty miles south, Lucille had begun to focus on every little sound she could distinguish both inside and outside of the vehicle.

Guessing that thirty minutes had elapsed since being abducted, she thought she would try one more time to get one of her captors to make a mistake.

"I suppose there's no chance of my being allowed to use any bathroom facilities, is there?" she asked in an annoyed tone.

"Not a chance," the one driving said, with a smile-like quality in his voice.

"Shut up, you fool. You drive, and I'll deal with her. Can't you get it through your head that she's attempting to exploit us to gain an advantage?"

The man sitting next to her turned toward her after warning his partner to keep his mouth shut and said, "Strike three. If it wasn't for the fact that we're only two or three minutes from our destination, I would put you out, and you wouldn't wake up until next week."

"Could I at least have a drink of water?"

He handed her a bottle of water, which still had the cap securely in place. She took off the cap of the bottle, took a nice, long swig, and put the cap back on the bottle.

She noticed the car began to slow considerably. It then made a long, sweeping right-hand turn.

We must be getting off the interstate, she thought.

The vehicle inched forward before turning left and then accelerated. She tried to time the distance but was interrupted by the ringing of a car phone in the front seat.

The conversation between the driver and whoever was on the other end of that call lasted about thirty seconds. It sounded to her more like a call confirming how much longer it would be before they reached their destination. She learned that whoever she was going to meet was called "the chief" and that he would be arriving by car as well. *This could be the script of a lousy B movie,* she mused.

Finally, the car came to a stop, and both men exited the vehicle. She heard at least three, maybe four people having a conversation outside the vehicle before she moved her blindfold enough to see who was doing the talking. From the corner of her right eye, she saw another car arrive. The driver's side rear window lowered slightly, and someone from inside the car tossed out an unfinished cigarette. The window was then rolled up, and the other car moved slowly behind the building.

Because the lighting was so poor, it was difficult for her to identify a building number or street name.

She moved the blindfold back in place, however, and sat patiently waiting for whatever was coming next.

Startling her slightly, the rear passenger door opened unexpectedly. She was then instructed not to remove her blindfold. She was helped out of the car and assisted up a short flight of stairs. She knew these stairs were the side entrance to the building she had seen.

Once she was inside the building, she was escorted to what someone called "the room." She was ushered through a series of doors before finally being given the okay to remove her blindfold.

Sensing very bright lights, she shielded her eyes from the initial shock of the stark lighting. She found herself sitting in a well-ventilated room on a fairly comfortable chair, looking directly into two very bright lights, which helped to outline the figure of a large, stocky man.

"Is this where you do the bamboo thing under the fingernails?" she asked of the person standing behind the lights. She couldn't make out his face but figured this had to be "the chief."

"No, sugar, this is where you answer questions, and then you go home. I'm all out of bamboo, but I believe you and I will get along well enough not to have to use such nasty methods."

"Why did you kidnap me, then? Whatever you think I know, I don't."

"Let us be the judge of that, sugar. How about we start with an easy one? Why don't you tell me what you know about your friend Lenny and what he's up to?"

"Lenny Yeager works from time to time for our office. Currently, he's hired to track down information about the Charles Durham case. How about you tell me who you are?"

"Sugar, I'm your best friend for now. Where is Lenny?"

"The last I knew he was somewhere in Orlando. You still haven't told me who you are. How about telling me whom you work for?"

"Sugar, you're not getting the hang of this." He motioned for one of the other men to approach her. "Sugar, this gentleman will put you in a very compromising place, if you do not stop running your mouth."

"Buddy, I'm not your sugar. I am—"

She felt someone grab both of her arms from behind and restrain her in the chair. Someone else tied her ankles together. She thought she was putting up a fight, but everything seemed to flow in slow motion. The man behind the lights began to approach her, but she began to feel a floating sensation come over her. Her head began to feel as if it weighed a ton. She heard someone say, "It won't take much longer…"

When she came to, she was still in the same room, in the same chair, but her hands and feet were untied. She felt the blindfold in place, but she was grateful for that. It kept the bright lights from making the pounding of her headache even worse.

"Thank you, sugar," he said as he headed out the door. "You can go home now. We're done with you."

She wasn't sure what made her furious, but she wanted to get up from the chair and hurt him. The problem was that her legs felt heavy and weak.

"You've drugged me. You're all a sorry lot. And you call yourself men."

Two men helped her to her feet, led her outside, and began helping her back into the same car that had brought her to the meeting. As soon as she sat down in the backseat of the car, all she wanted to do was go to sleep.

She tried to stay awake but couldn't.

"Something's not right about all of this. I cannot imagine what's delaying her, unless it's Craig," he said. "She doesn't seem the kind that would just walk away from a plan without notifying someone about what else she needed to do. She just seems like the kind of woman who has more class than that."

"Joseph," Sergeant Rothermel said quietly, "there's no accounting for any measure of class until you've had a chance to observe them close up. I'm sorry, but she's not here, and you're having a hard time with that. Maybe you need to focus less on her and a little more on this case that is biting you in the butt."

"When Carlisle gets back from New York, we've got to get in the middle of whatever he's up to. I think he's the key to this whole case. Lucille is just a minor player here and is likely to end up getting hurt because someone doesn't understand that. The fact is that Craig's wife has proven to be expendable. How long do you think it will be before Lucille, or even Samuel's family, for that fact, could end up the same way?"

"That's not the real problem," Sergeant Rothermel said. "What about the big picture? There has to be someone dancing the dummy."

"True, but I don't think we're close enough to anybody about anything at this point, except for Craig. We need him, and we need to find him now."

CHAPTER 26

"Mom, what exactly was it you wanted to talk to me about?" Samuel inquired.

She looked directly at him, then glanced at Vicky, who was seated next to him on the sofa, and decided to wait until Richard rejoined them.

"Would you like some more coffee?" Pat said as she gathered their coffee cups and then walked to the kitchen.

Samuel looked at Vicky, who was hugging one of the overstuffed pillows, and said, "Did I say something I wasn't supposed to?"

Richard, who had just spent the last twenty-five minutes reading bedtime stories to Joshua, entered the room.

"Story time is getting tougher every day," he said as he sat down in his easy chair. "Every night it seems like we have to read the same books, and in the same order, as we did the previous evening. What gives? When you were little, Samuel, I made up the stories every night, and you ate them up."

Vicky smiled and said, "Yes, but times have changed, Richard. Rachel and Joshua have a ton of books at the house. When it's time for them to go to bed, it's like they have to drag out their entire library, hopeful of delaying the inevitable."

Richard smiled and said, "So, you two started this."

"Yes, we know," Samuel said, pointing to several books on the bottom of the built-in shelving units at the far end of the living room. "You used to drag them out too. We did books when I was smaller, then your stories as I grew older. Finally, it was just the plain 'go-to-bed' routine after that."

"You did whatever you could to keep yourself from falling asleep. Your father had very little patience then but seems to have mellowed considerably with the grandchildren," Pat said as she returned from the kitchen with fresh cups of coffee and placed them on the coffee table.

"Regardless, people change," Pat said as she sat down in her recliner.

"Mom, what was it that you wanted to talk to me about?"

"Your father and I are planning to move to Florida, Son, as soon as we can take care of the business end here in New York. Our plan is to take a couple of weeks to check out possible locations, that is, if we actually decide to move the business and set up shop in Florida. We might even consider just opening another place and not sell the store here in New York," she said as she reached for her coffee cup.

"Your mother and I believe it's time for us to make this move," Richard said as he looked at Samuel.

Samuel sat quietly looking at his mother and father. The two of them shared a smile and what seemed to be a moment of pure joy. He glanced over at Vicky, who was peeking out from underneath the pillow she was still hugging, only to see a huge grin on her face.

"Are you sure, Mom? Dad?" he asked, pointedly looking at both of them.

Pat found it hard to resist the urge to jump up and dance around the room, but she calmly took another sip of her coffee, lowered her glasses enough so that she could look over the top edge of the rims, and said, "You bet we are."

"Of course, we're going to need your help with the legal stuff, Son," Richard added.

"I can help, but you would do better with an attorney who specializes in real estate law. I know one or two in the area who do really great work. I guess I can get in touch with them before I leave on Monday, but I will collaborate throughout. It would be better to have someone who deals with New York law to help you with the tax and property statutes."

"If that's what you think is best, then so be it," Richard said.

"When do you plan to start on this process?"

"We already have. We had a real estate agent in earlier today, and he's worked up an estimate for us on the costs and property value. What we need is to be able to put all of this together and to have someone figure out what our best options might be. We're not really sure whether we want to sell the business, relocate, or just open a second store in Florida. I guess we need to know more about the tax liabilities and what kind of costs we're looking at down the road. We're going to leave that to you, Son, if you don't mind."

"Mom, I don't mind, but this is something that folks specialize in. I really don't have a thorough working knowledge of this corner of the law. Have you thought about calling Donald Hampton? He's really pretty good at this kind of thing, at least that's what I've been told."

"But he's so expensive," she said. "We had Carlitto Berteloni start the process with us. He was the real estate agent we had in earlier today, and he seemed really interested in getting started."

"Mom, I meant someone who wasn't out to steal from you."

"Not to worry. We worked out a great deal, and I think you will be pleased with it. Let me get the papers for you to look over before we sign them," she said as she walked toward the back bedroom.

Just then the recognizable sound of Rachel's voice could be heard approaching them, making a pitiful whining sound.

"Mommy, I can't sleep," she whined, while rubbing her eyes.

Vicky looked at Samuel, moved her legs, got up from the sofa, and headed to her.

"I'll be right back," she announced.

"Dad, I need to make a few phone calls. Do you mind if I use the phone? I will charge them to my office."

Richard motioned to him that it would be fine and said, "Speaking of calls, the two of you will need to excuse me. Nature calls."

Pat and Samuel were alone in the living room for the first time in what seemed like years.

"Mom, are you sure you and Dad are ready for this? I mean, this will require the two of you uprooting and resettling in a very different place. Our family has been in Brooklyn at this location for years. The business, what about the business?" he asked as he leaned forward and clasped his hands.

"The business will take care of itself, even if we move and don't sell it. We have very good workers who know what to do. Besides, your father and I believe that the move is long overdue. Here or there, the only thing that matters is that we want to be close to you and the kids. If that means giving up the business, we'll start another one in Florida."

Samuel was captivated by how focused his mother seemed to be.

"What's with the look, Samuel?"

"Nothing, Mom. It's been a long time since I've seen you like this. The last time I remember seeing you like this was when I wanted to go to Jersey with Catherine and her parents. Only you, if I remember correctly, thought it would be better for me to stay here and work. I guess I didn't understand then, and I guess I don't understand now. What's going on here? Am I missing something?"

"No. Your father and I want to live closer to you and the kids; that's all. You'll understand one day, when your kids have kids of their own. We know it'll be different and maybe even a little hard at first. But we're still young enough to handle it. We'll deal with it. We really want your blessing and for you to know that this is something we want to do. No one is forcing anything here. It's what seems right to both of us."

"Okay, so what happens after the move? What happens when you and Dad begin to miss all of your friends and the customers you have known for years? What then?"

"We understand that we may run into that problem, and we've talked about that. We just think that what we have decided to do outweighs any of those kinds of things. We can make new friends and build a clientele in Florida. We're not dead, you know."

"You know what I mean."

"Don't worry. We think this is meant to happen. It is time for us to move on."

Richard returned, sat back down in his easy chair, and said, "I've got to start eating prunes or something."

She looked at Samuel and said, "That lends new meaning to 'moving on.'"

He chuckled at the thought. Even Richard chuckled, but he had no idea what they had been talking about.

"I guess we'll need to start putting things on the calendar," she said as she continued sipping her coffee.

Samuel didn't want to talk about the case he was working on. He wasn't exactly sure what to say or how to start, but he waited until all four of them were in the room. He figured he better tell them something because he knew the phone would start ringing with colleagues wanting to speak with him.

"I think I need to bring you all up to speed on a case I am working on. I may be getting phone calls from some people who are keeping an eye on things for me back in Florida. I am afraid that the news may not be good and that some of the news may actually involve life-and-death issues. So, let me work through all of this before you ask any questions. I cannot betray any attorney-client privilege issues, even though I'm not exactly sure who my client is at the moment. Let me explain."

As he began telling all the events that had transpired since Vicky left for New York on Wednesday morning, it occurred to him that the people who had sent the thugs to get to Dr. Rutledge might actually try to come to New York and make an attempt on his family as well.

He stopped in the middle of a sentence, stood, and began pacing the room before continuing to relate the events of Thursday and Friday.

"Son, you don't think these people would be foolish enough to try something here, do you?"

"Dad, I don't think so, but they made a conscious effort to get to Dr. Rutledge earlier today."

"Is he okay?" Vicky asked.

"Yes, he's fine, but I am still worried about him."

She sat up on the sofa, leaned forward while still hugging the pillow, and said, "How is Lenny? What about Lucille?"

"They're fine too. My main concern is for Carrie. She was brutally attacked at the hospital by Craig. He put her in there that afternoon and then he tried to finish her off. I am waiting to hear, within the next hour or so, more on that. Lucille is supposed to call me tonight. Lenny should be calling any minute to let me know where he is, and we're to discuss what he's doing tomorrow."

"Why don't you just let the police handle this for you? It sounds like Craig has lost his mind. What in God's name could have caused him to react this way? I mean, something had to cause him to go off," Richard said.

"Dad, the police are working this case pretty hard. Lieutenant Howard is on top of it, but they have not been able to find Craig. I'm not sure if he's even still in Daytona. There's nothing keeping him in the area that I know of, unless Carrie pulls through."

Vicky inched closer to Samuel as he sat back down on the sofa. She reached out with her right hand and began rubbing his left shoulder.

"Do you mean to tell me you think that he may actually escape?"

"Anything is possible, Mom, and no one seems to know where he is."

"It would seem more likely that he's hiding somewhere nearby that nobody knows about. You know, disguises so he can travel without being noticed. Doesn't that sound plausible? I mean, well, he's probably got someone helping him, someone you would least suspect, doing whatever," she said.

"Mother, you've been watching too many episodes of *The Rockford Files*," Richard said.

"Will you need to return to Daytona before Monday?" Richard asked as he stirred his coffee.

"Dad, that depends on the answers to questions I get from the calls I'm waiting on. Right now, I just need time to sort through things and try to make some sense out of what's been going on."

He paused for several seconds, looked around at each of them, and then continued.

"You know, some things just don't add up. It'll probably be sometime after midnight before I finish with the calls and have a chance to draft my notes."

Vicky inched closer still to him, put her arm around his neck, and asked, "Is there anything I can do to help you?"

"Actually, there is," he said. "I need for you to go to the downtown library tomorrow and look up some phone numbers for me. I will give those to you in the morning before I start working on the contracts with Mom and Dad. I guess the best thing we can do right now is wait on the calls. I thought about calling the hospital to check on Carrie, but I'll wait on Lucille."

The phone ringing at that very moment surprised all of them. Vicky was so startled that she put her hand across her mouth and let out a gasp. Pat spilled coffee on both the dress she was wearing and the chair she was sitting in. Richard reached for the phone, only to end up knocking it onto the floor. Samuel bent over, gathered the base and receiver, and finally answered the call.

"Hello, Carlisle residence."

"Samuel, it's Lenny. Can you hold on a minute while I go to a little more private setting? I just need to step around the corner because the cord won't reach much farther than it is already."

"Lenny, where are you, and what's going on?"

"I am under the radar, and believe me, I am planning on staying there for a day or two. Right now I am at a lovely lady's house and plan to stay here for the evening," he said as he looked at Sheri and continued to move away from her toward the doorway to the living room. "I don't have much more to tell you, Samuel, except that I think someone is on to me. I managed to lose the two of them late this afternoon. The problem is I'm not sure whom they are and whom they work for."

"Who knows where you are right now?"

"You, Sheri O'Bannon, and her dad."

"Who's Sheri O'Bannon?"

"Only the most wonderful woman I have ever met," he replied, while looking directly at her. She walked over to where he was standing and

SOMETIME AFTER MIDNIGHT

245

hugged his right arm. He reached around her and brought her closer to him. "Here, say hello to her."

He handed the phone to her and said, "Say hello to my boss, Samuel Carlisle."

She took the phone and introduced herself. She began an engaging conversation with Samuel that lasted for about a minute. It lasted long enough for Samuel to know that these two were very much into each other.

"Lenny, I need you to stay focused on this case. From the sound of things, I'm thinking that the weekend at this woman's house might not be a bad thing for the moment. I need you to do a couple of things for me tomorrow, however."

Lenny began taking notes regarding Samuel's instructions. He wrote as quickly as he could, but he had to ask him to slow down and repeat himself several times.

"Did you get all of that, Lenny?"

"I think so. None of this will take much time, Mr. Carlisle. I just need to stay out of the public eye while working on these things. I'll try to do as much as I'm able by phone, and I'll wing the rest of it."

"Just don't include Lucille in any of it, and keep Sheri out of it too."

"No problem. I can do this."

After going over the information once again, he was certain he had all of Samuel's instructions clearly written and understood. After the two of them discussed some other details and made sure that each other was clearly on the same page, Lenny said good-bye.

After hanging up, Samuel turned to Vicky and said, "I think Lenny's in love."

"Who's the lucky girl?" she asked, with a somewhat surprised look on her face.

"Someone named Sheri O'Bannon. That's all I know. But she did sound very nice over the phone."

"Do you think it's serious?"

"He's planning on staying the night there. Sounds pretty serious to me," he replied.

Lucille was being chauffeured back to her house. The two men who had taken her to the meeting with "the chief" were replaced by two men wearing ski masks. When they reached the end of the street where she lived, the driver spotted the patrol car parked in her driveway. The man in the back of the car pulled her down in the seat so she could not be seen from the outside.

The officer, standing near the north side of the house, noticed the vehicle as it approached. Using his flashlight to inspect the vehicle from a distance, he thought the make and model of the car to be the same as her neighbors had described as the "police car" that picked her up earlier in the evening. He got his partner's attention over the radio, and both of them headed toward the curb.

When the car approached the house, the driver, who saw the two officers moving toward the street, told his partner to hang on and stomped on the gas pedal. Lucille was thrown back into the seat by the accelerating vehicle. The two officers ran to their car, jumped in, and smoked the rear tires as the patrol car backed out of the driveway and on to the street. As the car leaped forward, the flashing red and blue lights came on. Seconds later, the siren began screaming.

"Base, this is bravo seven-six-one calling. We are in pursuit of a vehicle driven by a suspected kidnapper. The vehicle is headed south and is passing through the intersection of Valencia and Alabama. Request backup and instructions."

The dispatcher directed them to continue pursuit and to treat the suspects as armed and dangerous. They were to communicate every fifteen seconds, updating location and direction, to assist with a rolling roadblock that would be set up within the next couple of minutes.

"Now you've done it," said the man in the back of the fleeing vehicle.

"If we get caught with her, we're dead meat. Find a place where I can roll her out of the vehicle," he yelled at the driver.

"She might get hurt if we do that," he shouted back.

"Better her than us at the moment. Just keep looking for a spot. Turn left on Flomich and head for Old Kings Road."

The officers were gaining on the suspects. The turn onto Flomich by the fleeing vehicle caught them off guard, and they missed the turn. The officer driving the vehicle stomped on the brakes, slammed it into reverse, backed up the vehicle, whipped the steering wheel around, and headed east on Flomich, accelerating quickly.

"Where'd they go?" the officer driving the patrol car asked.

"Just keep heading east, and I'll call it in," the other officer said.

Realizing they had momentarily lost the pursuing patrol car, the man in the backseat of the fleeing vehicle opened the driver's side rear door. He told his partner to take a hard right turn anywhere within the next few seconds. No sooner had he finished barking out those instructions than the car, traveling in excess of forty miles per hour, turned quickly to the right, causing Lucille to be thrown from the vehicle.

As the car sped away, she lay unconscious in the street, near a dark street corner. After the repeated tumbling-like roll on the pavement, she lay motionless and bleeding profusely from her head. The officers in the pursuing patrol car spotted Lucille lying face down in the street.

CHAPTER 27

Mr. O'Bannon had been on his feet for most of the day, taking care of customers and cleaning up messes. He saw a chance to sit down for a few minutes during his fourteenth hour of a fast-paced day, away from the steady stream of customers. The evening dinner hour had been more challenging than the typical Friday evening, and the customers seemed more rude and argumentative than usual. It appeared to him as though he had spent more time, from five thirty that afternoon to eight o'clock that evening, cleaning up children's vomit than he had serving food.

"JoAnn, this has been a very trying day," he said as he propped up his feet on one of the chairs in the rear office area. "Not one of those families budged one inch to help me clean up the mess their kids made. I might just be getting too old for this—"

Stopping him before he could complete the sentence, she interjected a change of thought by asking, "Did you see how old that little momma was with the first kid that barfed all over the booth? She couldn't have been much older than sixteen."

"The so-called family, you know, the herd that came in right after Donna dropped that tray full of spaghetti, the one that had me in their sights from the time they walked through our door and strolled to the back table, who couldn't wait to get out of here? You know why? They stiffed me on part of the bill, and their little darling of a son crapped all over the men's room floor when nobody was looking. Plus, somebody tried to flush a diaper down the toilet to boot. I wonder if the police would allow me to put out an APB on them. Maybe there's a hunting season I haven't heard about. Wouldn't that make one trophy to hang over the grill for customers who waltz in here with an attitude?" he asked as he began chuckling slightly and rubbing the back of his neck. "What do you think my chances would be in front of a jury?"

"Well, look at you. I believe evil Thomas has come out to play," she said, while sitting down next to him. She kicked off her right shoe and began wiggling her toes. She too had been on her feet over twelve hours. Her feet felt as if they had been held in captivity in shoes two sizes too small.

"It definitely has been a very busy day, but all in all, it should be very profitable. I've got over seventy-five bucks in tips in my apron and a pretty fair prospect at table twelve. Speaking of prospects, what's happening with Sheri and that guy who waltzed in here this morning?"

"You know, I'm not sure," he said as he leaned back in the chair and stretched his arms over his head. "She said something about her having a date with him tonight, so I asked her to call me when she got home, you know, like I usually ask her to do. Just having met this guy, I'm not sure what to think. But I do kind of like this one. He's educated and seems to have an eye for her. He paid his own way today, even though he didn't have to, and that's okay in my book. Plus, he showed some table manners about himself as well."

"Sounds like a real charmer, this one. What was that other guy's name? You know, the one who ran off for some other woman in Wyoming? I mean, Wyoming, for heaven's sake. The only women out there live in log cabins and haven't seen a razor's edge under their arms since 1886," she said as she pulled out a cigarette.

"Careful, JoAnn. My great-aunt Sarah from Ireland, may God rest her soul, ended up in Wyoming, and she was drop-dead gorgeous. I'd offer to marry her today, except that she's been dead for about twelve years. Shoot, she was so beautiful. I still wouldn't rule that out as an option."

They both managed a smile.

JoAnn Spencer, with kinky red hair and all ninety-four pounds, had become Thomas O'Bannon's lifeline at the diner. When it came to running the business, Thomas was insightful, but it was JoAnn who had been able to put all of the pieces together to make the restaurant profitable. The diner, which had become a fixture in the Orlando area, had struggled to become profitable. That was long before his wife, Arlene, who had died almost twelve years earlier having succumbed to a long bout with cancer, could set things straight. JoAnn, however, arrived at the right time.

The diner was a place where the customers felt relaxed and enjoyed the casual conversation waitresses would serve with a welcoming smile. JoAnn had worked hard to make sure that happened for every customer every time they came to the diner. She had dedicated herself to her work, almost as much as Thomas had. Just about everything else in her life, including her two unhappy marriages, had been miserable failures. Her working relationship with him at the diner, however, was the only bright spot in her life at the moment. They had grown to be a perfect balance for each other.

"Are you serious, Thomas? She's out on a date with this guy, and she just met him today?"

"There was no stopping her. We talked briefly about it before she left this evening, but I'm not sure anything I said to her sunk in."

"Why don't you head home, take a nice long shower, and then call Sheri to see how she and her friend are doing? That might help you feel a little better," she said as she lit her cigarette.

"I guess my problem is that I'm not interested in going home tonight to a house filled with only memories. You know, since Arlene died, I've tried a lot of things to help pass the time at home, but I've usually ended up falling asleep from exhaustion or with the television on, unless one of the kids comes over to take pity on me. Rose visits with me more than the boys do now, but then she always has. Going home isn't what I need tonight. I think your idea of contacting Rose is exactly what would lift my spirits."

"I haven't heard you call Sheri by her middle name in a long time," she said.

"She is such a blessing to me. For the life of me, I just can't understand why she has had such miserable luck with men. I just want her to be happy. And this Lenny person, whatever his last name is, has caught her fancy."

"I could see in her eyes that she has a thing for him that wasn't there with, what did you say that other guy's name was, the one who ran off to Wyoming?"

"I didn't, and I really don't like repeating it," she said. "If you must know, his name was—"

Betty, one of the waitresses who was just coming on for the mid-shift, appeared at the door and said with an anxious tone in her voice, "Mr. O'Bannon, there's a gentleman at the counter who insists on seeing you."

"I'll be right there," he responded, while leaning forward in his chair. "I hope it isn't a health inspector or one of those blasted salesmen I had to throw out of here this morning. After the kind of day I've had, I hope he's a shrink."

"Thomas," JoAnn said quietly as he gingerly stood to his feet, "play nice."

"No problem. I just hope he doesn't toss his cookies all over the place."

JoAnn's break from her duties was well deserved, but about an hour and a half later than usual. She had managed to grab a bite to eat on the run, however, around six o'clock and had managed a bathroom break shortly after that. Sitting and thinking about the business end of the day and enjoying her cigarette, she started thinking about how she met Thomas a little more than twelve years earlier. Her recollection of the first time she met him began with remembering the confrontation she had with her first husband, Kevin Bidwell. That evening, their argument was not pretty.

"You'll never believe in me, even if your life depended on it," JoAnn recalled saying to Kevin. "Can't you get it through your thick skull that I just might know a little something about running a business? Or maybe you're drinking has cooked your brain," she said sarcastically.

As she remembered the incident, she recalled how annoyed she had been with her husband for his coming home late from a night out with the boys, four days earlier. Now four days later, he was standing in front of her, once again, fresh from his drinking with his pals from work. Like so many times before, he hadn't bothered to call or tell her he was going to be late—or feel the least bit apologetic for his behavior. This time he had forgotten that she had a job interview at eight o'clock the next morning. The interview would require both of them to leave the house no later than six thirty.

Her memories of those events of that evening were crisp and very clear. She could almost hear the sounds of that evening and remembered that he had been drinking heavily. When he finally walked into the house, reeking of hard liquor and cigarettes, she recalled how loudly he stumbled into their kitchen. She remembered not wanting to move as much as one inch for fear that doing so might disturb him or attract attention to her. She had learned not to bother him when he was drunk. Her two previous trips to the hospital's emergency room had been hard-learned lessons, permanently etched into her mind.

She recalled him laughing at her and pointing his finger at her when he said, "You need to be taken down a notch or two. Come here, woman." She didn't even bat an eyelash, let alone go to him, and that angered him even more.

As she took another drag off of her cigarette while reliving that event, the images of what had happened next were as if they had happened to her yesterday.

When he lunged toward her that evening, she avoided his outreached arms, causing him to lose his balance and hit the floor—hard. She bent down to check his pulse but couldn't find one. He was out, and she panicked. She called for an ambulance first and then her next-door neighbor, Marcey, for help. The ambulance arrived about eight minutes later, and it took him to the hospital. She couldn't recall all of the specifics, but she was just glad Marcey drove her to the hospital.

The doctors on call in the emergency room decided to admit her husband for a few days to run some tests. They wanted to monitor the very nasty bump he had sustained when he hit his head on the kitchen countertop on his way down to the tile floor. Once she was assured she had not killed him and that he was going to live, all she wanted to do was to go home and get some sleep. Frankly, she was grateful for their decision to keep him at the hospital. It provided her with two days of

253

relief from constant worry and fear. Still, she wanted something to eat before going home that evening.

She remembered looking at her watch to check the time before signing her husband's admission papers. While at the admission office, she recalled asking if anyone knew where she might get a decent meal that early in the morning. She was told by the admission's clerk that there was a restaurant on Harden Avenue and that it was roughly ten to twelve minutes from the hospital. That's when she recalled her first encounter with Thomas.

"Welcome to O'Bannon's," she remembered him saying with such energy.

She and Marcey had barely gotten through the door, and here was this husky guy in a white T-shirt, white pants, and white apron handing them menus. She couldn't remember if there were waitresses present, but she did remember that there wasn't one spot of grease or stains of any kind on his clothes or apron. The recollection of that image caused her to smile and chuckle slightly.

"Ladies, how about a nice cup of hot coffee?"

"That would be just fine," she remembered Marcey saying.

She had forgotten, until just that very moment, that Thomas then looked at her and said, "And for my lovely friend?" The memory of the event was clear and sharp and certain. She remembered his saying, "my lovely friend," and they hadn't laid eyes on each other until that very morning.

She finished her cigarette, put her shoe back on, and stood up. As she straightened her apron and adjusted her hairnet, she looked out toward the counter and saw him sitting down with the man who had so urgently needed to talk with him. He had managed to get him seated, poured him a cup of coffee, and had even worked a smile or two from him during their conversation. Break time was over.

She watched as the two of them discussed whatever it was that seemed important to the stranger. She couldn't stop herself from thinking about why she never tried to make a play for him. She loved how he could just sit down with you and begin talking and listening about anything, all the while making you feel special.

At the same time, she was sad for him. She had seen a piece of him die twelve years earlier when he said good-bye to Arlene on that Sunday morning, May 15, 1966. She had only known her for a little more than a year before Arlene died. Even a blind man could see how much in love they were.

She knew deep in her heart that she could be a great companion, lover, and life-partner to him, but Arlene was still very much alive to him.

"Fighting a ghost for twelve years will wear you down," she mumbled as she watched the stranger get up, shake Thomas' hand, and leave.

"What'd he want?" she asked.

"He wanted me to try some kind of new fangled gadget for the kitchen. I told him I had all the gadgets I needed at the moment. Once that was out of the way, I found out that his family was from Kildare. My mother was born in Robertstown and my father in Edenderry, all part of the same area. He seemed like such as nice lad too."

"Thomas, go home. If not a hot shower, take a nice long hot bath and then call Sheri. You've put in enough hours today. Leave a few for tomorrow. I'll get things ready for the morning. You go home," she said as she pointed to the door.

Thomas looked at Betty, who was filling the napkin holders on the tables, and said, "Betty, JoAnn is bossing me around. What do you suppose I should do about that?"

She looked at JoAnn, and then at Thomas, and said, "Go home."

CHAPTER 28

"Friday nights are not a particularly fun-filled time for us," Pat said.

"Yeah, we're real party animals," Richard said as he raised his eyebrows, tilted his head toward Vicky, and chuckled slightly. "We stay up until, oh, maybe, nine thirty or so before we both fall asleep in our chairs. There's usually been too much workweek by then. For us, Saturday night is usually a snoozer."

"Since you're considering moving, why don't the two of you think about retiring and doing something else?" Samuel asked.

"Son," she said, "we're moving for a particular reason. Your father and I are not ready to stop working. I'm not sure what we would do with ourselves if we both quit working at the same time. One of us would probably be in the morgue and the other in prison awaiting trial for murder one."

"Seriously, Mom, have the two of you considered doing something else besides what you are presently doing?"

"Like what? We've been in this business too long. We know this business like the back of our hands," Richard said.

"Well, suppose the two of you considered traveling a little bit before you think about something more permanent, like opening another store."

Richard's expression couldn't hide the delight he was feeling over such a notion. He had dreamed about visiting Europe, especially London, a long time. His sister Susan, who was two years younger than he, had married Sean Nelson from Kennington, England, and lived just south of London. His thoughts were racing so quickly, but they were clearly understood by the expressions on his face. Pat saw it immediately.

"Richard, it would give you an opportunity to see your sister," she said.

"Yes, it would. But what about the store and the move?" he said.

"It's just a thought. We can discuss the details for all of this tomorrow. For now, how about us just enjoying the night with our family being together?" she said.

"Speaking of that," Vicky said quietly, "does anyone want to play cards?"

"That would be nice. I'll get the cards and the score pad, unless these two mice-for-men are afraid we might take their cheese," Pat said, speaking directly to Vicky but pointing at both Richard and Samuel.

"You'll need the score pad," Richard said. "Just to keep track of how badly Samuel and I are going to thump you."

"I don't know, Dad," he said as he got up out of his chair and headed toward the kitchen table. "I haven't played Canasta in years."

"Who said anything about Canasta? Bridge is the game of the evening. We are going to extract a pound of revenge from these two women for the beating you and I took, at their hands, the last time we sat down at a card table."

Pat looked at Vicky and said, "They'll never learn."

Not long after the card game began, Doc Lafferty sat quietly next to Craig, repeatedly checked Craig's vital signs, and watched for any changes or abnormalities. The trip had been uneventful, except for the few minutes delay with the cops. Gina was doing an excellent job of avoiding the potholes and bumps. After they pulled away from the garage, Verna climbed into the front passenger seat and struck up a conversation with Gina. Craig was out cold.

"Are you sure he's just asleep, Doc?"

"Trust me, Verna. He will soon be his old self. The sedative probably has about another forty or so minutes before it should wear off. By then, we will be at the office working on him and as snug as a bug in a rug."

"Verna, where does he come up with these sayings?"

"Believe me, you haven't seen or heard anything," she replied.

"How much longer, Doc?" Gina asked.

"A couple of blocks, and we'll need to turn right at the next light," he said.

Todd had been at the office area quietly waiting for them to arrive. He had finished getting the things done that Doc had instructed him to do before their arrival. Once those chores were done, he decided to watch television to help pass the time. However, the phone rang.

Instinctively, he picked up the phone thinking it was Doc Lafferty calling. Just as he did, a man's voice on the other end could be heard asking to speak to Doc Lafferty. Todd looked down at the lighted phone switches and saw that this was an incoming call on line one. His first intention was to hang up and ignore the person. He wasn't exactly sure what to say, but he listened carefully to every word this person said. He began taking notes as quickly as he was able to write them down on a small notepad that was next to the phone.

Thinking instead of listening, he realized he had missed a part of what the other person had been saying.

"I'm sorry," he said, "but Doc Lafferty has stepped out. Something about rounds. He did say, however, that he would be back before too long. Would you like to call back, say, in about twenty minutes?"

"Who are you?" the other person asked.

"I'm just a friend who is answering the phone until Doc Lafferty returns."

"Well Mr. Just-A-Friend, tell Doctor Lafferty to call me at the meeting place. He'll know who called, and he'll know where to call me. You got that?"

"No problem. He should be here in a few minutes. I'll give him your message."

Todd hung up the phone, took a couple of deep breaths to steady himself, and then finished writing, word for word, the message given to him by the caller.

Just as Todd hung up the phone, Gina perfectly navigated the turn into the secluded parking area behind Doc Lafferty's office. She started backing up the van just as Todd had swung open the rear doors and, using a small wooden wedge, propped them open. After he opened the rear door of the van, he and Doc Lafferty pulled the gurney out of the van, pulled it through the doors to his office, and wheeled it into a small surgical room. Craig must have sensed something different about where he was because he started to come out from under the anesthetic Doc had given him.

"Verna, I'm going to need your help with the surgery part of it, if you don't mind," he said as he continued to check Craig's vital signs.

"I can handle it, Doc. It wouldn't be the first time I've helped in an O.R."

"Good. Go scrub up over there. I'm going to get him prepped and ready for the surgery."

"How long do you think it will take to get him done?"

"All total? Maybe about an hour or two."

"Be sure to count all of your sponges, Doc," she said, while smiling slightly.

"What do you want me to do?" Gina asked.

"I need for you and Todd to keep the lights off and answer only phone calls on line three."

"Doc," Todd said as he cleared his throat, "someone left a message. He said to call him at the meeting place and that you would know who called him."

"How did the caller know about line three?"

"He didn't. I know; I know. Only those calls on line three, but—"

"Todd, you've got to go back to the garage area and stake it out. Stay out of sight over there, but keep a keen eye on anyone who comes around. Do you still have your camera?"

"Yes," he said, somewhat relieved that Doc hadn't made a big deal out of the phone call.

"The one with the infrared lens capability?"

"Yes," he said, more confidently this time.

"Anyone who comes up to that area, I want pictures. Got it?"

"I won't mess up this time," he said as he grabbed his coat and headed for the back door.

"Be sure you don't. And bring me those pictures as soon as you can. Oh, by the way, there's a fifty-fifty chance we will probably be gone from here by morning. At least that's the plan. I won't get a good read on Craig's recovery probably until sometime after midnight."

When he had finished putting on his surgical gown, he removed both Craig's shirt and the makeshift bandages, which effectively had stopped the bleeding.

Craig began to become more aware of his surroundings as Doc finished taking the last of the bandages off. Verna walked around to where he was standing and stared at the injuries.

"That looks pretty bad, Doc. Are you sure the two of us can handle this?"

"We'll be fine. Now just hold on to him, until I give him this joy juice."

Doc looked down at Craig, who had been trying to focus more clearly, waved at him, and said, "Goodnight, sweet prince. See you in the morning."

The next two hours went by quickly, and Verna proved to be quite capable as a surgical assistant. Gina, who had decided not to play doctor, had fallen asleep on one of the couches in the waiting room. Doc Lafferty had done a superb job on both Craig's shoulder and collarbone.

Craig was resting comfortably.

CHAPTER 29

"Okay, what do we do now?" Sheri said after picking up Lenny's plate.

"We could just sit here and talk for a while. It's still raining pretty hard out there, and it doesn't look like there's any relief in sight. How about the two of us just stay in for a while? I've had enough of the rain for one day," he said as he collected the remaining dishes and followed her into the kitchen.

Her house was not large, but it did have seven rooms under the roof. It was well furnished, and her kitchen had all of the gadgets and appliances any person could want. What struck him was that everything in the kitchen was white. The dinette table and chairs were white. The cupboards and countertops were white. Even the floor tile was white. And all of it was immaculately clean.

Sheri rinsed the dishes slightly before putting them in the dishwasher. She took the cloth napkins, which she and Lenny had used, and put them in the washing machine. She wiped down the countertop as he took a seat at the table.

"How long have you lived here?" he asked.

"I guess it's been almost four years. My brother Shawn and I bought this place together in the fall of 1974. After he got married a couple of years ago, he bought a place of his own and moved out. He and his wife, Emma, have a little girl now. Besides, they needed a place of their own anyway."

"Is he younger or older than you?"

"He's eight years younger. Patrick is my youngest brother; there's ten years between us. Thomas Junior is the oldest of my three brothers. He's four years younger than I am. There are four of us in all, plus Poppa, of course."

"Whose clothes am I wearing?" he asked as he tugged on the shirt he had on.

"Those happen to be Shawn's," she said as she dried her hands.

"Remind me not to upset him," he said, with a grin on his face.

"How about joining me in the living room again?"

"Lead on," he said as he stood and put his chair back in its place. As she was walking by him, her hand touched his. She stopped, took hold of his hands, and led him from the kitchen. He followed, willingly, and sat next to her on the sofa.

"You must know my father is probably wondering what we're doing at the moment. I expect him to come by or at least call me this evening. He's probably on his way home from work as we speak. I just thought I better let you know."

"I kind of expected that, actually," he said before kissing her hand.

She looked at him and sensed she was blushing. "He's very protective, if you haven't noticed," she said.

"I do know what you mean. Believe me, I would not want to get on the bad side of your father."

"That's one of the reasons why I didn't stay in the bathroom. Aside from it being wrong, I don't want to have to lie to him. I have to admit, it was inviting, but it wouldn't be right. I'm not a prude. I just have the feeling that we could have something more meaningful. That's all."

He was listening to every word she spoke. She was making perfect sense as he followed her every word. Part of his attraction to her was how time with her was more than just fleeting moments. His thoughts were racing, wondering where this conversation was going. He wanted to take her into his arms and kiss her, but his inner voice kept telling him to slow down.

"Sheri, the moment I met you, I knew I wanted to be with you. I don't know what to call it, but it's like I am meant to be with you. It's like I've known you all my life, and yet I know hardly anything about you. Call it whatever you want to, but our being together just feels right. Am I making any sense to you at the moment?"

"Yes, a lot of sense. I feel the same way too. My father and I spoke of this earlier in the day. He's sort of old fashioned with these kinds of things, but I respect him and want to do right by him. That's why I want to do this right. I've only known you for about twelve hours, and already I believe I can trust you. I want my father to trust you too. Just having someone in my house, I mean a man, of course, is something I haven't done in three years. My father didn't react well to that situation then, and I was engaged to that person at that time."

"Engaged? Is he still in the picture? What's his name?"

"Oh no. He's long gone. Scott moved out of state and has since married. The last thing I heard anything about him was that he had married some woman from Wyoming. My father just can't seem to let that go for some reason."

"If I were in his shoes, I believe I would have a problem with that as well."

"Does that bother you? I mean, that I was engaged? What about you? Have you ever been engaged?"

He wasn't sure what to expect when he arrived at her house, but he wasn't prepared for this. He leaned back on the sofa, put his hands behind his head, let out a long sigh before looking at her, and said, "Once. Several years ago I was engaged to a gal named Leanne. Her family was from the upper crust of Boston. I met her while I was in law school. We dated for seven or eight months. Before I knew it, one thing led to another, and we became engaged. Her father announced it at one of their special family dinners one evening. I will never forget the look on her face, as if there was no warning. Blam! She was as surprised about our engagement as I was. I never once asked her to marry me, but her folks decided that it would be best for us to look as if we were engaged, for the family image, of course."

"Do you still communicate with her?

"No. I haven't spoken with her since leaving Boston in '66. I've often wondered how she faired. No doubt, she married into one of the landed gentry, of sorts. Her family would have seen to that. Don't you wonder what Scott might be up to?"

"Not one bit. That weasel deserved whatever he got. Knowing his luck, he probably found a rich widow in the backwoods and ended up living in the lap of luxury. He never worked a day in his life and probably never will."

Their conversation continued for the next two hours. They spent time inquiring about each other's past, laughing at almost any notion, and talking about things that each of them hadn't talked about for some time. For Sheri, Lenny proved to be a better listener than she had imagined. For Lenny, Sheri confirmed what he had suspected about her having been burned in previous relationships. Their time together confirmed their instincts about each other and went by too quickly for both of them.

For Lucille, her instincts were anything but rewarded. By the time the ambulance had arrived at the spot where she had been thrown from the car, she had lost consciousness and was not responding to anyone. The paramedics were preparing to transport her to the hospital when Lieutenant Howard's voice could be heard over the radio.

"Mobile Unit Three, this is Lieutenant Howard with the Daytona Beach Police Department. Do you have any identification on the female you will be transporting?"

"Lieutenant Howard, according to her driver's license, her name is Lucille Pierce."

"What is your ETA?"

"We should be at the hospital in about six minutes. We are loading our gear and preparing the victim to travel as we speak."

"What is her status?"

"She's unconscious, has lost a lot of blood, and probably has several severe internal injuries. It's obvious that her left arm is broken in at least two places."

He paused and took a deep breath before asking, "Did she say any-thing or mention any names during the time you've been there?"

"Negative," the paramedic responded.

"Let me speak to the officer in charge at the scene."

It took a little over a minute for Sergeant Allen to get to the radio and respond.

"Lieutenant, this is Sergeant Allen. I have established the perimeter for the crime scene and am waiting on the investigation unit to arrive. Anything else you need, sir?"

"One more thing. Has anyone started canvassing the neighborhood to find out what anyone might have seen?"

"One of the other officers has begun that process. The investigation unit will expand their canvass. So far, no one saw anything. They heard the squealing tires, but no one saw the vehicle."

He finished giving instructions and asking questions. Then he turned to Sergeant Rothermel and said, "If this doesn't beat all. Just what do you suppose she was doing in that part of the neighborhood?"

"Since we know that she was picked up by someone posing as police, why don't we start with that and work on getting a timeline put together for now?" Sergeant Rothermel asked.

"That's a great idea, for now. Go over to the scene and see what you can pick up on and get back with me. Someone out there holds the answers to our questions, and I need you to be the one who's doing the asking."

The ambulance announced its departure by turning on its flashing red and blue lights. The siren, once quiet and humble, began its painful scream-ing into the crisp spring night as the ambulance sped toward the hospital.

Lucille was not able to see or hear them.

CHAPTER 30

Saturday mornings were nothing special for Pat and Richard. They typically meant just another day—only with several more customers than usual. The lunch traffic and the afternoons seemed to drag on for hours. With Samuel, Vicky, and the kids staying for the weekend, Richard had made arrangements to bring in a couple of extra workers to open and help out for the day.

They were enjoying their first cup of coffee of the morning while relaxing in the living room. They had been watching the morning news for a few minutes but were more interested in getting everyone's day started.

"Pat, do you suppose anybody is stirring back there?" Richard whispered as he pointed to the two back bedrooms.

"If not, there ought to be," she said.

"Maybe we should wake up Samuel," he said. "He may have things he needs to do before the kids get all wound up."

"That may not be a bad idea. He mentioned something about Vicky going to the library this morning to look up phone numbers, or something like that," she said.

She got up from her easy chair, put her coffee cup on the end table, wrapped her robe snuggly around her waist, and headed for Samuel's room. As she stepped into the hallway, the phone rang.

"Are you expecting a call? I wonder if it's one of the help calling back?"

She walked over to the phone, which was on the small table where the hallway and the living room joined, and answered it.

"Hello? Who's calling? And do you know what time it is?"

"Yes, it's six o'clock in the morning, and this is Lieutenant Howard from the Daytona Beach Police Department. I'm sorry that I have disturbed you, but I need to speak to Mr. Samuel Carlisle. It is an emergency."

Pat covered the phone with the palm of her hand and whispered to Richard to get Samuel quickly because the police needed to talk to him.

"Richard, tell him it's Lieutenant Howard with the Daytona Beach Police, and he said it was an emergency."

Samuel came out of his room, just as Richard started down the hallway.

"Samuel, the police are on the phone for you. Do you want some coffee?"

"Who is it? Did he say what he wanted?"

Samuel took the phone from Pat and nodded at Richard that he would like some coffee.

"This is Samuel Carlisle," he said as he yawned quietly.

"Mr. Carlisle, this is Lieutenant Howard. Before I go any further, I want you to return to Daytona on the next available flight. There have been events that have occurred since your departure that you need to deal with. Plus, I need to know more about your investigation and findings regarding your so-called partner, Craig Myers."

"What events?"

"Lucille died last night from injuries when she was thrown from a moving vehicle. We don't have many clues to go on. I just figured you need to start filling in the gaps. Your getting back here this morning is requested, if that works for you. At this point, you could be considered a material witness and in possible danger. We can do this another way if you want to, but I'd rather you come willingly. I am also sorry to have to report to you that Carrie Myers died last night too."

Samuel looked at his mother.

"This can't be happening," he uttered in disbelief.

Lieutenant Howard spoke in greater detail for six or seven minutes about what had happened. He asked Samuel to call him back within the hour to tell him about his flight information, indicating that he would plan to pick him up at the airport.

The conversation ended when Samuel said, "I'll call you back within the hour."

Pat and Richard could tell something terrible had happened. She went over to Samuel and put her hand on his shoulder.

"Son, come sit down and tell us what's going on," she said as she put the phone back on the hall table.

Richard returned from the kitchen with a cup of coffee and placed it on the coffee table. Samuel sat down and said, "They're both dead. Lucille is dead. Carrie died last night too."

Pat placed her hand over her mouth and looked at Richard.

"Son," Richard asked as he leaned forward, "what happened?"

"I don't know, other than Lucille was apparently thrown from a moving vehicle. He didn't say by whom or why. He just said she was dead. I think he suspects Craig."

"Did you say that Lucille is dead?" Vicky asked as she came around the corner and into the living room. "My God, Samuel, what is going on?"

She sat down on the sofa next to him and put her arms around him. He pulled her close to him, kissing her on the top of her head. Thinking of Lucille, it suddenly came to him how little he really had control of this case. Nothing seemed certain to him, but he could sense a rage-like feeling beginning to build within him. Carrie's death, to him, seemed almost like a blessing now. But he was struggling with Lucille's.

"They will not stop. I don't know why they killed Lucille, but I do know why Craig tried to kill Carrie. This is getting out of control," he said, just before taking a sip of his coffee.

"Samuel, you're scaring me," Vicky said nervously.

While placing his coffee cup back on the table, Samuel looked at his father and said, "Dad, I need to be on the next flight out and back in Daytona as soon as possible. Would you mind making the arrangements with the airlines?" He then turned to Vicky and said, "You need to go to Aunt Ginny's for a while."

She started to say something, but he looked at her and gestured with his right hand that he was not going to listen to any arguments.

"Samuel, why can't she and the kids stay here? They will be perfectly fine here with us," Pat said confidently.

"Mom, it's better for them to be anywhere other than Daytona or Brooklyn for a while. Please, I don't mean any disrespect about this, but this would be the first place they would look. Got it?"

"Samuel, you're talking crazy. Who would come here for us?"

"The same people who want me and Lenny to stop digging into the Charles Durham case, that's who. Besides, it wouldn't be for just the two of you."

They sat there looking at each other as if they were in the middle of a poorly written stage play, waiting for each other to say their lines, but none of them knew what to say next. Even clichés seemed inappropriate at the time.

Richard, meanwhile, was seated in the kitchen and had begun working busily on airline arrangements for Samuel.

"How does nine thirty this morning sound?" he called out.

"Dad, that's fine. Just get me a seat on a plane. When's it due into Daytona?"

"You don't arrive in Daytona until sometime mid-afternoon. It's not a direct flight, but you might stay on the same plane."

"Dad, see if there's a flight to Atlanta and then to Daytona. If I have to, I can be at the airport in forty minutes. That will put me on a plane by seven fifteen this morning. I could do that."

While Richard went back to negotiating with the airline representative, Samuel returned to his room to start packing. Vicky, believing her worst nightmare was about to unfold in front of her, sat on the sofa, pulled her knees closely to her chest, and rested her chin on the top of her knees. She and Pat sat quietly staring at the television until Richard came back into the room.

"I've got him booked on an eight o'clock flight to Atlanta. He'll transfer to another plane that will get him into Daytona by one o'clock this afternoon. The best thing for him to do is to travel light and take just a carry-on bag with essentials. We can get the rest of his luggage to him later."

"How about some breakfast?" Pat said. "It looks like we have a very busy day ahead of us."

Vicky got up from the sofa and walked to the bedroom where Samuel was packing for his return flight. She walked over to him and hugged him from behind. He turned around, kissed her on her forehead, and pulled her close to him.

Looking directly into her eyes, he said, "I didn't want any of this to happen. When I left yesterday afternoon, everything seemed to be under control, and we were looking at a quiet weekend. Carrie's death was one thing. I just can't believe that Lucille is dead. Something has gone terribly wrong, and I haven't the slightest idea on what to do next. I just know that you and the kids are the most important things in my life right now. That's why I need for you to just do what I am asking. I need for you to promise me that you will go to your aunt Ginny's today."

"I still don't understand how you could get mixed up in a murder. There's something you're not telling me, and I'm not budging one inch until you do."

"Look, there are now at least three dead bodies tied to this case. I don't need any more. I just need for you to do what I'm asking, and we'll sort this out later."

"Why won't you talk to me about this?"

"Because…" He paused. "Because the more I tell you, the more I fear for you and the children. You've got to listen to me and realize the folks we have been investigating are up to their eyebrows in corruption, kickbacks, and now murder-for-hire. I just can't figure how Lucille got involved in this, unless—"

Samuel shot out of the room and headed directly for the telephone in the living room. He retrieved the piece of paper he used to write down Lenny's contact number and began dialing. He looked at Vicky as she entered the living room quickly behind him and said to her, "I think Lenny knows. The problem is, Lenny doesn't know he knows."

The phone rang on Lenny's end of the line for the second, then the third, then the forth time before he realized he wasn't dreaming.

Somewhat groggy, he rolled over, picked up the receiver, and mumbled, "This better be good."

"Lenny, it's Samuel. Do not, I repeat, do not make any more phone calls from the office. Is that clear? If I need to get you, I will call this number."

He rolled over slightly, trying to prop himself up on his right elbow, and repeated what Samuel had just told him.

"What do you mean, no more phone calls? How am I supposed to get my work done if I don't use that phone?"

"Look, we really don't have time to play twenty questions. Get up, get dressed, and get over to Dr. Rutledge's place as quickly as you can. Get him out of that house, and the two of you get lost. Do it now, and make sure that when you leave his house, you're not followed. Is that clear?"

"Yes, but why all the dramatics? I thought all we had to do was to lay low for the weekend."

"Carrie died last night. Lucille is dead. She was killed by being thrown from a moving vehicle. I think you're next, and they will probably try once more to get to Dr. Rutledge."

There was nothing but silence on Lenny's side of the conversation. He was stunned.

"Lenny? Lenny! Did you hear what I said?"

A few seconds went by, but Lenny finally responded. He and Samuel spoke for another minute or two. Before hanging up the phone, the two of them agreed on their contact times and locations. They both knew the office was off limits until they were satisfied that Craig and his henchmen were behind bars. It was then Lenny heard a knock on the door. He jumped out of bed, leaped toward the door, and pulled on it, only to startle Sheri.

"What's wrong, Lenny? I heard the phone, but I was in the bathroom," she said as she stood in the doorway pulling her robe around her waist more securely.

Lenny, still spinning from the phone call and the news of both Lucille's and Carrie's deaths, took a step back to take in how beautiful Sheri looked first thing in the morning. After just a few seconds of enjoying the view, he realized that he was standing there with nothing on but his boxers. Recognizing he was beginning to blush, he moved to where his borrowed pants were, picked them up, and put them on before turning around to zip them up.

"Are you okay? You look as if you've seen a ghost," she said as she entered the room.

"Do you remember the girl I told you about, you know, Samuel's secretary?

"You mean the one who's over six feet tall?"

"Yes, that's the one. She was killed last night. Something happened, because Samuel said her injuries were caused by her being thrown from a moving vehicle. That just doesn't make any sense," he said as he reached down, picked up his socks, and put them on. He stood up and then began putting on the shirt she had found for him.

"What are you doing?"

"Samuel gave me instructions, and I have to leave right now."

"What to do you mean, you have to leave? What is going on?"

"Don't ask. That way, you don't know. Let's just say that I need to go to work on the case right now, and I will call you later this morning. I know you got the day off and all so that we could spend some time together, but I've got to go to work."

With that, he rushed out of the room and headed for the clothes dryer. She followed quickly behind. He opened the dryer door and retrieved his coat. His shoes were still damp from yesterday's downpour, but that didn't matter. He slipped into them, put on his coat, and headed for the front door.

She attempted to block his leaving by leaning back against the front door, almost daring him to go through her.

He looked at her, again taking in the natural beauty he had noticed moments before. Although wearing a somewhat tattered robe over an even more worn cotton nightgown, she was gorgeous to him. He put his arms around her, pulled her close to him, and said, "Now get out of my way. I have got to go to work."

With that, he spun her around, as if she was a puppet on a string, and unlocked and opened the front door. Before leaving, he leaned toward her, kissed her gently on the lips, and said, "I will be back to finish this kiss."

She smiled as she leaned out the doorway, only to watch him rush to his car. He waved to her as he began backing out of the driveway and headed toward Dr. Rutledge's house.

"Be careful," she said softly, while waving back to him.

CHAPTER 31

Gina and Verna were up most of the night talking about old times and old boyfriends. Craig slept like a baby because of the sedative Doc had given him. Doc Lafferty, on the other hand, looked like death warmed over. He was exhausted from keeping an eye on Craig all night.

Waking slowly, Craig attempted to call for Doc. His throat was parched, and all that he could muster to get Doc's attention was a hoarse, hollow sound.

"Craig," Doc said, "did you say something? Here," he said as he handed him a wet washcloth to moisten his lips. "Let's check your bandages while we're at it."

"What time is it, Doc?"

"It's a little before seven in the morning. Why? Are you going someplace in a hurry?"

"Funny," he said, with a wry smile on his face. "What's the verdict? Am I okay to travel this morning? Where's Verna?"

"In due time, Craig. First things first. Verna is just down the hall, sound asleep with her buddy Gina. Do you think you could try to sit up for me, without rolling too much to either side?"

Doc was astonished by how easily Craig managed to sit straight up and throw his legs over the side of the table. Even more surprising was how little pain Craig felt in his right shoulder area.

"Easy, boy. It took me over two hours to piece your collarbone back together and set your shoulder, at least, I tried. You'll need at least three to four weeks of being somewhat immobile, without the use of that right arm."

"Doc, am I going to be okay?"

"Yes, Craig, as long as you keep from trying to stop bullets with your body. As it stands, you were very lucky. You lost a lot of blood, so don't start doing any fancy footwork this morning. Do I make myself clear?"

Craig nodded his head in agreement.

"Doc, I need to get a hold of a few folks. Do you mind if I use your phone?"

"I want you to promise me that you will not try to get off of this table."

"Okay, okay, I get the message. Just get me a phone, and I promise to be a good boy."

Verna, who was awakened by Craig's voice, walked into the room just as Doc was handing the phone extension to Craig. Craig settled the phone on his lap and began dialing.

"Craig," Verna said softly, "who are you calling at this hour? Whoever it is, I hope they work for you."

"Where's Todd? I need to talk to him right away. Is he here, or did he leave?"

"No, he's back. He's sawing logs a couple of rooms down. I'll go get him. Then I'll make some coffee for us."

Craig placed the receiver to his left ear and spoke.

"Charlie, get Anthony and meet Todd in a half hour at Rutledge's place. I want him alive and kicking when you bring him to me." There was a pause, and then Craig continued, "No, I don't care if you have to. Just get him and bring him here. I believe he needs to tell us about what that ratfink of a colleague Samuel is up to. Remember, I said alive, and that means all of you."

He paused again for a few moments and then spoke with even more urgency in his voice. "I couldn't care less about what that weasel Lenny is up to at the moment. I think Rutledge holds the part of the answer we need, and I'm counting on the three of you to handle this quietly, without waking up the neighborhood in the process. You got that?" With that said, he hung up the phone.

As Todd entered the room, he was tucking his shirt into his pants.

"Good morning, boss. How are you feeling?"

"I feel like something floating in the toilet bowl that wouldn't flush. Doc was poking around inside me for over two hours last night with who knows what. With my luck, I probably will end up peeing out of my elbow from now on."

The humor seemed to help, although Doc didn't laugh as loudly as the others.

"Todd, I just got off the phone with Charlie. Make sure the two of you take Anthony along, just in case you need some firepower. Do you still have your shotgun in the car?"

"Yes. And it's fully loaded with extra ammo available."

"Good. Try not to use it. I want Rutledge alive, and I want him here as soon as the three of you can get him here."

It didn't take Todd very long to get everything he needed and out the door.

"Doc, how many more times you reckon you'll have to patch up Craig?" Verna asked.

"I hope this is the last time," he said, while looking directly at Craig.

Craig tried to shrug his shoulders but had forgotten he had just come out of surgery a few hours before. He winced and lay back down on the table.

"Friend," Doc said, "you are not in any position right now to move that shoulder without feeling significant pressure."

"Why is it you doctors keep using the 'pressure' word when the pain feels like somebody's stickin' a knife in you?"

Verna returned with a cup of coffee for Doc and Craig. She asked if either of them wanted something to eat and offered to go get whatever they wanted.

"Nobody's going anywhere until Doc says I can travel," Craig said pointedly and directly at Verna.

"I'm sorry, but I'm hungry. Besides, nobody knows me around here or knows my vehicle. I could really be a big help here."

"Craig, she's got a point," Doc said as he began checking Craig's

blood pressure.

"You think so? I guess it wouldn't hurt to have something to eat and a few other things we might need for the trip. Verna, get a pen and paper and start writing."

The list began with the essentials: food items, bandages, sterile gauzes, and other medical supplies that he could think of. The list grew as the trip became more clandestine in nature. Verna wanted to make sure there were flashlights, batteries, and a battery-operated radio. Still, he instructed her to purchase additional ammunition for the revolver he was carrying. Doc added a few special items he thought might prove useful in the event of problems with Craig's shoulder during the long car ride.

She collected her things and left for the store, just two miles from their location.

"Will you sit back up for a couple of minutes while I change your bandages?"

"Yes, I can, if it will help me get on the road any sooner."

About the time Doc Lafferty began wrapping Craig's right shoulder with fresh bandages, Lenny arrived at Dr. Rutledge's home. He stopped short of the driveway, quickly got out of his vehicle, and sprinted to the front door. He knocked quickly and repeatedly on the door, while ringing the doorbell with his free hand. He could hear Dr. Rutledge approaching the door with a raised voice, saying, "Hold on to your britches. I'm coming."

Lenny's cue was when he heard Dr. Rutledge unlock the door. He nudged the door open and slipped inside quickly. He closed the door and suddenly realized he was standing with his back up against the door with both barrels of a large shotgun poking him in his chest.

"Dr. Rutledge, I'm Lenny Yeager. Samuel told me to come here and tell you that you are in serious danger. I am supposed to get you and take you out of here now."

"Young man, my instincts suspected there would be things happening this morning. Something just told me I needed to call Samuel and confirm my feelings. In fact, I just got off the phone with him a few moments ago, and he told me to ask you a question. Then he told me the answer I should listen for. He told me if you couldn't answer the question the way he said you should, for you to say your last prayer."

"And what question was that?"

"Samuel said to ask you what your favorite dessert is. So, what is your favorite dessert? Remember, I already know the answer."

"Dr. Rutledge, my favorite dessert is any dessert, as long as it has chocolate in it and on top of it."

"That's sick, but right."

Dr. Rutledge lowered the shotgun and turned slightly to go upstairs. As he was walking toward the stairs, he said, "I've already packed. I just need to get my things."

Lenny heard two car doors close. He looked through the sunburst at the top of the front door to see three men split up and begin to work their way around the sides of the house.

"We've got company," he said as he signaled Dr. Rutledge to move away from the entrance and into the hallway.

"Young man, I hope you've got a weapon of some kind besides your mouth."

"Sorry, I never carry guns."

"Take this," Dr. Rutledge said as he handed him his shotgun. Then he reached into his belt loop and pulled out a chrome-plated, pearl-handled .38 caliber pistol.

"This isn't just pretty. It makes a loud noise, knocks people down, and puts a huge hole into them," Dr. Rutledge said. "Right now, Lenny, you need to get to that phone behind you and call the police. I'll hold them off. They probably aren't suspecting lead for breakfast," he said coyly.

Lenny shook his head in disbelief. "I thought there were police on duty outside of your house?"

"I guess they took a break," he said.

I'm waiting for someone to yell, "Cut! That's a wrap," so we can go on to the next scene, Lenny said to himself. But the bullet that zinged by his head redirected his thoughts. Instinctively, he dropped to a prone position in the hallway and prepared to return fire. Dr. Rutledge stepped in front of him, raised his pistol, and squeezed off three rounds. Anthony Dortch, who had entered through the back door and taken a position behind one of the kitchen cabinets, fired off two more rounds.

"Get on the phone and call the police, now!" Dr. Rutledge yelled as four more bullets found their resting place in the wall area about three inches from Lenny's head.

Lenny rolled out of the way, crawled to where the phone was in the living room, and pulled it off of the shelf. He frantically dialed the operator and asked that the police send help immediately. As he was anxiously telling the operator what was happening, he noticed the bloodstained carpet, where Jack Ussery's body had been, from the day before. *Samuel doesn't pay me enough,* he thought.

Three more rounds were fired at them, only these came from Todd's weapon.

"Lenny, there are more shells for the shotgun in that brown box on the shelf behind you."

He located them while Dr. Rutledge fired two more rounds toward the kitchen. Charles "Frenchie" Puska decided not to take any more chances and scurried out the back door.

"Get back here, you idiot," Todd screamed. "Anthony, sit tight and don't let anyone come down this hallway. I'll circle around to the side of the house and get an angle on them through one of the windows."

Before he could get the words out of his mouth, Frenchie had run back into the house, yelling, "The cops are outside and coming this way. What do we do now?"

Todd looked at Anthony and then looked at Frenchie.

"Dr. Rutledge," Todd yelled. "We're coming out unarmed and with our hands up. Don't shoot."

Lenny peeked around the corner. He saw Todd standing at the other end of the hallway with his hands up and no weapon in sight. The next thing he saw was Todd on the ground with blood streaming from his motionless body. Three more shots came from the direction of the kitchen. Lenny ducked back out of the hallway. He could hear someone running down the hallway toward him. He raised the shotgun, steadied his nerves, and emptied both barrels with extreme prejudice.

There were pieces of Frenchie Puska's body strewed everywhere. The blast was so intense that it had turned what once was a human's upper torso into what looked like minced meat. Anthony Dortch threw his weapon down, walked into the hallway, and surrendered to the police who had entered the rear door.

"Good God, boy. One barrel at a time," Dr. Rutledge said. "One at a time is enough."

Lenny sat up, leaned against the wall, and stared at the lifeless bodies of Todd Koehler and Charles "Frenchie" Puska.

He heard a voice from the back of the house yell, "Dr. Rutledge, are you okay?"

"Yes, I'm fine; I'm okay," he said, raising his voice slightly.

Lenny stood up after dropping the shotgun at his feet. He looked at Dr. Rutledge and said, "One at a time?"

"Boy, you'll do. You'll do," he said as he went over to where Lenny was standing. He put his right arm around Lenny's left shoulder and said, "Next time, make sure that I'm behind you when you decide to do that again."

They both watched as Anthony Dortch was handcuffed.

"Do you know him?" Dr. Rutledge asked.

"I think that's Anthony Dortch," Lenny responded as he walked to the front door.

"He's the guy that was implicated by Samuel in our conversation yesterday," Dr. Rutledge said. "Have you discovered anything about him that might help with the Durham case?"

"If I hadn't by yesterday, I surely have today. There's a connection between Anthony and Craig that goes back several years," he replied.

"Any idea who these other two guys are?"

"Not a clue, but I'll betcha when the police ID them, we'll already have something about both of them. The connection to Craig will show up eventually as well," he said.

"We better call Samuel and let him know what happened. This might change a few things. The case is getting more complicated, certainly more personal."

Sergeant Rothermel entered the house through the front door, approached Dr. Rutledge, and flashed a huge grin.

"You sure throw one heck of a party at your place. The only problem is that you keep waking up your neighbors, and there are usually dead bodies involved. How about we try not doing this anymore, at least for the rest of today?"

Lenny looked at Dr. Rutledge and asked, "May I borrow your phone? There are two calls I need to make right now."

"No problem. Use the phone in my bedroom upstairs. Anybody I know?"

"Yes and no. I'll call Samuel first because he will want to know what's going on down here before next week. The other call is personal."

The conversation with Samuel was short and to the point. Lenny began to put the pieces together for Samuel about the behind-the-scenes effort by Craig and his henchmen. Samuel told Lenny to not go by the office without a police escort.

He seemed amused by Samuel's comment. *All the police seem to be able to do is show up late and process dead bodies.*

"You do realize that two of Craig's goons are dead and that Anthony Dortch is in custody, right?" Lenny asked coyly.

"Yes, and I am grateful that Anthony is still alive. He's the only person who can help us piece the puzzle together in the Durham case. When I get back there this afternoon, we need to get to Dortch and question him before he clams up."

"You're coming back here today? You just left yesterday."

"I know, but we've got a solid connection to Craig, and I want to exploit that possibility as quickly as possible. Just make sure that Dr.

Rutledge is safe. As soon as the police will allow the two of you to leave the house, do what I asked you to do."

He agreed. *The sooner we get back to Sheri's place, the better it would be for both Dr. Rutledge and myself,* he thought.

"Samuel, if I have to get shot at while in your employ, I need a raise," he said before taking a deep breath.

"Agreed. We need to meet as soon as we can. Tell Dr. Rutledge that we'll meet where we had dinner a couple of days ago. I will make reservations for the three of us for seven o'clock tonight."

"On your nickel, right?"

"Yep, my nickel."

"Do you mind if I bring a friend?"

"Lenny, just bring Dr. Rutledge and your appetite. Nothing or no one else."

Lenny hung up and dialed a new number.

"Sheri, I'm going to be later than I thought. Guess what?"

CHAPTER 32

"Vicky, why don't you just take a few things for you and the kids? Richard and I can see to the rest of your things."

"I guess that would be better. I just wish Samuel would reconsider," she said. "He is so stressed on this thing."

Pat, sounding slightly irritated, said, "I believe he thinks that what he's telling you to do is in all of our best interest. I'm with you. I just wish he'd reconsider this whole thing."

Samuel emerged from the hallway, fully dressed and toting his carry-on bag over his right shoulder. When he saw Vicky, he put down the bag and turned toward her.

"I will call you as soon as I land in Daytona. And no, I will not reconsider about your going to Aunt Ginny's. Until this thing gets settled, that's where you and the kids need to be. My mother and father know of her but do not know where she lives. I don't think they even know your aunt Ginny's last name, which is a good thing."

He went into the kitchen, hugged Rachel and Joshua, kissed them both, and said, "Please be good for Mommy. Okay?"

"Daddy, when will you be back?" Rachel asked.

"I don't know, but I will call you later today. Just be sure that you are a really good girl for Mommy."

He bent down one more time and kissed them both on the tops of their heads.

Pat and Richard were in the living room as he went to pick up his bag.

"Be careful, Son," Pat said as she hugged him. "Please keep in touch, okay?"

"Samuel, if there is anything we can do—"

"I know, Dad, but there really isn't."

He hugged Vicky, kissed her tenderly, and said, "I hope this will all be over by Monday."

Richard, who had been watching out the window of the living room, saw that the taxi had arrived. He motioned that Samuel needed to leave because the meter was running and he had a flight to catch.

As he went out the door, Vicky sat down on the couch and started to cry. Rachel came over to her, put her arms around her, and said, "Mommy, it will only be two days. Daddy said it will be Monday. Right?"

She looked at her daughter as tears continued to flow and said, "I hope so, sweetie. I truly hope so."

They both went to the front window and watched as Samuel emerged from the downstairs door, looked up at them, and waved good-bye before getting into the cab. They stood watching and waving as the cab disappeared on its way to the airport.

A little while after the driver had floored the accelerator of his cab in Brooklyn, Lieutenant Howard pulled into Dr. Rutledge's driveway, got out of his police vehicle, and entered the front door to the house.

He saw the blood spatters and human tissue on the walls, the two body bags in the hallway waiting to be carried to the two coroners' vehicles that were parked on the front lawn, and the handcuffed Anthony Dortch sitting on a chair in the living room.

He looked at Anthony and said, "I suppose you just happened by and wondered what was for breakfast?"

Anthony abruptly turned his head toward Lieutenant Howard and said, "Too bad you missed the fun."

"For your sake, you should be happy I did."

Lieutenant Howard turned to go down the hallway when he saw Lenny coming down the stairs. He paused for a moment, continued past the two corpses, stepped around a large pool of blood that had formed where Todd's body had fallen, and noticed the spent cartridges on the floor in the hallway and the kitchen. He made his way back to the front-door area before approaching Lenny and Dr. Rutledge.

Turning to Sergeant Rothermel, he asked if the forensics team had completed its work. He was informed that the team had not finished and was advised to wear gloves and to be sure to observe the forensic markers on the floor areas.

He turned to Dr. Rutledge and said, "We've met, but who is your new friend?"

Lenny stepped forward, extended his hand to introduce himself, and said, "I'm Leonard Yeager. I work for Mr. Samuel Carlisle. I came here to pick up Dr. Rutledge, before these three men started shooting at us."

"Dr. Rutledge, does this have anything to do with yesterday's little goings-on? I'm not exactly sure what went on here this morning, but somehow I just have to believe that we're not quite finished with this matter, are we?"

"Lieutenant, I certainly hope so," Dr. Rutledge said as he continued walking toward the front door.

"Where do you think you're going?" Lieutenant Howard asked.

"Lieutenant, Lenny and I were just on the way out to get some breakfast before all of this happened. Would you care to join us? Afterwards, we can go down to the station and complete your report for you. How does that sound? Besides, you can ask all the questions you want over a nice, hot cup of coffee and some pancakes smothered in butter and syrup."

"How about you go with Sergeant Rothermel? He does breakfast better than I do. I have other business to attend to before I head back to the station."

Dr. Rutledge turned to look directly at Lieutenant Howard and said, "Please be sure to tell your men to lock the doors when they're done."

Lieutenant Howard watched as the two of them drove away, followed closely by Sergeant Rothermel and two uniformed officers in separate vehicles.

Lifting his radio to speak, he said, "Base, this is Lieutenant Howard.

Please show my destination as the residence of Lucille Pierce. I'm taking Officer Lois Granger with me to help begin a preliminary investigation into Mrs. Pierce's death. I will contact you upon arrival."

The dispatcher acknowledged the call.

Verna returned to Doc Lafferty's office, frantically entering the room. She told Doc to turn on the television to the local station.

The two of them stood motionless as the reporter began telling the story of what had happened at Dr. Rutledge's house earlier.

"Saturday morning's quiet part of the Aberdeen Forest community, at a house belonging to Dr. Woodrow Rutledge, was upset earlier this morning with gunfire and the death of two yet-to-be-identified individuals. A third suspect, in what may have been a home invasion, has been identified as Anthony Dortch. He was taken into custody and transported to the Daytona Beach Police Department. No one has indicated the reason for the shooting, but—"

"This is not the start of a good day for Craig," Doc said.

"We need to get out of here," she said nervously.

"Probably not a bad idea, but Craig's shoulder is critical, and moving him could mess things up. We better tell him now and then start getting ready to leave."

"Why don't you just knock him out?"

Gina heard the noises the two of them were making and decided to see what all the fuss was about.

"What's going on?" Gina asked.

"We're getting ready to leave this place," Verna said to Gina. While glancing over her shoulder at Gina, she continued, "It might be best if you disappeared too. I'll take care of Craig from this point on."

Doc Lafferty decided to go tell Craig the bad news. He wasn't exactly sure where to start, but he knew that Craig would finish the conversation.

Doc looked at Verna and said, "You really won't have time to pack. You and Craig will need to leave as soon as possible. The traveling part might take his mind off a few things and beat the rush to your front door. After that, don't stop until you get to where you're going."

Gina walked over to Doc and hugged him. She took a small step back from him and said, "Will it be okay if the two of us get to know each other a little better, once she and Craig are out of town?"

"I don't see why not," he said as he headed to Craig's room. "Wish me luck."

"Gina," Verna said, "I will call you in a couple of weeks, you know, when things aren't quite so hectic. It's been really good seeing you again. I wish we didn't wait so long in between visits."

"I know, girl. Life is short, and our friends need to be near us. When you call, just be sure that the two of you are in a good place," she said, with a grin on her face.

The two of them heard Craig yell from the other room. They heard something hit the wall and then heard Craig say, "Samuel will pay for this."

Doc called for Verna to join them. Verna turned to Gina and said, "You better leave, because we'll be gone in a few minutes. I know I can depend on you to be discrete and trustworthy. I can't thank you enough for coming so quickly, girl."

With that, they hugged once more, and Verna watched her lifelong friend leave. Gina stopped at the door, looked back, flashed one of her patently face-wide grins, and said, "Aren't we the cat's meow!"

Verna, pointing her fingers at Gina, as if she was holding a pistol in her hand, said, "Back at you."

When Verna went to help Doc with Craig, Craig was sitting up, and Doc was standing on the other side of the room.

"Verna," he said, "finish getting him dressed. I need to call and speak with a doctor friend in Tarpon Springs. He's the one who will help you when you get there. I've known Lincoln, Dr. Lincoln Evans, for a long time, and I know he can be discrete. Besides, you will need someone to examine that shoulder tomorrow. He'll probably want to take an X-ray and run some blood work. Just know he is a capable doctor."

Craig's head had been down and looking at the floor the entire time Doc had been talking. Looking up and directly at Verna, he then looked at Doc.

"Doc, I can't thank you enough for what you've done and what you're doing. When we get to Verna's place and the dust settles, I will send you a little something in the mail. In the meantime, it would probably be best if the two of us not speak for a while. If the police decide to start nosing around, I know I can count on you being forgetful."

"Craig, you have nothing to worry about."

Verna finished helping Craig get dressed. Then she said she was going to move the car so it would be closer to the door. The items she had purchased earlier were already in the trunk of the car. Before going outside, she asked Doc if she could grab a couple of the pillows to take with them.

"Craig, I'm not much on speeches, but you've got a really good woman there. I think she loves you. She certainly seems devoted to you. You better take care of this one. Or sadly, you will not just find yourself alone in life; you will be without a proverbial paddle."

"Doc, I understand, but listen to me. Verna is the least of my worries because right now, there are a couple of thugs out there who want me dead. I have no idea who they are or who sent them. I have a suspicion or two, but your guess would be as good as mine at the moment. So you better understand that this boy will be underground for a good while.

"Verna and I are about to disappear off the face of this earth. Don't come looking, because we won't be in Tarpon Springs very long. If you get pushed into a corner, tell whoever is doing the pushing that we left for Tarpon Springs, because that's where we're headed. After that, you won't know, and no matter what anyone does, you'll be telling the truth. Maybe it's time that we both consider making an effort to start over. You know, and to try to get things right this time."

"Craig, that's the first thing you've said to me that has made any sense."

Verna returned and said, "Come on, the motor's running."

Doc helped Craig down from the table, walked slowly with him to the car, and helped him into the front passenger seat.

"Craig, if you rip open those stitches, get to a hospital, or at least call this number," he said as he handed him one of his business cards. "The number to Dr. Evans is on the back. I know he will handle this for you, and I know I can trust him."

"Don't worry, Doc, I'm in good hands," he said as he turned and looked at Verna.

"Nothing personal, Doc, but we've got to go," she said sternly.

Doc pointed at Craig and said firmly, "I meant what I said about those stitches. And Verna, those bandages will need to be changed by late this afternoon. Hold on for just a minute," he said as he hurriedly went back into the building. "I'll be right back."

When he returned, he handed Craig two small medicine bottles.

"The yellow one is for pain, and the one that is red and blue is for infection. Follow the instructions on the bottles."

"Thanks, Doc," Craig said, and then motioned for Verna to leave.

As the car pulled slowly out of the driveway and into traffic, Doc somehow felt this might be the last time he would see Craig for several months or even years. He wasn't exactly sure why or even if it was just wishful thinking.

Lieutenant Howard and Officer Lois Granger were just pulling up to Lucille's house.

"When we go inside, be sure you wear your gloves and that you don't touch anything. We are looking for some reason why Lucille would have been thrown from a vehicle and why she mistook whoever abducted her for the police," he instructed.

They exited the vehicle and walked to the front door. They saw no signs of forced entry or broken windows on the front part of the house. Lieutenant Howard directed Officer Granger to check both the sides and back of the house to be sure no one had attempted a break-in.

When she returned, she indicated that the house was secure, and there was no physical evidence of forced entry anywhere.

Using the key the coroner recovered from Lucille's purse at the scene, he opened the door. They drew their weapons and slowly entered the house. She went to her left, and he went to his right. Using and following their training, they began looking for anyone who might be in the house.

Once they had cleared the house and believed no one else was in the house with them, they began their search for clues that might help answer some questions about Lucille's abduction.

Officer Granger turned to Lieutenant Howard and said, "I'll start in her bedroom." He instructed her not to move anything—just to look. He figured the forensics team should be there around ten o'clock, and pictures would need to be taken before moving anything.

When Officer Granger entered Lucille's bedroom, she could smell the lingering aroma of the perfume Lucille had put on less than fifteen hours earlier. She noticed hangers on the perfectly made bed, as well as the wrappings and packaging for a new pair of pantyhose. When she walked by the dresser, she noticed the perfume bottle and bent down to smell its contents. She saw a tube of lipstick next to the perfume too.

She was into some guy for sure, she thought. *You don't wear Eden's Journey lipstick and put on Bonsoir Monsieur perfume unless you're expecting a big evening.*

She saw several pictures from what must have been her childhood. They were stuck into and all around the edges of a large mirror frame. She noticed one picture of Lucille, which had to be taken when she was about three or four, dressed up like a ballerina. She glanced at the others before she continued her inspection of the room.

Satisfied that there were no real telling clues into her disappearance or death, she left Lucille's bedroom to find Lieutenant Howard. He had been looking through some of Lucille's recent mail.

"Lieutenant, I can tell you this. The only clues in that room told me she had a hot date lined up for last night."

The words cut Lieutenant Howard deeply.

"Are you okay, Lieutenant?"

"No, I'm not. I think we better wait until forensics shows up before we do anything else."

With that said, he motioned for them to go outside and began walking toward the front door. That's when he spotted what he had hoped to find all along. There, on the corner of the end table, partially covered with a local food store advertisement, was Lucille's diary.

He instructed Officer Granger to call the dispatcher from the car and to check on when the forensics team would be arriving. After she went outside, he picked up the diary, opened it, and read an entry dated two months earlier.

> *Dear Diary: Today was a wasted day. I spent the entire time at the office trying to finish a brief for Carrie but was sidetracked every time I turned around. The worst part of it was that Samuel didn't even notice my new dress. He can be such a cad at times. And that Mr. Kellerman, he would be the one that noticed my dress! What a creep. When he touched me, I thought I would break out with hives. He's a very odd sort. I really don't understand why he and Craig meet so often. Gotta go! xoxoxo*

He looked around to be sure that Officer Granger had not been watching and slipped the diary into his coat pocket. Once secure in knowing he had found what he had hoped to find, he went outside and waited for the forensics team to arrive.

"By the way, Officer Granger, do you mind if I call you Lois?" he said.

CHAPTER 33

It didn't take long for Craig to settle in for the four-hour ride to Tarpon Springs. They hadn't been on the road ten minutes before he had fallen asleep. Verna snickered under her breath and mumbled, "Not so big and so bad now, are we, Craig?" as she drove along US Highway 92 headed for DeLand.

Seeing him asleep in the front seat brought back memories of high school, when the two of them were dating exclusively. She couldn't help remembering the Friday night dances, the 1951 two-door Chevrolet, and the drive-in movies they shared. Those few years they had together in high school, before she and her family moved to Atlanta, were precious to her because Craig made her feel important. *He was different back then,* she thought.

The most cherished memory for her, of all the times the two of them spent together, was a picnic just off of River Street in Savannah, Georgia. They had spent the day sitting under a large oak tree on the bank of the river, talking and making plans focused on what he called "grown-up stuff." She recalled how he was so clumsy when he tried to kiss her for the first time, and that brought a smile to her face.

Also, watching him sleep reminded her of the time the two of them had gone out in the spring of 1955 on a Friday night to see James Stewart in *Rear Window*. He was exhausted from having finished school that same afternoon and then working three hours at the feed store. They ate dinner, went to the theater, and, while waiting for the movie to start, shared a large bag of popcorn. Sometime between the cartoons and before the feature presentation started, Craig had fallen asleep with his head leaning gently on her right shoulder.

While driving toward DeLand, she glanced over at him, smiled, and then said softly, "We were made for each other, sweetheart."

When she brought the car to a stop at a traffic light in DeLand, he awoke for a few seconds, looked around at the surroundings, smiled at her, and then went back to sleep for another two hours. When they stopped in Brooksville for gas, Craig woke up enough to get out of the car to use the restroom. Almost as soon as she pulled the car out of the station and back onto the road, he went right back to sleep. Verna knew the medication Doc Lafferty had given him was causing his sleepiness.

The trip, for the most part, was uneventful. For Verna, the trip down memory lane helped to pass the time. For Craig, he couldn't wait to get out of the car and into a comfortable bed. Although his shoulder had not started bleeding again, it ached something fierce because of the sitting and leaning, and the pain medication he had taken in Daytona had begun to wear off. He insisted, however, that he did not want to take another pill until he got settled at her place.

Pat and Richard were sitting across from each other at their kitchen table.

"I don't like that Vicky and the children had to leave this house," she said.

"I understand, but don't second guess Samuel. He's pretty smart and wants what's best for us all," Richard said as he put down the newspaper he had been reading.

"You can be such a, sometimes, lame brain," Pat said as she stood to go to the sink.

"What would you do? Have them stay here and possibly put their lives in jeopardy?"

"It doesn't matter now, anyway," she said.

"It sure does," he said, placing his hand over his mouth to muffle a yawn.

"No, it doesn't. Samuel is just like you. He is you all over again," she said, pointing at him.

"And that's a bad thing because ..." he said.

"Because—you know what I mean. Stop trying to confuse the issue," she said.

Richard decided this conversation was going nowhere. He got up from the table with newspaper in hand, went into the living room, sat down in his chair, and started to read the paper again.

She raised her voice enough to make sure he could hear her clearly.

"When will you ever understand? Our son may not be a momma's boy, but when he says he is going to do something, he does it and expects everyone to be on board with him when he does whatever it is he intends to do."

"Pat, did you just hear yourself? What are you talking about?"

"Never mind," she said. "Just know that this is driving me nuts. I worry about him, and now with whatever he's got himself into, I worry even more about him and his family. He's making me crazy."

Richard walked over to her, placed his arms around her, and said, "He'll be fine. Trust him; show some faith in him. I know you didn't like discussing this with him, about their leaving, that is, but it's what he wants. Be happy that he's taking control of the situation."

They both stood quietly for a minute, taking in the fact that their grandchildren were no longer with them and that Vicky left in a controlled panic.

"I can't help thinking that those babies might get hurt or that someone might try to grab them just to get at Samuel," she said, with contempt in her voice.

"Nothing like that is going to happen. Samuel made a good decision, and we need to honor it by not making a big issue out of it. Vicky has our phone number. If she should need anything—"he said, trying to console her.

"I would feel better if they were still here," she said, cutting him off in mid-sentence and fighting back a deluge of tears.

"Me too," he said before kissing her forehead. "Me too."

CHAPTER 34

About the time Samuel's flight was landing in Atlanta, Doc Lafferty's nursing assistant entered his office and told him there were two gentlemen, dressed in suits and flashing U.S. Marshal's badges, who wanted to speak with him. He asked her to tell them to have a seat for a couple of minutes and that he would meet with them in the conference room.

Within seconds after his assistant returned to her workstation, the two men pushed their way through the doorway and into his office. One of the men circled behind Doc, while the other stood directly in front of him, pushed Doc's name plate out of the way, leaned forward on the desk, looked directly at Doc, and asked, "Where is Craig Myers?"

Doc knew immediately these two men were not law enforcement of any kind. They were enforcers of another kind. He knew about these things and could tell these two men were seriously rough around the edges.

"May I ask who you gentleman are, and would you mind showing me your identification badges, please?"

"I'm your mother's boyfriend, that's who," the man behind him said, in a stern and unyielding voice.

"I get it," Doc said. "You must be the good cop, so that makes him the bad cop in the routine, huh?" he said, while pointing toward the man standing in front of him.

"I am anything but a good cop, and I'm about to pound you pretty hard. Just tell us where Craig is, and we'll leave. Be a good doctor and heal yourself by telling us what we want to know."

"What makes you believe that I know where Craig is?"

"We know you're hooked at the hip with him. Don't be so cute. Just tell us where he is, and like, now, or we start messing up the place. I think we need to start with your face," he said as he looked directly at his partner standing behind Doc Lafferty.

He recognized the body language and knew these two meant business. Although stalling seemed to be his only option, he decided to take back any advantage he might have had before they muscled their way into the office.

He reached for his phone, pushed the assistant's call button, and waited for a moment. His action caught the two of them off guard for just a second. Realizing that the assistant was not picking up, he also hoped that she was not sticking around for what might happen next. He began an imaginary conversation, thinking that it might throw these guys off their game plan for a couple of minutes. Hoping it would allow him more time to think about how he was going to get out of this mess, he tried to make it look real.

Holding the phone to his left ear, as if he was speaking to his assistant, he said, "Mrs. Johnson, would you call the hospital and check to see how Mrs. Reed is doing? Have them report their last findings of her vital signs to me. Also, contact whoever the radiologist is for Mr. Hafner and have the X-rays sent to us as soon as possible. And please bring me the appointment calendar, you know, the one that has address information in the back of the book. And, while you're at it ..." pausing and acting as if he had asked the two men if they wanted something to drink, "please bring me and the two marshals a cup of coffee. Make that two with cream only and one with cream and sugar."

"Doc, I truly hope you are not messing with us. You've got about fifteen seconds before we use you to redecorate your office," the man leaning on his desk said as he pushed all of the papers, which were stacked neatly on the corner of his desk, onto to the floor.

"Wait," Doc said as he put his hands on the desktop. "Okay, okay! You don't have to get all uptight about this. Yes, I did see Craig yesterday. He came in here needing to be patched up because someone shot him. He had lost a lot of blood and was messed up pretty good. I took care of him, and they left."

The man standing behind him grabbed Doc around the neck and began squeezing, slowly at first.

"What do you mean, 'they left'? Who is 'they' you're talking about, and where did 'they' go?"

Doc's eyes were beginning to burn from the pressure being applied to his neck. He was having difficulty breathing, causing him to move his legs erratically. He tried to stand up but was forced back down into his seat.

"Doc, I'm only going to ask one more time. Who is 'they' and where did 'they' go?"

Doc knew they were about to hurt him badly. He waved his arms as if he was about to tell them everything they wanted to know, but one of the men realized that the police had pulled up in the parking lot.

"The cops are here. We better get out of here, now."

The man standing behind him lifted Doc up by the grip on the back of his neck and dragged him to the side entrance of the office. Doc managed to free himself. He ran toward the front of the office complex where the police were entering. Within seconds, the two thugs had exited the building and had gotten into their vehicle. Before the police could stop them, they sped out of the parking area, into traffic, and disappeared. The officers attempted to give chase but were not able to locate the car or the two men.

The attempted abduction of Doc Lafferty was the lead story on the local television channels that afternoon. It was all over the news that evening as well. Not one word of any connection between Craig Myers and Doc Lafferty, however, was mentioned in any of the stories reported that evening.

While Lieutenant Howard was in his office at police headquarters, waiting for Samuel to get back to Daytona and trying to figure out why Lucille had been killed, he overheard the radio discussion between the dispatcher and the police officers who responded to the phone call made by Doc's assistant. Knowing that she was able to provide an insight into what went on in the office between the two men and Doc, he thought this might be the break in the case he needed. He called the officers, advised them he would be at Doc Lafferty's office in a few minutes, and instructed them that no one was to talk with the assistant and that they were to keep Doc in sight until he got there.

By the time Samuel's plane was rolling down the runway at Atlanta's airport and taking off for Daytona Beach, Lieutenant Howard had begun to chart the events of the day and the information acquired from eyewitnesses. He methodically began to build a much clearer picture of what had happened over the past three days. Further, his investigative team had located the garage area that Craig used as a safe house for more than six years. He connected Doc Lafferty to Craig Myers through both medical records at Doc's office and the testimony from the nursing assistant. As badly as he wanted to, he still was not able to make any connection to Lucille's death. He knew, however, that he was close to breaking the main part of the case wide open, but he still felt a major piece of the case was missing.

"Perhaps our dear friend Samuel Carlisle will enlighten us," he said sarcastically to Sergeant Rothermel. Having just returned from breakfast, Sergeant Rothermel had started logging the evidence discovered at the garage site by the investigative team earlier that morning.

"Samuel's office must have been a zoo," Sergeant Rothermel said.

"Sometimes, it makes you wonder on which side of the animal cages you're standing," Lieutenant Howard commented. "Right now, I'm headed to Doctor Lafferty's office. I need for you to stay put for a while, just in case those two hoodlums surface again."

Sergeant Rothermel nodded in agreement and said, "Good luck with the good doctor. He's a real piece of work."

CHAPTER 35

Aunt Ginny had lived in Brooklyn for several years before moving in 1967 to Bridgeton, New Jersey. When her daughter, Allison, graduated from high school that year, Aunt Ginny's moving to Bridgeton seemed like the thing to do. After all, Vicky had lived with them for two years but had graduated from high school the year before Allison. For Aunt Ginny, having the two girls around was gratifying and enjoyable. When they both had left, moving back to her hometown had not been a big reach for her. There were several of her friends and members of her church still living in Bridgeton. That alone helped to make the decision a little easier for her.

Visiting with Aunt Ginny until the case was settled was not viewed as a punishment by Vicky. It actually made sense to her, once she set aside her initial emotions. Very few people knew of her aunt Ginny and that side of her family. For Samuel, he could rest easier knowing that his wife and children were, for the most part, out of harm's way. For Vicky, it would be like an adventure for her children, getting to meet someone she had spoken of frequently. Pat, however, was the only person who seemed annoyed with the decision.

The trip to Bridgeton was uneventful. Her only stop was on Carmel Road in Vineland where she purchased gas, picked up cold drinks for Rachel and Joshua, and purchased a couple of Sophie's subs. *These subs will be a nice surprise for Aunt Ginny,* she thought.

As she pulled out of the parking area from Sophie's Deli and merged into traffic, Rachel asked, "How old is Aunt Ginny?"

"Sweetheart, Aunt Ginny is sixty-three. You're going to love her.

She always made me feel so special when I lived with her. She's a great cook too."

"Do you think she will make us some cookies like you do?"

"Why, yes, of course. She's the one who taught me how to make cookies."

Joshua, sitting in a booster seat in the back, clapped his hands, applauding the idea of cookies. His eyes widened, and a broad smile filled his face.

"Of course," she said, "she makes a really good potato salad too. I just know you will enjoy our time with her."

"How long will we stay there?"

"Oh, probably a couple of days. We'll need to make sure that we go to the beach at Fortescue. It's only a little ways from where Aunt Ginny lives."

About the time they were forty-five minutes from Aunt Ginny's, Joshua had fallen asleep, while Rachel continued coloring in a coloring book.

"Rachel, would you mind reaching into Mommy's bag and getting a piece of gum for me?"

"Can I have one too?"

"I suppose so, but please don't swallow it. We're almost there, and I wouldn't want you to get an upset tummy."

When they finally reached her aunt's house, Aunt Ginny had just stepped onto her front porch to greet them. Rachel turned to her mother and said, "Are we staying in that house tonight?"

"Yes, we are. You'll love it. There's a huge screened-in back porch with a large dollhouse and lots of stuffed animals."

Rachel threw open the door, got out of the car, and made a mad dash for the back porch. Aunt Ginny called to her, but Rachel ran as fast as she could to see the dollhouse.

"Hi, Aunt Ginny. I'm Rachel, and I want to see your dollhouse," she screamed as she disappeared around the side of the house. Through it all, Joshua remained fast asleep.

Vicky got out of the car. She and Aunt Ginny met about halfway up the walkway to the house. They exchanged hugs and kissed each other on the cheek.

Holding Vicky by both arms and looking directly at her, Aunt Ginny asked, "Vicky, are you all okay? When I got the call, I was a little nervous, not knowing the details and all, but I'm glad you're here. We can catch up on all that's happened later. Was that your Rachel I just saw running toward the backyard?"

"Yes, in all of her glory. I made the mistake of telling her about your dollhouse."

"She'll be fine, and so will the dollhouse. After all, it did survive both you and Allison. Why don't you go ahead and get Joshua out of the car? We can put him in the downstairs bedroom for now and can make sleeping arrangements later. Right now, I think I better see what Rachel is up to."

Lenny and Dr. Rutledge finished their breakfast and headed for Sheri's house. Sergeant Rothermel had collected contact information from them both before leaving the restaurant for the station. He offered stern advice by reminding both of them that someone wanted the two of them dead badly enough to commit murder to make it happen.

"You know," Sergeant Rothermel had said, "if that thought doesn't get your attention, you're either foolish or just plain stupid. Would one of you so-called scholars mind explaining which one of those two choices you happen to resemble?"

Lenny looked at Sergeant Rothermel and said, "Frankly, you're a tad off base. We are neither stupid nor foolish. We got you to pay for breakfast this morning, didn't we?"

"Actually, Lieutenant Howard picked up the tab," he said. "That's his way of saying *don't even think about leaving the area*, unless you check in with him first."

Lenny glanced at Dr. Rutledge, chuckled slightly, looked directly at

Sergeant Rothermel, and then said, "Just make sure you guys keep the rest of Craig Myers' goons away from us."

"We can do that," Sergeant Rothermel said as he turned to leave the table where the three of them had been sitting.

"Just be sure you do," Dr. Rutledge said, while looking directly at him. "So far your record has been less than stellar."

On the way to Sheri's house, Dr. Rutledge and Lenny began discussing more of the details of the Durham case. Their conversation focused on the events and individuals surrounding Craig Myers. When Lenny began talking about the material he had gathered at the library, a clearer picture emerged for Dr. Rutledge of a wicked web, which Craig and his goons had spun.

Several contacts with a Jason Mayer from Tallahassee, the names of Herman Jackson and T.D. Ziegler, along with Roger Matheny's name surfacing again and again, seemed to draw what Lenny referred to as "a circle of criminal misconduct." The information that Lenny used to envision a network of illegal dealings came from the news articles on Roger Matheny, from Orlando, and the several articles he had found on how Charles Durham ended up in the middle of the Herman Jackson investigation. Between the documents he and Samuel had located and discussed, it was as if they had found all the corner pieces and outside edges of the puzzle. All that was left was to paint the picture.

About halfway to Sheri's house, Dr. Rutledge began writing down the connection of the names and events that Lenny spoke of during the car ride. Lenny, excited about how the case was beginning to come together, couldn't wait to see the news clippings that Samuel had found in Craig's wall safe.

When they drove into Sheri's driveway, she had opened the front door of the house to greet them. Dr. Rutledge shook her hand as he entered, but Lenny reached out and hugged her before kissing her tenderly.

"Welcome home," she said. "Who's your friend?"

"Sheri, let me introduce Dr. Woodrow Rutledge. He's a retired professor from Stetson University."

"Lenny, so, how did your errand go this morning?"

"You're looking at him. Do you mind if he stays here for a day or two, just until Samuel figures out what we do next?"

"Of course, he's welcome to stay," she said, looking at Dr. Rutledge.

"You're as gracious as you are beautiful," Dr. Rutledge said, bowing slightly toward Sheri.

"My, my, a Southern gentleman," she said, while smiling at Lenny. "I think I like your friend already."

Lenny and Dr. Rutledge went into the living room and sat down.

"Can I get y'all something to drink?"

Dr. Rutledge declined, but Lenny asked for a glass of water.

Sheri excused herself and headed toward the kitchen.

Lenny watched her as she walked toward the kitchen and then said, "Dr. Rutledge, Samuel is on his way into Daytona as we speak. I would like to meet him at the airport, but we are supposed to stay put and lay low."

"I suggest we follow his instructions. Lately, it seems like I must have upset someone considerably because of the unannounced and heavily armed visitors to my house," he said as he picked up one of the magazines from the coffee table.

Lenny leaned back, let out a sigh, and said, "We must have rattled a few cages and must be getting close to something. Otherwise, we wouldn't be worth their time of day. Whatever it is, we're close, and they know it. Once Samuel and the two of us can sit down together, I just know we'll figure it out. Those clippings he has squirreled away somewhere will be the final part of the puzzle. The problem is I just don't know what the puzzle is supposed to look like, at least not all of it."

"Not to worry, young man. The picture has become quite clear since our little discussion this morning. And you're right about Samuel's joining us. Each of us needs the other two at the moment to make the picture more complete. I'm confident by this evening we will have dotted our i's and crossed our t's.'"

"Let's hope so," Lenny said.

CHAPTER 36

Spending Saturday afternoons playing peek-a-boo with the police and recuperating from surgery were not among Craig's top two fun things to do. Verna went about doing everything to make Craig as comfortable as possible, but she could tell his mind was on other things. He managed to get settled, finally, on a very comfortable bed in one of the upstairs bedrooms that overlooked the backyard and the boat dock. There, moored securely to the dock's support poles, he saw what he believed would be his and Verna's ticket to freedom.

He couldn't help it. He had to sit up and take it all in. Verna's ninety-five feet, ocean-going boat, which she had affectionately named *Heaven's Gate,* was secured safely to the dock. It was bobbing slightly from the wakes caused by other boats passing as they went farther inland. He could see the open water of the Gulf of Mexico not too far in the distance. The boat seemed enormous and powerful to him. His eyes followed the sleek, nautical lines of that marvelous vessel, which called to him to be boarded and taken out to sea. He intended to answer that calling—and soon.

As she entered the room carrying a small silver tray, on which was a pitcher of lemonade and two Dagwood-like roast beef sandwiches, she commented, "Isn't she beautiful?"

"She's mighty pretty. I see now why you speak of her in the manner you do. She's enough to make you forget your own momma."

"You wouldn't forget me, would you, darling?" she said as she put the tray on the bed next to him. "How about a little something to eat?"

"This looks great. Is she ready to take out?"

"Fuel tanks are full, the galley is fully stocked, and she's armed to the teeth with the latest weaponry, including short-ranged intercept missiles."

Craig's jaw practically became unhinged.

"Is this part of your navy?" he asked, laughing ever so quietly to himself.

"You could say that," she said matter-of-factly.

Craig poured himself a glass of lemonade as she searched through her purse for the phone number to Dr. Evans.

"We better make contact with him and get you checked on today," she said.

Craig, not wanting to disagree, said, "The sooner we're on open water, the more comfortable I will feel. Those two criminals who tried to kill me are still out there and are looking for me. When you speak with Doctor what's-his-face, make sure he's talked to Doc before you discuss me and my situation."

"Craig, I will handle it," she said as she raised a glass of lemonade and mimicked toasting him.

"Just be sure he makes house calls, because the next trip I take will be on that," he said as he pointed at the yacht.

Lieutenant Howard got out of his vehicle and went into Doc Lafferty's office area. The nursing assistant who had called the police verified the lieutenant's identification and announced him to Doc Lafferty.

Within seconds, Doc came out of his office area and met Lieutenant Howard. They shook hands and then went into his office to continue their conversation.

"Are you okay, Doctor Lafferty?"

"I'm fine, but they sure put a scare into my assistant."

Lieutenant Howard noticed the files and papers that had been knocked to the floor. He looked around the remaining parts of the room, noticing that everything else seemed to be in place.

"Sir, would you mind if my forensics guys came in here and checked things for prints? It may provide us with a little more about who they were."

"No, I don't mind."

"Doctor, why do you suppose these guys were pressuring you about Craig Myers?"

"He's a patient of mine and has been for a number of years."

"Your assistant believed that they were pressing you to tell them where they could find him. The funny thing is that she indicated you told them that he had been shot, that you patched him up, and this is where it gets really uncanny: she remembers hearing you tell them that 'they' left. When you said, 'they left,' that's when she remembered them really getting physical with you. Tell me, Doctor Lafferty, can you explain what you meant by that and why they were so insistent about finding Mr. Myers?"

"Did she also tell you about the phone call I supposedly made to her? Look, I was trying to throw them off because those guys looked like they were going to seriously hurt me and possibly my staff members. I do not know why they wanted Mr. Myers, but I do know they said they were U.S. Marshals, badges and all. Why? Is Craig wanted for something?"

Lieutenant Howard wasn't buying it—and Doc Lafferty knew it.

"Look," Lieutenant Howard said as he walked toward the window, and then continued, "you've decided to play a game that's only going to get you dead. When I leave here and my folks go with me, you're on your own. When these two guys come back, and they will, believe me, they will, it'll be too late to help you or any members of your staff. And by the way, why would you tell them that he had been shot? Why not just a bad cold? Besides, there have been no reportings of gunshot wounds from any doctors within the last four weeks."

Doc knew he was in trouble, the kind of trouble that was going to send him to prison. Lieutenant Howard knew Doc was lying, but Doc didn't want to stop the conversation.

"You and I both know that those guys weren't here about Mr. Myers' runny nose. If I had any chance with them, I needed for them to believe me. A gunshot wound sounded more plausible to me," Doc insisted.

"You know, you could lose your license over stuff like this. Is he really worth all of this?" he asked as he looked out the window. "I mean, you have a seemingly very successful practice here, well established in the community, probably knocking down two or three hundred thousand a year. You must be a really loyal friend, or he's got something really big on you from way back."

Doc Lafferty sat there taking in all that was being said, without so much as flinching or even batting any eyelid.

"Lieutenant Howard, I'm telling you the way it is. When you catch these two hoodlums, you'll see."

Lieutenant Howard went out into the reception area and called for and instructed the forensics team to go through the entire office area. They were to collect prints and any other pertinent items that might help determine the identity of the two men.

Satisfied that he had gotten a good physical description of the two men and that the assistant was willing to help a police artist to sketch a likeness of the two men, he got into his car and headed back to the station.

While he was driving back to his office, Lieutenant Howard began to see how Doc Lafferty could be a major player in the case. His mind raced with questions that needed to be answered about Carrie's death. His experience told him that Lucille's death may have appeared to be an accident, but he believed it was a result of events surrounding Craig's murdering of Carrie. The odd players in this production, it seemed to him, were Dr. Rutledge and Lenny.

As he drove, he kept coming back to thoughts about Carrie's murder. It had been the starting point for all of this, including Lucille's death. He tried to connect all of the players and identify some common piece of information. He kept ending up with two connecting pieces—the hospital and Craig.

He picked up his radio receiver and called the dispatcher. He asked her to reach Sergeant Rothermel. He instructed her to tell him to go to the hospital and that he would meet him there in about thirty minutes. *Craig, I am all over you. I have picked up your trail*, he said to himself. *It's only a matter of time before I corner you. I know where and what the missing piece is, and I'm about to ruin your Saturday morning.*

As far as flights go, Samuel's return flight to Daytona was without incident, but tiring. As he felt the cabin pressure return to normal and listened to the pilot announce that the plane would be on the ground in less than fifteen minutes, he sat quietly running through all of the pieces of the puzzle that he and Lenny had discussed. He kept coming back to the question of why Craig felt compelled to attempt to murder Carrie. He knew that the obvious answer was to keep her silent. He felt there was more to it than that.

Just as the plane touched down on the Daytona runway, it was as if the jolt from the plane landing had sent a surge of electricity up Samuel's spine, shocking his brain.

He didn't know why he did what he did next, but he turned to the passenger sitting next to him and said, "It wasn't just what Carrie knew. It was what Craig knows, and I have that information, I think. That's why they want us dead. It's bigger than Craig, much bigger than Craig."

The passenger sitting next to him, somewhat surprised by Samuel's statement, leaned over toward him and said in a thoughtful manner, "If that's the case, Craig's not the big fish. Why don't you use him as bait?"

The look on Samuel's face was priceless.

CHAPTER 37

"May I speak to Mr. John Courson, please?" Lieutenant Howard asked as he leaned on the receptionist's counter for the administrative offices at the hospital.

"I'm sorry, but you just missed him. He said he was headed for the bank with the overnight deposits but that he would be right back."

"What bank would that be?"

"The Centennial Bank, three blocks from here."

"What does Mr. Courson drive?"

"Oh, he's not driving. Mr. Lynch is."

"Who's Mr. Lynch, and what is he driving?"

"He's our security chief. He's driving a beige-colored two-door sedan."

Lieutenant Howard called and instructed the dispatcher to send a squad car to that location. His further directions were for the officers to approach quietly and only observe the vehicle and its passengers. After giving her the description of the vehicle and passengers, he turned to locate Sergeant Rothermel.

"Sergeant," he said, with a sense of urgency in his voice, "stay here and find out all you can about Mr. Courson and Mr. Lynch. Start with this lovely young lady behind the counter," he instructed, while looking directly at the receptionist. "I'm on my way to make a withdrawal."

Samuel sat in one of the airport's phone booths, dialing Lenny's contact number.

"Hello," Sheri said as she answered the phone.

"Sheri, this is Samuel, Lenny's boss. Is he there?"

"Why, Mr. Carlisle, it is so nice of you to call. We were just speaking about you and how much Lenny enjoys working for you. I'll get him. Just a minute, please."

Samuel couldn't help smiling thinking about how genuine and truly "Southern" she sounded over the phone. Hearing her speak with such a Southern accent reminded him of the sweet tea, cornbread, and sweet potato pie his neighbor would serve each time they had a backyard cook-out. Only his neighbor, Beth Alderson, was from Meridian, Mississippi. He believed Meridian was about as Southern as anyone could get. Her accent was neither forced nor overly thick. Sheri's accent sounded similar.

"Yes, sir," Lenny said sharply as he took the phone from Sheri. "How was your flight, and are you still at the airport?"

"The flight was fine, and yes, I am still at the airport. My plane landed about ten minutes ago. I wanted to get in touch with you. I want you to stay put for a few more hours. I need to go downtown to see Lieutenant Howard, since I promised I would take care of my statement for him as soon as I got back today. Make sure that you and Dr. Rutledge are at the restaurant tonight by seven. We have a lot to cover in a short time."

"Mr. Carlisle, is there anything else we can do?"

"No, just sit tight and enjoy your time with Sheri for now."

"That, sir, I can do."

After hanging up on Lenny, he called the police station, trying to connect with Lieutenant Howard. Learning that he had left a message for Samuel to meet with him at the hospital, he headed for his car, knowing all along that the hospital was the place he needed to be, for more than one reason.

After hanging up from his conversation with Samuel, he returned to the living room, where Sheri was sitting on the sofa. She was gently patting the seat cushion next to her, as if to say she had reserved the seat for him.

As he sat down, he said, "Samuel instructed me to stay here until it was time for Dr. Rutledge and me to meet with him tonight at the restaurant. I told him that would be really hard work, and he should appreciate my willingness to handle such difficult tasks."

She reached over and playfully thumped his left arm.

"Well, you have a very insightful boss, because I need attention too," she said softly and coyly.

"Then, by all means, I will shower you with my undivided attention, right after we watch this afternoon's ball game. The Braves are playing the Mets today. Besides, Dr. Rutledge is in the next room and—"

"Yes," she said, slightly interrupting his sentence. "He's in the next room, but he is also sound asleep, and it looks like he's going to be out for some time."

"It would be a terrible thing for the game to be rained out this afternoon. We'd have to find something else to keep us busy."

She put her arms around him and hugged him gently.

He returned the hug and kissed her tenderly.

"Isn't it nice we're having weather?" he said.

It didn't take Samuel long to get to his car, pay his parking fees, and exit the airport area en route for the hospital. As he drove, his thoughts turned to his concern for whether Lucille's brother had been contacted about her death. Depressed by knowing that he would be without Lucille's help on this case, it hit him that some of the information about understanding her brother's background was lost. His main concern, however, was to make contact with Lieutenant Howard. He believed the two of them had pieces of the same puzzle that, when connected, would answer several questions.

That's when the proverbial snowball will start going downhill, he thought.

Finally locating and identifying the car being driven by Mr. Lynch, a patrol officer pulled over to the side of the road and called in his status. He was instructed that Lieutenant Howard was en route. Further, he was instructed that when Lieutenant Howard arrived, he was to move his vehicle to a location nearby but to keep it out of sight.

It didn't take Lieutenant Howard very long to find the bank. He pulled over and parked his vehicle about thirty yards south of the entrance, got out of his vehicle, and started walking toward the front door of the bank. The uniformed officer pulled the patrol car into traffic heading south, passing Lieutenant Howard, turned right at the next intersection, and positioned the car such that he could keep the entrance to the bank in sight and still remain somewhat veiled. His partner exited the vehicle and positioned himself about thirty feet south of the bank entrance. Lieutenant Howard motioned for him to stay put and to keep an eye on the door to the bank.

As he neared the bank's entrance, he observed a late model maroon-colored van approach from the west. It had stopped in a no-parking zone at the intersection. The windows were tinted so darkly that it was impossible to see any passengers. He continued walking toward the bank entrance, one eye on the van and one on the entrance. He turned the volume down on his radio receiver so that the chatter could barely be heard.

When he entered the bank, he saw whom he determined to be Mr. Courson and Mr. Lynch speaking with one of the tellers at the counter area. To his left, he noticed two small office areas and what appeared to be a locked gate to the vault. An assistant, presumably helping with the safe deposit boxes, was seated in front of the locked gate and was working on a stack of filing cards. Glancing to his right, he saw a corridor to a couple of conference rooms, other office areas, and the entrance to the stairway leading to the second floor. There were three other customers standing in line waiting their turn. He positioned himself behind those three, taking up the posture of one waiting to be served. After all, it was Saturday, and this was the only bank in the area open on Saturdays.

After Mr. Courson secured the night-deposit bag from the teller, both he and Mr. Lynch walked right past Lieutenant Howard as they moved toward the exit.

Lieutenant Howard turned around, took out his badge, took the safety off his revolver, and said, "Mr. Courson and Mr. Lynch, I'm Lieutenant Howard with the Daytona Beach Police Department. May I have a moment or two to speak with you?"

"Of course you may," Mr. Courson said, turning to face him.

Mr. Lynch continued walking toward the door, however.

"Mr. Lynch, would you please join us?"

"Mr. Lynch has another appointment that he must attend to," Mr. Courson said as he approached Lieutenant Howard.

"Mr. Lynch, do not go out that door until you have answered a few questions," Lieutenant Howard demanded.

He bolted out the door, turned right, and began running north as fast as he could. The maroon van, which had been waiting at the intersection across from the bank, squealed its tires as it too turned north and began pursuing Mr. Lynch.

"Mr. Courson, you wait here and don't move one inch," Lieutenant Howard yelled as he grabbed for his pistol and headed out the door.

The uniformed officer, who had remained out of sight, saw what was happening and entered the chase. He pulled alongside of Lieutenant Howard.

"Pursue the van no matter what," Lieutenant Howard yelled. "I'll continue on foot after Lynch. Call in and get backup on the scene now!"

The patrol car sped after the van as he picked up his pace in pursuit of Mr. Lynch. Lieutenant Howard instructed the officer on foot near the entrance to the bank to detain Mr. Courson and not let him go anywhere.

He saw his suspect run into an alley about fifty yards ahead. The van turned in as well, followed closely by the patrol car. A flurry of gunshots could be heard—then nothing but silence. Those pedestrians in the area all turned and looked toward the entrance to the alley. Some got down on the ground, while others ducked into businesses whose doors were unlocked. He ran as fast as he could to get to the entrance of the alley.

When he turned the corner, he saw the patrol car had stopped about forty feet into the alley. The van was nowhere in sight. He saw the uniformed officer standing with his back against a wall, motioning for Lieutenant Howard to join him.

"What happened?"

"All I know is that the van opened up on the guy who came out of the bank. He's holed up behind some boxes and a large dumpster around the corner. There's no way out, and this is the only way in."

"Did you see which way the van went at the end of the alley?"

"Yes, he turned left; that's all I could see from here."

"You stay right here, and do not let Mr. Lynch escape."

With that said, he ran back to the squad car and radioed the dispatcher with information about the van. He requested backup for his location.

As the dispatcher could be heard reporting the incident and requesting all vehicles in the area to close in and locate the van, he headed back to the bank to speak with Mr. Courson.

By the time that incident was over, Samuel had pulled into the parking lot of the hospital, gotten out of his vehicle, and entered through the main entrance. He asked one of the volunteers seated at the table near the entrance where he might find Lieutenant Howard and Sergeant Rothermel. She handed him a note, left there for him by Sergeant Rothermel, that instructed him to join them in the administrative offices. He thanked them both and headed for the office area.

"We've been waiting for you, Mr. Carlisle," Sergeant Rothermel said. "You need to follow me so we can all gather as one big happy family."

"Where are we going?" Samuel asked.

"We're headed for the bank, which is right down the street. Come on, I'll give you a ride," Sergeant Rothermel said.

There wasn't a lot of conversation between the two of them on the way to the bank. Sergeant Rothermel wasn't interested in talking with someone he had once called "college boy." He never had much time for college or college-types. His attitude toward lawyers was even worse.

Samuel quickly picked up on the attitude. Instead of letting it get to him, he thought about how Lucille's parents were going to feel when he called them later that evening.

"Here we are," Sergeant Rothermel said.

They both got out of the car and went into the bank. Lieutenant Howard was seated at a table in one of the conference rooms with Mr. Courson.

"Samuel," Lieutenant Howard said gleefully as he stood to shake hands, "what a pleasant surprise. I didn't expect you until later this afternoon. Now that this gentleman seated at the table with me has caught his breath from my tackling him ten minutes ago, would you care to be introduced to him?"

"I was able to catch an earlier flight. Let me guess," he said as he turned and looked directly at the man seated at the conference table. "This would be Mr. Courson, correct?"

"How did you know who he is?"

"I remember seeing his picture at the hospital, hanging in the hallway near the administrative office areas, when I was looking for help the other night. That, by the way, was before Mrs. Myers was murdered. I was told that you were sick, when in fact you were off gallivanting, somewhere only heaven knows, probably doing something hateful, no doubt."

"Now, Samuel, be careful how you speak of Mr. Courson, because he's going to tell us all about Mr. Lynch. I have a warrant coming to search their offices as well as their personal effects at both his and Mr. Lynch's house and both of their vehicles. You're going to help me question him about Mr. Myers' activities, sort of like a great tag team in wrestling, if you know what I mean."

Samuel's heart felt like it had skipped a beat, knowing that he was finally getting close in this case. Although Mr. Courson's name had not surfaced until now, he could feel in his bones that either he or Lieutenant Howard would be able to get Courson to talk. Samuel sat down at the conference table, poured himself a glass of water, and then looked directly at Courson.

After taking a nice, long drink of water, Samuel turned to Lieutenant

Howard and said, "I'll bet you Mr. Courson knows who Anthony Dortch is. In fact, I'll even bet you Anthony Dortch knows who Mr. Courson is. Do you think if we asked Anthony Dortch about Mr. Courson, he'd continue to talk as much as he has?"

As he was speaking the entire time to Lieutenant Howard, he wanted to see if Mr. Courson showed any reaction.

"Even if I lose those bets, I know I'll win the one where I bet you, Lieutenant Howard, that he knows who Herman Jackson was because there is a picture of the two of them together about three years ago with Councilman Kellerman, which was found in a local newspaper."

"Okay, okay, so I know these guys. It doesn't make me a criminal. I think I'd like to talk to my attorney now," he said.

Lieutenant Howard looked at Samuel, smiled, and then said, "Samuel, aren't you an attorney? Wouldn't you like to talk to Mr. Courson?"

"Mr. Courson," Samuel said. "I have only one question for you. Why Lucille?"

He got up from where he was sitting and stared at Samuel.

"What do you mean, 'why Lucille'? I never touched her."

Samuel looked at Lieutenant Howard and motioned for him to step outside for a moment.

When Samuel and Mr. Courson were the only ones left in the room, Samuel turned to him and asked, "Why did Lucille have to die? She did no harm to anyone and really knew nothing about what was going on. This whole thing isn't about her. It's about her brother, Charles Durham, and the murder of Herman Jackson."

"I swear to you, when she left us, she was alive. Groggy, but alive. They were taking her back to her house. After that, I don't know what happened. I was against her being picked up from the beginning. If you think that this case is only about Charles Durham and Herman Jackson, then you're an idiot. Don't think for a minute they don't know who you are and what you do. I have nothing else to say to you or anyone else, unless you plan to be my attorney."

Lieutenant Howard came back into the room and announced,

"Samuel, he may need your services in a moment or two. The DA's office has agreed to issue a warrant for Mr. Courson's and Mr. Lynch's arrest for the murder of Lucille Pierce. We're going to detain Mr. Courson now, until the warrant arrives. There may be enough evidence to tie him to the murder of Mrs. Myers as well."

"I had nothing to do with that. That one was Craig's idea," Mr. Courson said as he stood and pointed his finger at Lieutenant Howard.

"Mr. Courson, I would not say any more at the moment, because you're under arrest. You have the right to remain silent..." he said as he began to place handcuffs around Mr. Courson's wrists.

CHAPTER 38

"Verna, something tells me we need to leave. Let's get on the boat and leave, now. I understand it's really nice this time of year in Argentina."

"Craig, let's first go by Dr. Evans' office and get you checked out. It won't take long. I really would feel better about the whole thing."

"Really, you don't need to worry, because I feel better now. I really don't have any pain, and I haven't taken one of those pills for almost six hours. Something tells me I need to get out of here now, and I have learned to trust my instincts."

She called the captain and instructed him to begin preparations for leaving. She informed him that he would not need a full crew, since she could take care of a lot of the things the others normally did.

"I'll be back in about twenty minutes to get you. I just need to run to the corner drugstore and pick up a few personal items. Just sit tight. I'll be right back before you know it."

She drove off as he watched her disappear toward town. Late afternoon was approaching quickly, and he felt the need to be on that boat and out to sea.

Samuel finished working on his statement concerning the weapon from Craig's safe. His approach seemed to appease Lieutenant Howard. He believed Lieutenant Howard also needed to be at the restaurant with the others so the entire story could be unraveled with all the players present. He felt that with all four of them together, the process might be pushed along faster and more details uncovered. He was ready for this case to be nothing more than making a simple appearance before a judge to get Charles released from prison.

As he prepared to leave the station, Lieutenant Howard asked him to join him and go to the alley near the bank with him. The call he had taken was from his forensics team. The maroon van had been found just west of Ormond Beach. There were multiple blood splatters and stains on the inside the van. The van had been abandoned, but still it may have held several clues. He agreed to follow him.

"Before we head to the van, we need to stop by the alley area where Lynch was holed up earlier in the day. They just radioed in that he is dead. Apparently he died from gunshot wounds he took earlier in the day. The officers on the scene said he had been hit at least five times in the back, center mass."

"That sounds like not just a professional killing, more like an execution," Samuel said.

"Maybe that's what he meant when Courson told me that Lynch had an appointment he needed to attend to. Courson seems to know a lot about a lot of things going on around here. Maybe we need a little more time to talk to him before his lawyer shows up," Lieutenant Howard said.

"You won't be able to use it in court," he reminded him. "You might want to wait until his lawyer shows up and have the DA start negotiating a deal for his client's testimony. Courson may not be the most honest thug, but I believe he'll do whatever it takes to stay away from 'Old Sparky.' I get the feeling he knows more about the Herman Jackson murder as well. Let's spend a few more minutes with him before we go to dinner. Tally-ho, Lieutenant."

Craig saw the headlights of Verna's car as it drove toward the house. He checked his watch and noticed that it had taken her almost forty-five minutes to return from a twenty-minute errand. He heard the door close, heard her footsteps as she came up the stairway, and finally watched as she entered the bedroom.

"That was the longest twenty minutes I can ever remember," he said as he prepared to stand.

"I'm sorry, but I picked up some extra cash just in case. I remembered that I had some clothes at the cleaners, so I picked them up before going to the store. Now we have everything we need, including personal female things. Here, let me help you to the boat."

As they exited the house, the sun was falling quickly to the horizon. The boat appeared to glisten and sparkle as the reflection from the water seemed to dance on the hull of the boat. The shades of violet and orange were very soothing to him.

"Every step I take toward your boat, I feel like a ton of weight is being shed and left behind. I can't tell you enough how much I appreciate how you have come back into my life after all these years."

He needed her help to take that final step to get on to the boat. First, he went to the bow of the boat and watched the deckhand release the ropes. The captain fired up perfectly matched diesel engines, whose sounds were like music to his ears. He could feel the deck begin to vibrate slightly beneath him as the captain began to ease the boat gently away from the dock and out into the canal. She suggested they go down below and make themselves comfortable because it would be several hours before they would be able to make their first stop.

"When do we reach our first stop?" he asked as he took a seat in one of the easy chairs in the lounge area.

"If we stay on course and don't encounter any problems, we should reach our first stop sometime after midnight."

He was fascinated with the plush interior of the boat but preferred the fresh air on the open sea.

"Do you mind if we stay up top for a while? The fresh air would really feel good to me," he said.

"No problem. You go on. I'll join you in a minute. I'd like to grab a sweater before I join you up there."

He carefully climbed the stairs that led to the open deck on the fantail of the boat. He found a comfortable area where the plush cushions helped to relieve some of the pressure on his shoulder. As he sat there enjoying the evening breeze and watching the boat slice its way toward the Gulf of Mexico, he thought how lucky he was to have such friends as Doc Lafferty and Verna in his life. He actually began to feel like he was a free man and that his past would be a distant part of his life.

He never heard the gunshot. He slumped over on the seat cushions and bled out in a matter of seconds.

"Captain, we need about another thirty-minute ride, if you don't mind. We have a little more cleanup than I had originally planned for," she said.

"Yes, ma'am," he said as he increased the engines to full throttle.

She went below and put her Colt .45 caliber pistol back in its case. She removed the silencer and would toss it overboard later. Next, she got on the boat's radiophone. Using the ship-to-shore system she had installed on the boat only two months earlier, she made one very brief phone call.

"We're done here," is all she said before hanging up.

At the same time Verna finished hanging up from that call, Samuel was calling his wife. He wanted to let her know that he was fine and that he was about to have dinner with Lenny, Dr. Rutledge, and Lieutenant Howard. He explained the breaks in the case and how hopeful he was about the outcome for reopening the Durham case.

They spoke for about three or four more minutes before each said their good-byes. As soon as he had finished speaking with her, he and Lieutenant Howard headed for the restaurant.

"Dr. Rutledge, we've got to go, or we'll be late for dinner," Lenny said.

"Don't get your bowels in an uproar. We have plenty of time. By the time you kiss Sheri good-bye, I will be ready."

Sheri was standing right next to him when he said that. She reached out and gave him a hug before he could get his coat on.

"Thank you, sweetheart," he said, "for making this old man feel at home."

"You are welcome here any time, kind sir," she said in response.

Lenny opened the door for him, hugged Sheri, and said, "I'll be back around ten o'clock. Maybe we can go down to the diner, you know, to see if your father is still there. He might like some company," he said as he kissed her good-bye and headed toward his car.

Dr. Rutledge turned, waved good-bye to Sheri, got into the car, and buckled his seatbelt. He turned, looked at Lenny, and said, "If you don't marry that girl, let me know. I got dibs."

Dinner lasted about an hour. Their conversation continued for over two hours after the dishes had been cleared from the table. What caused the conversation to shift from the events of the day to a deeper level of understanding was Lenny's "circle of criminal misconduct" theory he and Dr. Rutledge had worked on earlier.

"Look, the whole thing seems to be tied to bigger fish, so to speak," Samuel said.

"The execution-style murder of Lynch and Jack Ussery's connections to the Hank Watson murder tell me that someone else was calling the shots besides Craig. All of this is somehow connected to both Carrie's and Lucille's deaths. My bet is that we got too close to some information someone didn't want us to know," Lenny said.

"Too close is an understatement. I believe Durham somehow let too much information slip to Lucille. Someone much higher than Craig saw that as a threat and caused her to end up high on the hit list. Durham's got to be taking a fall for somebody else. He has not been as cooperative as you think someone would be who has tried repeatedly to convince us of his innocence," Samuel said.

Dr. Rutledge sat quietly during most of the evening's conversation, until the issues began to focus on the attacks at his house.

"You've got to give them credit," he started, "they were a persistent bunch. From where I'm sitting, there's something that doesn't fit about why they would come back after a failed attempt on my life. The fact that they came back a second time armed to the teeth, you would think that I really knew something or had something they wanted. At that point in all of this, I knew very little. Lenny and I put a few things together this morning, but that was after a second rendition of the OK Corral in my house.

"Try this on for size: Jack Ussery, Todd Koehler, Anthony Dortch, and Frenchie Puska were very close and faithful servants of Craig. The only one left standing is Dortch, and he's not talking. Craig is somewhere, but I bet his turn is not far down the road. His wife is dead, and Samuel's secretary, may God rest her soul, could have been considered by these thugs as the hub of our communication wheel as well as a millstone around their neck because of her brother. One of Craig's probable contacts at the hospital, Lynch, is also dead. Anthony Dortch is supposed to be dead too, probably someone hoping that he'd be done in during the second shootout at my place. And Courson? He was supposed to die with Lynch on their way back from the bank. If you ask me, it sounds more like someone was cleaning house. I guess the real question is who?"

Lieutenant Howard, realizing that Dr. Rutledge's assessment put all of the players on stage and the roles they played, reminded everyone at the table that Courson and Dortch weren't talking.

"These two have clammed up," he said. "You know what else bothers me is that there is this Doctor Lafferty who is somehow in the mix. A couple of goons posing as US Marshals were about to dance on his face today when we showed up at his place. He's dirty, and I can feel it. If I can feel it, I can cuff 'em."

"We need to keep Dortch and Courson in a very safe place," Lenny added as he pointed at Lieutenant Howard. "And I agree with Dr. Rutledge. It looks as if is someone out there is trying to cover his tracks as fast as he can."

Samuel brought everyone's attention back to the original conversation when the evening first began.

"What about Kellerman and Herman Jackson? How do we connect the dots on them?"

"Easy," Lieutenant Howard said. "Let's show Durham the list of names that Dr. Rutledge just gave us and their current condition or prognosis. Let's help him understand that if Dortch starts talking, his life won't be worth a plug nickel in prison. Maybe the DA will listen and work with us on making some kind of deal with him."

Lenny couldn't restrain himself.

"You know…if we can get Durham to start talking about Herman Jackson and Kellerman, it might just help us tie a ribbon on the whole package. Between the information Samuel and I have put together about some of these bad apples we've been talking about tonight, there's bound to be money somewhere. Besides, some of the names we haven't mentioned yet are elected officials. Shoot, there's no telling where this could lead."

"You're right, Lenny. There's money involved in all of this, and the question is who has it," Samuel said. "All we should have to do is to follow the contracts. Remember, there are other lawyers involved in this besides Craig."

"That figures," Lieutenant Howard said.

Samuel leaned over and whispered to Dr. Rutledge, "There's something I need to tell you, but not here and certainly not in front of them."

Lenny looked at his watch, pushed his chair back as if to leave, looked at the other three, and said, "I need to leave in a couple minutes. What say we set a time for us to meet tomorrow and continue this, after church, over lunch? I know a great little place to eat where the service is first rate."

EPILOGUE

Sunday morning started quietly. Samuel had tossed and turned most of the evening. Dr. Rutledge managed to sleep but was on the ready just in case he should have more uninvited guests for the third day in a row. Lenny had returned to his own house late Saturday evening and fell quickly asleep. Lieutenant Howard fell asleep while reading Lucille's diary.

The puzzle, although not completely finished, was missing very few pieces. Tuesday's upcoming visit to Starke and the answers to the many questions that arose from the previous evening's discussions would probably help complete the picture for all of them.

Eight o'clock Sunday morning came quickly, however. About the time that Samuel was just crawling out of the bed at his house, Verna was using the ship-to-shore phone from her yacht.

"I told you he has been handled," Verna said resolutely.

"Thank you. I know you really didn't want to have to do this for me, but I am grateful to you."

"For a while I wasn't sure I could do this. But I knew you needed this done. Besides, I was better suited for it than you."

"I am grateful that you did this. I probably would have done it differently and left some kind of evidence behind."

Verna looked at her watch as she sat in one of the chairs on the bridge of her yacht.

"Hey, it's just about that time when you need to make contact with them by phone. Let me know if I need to be in on that conference call. I can help you, you know," she said as she got up out of her seat and motioned for the captain to begin heading for shore, which was about two miles away.

She listened intently as instructions were provided to her. She didn't need to write anything down.

"I'll see you just before ten," she said just before lighting a cigarette and sitting back down in the chair.

When the phone call was finished, a conversation between four men began in a closed conference room in a tall building near the center of Miami, Florida.

"She's good. It is done, and there are no trails to follow," the man sitting at the table said.

"I told you, she's not only good … she's thorough," the man said as he began filling his plate from the buffet breakfast that had been set up in the room.

"Now what about Samuel? Are we still in agreement about what we think is best for him?"

They all nodded in agreement.

The man standing and looking out the window of this very plush room said, "I believe our company needs him. He will bring legitimacy to our new efforts. Don't you think so?" he asked as he turned and faced the man sitting at the table.

"I hope so. If not, we're not done. As it is, I have made arrangements for Courson and Dortch. We still have to deal, however, with the missing money. And one other thing, somebody has to contact Sidney Dorn and Ziegler. We promised to keep them underground for a while."

"We'll find the money. Just make sure that Courson and Dortch are out of the way before Tuesday morning … and make sure that Dorn and Ziegler both know they're covered. We'll need them later on. That's how the plan has been put together."

"I have been told that it will be done just before noon tomorrow. The only thing that will be left is the money. Maybe we should have pressed Craig a little longer, since we don't know what he did with the money."

"Too late. He's sleeping with the fishes and he's their problem now. The money is a secondary issue, and I know just who can handle that for us."

 LIVE

---

listen|imagine|view|experience

AUDIO BOOK DOWNLOAD INCLUDED WITH THIS BOOK!

In your hands you hold a complete digital entertainment package. Besides purchasing the paper version of this book, this book includes a free download of the audio version of this book. Simply use the code listed below when visiting our website. Once downloaded to your computer, you can listen to the book through your computer's speakers, burn it to an audio CD or save the file to your portable music device (such as Apple's popular iPod) and listen on the go!

How to get your free audio book digital download:

1. Visit www.tatepublishing.com and click on the e|LIVE logo on the home page.
2. Enter the following coupon code:
   7a20-d4a5-33c2-2ec0-fa71-dc43-c1be-12f1
3. Download the audio book from your e|LIVE digital locker and begin enjoying your new digital entertainment package today!